BULLETS AND BONES

DESA KINCAID BOOK 2

R. S. PENNEY

Copyright (C) 2020 R.S. Penney

Layout design and Copyright (C) 2020 by Next Chapter

Published 2020 by Beyond Time – A Next Chapter Imprint

Edited by Jourdan Vian

Cover art by Cover Mint

This book is a work of fiction. Names, characters, places, and incidents are the product of the author's imagination or are used fictitiously. Any resemblance to actual events, locales, or persons, living or dead, is purely coincidental.

All rights reserved. No part of this book may be reproduced or transmitted in any form or by any means, electronic or mechanical, including photocopying, recording, or by any information storage and retrieval system, without the author's permission.

PROLOGUE

Wind swept through the narrow canyon with a howl like a banshee, a sound made only more terrifying by the moonless, night sky overhead. There were a few stars twinkling faintly, but otherwise not a speck of light to be had. Well, except for Sal's lantern.

The small lamp cast an orange glow on the canyon walls, walls that stood so close together he could barely stretch his arms out to the sides. Night in the desert was cold, and that relentless wind only worsened matters.

Sal scrambled over the rocky ground, panting with exhaustion. The lantern swung like a pendulum on its metal ring, the flames dancing and nearly winking out more than once. He tripped on a rock.

Falling onto his knees deliberately, Sal held hard to the lantern. He managed to keep his grip on it, though the hot glass smacked against his cheek and burned him.

Wincing, he hissed air through his teeth and then shook his head. "Keep going," he whispered to himself. "Get up!"

And then he was on his feet again.

He ran as if Death itself chased him. His actual pursuer

was much, much worse. He jumped over a rock, landing in a crouch, then forced himself to rise again and darted through the canyon like a madman.

A shadow leaped across the canyon above him.

Craning his neck when he noticed the flicker of motion, Sal squinted at it. "No," he breathed. "No, she can't be this close."

The ground beneath his feet had a slight upward tilt. Rocks crunched under his shoes as he sprinted up the tiny hill. He had to reach the end of the canyon before his pursuer caught up to him. Except she had already caught up to him. Perhaps he should turn back? No, that would put him back inside the network of caves where she had found him in the first place. He didn't want to die in there.

A few minutes later, he emerged from the canyon onto hard-packed, sun-beaten clay only to find the shadow waiting for him. A hooded figure that stood with a knife clutched in one hand. "Did you really think you could outrun a bounty hunter?"

Sal shut his eyes, tears leaking from them, streaming over his cheeks. "Please," he whimpered. "Whatever they're paying you, I'll double it."

"With what money?"

"I...I have gold."

The shadow strode forward, chuckling softly. "A little-known but easily-deduced fact about bounty hunters," she said. "We can't be bought. Because, you see, if I were to break the contract that set me after you simply because you offered more money – and I have serious doubts that you could make good on that promise – well, my reputation would be worthless. In fact, such a betrayal would impugn the dignity of all bounty hunters, and thus my brothers and sisters would have no choice but to hunt me down to clear their good names."

Snot dripped from Sal's nose. His tears flowed freely, and his body trembled. "Please," he mumbled, his voice cracking. "Please, I beg you not to do this."

"They all do in the end."

Sal turned and tried to run.

A coin landed at his feet, and then he was pulled down to his knees, anchored to the ground by a force that he could not explain. His arms and legs felt so heavy. The lantern fell from his grip, glass shattering on impact. The flame was helpless before the wind's terrible onslaught.

The hooded figure held up her hand, and the ring around her finger began to glow, providing more light than ten lanterns could. Sal could see her as clearly as he would if the blazing sun hung overhead. Her footsteps were so light he could barely hear them. Somehow, she seemed to be unaffected by whatever held Sal pinned to the earth.

With her free hand, she pulled back her hood to expose a pale face framed by curly, brown hair. Her large, dark eyes gave her a girlish quality. "You ran," she said. "I hate it when they run. So, I'm going to have to make this as painful as possible."

"No!"

She brandished the knife, its blade reflecting the light from her ring. "You have the honour of dying by the hand of Azra Vanya. Take comfort in that."

PART I

1

Aladar was a city of shining light, a place of electric lamps and horseless carriages, a beacon of civilization. But its prison cells were the same as every other one Desa Kincaid had seen across the face of this continent. Three stone walls and a set of bars that cut her off from the cellblock. The only window was about the size of her palm and also blocked off by bars.

Desa sat on a bench with her elbows on her thighs, covering her mouth with both hands. "Well," she said. "This is quite the predicament."

"That's all you have to say?"

"Need I say anything more?"

Miri stood with her back turned, one hand braced against the wall. The woman hung her head in frustration. "I don't know," she muttered. "Perhaps you could offer some suggestions as to how we get out of here."

A smile grew on Desa's face, and she shook her head slowly. "After all our adventures," she said, "you still have so little faith. By the way, I'll need your belt."

Spinning around to face her with a scowl that could

ignite dry kindling, Miri took one step forward. "Sweet Mercy!" she growled. "What in the name of all that's holy are you gonna do with my belt?"

"Just trust me."

Grumbling to herself, Miri undid her belt and yanked it free of the loops. "Here!" she said, thrusting the thing at Desa. "Anything else?"

"Yes," Desa replied. "I need you to distract the guard."

"And how exactly am I to do that?"

Tilting her head back to study the other woman, Desa blinked a few times. "You have a quick wit," she said. "I'm sure you'll think of something."

Miri sighed and stalked off toward the bars, grabbing one in each hand. "Hello!" she called out to the guards at the end of the cellblock. "Might I have some water, please? You see, I was traveling for several days in the desert, and I…"

Desa closed her eyes.

Miri could handle the guards. The woman was a fast talker. Now, hopefully, those louts out there would focus on the loud-mouthed woman and not on the one sitting quietly. Centring her emotions, Desa reached out to the Ether.

It came reluctantly – her mind was frantic after Adele's betrayal – but years of training helped to put the anger aside. She focused, and the world broke apart into a sea of particles, all swirling and dancing around her. Only a few moments. That was all she needed

Desa began a Field Binding, building a lattice of energy in the molecules of Miri's belt buckle and in one of the bars of their cell door. She was vaguely aware of a human-shaped collection of molecules stepping into view. The guard began chastising Miri.

He wasn't focused on Desa; she could tell. Now, if Miri could just keep him busy a few moments longer. The lattice grew as she Infused the metal with a connection to the Ether. Only a few moments more. She had to make sure her Infusions could release enough energy.

"But you see," Miri went on. "Dehydration leaves one vulnerable to all sorts of nasty pathogens. Pathogens that you lot might contract now that we're staying under your roof and all. So, in the interest of continued health – mine and yours – I highly recommend that you get me some water."

The guard rapped on the bars with his truncheon. "You'll get your water when we decide to feed you," he said. "Now, sit quiet and respectable like your friend there."

Desa had to suppress a smile.

The Infusion was complete.

She opened her eyes, clouds of molecules snapping together into solid objects. She saw the man on the other side of the cell door. He was a rough-looking fellow with tanned skin and a stubbly beard. "Both of you, stay quiet and still," he said. "I'll suffer no more trouble from either of you."

Sitting primly with hands folded on her lap, Desa smiled and shook her head. "Perish the thought," she murmured. "Thank you, sir, for your kind indulgence of my friend's difficulties."

With a grunt, the man turned on his heel and walked away.

"Are you ready?" Desa asked Miri.

The woman spun around, resting one hand on the bars and grimacing as if Desa had just spoken nonsense. "Ready for what?" she asked. "Whatever plan you've got, it better be a good one. They might show Marcus some respect, but Tommy...He's an outsider."

Desa rose from her seat, stretching her arms above her head as she drew in a breath. "I suggest you move to the back of the cell," she said. "And stay behind me."

Miri did as she was told, pacing to the small window in the back wall, turning around to stand under it with her arms folded. "Whatever you're going to do..."

Desa put herself in front of the other woman, lifting Miri's belt as a shield. Then, with a thought, she triggered the Force-Sink in the buckle and the Force-Source in one of the cell door's bars.

An explosion of kinetic energy knocked the other bars off their mountings, energy that expanded into the cell and out into the cellblock, hurling bits of metal and debris. All of it came to an abrupt halt about two feet in front of Desa, bits of it hanging in the air.

She heard the footsteps of guards running to check on the cacophony.

Gritting her teeth, Desa seethed with anger. "Now it begins."

She ran out into the cellblock.

One guard was coming toward her, his hand resting on a holstered pistol. He drew the weapon just as he got within arm's reach of her.

Desa swung the belt like a whip, its buckle lashing him across the cheek, stunning the man. He stumbled, clapping one hand over the wound.

Spinning like a whirlwind, Desa lashed out again, the belt buckle striking the gun and tearing it out of his hand. The startled guard gasped as she came around to face him.

A swift kick to his belly made him fold up on himself. Desa grabbed a fistful of his hair, yanked his head down and brought her knee up to smash his face. Down he went, crumpling to the floor in a heap.

Three more guards appeared at the end of the cellblock.

Falling over backwards, Desa rose into a handstand. She grabbed the fallen gun, flipped upright and pointed the weapon at her enemies. Drawing back the hammer with a *click,* she watched them hesitate.

"Now," Desa said. "You're going to let us out of-"

One of the guards surged forward.

Dropping to one knee, Desa extended her arm with the gun pointed at him. She fired once, filling the cellblock with a thunderous roar. Her bullet pierced the man's leg, and he fell flat on his face.

The other two had their weapons up.

Desa threw herself sideways, rolling into the open cell. She came up and backed away from the door, positioning herself beside Miri. "This is going to get ugly…"

Miri had fists balled and teeth bared. There was fury in her eyes. "The next time I don't have any faith in you," she muttered, "feel free to give me a good slug in the gob."

"Noted."

Miri moved like a striking snake, pressing her back to the wall near the door. When the first guard appeared, thrusting his gun into the cell, she grabbed his outstretched arm with both hands and gave a twist. His weapon fell to the floor.

Elbowing him in the face, Miri sent him careening into the wall on the other side of the cellblock. The final guard spun around the corner, lifting his weapon, firing blindly into the cell.

One bullet whizzed past Desa's ear, burrowing into the wall and sending bits of stone flying. Some of it grazed the back of her head.

Miri brought her hand down on his wrist in a chopping motion. His fingers uncurled, and the pistol fell to land beside its twin. Miri was lightning quick. Her next chop hit his throat, producing a gurgling sound.

Rounding on the man, she kicked him in the belly, then punched his face with one fist and then the other. Bloody and disoriented, he staggered. Miri seized two handfuls of his shirt and shoved him backwards.

He fell on top of his partner.

Dropping to a crouch, Miri picked up both pistols. She twirled one around her index finger, caught the grip and then pointed the smoking barrel up at the ceiling. "Yes, this will do."

"Let's go."

Desa went out into the cellblock to find it blessedly free of guards. Well... free of guards that could pose a threat to her. One man was moaning on the floor, clutching his bleeding leg. Another was unconscious, sprawled out on his belly.

As she strode through the corridor, Desa stooped to pick up the belt she had abandoned. She rose in one fluid motion and went to the door.

"Tommy and Marcus? And that sheriff from Dry Gulch?"

Closing her eyes, Desa took a moment to centre herself. She nodded slowly. "Grab the guard's keys," she muttered. "Kalia! Are you here?"

"Back here!"

The voice came from a cell at the far end of the block. Without hesitation, Desa turned and ran toward the sound. Miri tossed her the keys. Desa caught them without even looking and went to the door.

She found the sheriff on the other side of the bars,

staring at her with wide eyes. "What are we going to do?" Kalia asked.

"We're going to get out of here."

Shoving the key into the lock, Desa jiggled it a few times, and then the door slid open. Kalia stepped into the hallway, panting. The woman glanced this way and that as if she expected more guards to leap out from every shadow. Sweet Mercy, she might not be wrong.

As they made their way out, Kalia retrieved the last fallen pistol. Now, they were all armed.

Desa strode through the cellblock, flanked by both women. "All right," she said with a curt nod. "If we're quick, we can escape without any more trouble."

"What about Tommy?" Miri demanded.

"He'll be in the men's section," Desa protested. "There's no way we can get to him without running into more guards. And I'm out of Infusions. The best thing we can do is find someplace to hide while I create more."

Kalia went into their open cell, stood on her toes and placed a copper penny between two of the window bars. She came out and then pressed her body to the cellblock wall. "Stand clear."

Desa was about to ask what the other woman was planning, but she felt a stirring in the Ether, and then the cell's back wall exploded, chunks of stone and metal flying out in all directions. The coin had been a Force-Source! Now there was a big hole in the wall.

Bent over with hands on her knees, Desa looked up at the woman with the gaping mouth. "You know…" she stammered. "You know how to…"

Kalia shut her eyes and shook her head in dismay. "I told you," she said. "The Aladri aren't the only ones who know how to Field Bind."

"I regret my arrogance..."

"Let's go."

The hole in the wall led out to an alley between the police station and the next building over. Even in the shade, the afternoon was hot. A cloudless, blue sky loomed overhead.

Desa fell back against the alley wall, shutting her eyes and formulating a plan. "They'll be on us in a moment." The guards had to have heard that commotion. "I need time to make new weapons."

Jerking her head toward the street, Miri grunted. "No sense in staying here," she muttered. "Let's find ourselves some privacy."

They ran out to the sidewalk, pausing there. Kalia stood slack-jawed, taking in the sight of a paved road and lampposts that stood two stories high. A car came rumbling towards them, honking its horn as if the driver saw that they might thoughtlessly step into the street. Kalia leaped back with a squeak.

Desa's heart went out to the other woman; she had ridden in a horseless carriage last night when the police imprisoned them at the Prelate's command. But riding in one and seeing one coming at you were two different things.

Across the road, a red-bricked building with arch-shaped windows stood four stories high. Things were changing in Aladar; ten years ago, when Desa left on her adventure, automobiles had been a rarity, and electric lights were a pleasure reserved for those who could afford them. Now, both were becoming common.

"Over there!" Miri said, pointing across the street.

That seemed as good a direction as any.

Together, they ran across the empty road, onto the opposite sidewalk. They ducked into another alley, slipping out of sight. A good thing too. Desa ventured one glance back the way they had come and saw three uniformed police officers coming out of the hole that Kalia had put in the wall.

Hiding behind the red building, Desa sucked air into her lungs. "This will do," she mumbled. "Yes, this will do."

There was a thin, wooden fence between this building and the one behind it. While the police might think to look in nearby alleys, they would search the street first. She only needed a few moments.

Desa opened herself to the Ether, and the world became a place of dancing particles once again. She saw the collection of molecules that represented Kalia. The sheriff looked at her, eyebrows rising. "You can find it that quickly?"

Desa said nothing. It was difficult to speak or move her body while she was in the Ether's embrace. And she didn't want to admit it, but ever since her time in the ancient city, finding the Ether was easier.

The belt buckle was just simple brass again; the Force-Sink she had Infused was gone, used up absorbing the kinetic blast that had freed them from their cell. Now, she could make it into something new.

Quickly, she made a new lattice between the buckle's molecules, one attuned to gravity. She made sure to specify that it would only pull on things from one direction so that it wouldn't affect her when she triggered it. She found a small rock on the ground, one that she could conceal in her hand, and she built a lattice inside that as well.

The Ether showed her police officers fanning out in the street. They were searching for her. Only a few moments longer. She had to make the Infusions strong enough.

"Almighty preserve us," Kalia whispered. "She's so fast..."

"She's one of the best Field Binders Aladar has ever known," Miri replied.

A bottle cap on the alley floor. Desa Infused that with a thirst for gravitational energy. Yes, that would do nicely. Now, she needed something to deal with the bullets. Of course! The shirt they had given her had metal buttons. She Infused two of them with a connection to the Ether. And the guns...

She moved quickly from bullet to bullet, making a Heat-Sink, a Force-Source, and another Gravity-Source. Kalia and Miri... They would need protection as well.

Out on the street, one of the officers was gesturing towards the nearby alleys. She was running out of time. Working as fast as she could, she chose Kalia's belt buckle and one of the buttons on Miri's blouse, making each one a Force-Sink. She gave each one a physical trigger so that its bearer could choose when to use it. Then she released the Ether.

Opening her eyes, Desa took a moment to collect herself. She wiped sweat off her forehead with the back of one hand. "The third button on your shirt, Miri," she said. "Tap it once if someone's about to shoot at you. Tap it again when you're out of danger. Kalia, for you, it's your buckle."

Both women nodded.

"I'll keep the guards distracted," Desa said. "The two of you go free Lommy... *Tommy* and Marcus. Wait until they're busy shooting at me, and then make your move."

"Works for me," Miri muttered.

"Let's go to work."

She picked up the pebble and the bottle cap, stuffing them both into her pocket. Giving the others one last nod, she slipped into the alley and moved cautiously toward the street. When she was close enough, she peered out from the shadows.

There were three men in blue uniforms and billed caps standing in the middle of the road, looking this way and that, searching for any sign of her. All it would take was for one of them to glance in her direction.

Desa fished the pebble out of her pocket.

Tossing it into the street, she watched it land in the middle of the group of men. They looked down at it, bewildered. And then she triggered the Light-Sink that she had Infused into the rock.

A patch of gloom, dark beneath the blazing afternoon sun, appeared in the middle of the road. All three men began shouting, crying out in surprise. Time to press her advantage

Desa ran into their group.

Once she was within range of her Light-Sink, the world around her seemed to darken. The sky above was now a deep, twilight-blue. The buildings were blocky shadows. Not total darkness, but it would do.

The nearest man, a silhouette to her eyes, spun around at the sound of her footsteps. He tried to lift the pistol in his right hand.

Desa swung the belt like a whip, striking his wrist with the buckle. His fingers uncurled, the revolver falling to the ground. Hissing in pain, he tried to advance on her. Desa whipped him again, lashing him across the cheek.

The poor fool stumbled.

With a thought, she killed the Light-Sink. Full brightness returned, and all three men winced, their eyes smarting. Desa's eyes were sore as well, but she had learned to rely on her other senses.

She kicked the man in front of her.

He went staggering backward into one of his companions, and they both fell to the pavement. The third man rounded on her, baring teeth in the snarl. In an instant, he had his gun up and pointed at her. Desa activated her shirt buttons.

CRACK!

The bullet came to an abrupt halt right in front of her and fell to the ground a second later when she killed the Force-Sinks. She could see the shock on her enemy's eyes, and she capitalized on it.

Desa flung the belt out toward him, briefly pulsing the Gravity-Source that she had infused into the buckle. The policeman was yanked toward her, nearly falling over as he stumbled the few steps that were necessary to bring him within reach of her weapon.

Desa whipped him across the face, leaving a red welt on his upper lip. Her next lash tore the gun right out of his hand. Then she sent the buckle into his groin for good measure. Squealing in pain, the poor fellow clutched his pelvis and fell to his knees.

The other two were rising.

One was down on all fours and pawing at the ground for the pistol he had lost. The other was standing up slowly, holding his weapon tight in one hand. He turned a hateful stare upon Desa.

She triggered the Light-Sink, forcing it to drink as deeply as it could.

This time, the world became a place of utter darkness. Pure black in all directions. The Sink wouldn't last long, gobbling up light energy that quickly.

Swift and silent, Desa moved off to her right to avoid being where the man had last seen her. The thunder of gunfire filled the air, and by the sound of a bullet ricocheting off bricks, she was fairly certain that the shot had gone into the alley.

"Where is she?" one officer shouted.

"I don't know! I don't know!"

They were all breathing hard and moving awkwardly, feet scuffing on the pavement. It wasn't difficult to estimate the position of each man. Desa crept up behind one of them.

"Where is she? Where is she?"

"Right here," Desa whispered.

She looped the belt over his head, pulling it tight over his throat. And then she yanked him backward onto his ass. A swift kick to the head knocked him senseless. She left the belt where it was.

Triggering the Gravity-Sink in the bottle cap, Desa leaped and soared right over the remaining two men. At the apex of her jump, the Sink gave out, and the harsh light of day returned in full force.

Allowing gravity to reassert a tiny fraction of its power, Desa landed a little ways up the street. She whirled around to find two uniformed men standing in the middle of the road, shielding strained eyes from the sun's relentless assault. Now to end this while she had them distracted.

Desa triggered the Gravity-Source in the belt buckle.

Both men were pulled backward, falling hard on their backsides and skidding across the pavement toward their fallen companion. The legs kicked feebly. Their hands clawed for purchase, but they couldn't escape. The discarded guns were drawn toward the belt as well. Not a good idea, putting her enemies and their weapons in the same spot, but she wouldn't give them a chance to do her any harm.

Finally, Desa killed both Source and Sink.

She drew her own pistol, cocking the hammer, and then pointed it at the pile of men. "Easy now," she said. "Nobody reaches for a weapon, and nobody gets hurt."

Desa closed her eyes, a fat bead of sweat rolling over her forehead. Her breathing was laboured, her body aching from the exertion. "Now," she went on in a husky voice. "My friends and I are going to leave the city peacefully. All you have to do-"

A whistling sound behind her.

She turned around to find a man in billowing, yellow robes descending from the rooftop of a nearby building. He landed on the sidewalk with barely a sound and then rose to stand at full height.

His face was hidden under a yellow hood. Even without the obvious use of Gravity-Sinks, Desa would have recognized the uniform and the sleek, metal staff of an Elite Guardian. "Desa Nin Leean," he said. "You are charged with treason."

He began a slow, inexorable march into the middle of the road.

Desa stood there with her mouth agape, blinking slowly as she tried to put a name to that voice. "Radavan?" she stammered. "Is that you?"

He put himself in front of her, holding the staff out before himself in two hands as if he were a guard on a bridge who meant to bar her passage. "You are charged with treason," he said again.

Clenching her teeth, Desa shut her eyes tight. She shook her head with a growl. "I have done no treason," she declared. "I'm trying to save this world. All of it. Aladar included."

"You will report to the Prelate," he said.

"Vengeance spit on my grave if I will."

Taking that as a sign that further talk was pointless, Radavan strode toward her with the staff in one hand. He pulled back his hood to reveal a pale face and a shaved head. "In the name of Aladar, I arrest you."

He stretched a beringed hand out toward her.

Without warning, Desa was pulled forward. The sudden tug was so strong it ripped the gun right out of her grip. The butt end of that staff struck the side of her head, and then her vision was filled with silver stars. Reacting by instinct, she let herself fall over backward.

She rose into a handstand, stretching her legs into the air, and then flipped upright. When her vision cleared, she saw Radavan coming at her with determination in his eyes. He thrust the staff at her face.

Desa leaned to her right, the weapon flashing over her left shoulder. Her first instinct was to grab it and take it from him, but only a fool touched another Field Binder's weapon. She retreated and waited for an opening.

Radavan tried to take her legs out from under her.

With a screech, Desa jumped and back-flipped through the air. She landed just in time to see the stubborn fool of a man bearing down on her, raising his weapon for yet another blow. He swung at her head.

Desa ducked, allowing the staff to pass over her.

He's got reach. She fell onto her side, bracing one hand on the pavement, and kicked Radavan's knee. He yelped.

Curling up into a ball, Desa sprang off the ground and landed with her fists up in a guarded stance. "Listen to me!"

Twirling the staff with expert skill, Radavan backed away to put some distance between them. He raised the weapon high and slammed it down onto the road, releasing a wave of kinetic force.

The blast hit Desa like a tidal wave, throwing her backward. She landed on her bottom, groaning. *That* was why you never touched another Field Binder's weapon. If he had triggered that Force-Source while she was holding the staff, she would have lost a hand. She somersaulted and came up in a crouch.

Wiping her mouth with one hand, Desa squinted at him. "All right," she said, rising. "You don't want to talk? We don't have to talk."

Radavan tossed the staff at her.

It landed with a clatter right between her two feet. Instantly, Desa threw herself down on her belly and triggered the Force-Sinks in her buttons. The explosion of kinetic energy that should have hurled her four stories into the air was instead absorbed into the Ether. But the staff released more than her buttons could take.

Desa was launched about five feet off the ground, and then she unceremoniously dropped to the pavement, bouncing like a stone. She pushed herself up on extended arms. Her head was swimming.

She barely even felt it when the tip of Radavan's staff found its way under her chin. He tilted her face up so that she was forced to stare into his eyes. There was nothing but grim resignation there. This man was as bad as Marcus. Worse.

"You are no longer Desa Nin Leean. You forfeited any right that name when you left this place. No, you are Desa Kincaid now. And your skills have atrophied."

He thumped her on the head with the staff.

Everything went dark.

2

A fog of confusion filled Desa's mind, receding only reluctantly to be replaced with pain. Her head hurt, and the dizziness that came with that made her nauseous. The voices that were speaking somewhere nearby sounded as if they were coming from the depths of some ancient cave.

The first pleasant sensation she experienced was the feeling of soft, red carpet beneath her. The walls of this room are also red, and its vaulted ceiling was supported by thick, golden pillars. She knew this place. The Prelate's office.

Desa was lying on her side, dressed only in gray pants and an undershirt that barely let her maintain modesty. Her short, brown hair was a mess, thin strands of it falling over her face. She tried to sit up.

Tried and failed.

"She's awake," someone said.

Without thinking, she reached for the Ether and wrapped herself in its warm embrace. The world around her became a tempest of swirling particles. The walls, the chairs, the Prelate's desk and the people surrounding it:

each one a small galaxy of tiny molecules. There were three Elite Guardians in this room. Radavan was one. "She's trying to Field Bind," he barked.

"Desa Nin Leean!" the Prelate snapped.

Desa released her hold on the Ether, and the collection of molecules on the other side of the desk became a tall and willowy woman with a leathery face. Her gray hair was pulled back in a bun. Daresina Nin Drialla looked even more cantankerous than Desa remembered.

Standing by the wall with his metal staff in the hand, his yellow robes seeming to hang off his body, Radavan sneered at her. "She's released it," he said. "You're in no danger."

Desa realized that she could feel the Sinks and Sources that she had Infused earlier. They were somewhere to the south-west, several miles at least, and if her memory of the city's layout was still accurate, it was a good bet that every single one of those weapons was sitting in a vault in the police station. Desa ordered them all to release their power at a glacial pace. At this rate, it would take the better part of two weeks for them to revert to ordinary objects, but if she couldn't have them back, it was best to defuse them. An Infused weapon was like a drawn bowstring: tense and ready to release its power at the slightest provocation. Her sudden death might trigger any one of those devices.

"Desa Nin Leean!"

Covering her face with one hand, Desa rubbed her eyelids with the tips of her fingers. "I heard you the first time." She looked up, blinking. "Frankly, I'm surprised you didn't put me back in that cell."

Daresina sat behind her desk with arms folded. Her mouth was twisted like she had forgotten to add sugar to her lemonade. "Would it do any good?" the Prelate countered. "You would only make another escape attempt."

Radavan's wolfish grin made Desa shiver. "Leave her with us," he suggested. "The Elite Guard knows how to deal with one such as her."

"Is that really necessary?"

Desa froze.

She had not realized that Marcus was present, but his voice was unmistakable. One glance around the room, and she found him standing by the door with the wide brim of his hat pulled low over his eyes. He still wore the dungarees and brown jacket that he had donned during their journey.

The others were here as well.

Kalia was on her knees, staring into her lap with lips pursed. There was an ugly, purple bruise on her cheek. For some reason, that made Desa very angry.

Tommy was in the corner, doing his best not to look at anyone, and Miri was next to him. Unlike everyone else, she seemed to be uninterested in what the Prelate had to say. She just kept close to Tommy and whispered comforting things in his ear.

"It's clear," Daresina began, "that you cannot be trusted as you were tasked with bringing Desa home, and you betrayed that charge."

Contact with the Ether accelerated the body's natural healing process. Desa would need an hour at least in its embrace to recover completely from her injuries, but those brief few seconds had given her enough lucidity to carry on this conversation.

Drawing breath through her open mouth, Desa shut her eyes and tried to keep her voice steady. "He had some good reasons for doing so," she said. "There is something dangerous out there."

The Prelate sniffed.

Hunching over her desk, she rested her elbows on its

surface and balanced her chin atop laced fingers. "Oh yes," she mocked. "This mysterious force you keep speaking of. This creature from beyond the confines of our universe..."

Her tone betrayed more than skepticism.

"All of it is true," Desa said. "And everyone here will tell you the same."

"You will forgive me," Daresina replied, "if I don't find your new friends to be the most credible witnesses."

Tommy perked up at that, pulling away from Miri and striding across the room, planting himself right in front of the desk. His blue eyes were as hard as diamonds. "Seems to me that simple logic would mark our words true," he said. "How do you think we arrived in Aladar?"

"By ship or by train."

"And yet we just happened to show up in your temple? No one saw us come into town? No one made us go through customs? Is your bureaucracy really that incompetent? Or is there more going on here than meets the eye?"

Desa blinked.

When had Tommy developed such a backbone?

Daresina was focused on him now, shaking her head slowly as she considered his questions. "I am sure there are perfectly rational explanations," she said. "Explanations that are far more plausible than claims of some mysterious force transporting you across the face of the continent."

Desa seated herself in a cushioned chair, crossing one leg over the other and facing the Prelate with as much serenity as she could manage while she was trapped in the grip of dizziness. "A month ago, I told you that we need Field Binders," she said. "Since then, the situation has become more dire."

She leaned forward, squinting at the other woman. "Our people are not the first ones to discover Field Binding," she said. "There is an abandoned city in the desert, about a day's ride south of Dry Gulch. They have technologies there that surpass anything we have ever created."

"Are you saying we should send an expedition?"

"I'm saying that Bendarian tried to use those technologies to rip a hole in the Ether. He tried, but I stopped him. Unfortunately, a companion of ours – Adele Delarac from Ofalla – managed to succeed where Bendarian failed. She created a rip in the Ether, and something came through it. It claimed Adele as a host."

"A truly fascinating story."

"This is not a game!" Desa hissed. "This is not a tale I've invented to impress travelers around a fire."

Marcus strode forward, set his jaw and stared down the Prelate. "I have seen this thing with my own eyes," he said. "Its power is unimaginable."

"It seems to warp the very laws of reality."

Planting elbows on the arms of her chair, Daresina regarded them over steepled fingers. "Say I believe you," she began. "What would you have me do?"

"Send Field Binders with me. They have the best chance of stopping this thing."

"So, you're planning to leave again?"

Desa stood up and immediately regretted it. A wave of dizziness nearly took her feet out from under her. "I don't see that I have much choice," she replied. "This thing has to die."

Daresina's eyebrows tried to climb up her forehead. "Impressive," she said. "Ten short years among the mainlanders have taught you to solve every problem with violence."

"Well, perhaps we could make peace with it," Miri suggested. "Hello, Mr. Cosmic Entity. Would you mind terribly if we ask you to stop rewriting the laws of our universe? Thank you ever so kindly."

Radavan had one hand braced against the wall, and his patronizing grin made Desa want to punch him. His soft laughter was even worse. "Forgive my intrusion," he cut in. "But if this thing is so powerful, how do you plan to kill it?"

"It is currently in possession of Adele's body," Desa explained. "Every time we attacked her, the entity defended itself, unwilling to risk harm to that body. Which leads me to believe that it needs a vessel and that the body it chooses is still vulnerable to physical harm."

"So," Daresina replied, "you will kill an innocent woman to defeat this creature."

Clenching her teeth, Desa hissed air through them. She shook her head slowly. "Adele is anything but innocent," she growled. "She welcomed this thing into her body. She made her choice, and now she can pay for it."

Betrayal did not sit well with Desa Kincaid. The frenzy of the last few days had prevented her from indulging in some much-needed introspection, but she realized that her blood boiled every time Adele entered her thoughts. She would put a bullet in that treasonous woman: that much was certain.

Perhaps…Perhaps…Desa didn't want to admit it, but it stood to reason that some of her anger had come out of the fact that a small part of her had started to believe all that talk about soulmates. Fool's talk, all of it. She should have known better than to let herself get carried away by flights of fancy. Like a girl half her age.

Daresina was silently watching all of them. Desa could see that she wasn't sure what to make of any of this, but while the Prelate might be set in her ways, she wasn't completely closed-minded. "You're free to go," she said at last. "Though I would ask that you remain within the city for a period of at least one week so that we may speak more on what you have shared today."

Tommy stood in front of the desk with his eyes downcast. His face was pale, but he licked his lips and spoke words that Desa would have never expected. "Madam," he began. "I would like permission to visit your libraries."

"For what purpose?"

"To learn more about your history."

Daresina shut her eyes, nodding slowly as she considered his request. "I see no harm in that," she said. "Perhaps, young man, you will speak with me as well. So that I may learn more about the world beyond my borders."

SETTING his hat atop his head, Tommy pulled the brim down to shield his eyes. "That went about as well as could be expected," he said. "Half thought she might order us executed, myself."

Miri joined him on the top step of the Hall of the Synod, standing tall with her hands clasped behind her back. She wore a smile that made him want to kiss her. "Oh, old Daresina's not as bad as all that."

They stood between two pillars that supported an overhanging roof. At least a dozen stone steps led down to an open area where a round fountain sprayed water into the air, and beyond that, a paved road like nothing Tommy had ever seen was filled with those strange horseless carriages.

There were buildings on the other side of the street, tall buildings made of white brick. At least three or four stories high each. When Desa had told him about the wonders of Aladar, he had pictured many things, but this exceeded even his wildest expectations.

He began his quick trek down the stairs, his brown duster flapping against the backs of his legs. "Guess you have to take me to the library," he said, glancing back over his shoulder. "Got a lot to learn."

Miri was right behind him, shaking her head with a rueful smile. "See, that's what I love about you, Lommy," she said. "Always eager to fill your mind with new facts and ideas and philosophies."

She was mimicking his style of speaking, the rougher dialect you heard in the outer villages near Sorla. Tommy wondered if she was doing it on purpose – Miri prided herself on her ability to blend in – or if it was just another sign of affection.

Desa and Marcus were still at the top of the stairs, standing between two of those fat, round pillars and facing each other with grim expressions. What exactly were they talking about? Something to do with the entity that Adele Delarac had unleashed, no doubt. He felt a mix of emotions at the sight of his mentor. Just one day ago, they had been in Dry Gulch. Miri had been trying to make him sort out his difficulties with Desa. He still wasn't sure how he felt about her killing Sebastian. But it was amazing what twenty-four hours could do to change one's outlook.

The fact was Sebastian *had* been a dangerous man. Treacherous and deceitful. There was just no denying that. And it seemed they had much bigger problems on their hands.

Scratching his forehead with the knuckle of his index finger, Tommy grunted. "Knew we shouldn't have taken that priss along with us," he said. "Rich girl like that is nothing but trouble."

"She said she could help us find Bendarian."

"Yeah, but only so she could take the power he wanted for herself."

Miri nodded curtly, and Tommy smiled. Whatever he felt for her was no less complex than anything else he had been feeling over the last few weeks. But he could say one thing for Miri Nin Valia: she had a talent for seeing through to the heart of an issue.

Tommy went down on one knee in front of the fountain, dipped his hands into the water and splashed it over his face. "Don't suppose they'll give us rooms," he muttered. "Someplace we could freshen up. I haven't had a decent bath since Thrasa."

He looked up to find people sitting on benches on either side of him. There was a dark-skinned woman in a purple dress and a pale fellow who wore black suspenders over his white shirt. There were children as well: a young boy and girl, both with sandy hair and wide eyes. And they were all watching him.

Tommy felt heat in his face that had nothing to do with the sun's glare. "I just named myself a country bumpkin, didn't I?"

Miri came up behind him, resting her hand on his shoulder. Then, to his surprise, she fell to her knees and washed her face with the bubbling water as well. "Don't pay them any mind, Lommy," she said. "You're more civilized than half the men in this city."

LEANING against the pillar with her arms folded, Desa frowned at Marcus. "And that's it?" she said, her eyebrows rising. "We just stay here and enjoy the comforts of home while Adele does Mercy alone knows what?"

Marcus had his back pressed to the next pillar over, and

his eyes were focused on the ground under his boots. "We have no idea where she is," he insisted. "She seems to be able to travel hundreds of miles in the blink of an eye."

"Your point?"

When Marcus looked up at her, his face was as hard as granite. "At least here," he began, "we have the assembled knowledge of our people. For once, Tommy seems to have done something useful. He had the right idea about the libraries."

Desa paced through the space between the pillars, stopping next to Marcus. Her head drooped with the weight of her fatigue. "I know almost everything our people have ever discovered about Field Binding," she hissed. "Believe me when I tell you that there is nothing in those books that we can use against Adele."

"Not Adele."

Desa opened her mouth to protest but quickly snapped it shut again. Annoying as he was, Marcus was right. Whatever had taken residence in Adele's body was not Adele herself. Though remnants of her seemed to remain. Perhaps that was a weakness they could exploit.

"You should visit your mother," Marcus grunted.

A stab of pain – like a blade slammed right through her heart – made Desa tense up and shiver. Her mother. Ten years had passed since she had fled the city in pursuit of Bendarian. She hadn't left a note or any explanation. Would Leean even want to see her after all that?

"There's one way to find out," Marcus said as if reading her thoughts.

Trembling as a chill ran down her spine, Desa scrunched up her face. "You're right," she muttered. "The odds of my mother forgiving me after all this time are...not good. But a small chance becomes no chance if I leave again without even visiting her."

"Do you want me to go with you?"

"No," Desa grumbled. "There are some things we have to do on our own."

3

The horseless carriage rolled smoothly along the wide, black road. Well...More smoothly than a horse and buggy would. From his position in the back seat, Tommy gazed out the window and watched the buildings scrolling past. They were so tall, and they came in a variety of colours. Some were pressed together without an inch of space between them; others stood on their own. He noticed elaborate architecture that rivaled even some of what he had seen in Ofalla. What a marvelous city!

His own reflection stared back at him, barely visible in the glass.

He felt his lips curl into a smile, then leaned forward until his forehead bumped the window. "If you had told me, just three months ago, that a device like this was possible, I would have said you were crazy."

Miri was next to him, sitting with hands folded in her lap. He wasn't used to the sight of her in a dress, and especially not one made of thin, blue cotton that left her shoulders bare. "There's a wide world out there beyond the confines of your little village."

"I wish I had seen it sooner."

The driver watched them with a skeptical frown.

Once again, Tommy clamped his mouth shut. It seemed that every time he spoke, he said something that revealed his lack of sophistication. That shouldn't bother him – it certainly didn't bother Miri – but it did.

Earlier this morning, the two of them had met with Desa, Marcus and Kalia to discuss their plans. Tommy had tried to convince the sheriff to join them on this trip – she deserved to see Aladar as much as anyone – but she was committed to going with Desa on some errand they wouldn't speak about.

Miri put her hand on his thigh.

Pressing a fist to his mouth, Tommy shut his eyes and cleared his throat. "Well," he began in a hoarse voice. "Do you think that the library will have many books on Field Binding?"

"This is Aladar, Lommy," Miri replied. "If there is one subject that you will find thoroughly documented in our libraries, it's Field Binding."

The carriage went around a corner, onto a curving street that encircled a bronze statue of a man on horseback. There were other carriages driving beside them. Some went down other streets that branched off from the circle.

Tommy breathed slowly, grief tying his insides in knots. "If only Lenny could see this," he muttered. "Maybe it would finally open his eyes."

The look that Miri gave him was full of sadness. "You miss your brother?" she asked softly.

"Yes," he answered. "And no. Lenny would never accept me for who I was. Not back in Sorla, anyway. But sometimes I think that if he could see how little he understood the wider world…"

Miri leaned in close to kiss his cheek, and when she pulled away, a slow smile grew on her face. "Perhaps we could go back for him, one day," she suggested. "Maybe he'll come with us to see the great city."

"I'm worried that he might take to all this the same way Sebastian did."

"Do you think so?"

Tommy shuddered as he considered the question. Unconsciously, his hands gripped the fabric of his parents until his knuckles whitened. "He was willing to see me executed simply for loving another man," he said. "Forgive my bluntness, but I'm not holding onto hope."

For a little while, they sat in silence, which was just fine with Tommy. He was content to just enjoy the scenery. They were now traveling down a narrow street lined with white-bricked townhouses with flat roofs. Most of them had a little garden in the front yard, and even the smallest was twice the size of his father's home.

When they finally reached the library, Tommy got out of the carriage and found himself face-to-face with a building that he could only describe as majestic. It was massive with a white façade and two large wings that took up most of a city block. The heavy, wooden door was nestled into the middle of an arch-shaped entryway.

Tommy ascended the steps slowly, reaching up to remove his hat. He sighed. "If I felt like a country pumpkin before..." he muttered under his breath.

At his side, Miri moved gracefully, and her smile was so bright it rivaled the sun. "You know, it's nice to see you like this," she said. "The whole time we've known each other, it's been one desperate chase after another. It's nice to see you happy."

Tommy opened the door and stepped into a huge lobby

where thick pillars supported a vaulted ceiling. The white floor tiles were polished to a shine. On the far side of the room, a gray-haired man with spectacles over his eyes sat behind a wooden desk.

Tommy hesitated, then forced himself to approach.

The clerk looked up to blink at him through lenses that reflected the light. "Yes?" he said. "Can I help you?"

"I'm looking for books on Field Binding."

The clerk narrowed his eyes as he studied Tommy. Grunting, he stood up for an even closer inspection. "Forgive my impertinence," he said, "but you look like a foreigner. We usually don't share such knowledge with outsiders."

Miri stepped up beside him, resting a hand on Tommy's shoulder, and though her smile was still bright, it promised...something. Not pain exactly. But there was no doubt in Tommy's mind that it was in the clerk's best interest to go along with whatever she wanted. "He has special permission from the Prelate."

The clerk was unconvinced as he glanced from Miri to Tommy and back again. "I shall need to see this permission, of course."

Tommy produced a folded-up sheet of paper from his satchel and handed it to the other man. When the fellow opened it, he saw that it was stamped and notarized with the Prelate's seal of office clearly visible.

The old man's brow furrowed, and then he lowered the paper to stare at them with his mouth hanging open. "Well," he stammered at last, "this seems to be in order. You will find what you need in the eastern wing, third floor."

· · ·

The heavy tome that Tommy had set atop his wooden table had a musty scent and pages that had turned yellow with age. He flipped through them with the utmost care. It wasn't as if he thought they might crumble at his touch, but he would not risk harm to something so ancient.

Most of the text was in Old Aladri, which made it indecipherable to Tommy. Fortunately, Miri was able to translate. Learning languages – even dead languages – was part of her training with the Ka'adri.

They sat together in the light of an arch-shaped with gray muntin separating the individual panes. The small table they shared was hidden behind multiple stacks of books just like the one that now sat in front of him.

Pursing her lips, Miri scanned the page, her eyes flicking back and forth. "This one is about the proper techniques of concentration," she explained. "The state of mind that one must be in to commune with the Ether."

Tommy slouched in his chair, pressing the heels of his hands to his eyes. A groan escaped him despite his efforts to restrain it. "Just like all the others," he lamented. "So far, we haven't found anything that we couldn't learn from Mrs. Kincaid."

Miri chuckled.

Sometimes Tommy still slipped into his habit of referring to Desa with a formal title. Well, he had been raised to be polite, and that was all there was to it.

Snuggling up, Miri closed her eyes and rested her head on his shoulder. "So, what exactly are you looking for?" she murmured. "If you're thinking about continuing your studies without Desa's tutelage, I would advise against it. You're not that advanced yet."

"I'm looking for some indication of what might have happened in that ancient city," Tommy replied. "From what

Bullets and Bones

Desa told us, Bendarian spoke of another force, an antithesis to the Ether, you might say."

"And you think my ancestors knew something of this other force?"

Clamping a hand over his mouth, Tommy tapped his cheek with one finger. "If anyone did," he muttered into his palm, "it would have been the people who spent centuries learning everything there was to know about the Ether."

The sound of footsteps made him tense up – and he couldn't suppress a moment of elation at the realization that he was becoming more observant – but it had no effect on Miri. No doubt she heard them as clearly as he had, but from what he understood of the Ka'adri, Miri was something of a spy. And he had seen first-hand that she could take care of herself. He shivered at the memory of those gray people in Thrasa.

A young man stepped out from between two stacks, a tall and handsome fellow with a coppery complexion and chestnut-brown hair that he wore parted in the middle. "I didn't realize there was anyone back here," he said. "I heard voices, and I thought it best to check."

"You're one of the librarians?" Tommy inquired.

"Indeed," the young man replied. "Dalen Von Sasorin at your service." He had a strong Aladri accent, a lilt even more pronounced than anything Tommy had heard from either Miri or Marcus. And of course, Desa must have lost her accent years ago.

Tommy rose from his chair and thrust out his hand. The other men took it after only a moment of hesitation and gave it a firm shake. "Thomas Smith," he said. "I was hoping you could tell me where I might find some of your earliest texts on Field Binding."

"Well, the earliest texts are nearly two thousand years old."

"Do you have them here?"

Dalen eased himself into a chair, sitting with his hands on his thighs. He leaned forward and regarded Tommy for a very long moment. "We do," he admitted almost reluctantly. "But they aren't available to the public."

"I have permission from the Prelate."

"It won't do any good," Dalen said. "Even Daresina Nin Drialla can't authorize access to those documents. It would take nothing less than the approval of the entire Synod."

"And if the information that we need is in there?"

"What exactly are you trying to find?"

"Specifically, I want to know how your people discovered Field Binding." He wasn't sure what drew him to that subject; it was more of a hunch than anything else. But it seemed to him that when people were still learning the basic theory, they might be more willing to experiment. Something had alerted Bendarian to the presence of this other force. Which meant that it was possible to discover it using the same methods that one employed when communing with the Ether.

"Our people discovered Field Binding long before we ever came to Aladar," Dalen said. "Records from that time are spotty at best."

"All right," Tommy said. "What about holy books?"

He noticed Miri watching him with avid fascination. He wasn't sure what it was about a simple information inquiry that had her so enraptured, but it made him blush.

"Holy books?" Dalen asked.

With a heavy sigh, Tommy shuffled over to the window. He turned his face up to it, allowing the warm sunlight to fall upon his skin. "Your people have been practicing Field

Binding for centuries," he said. "It's bound to have some religious significance."

Dalen was nodding as if everything that had come out of Tommy's mouth was just plain, common sense. "Of course!" he exclaimed. "We have many copies of the *Tharan Vadria*."

"Excellent," Tommy said. "Let's start with that."

"THAT ONE," Desa said, pointing to a bracelet on a blue cushion. It was nothing fancy. Just a thin band of steel or iron; she couldn't tell which by sight alone. But it was cheap, and that was what mattered.

This jeweler's shop in Aladar's eastern quarter was blessedly cool. A welcome reprieve after over an hour of walking in the hot sun. The walls were painted a soft blue, and there were display cases positioned along every one. One contained rings of gold, each marked by an emerald or ruby or some other stone. Another contained necklaces forged from other precious metals. Some silver, some gold. Desa wanted another necklace, but she would not waste money on anything ornate.

The jeweler, a bald man with a face darkened by stubble, looked up to favour her with a quizzical stare. "That one, ma'am?" he asked. "It's not a quality piece. I'm sure I can find something better that is still within your price range."

Desa wore tan pants and a blue shirt that she left untucked, its buttons done up all the way to her neck. Her bob of short, brown hair was a mess. With her accent at least five years gone, there was nothing to mark her as Aladri.

That was why it must have been a shock to the man when Desa lifted her hand and pulsed the Light-Source in her ring. "It's metal, and it's cheap," she said. "That's all I need."

"Say no more, ma'am. I can offer you a Field Binder's discount."

"Field Binder's discount," Kalia murmured behind her.

Desa felt her lips curl into a small smile. She bowed her head to the shopkeeper. "That won't be necessary, sir." Her talents had not been employed in the service of Aladar for over a decade. She had no right the boons that came from such service.

The jeweler clasped his hands together behind his back and then offered a shallow bow. "As you say, ma'am," he replied. "Is there anything else you might like?"

"Do you have another bracelet like that one?"

"Several more, ma'am."

Desa twisted around to find Kalia standing in the middle of the shop with her eyes about ready to fall out of their sockets. The other woman was transfixed by the wealth that surrounded her. "Then I will take one for my friend as well," Desa said.

"Very good, ma'am."

By the time they had finished, Desa had purchased an iron necklace and several more rings as well. She had to pay for it all with Aladri currency that she had borrowed from Marcus. Knowing him, he wouldn't come to collect any time soon. In fact, he might forget the debt entirely, but it still irked her. Her own coins had melted when that strange entity took possession of Adele. As had every other piece of metal on her person. And besides, foreign money wouldn't be worth much here.

When they were back out on the street, the hot sun assaulted her. It was a muggy afternoon, and the heat was oppressive. She felt sweat plastering her shirt to her back.

The street they were on ran down a gentle slope toward the rippling waters of the ocean. From the top of the hill, Desa could see all the way to the eastern horizon. There were only a few clouds in the sky.

They walked in silence for a time, passing a small market where men and women sold fish that had come in on boats that went out this morning. Many of them kept their wares cool with Heat-Sinks provided by Field Binders.

The docks were mostly empty, but there were a few metal ships in the harbour. Kalia gasped at the sight of those and muttered a prayer to her Almighty. Desa chuckled but made no comment. Gulls swooped low over the water, some scooping up small fish.

Being here brought back memories and emotions that Desa had buried long ago. She was thirty, but the sights and sounds of Aladar made her feel like an adolescent girl again. And that let her ignore the heaviness in her heart for a few minutes.

"It wasn't your fault, you know," Kalia said.

Desa stood on the dock with her fists clenched, a salty breeze ruffling her hair. "I trusted her," she growled. "Even when every instinct told me not to, I gave Adele the benefit of the doubt. How is it not my fault?"

"Why did you do that?"

A tear slid down Desa's cheek as she gazed out on the water. "I don't know," she muttered. "I suppose it's because I believe we all deserve a chance to prove ourselves. And maybe I was feeling guilty for killing Sebastian."

Kalia made very little noise as she stepped up beside Desa. The woman wore a thoughtful frown as she gazed out on the ocean. "Is it at all possible that you trusted Adele because you were in love with her?"

"Oh, that was part of it," Desa agreed. "But it was infatuation more than love. Perhaps, if things had gone differently, it could have blossomed into something more. But when I look within my heart, I find that I never really felt safe with Adele. There was always a part of me that insisted on keeping my guard up. I should have listened to that part of me."

Kalia put a hand on Desa's arm. "If you ask me, this is something we do far too often," she said. "When someone betrays us, we blame ourselves for trusting them in the first place. In doing so, we imply that it's better to not trust. And I don't want to live in a world where trust is foolish."

Desa couldn't suppress her small smile or the blush that singed her cheeks. "You've thought a lot about this," she said. "The sheriff philosopher."

"I live in a small trading outpost in the middle of the desert," Kalia replied. "There's not a lot to do."

"Well, then let me show you a city full of activity."

IT HAD BEEN years since Miri last read the *Tharan Vadria* – she wasn't exactly a religious person – and flipping through those pages brought up some childhood memories she would rather not think about. The clerics had always considered her to be a most unteachable student. She wasn't sure what Tommy hoped to find in her people's holy text, but she had come to realize that he had a shrewd mind. So, she would help if she could.

Miri stood between two long bookshelves with a leather-bound copy of the text in hand, frowning as she read through it. "Here's something," she murmured. "The story of Len and the Great March."

Her words fell on deaf ears.

At the end of the corridor that ran between the bookshelves, Tommy and Dalen sat in two wooden chairs, facing one another. A massive window spilled light into the room, leaving both men as little more than silhouettes to Miri's eyes. "No, no, no," Dalen insisted. "The text is quite clear. It was Mercy who led our people north through the jungle."

"Yes," Tommy replied. "I'm aware of what the text says. But my question remains. How would a primitive man, someone for whom a simple spear is a marvel of technology, distinguish between a god and a powerful Field Binder?"

Dalen sat forward with his elbow on his thigh, resting his chin on the knuckles of his closed fist. "I would have loved to have had you in the university," he said. "You'd give Professor Loran a challenge."

"My question?" Tommy pressed.

"Well, if you're taking the text as literal history," Dalen began, "that's probably a mistake. Most scholars agree that the *Tharan Vadria* was never intended to be a historical record."

It seemed silly, but Miri couldn't ignore the little flutter in her belly. Those two had been wrapped in serious discussion for the better part of an hour. There were moments when it seemed as if both men had completely forgotten her presence. She found herself presented with the uncomfortable revelation that she might just be falling in love with Tommy. Not a simple infatuation, but a real connection. For the first time in a very long time, she felt jealousy, and she didn't like it one bit.

She tried to put the thought out of her mind. They would not be staying in Aladar very long, and it was very unlikely that Dalen would come with them. In a week, she would have Tommy to herself again. That should have been comforting; so, why did it leave her feeling empty inside?

Miri marched through the space between the shelves,

approaching the two of them and thrusting her book at Tommy. He flinched, recoiling as if he thought she might smack him with it. "Len and the Great March," she said. "He offers some very vivid descriptions of Mercy."

Tommy stared at her, his face as pale as snow. Eventually, he forced his eyes shut and gave his head a shake. "Thank you," he mumbled. "I'm sure that will be helpful."

Miri dropped the book in his lap, and that made him jump.

Without another word, she turned and stomped out of the room. There was little she could do here anyway.

4

In the ten years since Desa had left the city, her mother had moved to a small apartment building. The hallway outside her door had white walls and a wooden floor that creaked at the slightest touch.

Desa stood in that corridor with one hand on the wall, frowning down at her own feet. "Hello, Mama," she murmured to herself. "I know I've been gone for a long time, but I had to stop Bendarian..."

Squeezing her eyes shut, Desa trembled. "No matter how many times you rehearse it," she hissed, "it's never going to sound right."

She slumped against the wall, air rushing from her lungs, and brushed a lock of damp hair off her forehead. "Best to just get it over with." Her stomach was tied up in knots, and she could feel her heart pounding.

Desa knocked on the thick, wooden door.

A moment later, it swung inward to reveal an olive-skinned woman who wore her gray-streaked hair tied back in a bun. Leean Nin Alora had changed since the last time Desa saw her. Her face had a few more wrinkles; her eyes looked tired, and she wore a thin pair of glasses. "Desa?" she exclaimed.

Quick as a bolt of lightning, she rushed out the door and threw her arms around her daughter. "It's so good to see you!" She stepped back with her hands on Desa's shoulders and smiled beatifically. "I've heard so much!"

Tears welled up, blurring Desa's vision. She sniffled and shook her head. "I'm sure much of it was exaggerated."

"Well, you'll have to tell me everything!" Leean insisted.

"Mama, I'm so sorry-"

"Not a word of that," Leean said sharply. "This is a happy day. Come in! Come in! Let me show you my new home."

It was a modest-sized apartment with hardwood floors and pale-green walls. A small, round table sat in the light of a rectangular window. On the far side of the living room, a narrow doorway led into the kitchen.

Leean's old rocking chair was in the corner with an open book waiting on the adjacent table. Desa remembered that chair all too well. When she was a little girl, she would sit in her mother's lap while Leean read her a story and rocked her to sleep. So much had changed, and yet so much was still the same.

Desa strolled across the room, blinking slowly as she took it all in. "How long have you lived here?" It was the only question she could think to ask, and it sounded feeble to her ears. It was the sort of thing she should have known, *would* have known if she had not left on her adventure.

"About two years," Leean said behind her.

Approaching the wall with her arms folded, Desa nodded. "I suppose you wouldn't need that much space," she said. "With me gone..."

When she turned around, her mother was standing in the middle of the room and smiling. For reasons that she couldn't even begin to explain, Leean's gentle laughter eased some of the tension.

"I'm sorry, Mama." Desa knew that her mother didn't want an apology, but one came tumbling out of her mouth anyway. For years, she had tried not to think about how her decision to leave might have affected the people she loved most. She justified that by reminding herself that if she let the guilt claim her, she would never catch Bendarian. Now, she was back, and there was no denying her remorse any longer. "I never meant to leave you alone for so long."

Leean waved her concerns away. "You did what those idiots in the Synod refused to do," she said. "'The problems of others are not ours to solve.' Radharal Bendarian escaped their leash, but since he was gone, he was no longer a priority. The rest of the world could burn so long as Aladar was safe."

"Well, they had the luxury of such apathy," Desa grumbled. "They didn't make him into the monster that he was."

Leean nodded.

A moment of silence passed between mother and daughter, a moment in which Desa had to struggle to prevent all of her anxieties from spilling out of her mouth. Guilt or no guilt, this *was* a happy day; she had no intention of ruining it.

Finally, Leean seated herself in the rocking chair with skirts arranged neatly and hands folded in her lap. "Past tense," she said. "I take it then that Bendarian is no more."

"That is a difficult question."

Leean raised an eyebrow.

With some reluctance, Desa told the story of the final adventure that had brought her back to Aladar. She began with her visit to Sorla, rescuing Tommy and Sebastian and the trip south to Ofalla. After that, the dam burst. She couldn't have held anything back even if she had wanted to. She told her mother everything: Adele, the ancient city, her battle in the pyramid. By the end, she was crying.

Desa more than half expected condemnation from her mother, but Leean only stood up and wrapped her up in a warm hug. "My poor girl," she whispered. "You've carried this all for too long."

"I love you, Mama."

"I love you too."

They stayed like that for a little while. Desa allowed her mother to just hold her. She felt like a girl again, which was embarrassing and comforting at the same time. Somehow, Leean sensed her chagrin and started laughing.

Her mother made tea, and they shared a little chitchat. Apparently, many things had changed in Aladar. Under direction from the Synod, electric power had been expanded to every building in the city. They were drilling for oil on the north side of the island. That had been going on since before Desa was born, but the operation was growing at an almost alarming rate.

Leean's friend Morena had passed away three years ago. Desa regretted not being there for her mother. Guilt. That seemed to be the defining emotion of her life. She felt guilt for leaving her friends and family behind, but if she had stayed, she would be blaming herself for letting Bendarian go.

Leean sensed her apprehension and changed the topic. Desa was thrilled to learn that after years of trying, her mother had finally found the Ether. If only she had been here to see it…Well, at least the reunion had gone better than she had expected. Her anxiety was almost gone, and then Leean asked the one question that she did not want to answer.

"You have to go again, don't you?"

Sweet Mercy, did it have to be so warm in here? The window was open, allowing a muggy breeze to drift in from the street. Aladar was located on a small island off the southern tip of the Eradian continent; summers here were always hot. But this was too much.

Desa sat in a wooden chair with her shoulders hunched up, a sheepish grin on her face. She had forgotten how easily her mother could intuit her thoughts. "The entity that invaded Adele's body," she mumbled. "Somebody has to stop it."

Leean had a cup of tea raised halfway to her mouth, and she watched Desa over the rim. Her arched eyebrow spoke volumes. "And that someone has to be you?" she asked. "No one else can take up this duty?"

Shutting her eyes, Desa drew in a ragged breath. "I started it," she said, nodding once. "I'm the one who has to finish it."

Leean grunted.

Desa almost wished that her mother would protest and ask her to stay. It wouldn't work, but the effort would count for something. Of course, that wasn't Leean's way. If something needed doing, there was no point in complaining about it. Best to just roll up your sleeves and get the job done. That was why it was no shock when her mother said, "How long can you stay?"

"A few more days, at least."

"Well then," Leean replied, setting cup and saucer down in her lap. "We'll have to just make the most of the time we have. So, tell me about this Eradian surname you've acquired. How did you become Desa Kincaid?"

Hiding a smile behind her hand, Desa tried to ignore the blush that set her face on fire. "His name was Martin

Kincaid," she said at last. "I met him about six months after I left Aladar, in a trading port about two hundred miles north of here. I think he fancied me at first, but..."

"You've never had an interest in men."

"No," Desa agreed. "But he was a kind soul. You wouldn't think so, given his choice of occupation. Martin was what the locals called a bounty hunter, someone who would pursue criminals who had escaped beyond the jurisdiction of the local sheriff. I was young then, and I knew nothing about tracking. Bendarian had long since eluded me, and there was nothing left for me to do but return home in disgrace.

"I offered to help Martin capture a particularly dangerous man if he would teach me everything he knew. He didn't think that a painfully naïve girl from Aladar would be of much use to him, but Field Binding gave me an edge. It took us another six months before we even got a whiff of Bendarian's trail, and in that time, we brought several despicable people to justice. Murderers, rapists."

When Desa looked up, her mother was sipping tea with a thoughtful expression on her face. "So, I have to ask," Leean began. "Why did you marry him?"

Desa had been expecting this question. Steeling herself against the pain of long-buried memories, she dragged the answer out of herself syllable by syllable. "Well, for one thing, it made me an Eradian citizen, which meant that I could work on my own," she explained. "Also – and I didn't know this until the poor fool was on his deathbed – Martin stood to inherit a sizeable sum of money, and he wanted me to have it."

"So, you're rich?"

"I wouldn't go that far," Desa replied. "Fairly well-off by

Eradian standards, but I never bothered to collect the money. It's sitting in a bank in Amondale."

Leean stood up with a sigh, shuffling over to the kitchen. A moment later, Desa followed her and found her mother depositing her cup and saucer in the sink. Running water. How she had missed that simple comfort.

Leaning against the door-frame, Desa frowned at the other woman's back. "I have grown more observant over the last ten years," she said. "And right now, I'm sensing disapproval."

"Not for you," Leean assured her. "But you should never have had to make such difficult choices."

"It wasn't all bad," Desa said. "There were happy times."

Turning slightly, her mother smiled. "Well, that sets my mind at ease." She went back to washing the dishes, humming quietly as she scrubbed a plate until it shone. "So, where will you be staying tonight?"

"Last night, I stayed with Miri and Marcus," Desa said. "I suppose I will do the same tonight."

"You could stay with me," Leean suggested. "I could make you some breakfast in the morning."

"I would like that."

Marcus watched as Radavan instructed his students. They stood under a wooden pavilion at the top of the hill, surrounded by trees in full bloom. Through the tangle of branches, Marcus could see a few old buildings with roofs that had once been pure copper but had since turned a faint, pale green.

The students all wore loose-fitting gray pants and sleeveless shirts, standing in three rows of four, each one of them barefoot. They were a motley group, boys and girls, some light, others dark. Some tall, others short.

Radavan stood before them with his metal staff in hand, stiff as a board and with half the personality. "Focus is key," he said. "The life of an Elite Guardian is one of eternal vigilance."

"Yes, Master!" the students yelled in unison. *And they call me rigid.* It would not do to voice such thoughts aloud, of course. Radavan would take it as a challenge.

"A bit of a ponce, isn't he?"

Marcus stiffened at the sound of a woman's voice. His mouth tightened with disapproval. "It takes a great deal of effort to sneak up on me," he said. "I really must commend you."

He turned to find a young woman with wavy, auburn hair leaning against one of the wooden pillars that supported the pavilion's roof. She was a tall, olive-skinned beauty with eyes that a man could fall into. "Well, I've been practicing."

"Good to see you, Andriel."

"I didn't think you'd be back so soon."

Shoving his hands into the pockets of his duster, Marcus shut his eyes and drew a deep breath through his nose. "Nor did I," he admitted. "I thought I would have to drag Desa back here tied up in a sack."

Andriel was studying her nails, seemingly unconcerned with whether or not Desa ever returned to their homeland. "You could have just let her go," she mumbled. "It's not as if we're starved for Field Binders."

"Desa was one of our most talented initiates. It makes sense that the Prelate would want her returned to Aladar."

Andriel stretched, arching her back and folding her hands behind her head. "If you ask me," she began, "it wasn't about bringing back a talented Field Binder. It was about preventing Desa from sharing her knowledge with the 'savages' on the mainland."

"You may be right."

In the middle of the pavilion, Radavan had his students performing a pattern with their staves. Each child stepped forward with their left foot and thrust their weapon out. Then they pivoted, raising their staves as if to block an incoming attack. They moved in perfect unison, disciplined, orderly.

Marcus felt a stirring in the Ether when Andriel triggered what must have been a Gravity-Sink. The young woman jumped, landing on the pavilion's slanted roof with cat-like grace.

Looking back over her shoulder, she favoured Marcus with a smile that would have ignited his blood when he was a younger man. "Think you can catch me?" She was fleeing before he had a chance to answer.

Tilting his head back, Marcus narrowed his eyes. "Oh, no," he muttered under his breath. "It's not that easy."

He had his own Gravity-Sinks Infused into the metal studs on either side of his boots. Triggering them required only a thought. He jumped and practically flew up to the roof, landing near the peak.

He could already see Andriel soaring toward the branches of a tall mahogany tree. She grabbed one near the top, swung like a pendulum and launched herself into the thicket with an enticing giggle.

Marcus leaped after her.

Branches came rushing toward him, the thinner ones snapping as he crashed right through. The patch of woodland around the high hill wasn't thick, but the trees stood close together. Obstacles to bar his path.

He kicked off the trunk of an oak and pushed himself forward, crossing his arms in front of his face to shield himself. He earned a few scrapes from branches that tried to claw at him, but within a few seconds, he was back out in the open air.

Being this high gave him a good view of the city.

A grassy hill sloped down to a winding road that hugged the perimeter of the park, and beyond it, a six-story building with a slanted, green roof rose up before him. There were ornate frames on every window and stone outcroppings shaped like roaring lions.

The Academy was one of the most beautiful buildings in the city. Inside, students learned the basics of Field Binding. Even from out here, he could feel some of them manipulating the Ether.

Andriel was perched on the rooftop, looking back at him, the wind teasing her long hair. Before Marcus closed even half the distance, she stood up, climbed to the peak and disappeared from sight on the other side.

He followed her.

Letting gravity regain a fraction of its power, Andriel descended to a smaller building behind the Academy. She landed with a grunt and took off in a sprint.

Saladrin Street was lined with free-standing shops built of red bricks. Andriel loped across one and the next, and the next like a nimble dear running through the forest. Marcus was always right behind her.

There were people on the street below, but none of them paid any mind to two Field Binders at play. They probably thought it was just another exercise. The Academy was known for its unorthodox training methods.

Andriel turned down Helvin Avenue, a narrow street where the white-bricked buildings were packed close together. She never seemed to tire, leaping from one roof to the next.

Finally, when they must have been at least a mile from their starting point, she stopped and stood with her fists on her hips, gazing out on the city. When Marcus got close enough, he could hear her heavy breathing. Well, at least he had given her a challenge.

Andriel closed her eyes, her face glistening with sweat. "How do they do it?" she asked. "All those people down there. How do they live without the freedom to fly?"

Marcus removed his duster, letting it fall to land at his feet. His hat followed it, and even then, he was still uncomfortably warm. "The freedom is theirs if they want it," he replied. "Many of them do not."

"And if there is a better argument for why the majority of people are fools," Andriel countered, "I haven't heard it."

"Why exactly did you lead me on this little chase?" Marcus asked.

Her answer was a shrug and an impish grin. "I wanted to see if your skills were still sharp," she said. "You don't disappoint."

Marcus strode forward until they were almost toe-to-toe. His frown could make even the most aggressive men back down, but it had no effect on Andriel. "Was there ever any doubt?" His skill with Field Binding was a matter of personal pride.

Looking up to meet his gaze, Andriel batted her eyes. "Perhaps a little," she murmured. "You *have* been gone a long time."

"And do I meet with your approval?"

"I don't know yet."

Marcus felt his eyebrows rising.

"Field Binding is only one essential skill," Andriel said.

"As I recall, you have other talents that we must put to the test."

He was about to ask what she meant when she jumped and threw her legs around his waist. Her arms went around his neck. Her mouth found his, and then they were both falling, landing on the hard roof. The impact sent a jolt of pain through Marcus, but he barely even noticed. He was too busy removing Andriel's shirt.

NIGHT HAD FALLEN, and the stars had come out. It was harder to see them with the city lights drowning out their faint twinkle. All those months on the road had given Marcus an appreciation for a clear night sky.

He was lying on the rooftop with hands folded behind his head, smiling lazily at the heavens above. "Well," he said. "I can think of worse ways to welcome a man home."

Andriel was curled up with her head on his chest. For a little while, she just stayed there, nuzzling him. "You'll be pleased to know that your skills have not atrophied," she purred. "I was most impressed."

"Then I can rest easy," Marcus said through a fit of laughter. "The prospect of your approval was the one thing that kept me going all these long lonely months."

"A joke from Marcus Von Tayros?"

"Mark the date on your calendar."

He sat up and allowed himself to really look out on his surroundings. The city was aglow all around him, lamps shining bright on the street below. The distant buildings were like blocky shadows, but he could see lights in their windows.

Snuggling up behind him, Andriel wrapped her arms around his neck and kissed his cheek. "I'm afraid I have a confession," she whispered in his ear. "As much as I enjoyed this reunion, I had an ulterior motive for speaking with you."

"And what motive is that?"

"Jonas wants Desa to teach Field Binding at the Academy."

Marcus crossed his arms, irritation tightening his mouth. "Then why not ask Desa herself?" he snapped. "You don't need my permission to approach her."

"You've traveled with her for some time," Andriel muttered, trailing soft kisses over the back of his neck. "She trusts you. Jonas believes that she will be more receptive if the offer comes from you."

Unable to suppress his anger, Marcus ground his teeth. "And does Jonas realize that I also know the art of Field Binding?" he spat. "And unlike Desa, I haven't been gone so long that I've forgotten the Academy's teaching methods."

Andriel rested her chin on his shoulder, sighing softly. "Years away from the Academy is precisely what Jonas is looking for," she said. "He believes that Desa can bring a fresh perspective."

"And since when have I been the Academy's emissary?"

"Just make the offer, Marcus," Andriel grumbled. "We have better things to do than sit here and argue with each other?"

"Like what?"

She pushed him down onto his back again and then kissed him before he could protest. Well, in all honesty, if Jonas had made up his mind on this point, there was little that Marcus can say to dissuade him. Perhaps Andriel was right; of all the many ways they could spend their time together, arguing was not one that Marcus would have preferred.

It was well past midnight when Desa woke up on her mother's sofa. She was curled up on her side, wrapped in a blanket. The thin pillow that barely supported her head seemed to deflate even further when she moved.

Desa exhaled.

There was just no getting around it; she was wide awake now. Getting back to sleep would not be easy, and her mind kept spinning with thoughts. Thoughts of what Adele might be doing with her demonic powers. Thoughts of how this was all her fault. If she had trusted her instincts, if she had refused to let Adele journey with them...But no.

Trusting Adele was not her first act of hubris. That honour belonged to a decision Desa Nin Leean had made at the tender age of fifteen. If she had listened to the Synod, if she had avoided the temptation to take matters into her own hands, Bendarian would never have become the menace that set her on a ten-year hunt. No, there would be no sleeping while these thoughts fluttered through her head.

The apartment was dark, but the electric lamps on the street outside provided just enough illumination for her to make out the shadows of walls and furniture. Perhaps a drink would settle her down.

Tossing the blanket aside, Desa rose from the sofa. She yawned, stretching her arms high above her head, straining for a ceiling that was well out of reach. "Perhaps you were always right, Radharal," she said. "Perhaps I was always the villain of this piece."

She padded over to the kitchen, passing through the narrow doorway. The tiles were cool beneath her bare feet, a sharp contrast to the warm air.

Dropping to one knee, Desa opened a cupboard and

retrieved a glass from it. "Always the villain," she muttered to herself.

She rose and ran the sink, filling the glass almost to the brim. The water tasted better than anything she had had in recent memory, and that included some very fine wines. How long had it been since she had poured herself a glass of water? At least ten years, of course. But she couldn't remember the last time. Was it right before she had left in pursuit of Bendarian? Or earlier than that? She almost laughed. Some very strange things occurred to you in the middle of the night.

Desa turned around.

A hooded figure stood in the doorway between the kitchen and the living room, a wraith that was blacker than the darkness all around her. And its gaze was fixed upon her with singular intent.

Desa stumbled backward, slamming into the counter. Water sloshed over the rim of her glass, spilling onto her feet. "Who are-"

She blinked, and the creature was gone. There was nothing there but an open doorway, and she could faintly make out the living room on the other side: the sofa and her rumpled blanket, the tall, unlit lamp in the corner.

It was as if the apparition had never been there, but Desa knew better. She recognized that thing; it was the watcher from the dead city. How could it have escaped the confines of its domain? How could it have come all the way to Aladar?

One thing was certain: she would get no more sleep tonight.

5

"That thing..." Kalia hissed.

With morning sunlight streaming in through the window and the sounds of a bustling city outside, it was hard to feel the terror that had gripped Desa just a few hours ago. In the harsh light of day, the fear of spooks seemed... well, silly. The sheriff, however, did not share that opinion.

Kalia squeezed her eyes shut, shivering as if someone had tickled her with an icicle. Absently, she tapped her fork against a plate of sausage links, strawberries and orange slices. Some of that fruit had come from the mainland, purchased from local farmers in exchange for Infused tools. Not everyone on the Eradian continent despised and feared the Aladri. "I told you that you would see that thing again."

Desa sat across from her with lips pursed, squinting as she considered the other woman's words. "You did," she said, nodding. "But I must admit that I thought you were exaggerating."

"If you encounter that thing even once, it's with you for the rest of your life," Kalia snarled. "There are old men in

Dry Gulch who saw it as boys, and it still haunts them to this day."

Desa stabbed a piece of sausage with her fork and held it up in front of her face as if inspecting it. It wasn't the meat that held her attention; she wasn't fond of the idea of being some ghost's plaything for the rest of her life. "Has it ever hurt anyone?"

Kalia lifted her shoulders in what might have been a shrug and then exhaled roughly. "Not to my knowledge," she said. "After a while, those people who saw it find its visits to be something of a nuisance."

"What does it want?" Desa wondered aloud.

"What does any ghost want?"

Tommy had also joined them for breakfast, but until now, he had been silent, content to shovel food into his mouth with surprising gusto. Well, perhaps it shouldn't have been a surprise; Leean *was* a good cook. "Pardon my interruption, Sheriff," Tommy said. "But I don't think this thing is a ghost."

"What else could it be?"

"I'm not sure," Tommy admitted. "Some life-form that we haven't defined yet. But what I have learned in three months of traveling with Mrs. Kincaid is that 'magic' is just a word people use for a process they don't understand. I would imagine that the same is true for ghosts and demons and all other forms of superstition."

Despite herself, Desa couldn't help but smile. Her student had come a long way in such a short time. "He's probably right," she said. "Perhaps the key to getting rid of it is simply understanding it."

"Whatever it is," Leean said, emerging from the kitchen. "I do hope you find some way to escape it. I don't mind you bringing friends into my home, Desa, but I draw the line at spirits."

A knock at the door interrupted their conversation.

Leean shuffled across the room with a soft sigh and then pulled the door open to reveal Marcus standing in the hallway outside. He tipped his hat to her and then stepped into the living room. "Good morning to you all."

"Good morning," Desa said cheerfully.

Approaching her with his hands in his pockets, Marcus offered a smile. "I have news," he said. "It seems that Jonas wants you to return to the Academy and teach a few classes while you're here in Aladar."

Desa blinked.

Her mother shut the door and then joined them at the table. Marcus's smile was nothing compared to the one that Leean wore. "That sounds like a wonderful idea!" she exclaimed.

"I'm not so sure," Desa muttered. "Why would Jonas want *me* of all people to teach his students?"

It wasn't that Desa lacked the skills or the knowledge, but Field Binders in Aladar employed a certain theoretical approach to the Great Art. After ten years of wandering the world, her methods were bound to be unorthodox by Academy standards.

"He says you have real-world experience," Marcus explained.

"I do at that."

"And he's willing to pay."

Leean eased herself into an empty chair, studying Desa through the lenses of her glasses. "Little one," she began, "I don't mean to tell you your business, but I do hope that you will return home for good one day. So, it may be wise to cultivate goodwill while you are here."

"I suppose you're right," Desa said. "Tommy, you should come as well. It's past time that we resumed your instruction."

"I-" He paused, his mouth moving silently as he racked his brain for an excuse to stay behind. Desa's chest was tight with anxiety. She had hoped that Tommy might have had time to sort through his feelings about her killing Sebastian, but it seemed that he was still uneasy around her. "Yes, Mrs. Kincaid," he said when no excuse presented itself

---

SILVER RAYS of sunlight streaked through the forest as Radavan led a group of two dozen students along a path where roots poked out of the ground. The oaks and elms that surrounded them provided plenty of shade, making the air cool and damp.

Wrapped in loose, yellow robes, Radavan carried his staff in one hand. He didn't look back even when he was speaking to someone behind him. "I strongly object to this foolishness," he said. "What can these children learn from you that they cannot learn from me?"

A little humility, for one thing, Desa thought to herself. She didn't give voice to her reflections; she would *not* be baited into a verbal sparring match with this pompous oaf of a man. Any respect the students had for her would evaporate the instant she gave into that inclination. They didn't know her as they did Radavan. Many of them had been little more than toddlers when she left Aladar.

Pressing her lips together, Desa looked up toward the treetops and blinked several times. "It never hurts to learn a new perspective," she replied. "My time in the Academy did not prepare me for what I would find beyond our borders."

Radavan snorted.

Tommy was shuffling along behind Desa, frowning at the ground under his feet. Every time she glanced in his direction, he looked up just long enough to make eye-contact and then averted his gaze. He must have felt terribly out of place among the students. Desa had heard some of their whispered comments about the primitive man who thought he could learn Field Binding.

Radavan stopped abruptly between two gnarled trees. He planted the end of his staff in the ground and then nodded curtly. "Yes," he said as if speaking to himself. "This will do."

He had chosen a small grove where twisted trees reached for the sky. One had a trunk so thick it would take at least four people to form a ring around it. Thin shafts of sunlight broke through the leafy canopy above them. The scent of moss filled the air.

Radavan positioned himself in front of the massive oak tree, facing her with a smirk on his face. "Students, look at your would-be instructor," he said, pointing at Desa with his staff. "She carries a gun like a common police officer."

Standing there with her arms hanging limp, Desa closed her eyes and let the anger drain out of her like water through a hole in the bucket. Calm serenity: that was the way to win this. "Actually," she replied. "I've found that firearms provide many opportunities for creative Field Binding."

"Then perhaps a contest is in order."

Desa had been expecting this. Ever since the first confrontation three days ago, Radavan had been eager to prove his superiority. Or perhaps it was the superiority of formal Aladri training that he was desperate to assert. Either way, his bravado would be a problem. Desa had Infused a few trinkets just in case he decided to resume their duel. "I think that would be most unwise," she said. "We are here to teach the students effective tactics, not to bluster like drunkards in a tavern."

Any hope of ending this with words died when Radavan stepped forward with his teeth bared. "I'm sure your methods were quite effective against the drunkards that you so obviously disdain," he said. "Are you afraid of a real challenge?"

Desa could see it in the eyes of the students; they were watching her to see what she would do. No doubt Radavan believed that since he had bested her once, repeating that feat would be easily accomplished. That she had been exhausted from a fight with three other men did not enter into his calculations.

She could leave, of course; these students didn't *need* her instruction per se. But they would be poorly served if they walked away from this believing that Radavan's methods would leave them prepared for what they might find beyond Aladar's borders.

"Men..." Desa muttered. She discreetly slipped her hand into her pocket, closing her fist around one of the trinkets that she had prepared. Radavan stepped forward with his staff at the ready. His eyes were fixed upon her, sizing her up, looking for a weakness.

He swung for her legs.

Desa jumped, allowing the staff to pass beneath her. She landed with a grunt. The man reversed his swing, aiming for her ear.

Desa ducked and felt a whoosh of air above her. Her hand flashed out, a coin flying from her fingertips. Radavan triggered Force-Sinks that made it stop dead a few inches away from him. He had been expecting a kinetic attack. Instead, Desa triggered the Light-Source.

The coin became a tiny, blazing star that made Radavan stumble backward and kill his Sinks. He raised a hand to shield his eyes.

In that moment of confusion, Desa rushed in. She kicked him in the belly, then spun and hook-kicked, her foot whirling around to strike Radavan's chin. He stumbled, dazed by the hit.

He stretched to hand out toward her.

The instant Desa felt the slightest tug of gravity, she triggered a Sink in her belt buckle and made herself weightless. Several rocks flew past her, drawn by the Gravity-Source in Radavan's ring.

Growling, Radavan drove the end of his staff into the ground, releasing a wave of kinetic energy that hurled Desa backward. She didn't fight it; she just used the Gravity-Sink to stay aloft.

Tumbling through the air, Desa planted her feet against the trunk of an elm tree. She compressed like a spring and then pushed off flying right over her adversary's head. Allowing gravity to reassert its power, she dropped to the ground behind him.

Desa drew her pistol and spun around to face him.

Radavan was already coming toward her, but he stopped when the barrel of her gun poked his chest. Desa thumbed the hammer. "And you're dead."

His eyes widened.

Several of the students clapped.

Backing away from her with his cheeks flushed to a furious red, Radavan snarled. "Cheating," he snapped. "A dishonourable way to win."

Desa threw her head back and roared with laughter. Her sudden outburst made some of the youngsters jump. "There are men beyond our borders who would put a bullet in you because they believe that Field Binding is a form of witchcraft," she said. "Do you think they care about Aladri honour?"

Holstering her pistol, Desa rounded on the students. She strode forward with fire in her eyes. "Your first lesson!" she barked. "Never expect your enemy to abide by the rules you have learned here in the Academy."

"Yes, ma'am!" a few of them shouted.

"Now," Desa went on. "Since your teachers disdain the use of firearms, perhaps it's time to expand the curriculum. Why don't you tell me some creative ways that we might enhance an ordinary pistol with Field Binding?"

It took them some time to come up with any viable ideas. The Elite Guard did not use guns. These students were used to thinking in terms of rings that could unleash a kinetic blast or coins that could hold an enemy anchored to the ground. Useful tactics, but if any one of these children ever left Aladar, they would find themself confronted with any number of outlaws who were eager to shoot them.

It pleased her to see that Tommy had some of the best ideas. He must have been paying attention during their long journey. Now, if only he could find the Ether. Desa clicked her tongue and annoyance. Tommy's difficulties in that regard were as much her doing as anything else. She had neglected his training ever since Thrasa.

It's time to correct that mistake, Desa thought to herself. *Long past time.*

6

Clay cracked beneath her boots as Azra walked through the streets of Dry Gulch. She was wrapped in a thin, brown poncho, and so long as she kept her eyes downcast, her face would be hidden by the brim of her hat. No need to announce her presence to the deputies.

The wooden buildings on either side of what could hardly be called a road had been bleached by the sun. People walked along the boardwalks: women in thin dresses, men in straw hats who wore their shirts open. Lambs, the lot of them, and she was a very hungry wolf. But not today. Today, she had business.

Azra strode into the saloon.

A dozen wooden tables stood in the light that came in through the front window, and only three of those were occupied. An old man with a fluffy, white beard sat staring into his cup. There was a woman in tan pants and a red shirt who idly flipped a coin.

The final patron was the one that Azra had come to see, a man in his middle years with dark hair turning gray at the temples. He sat with a deck of cards on his table, flipping them one by one in a game that Azra didn't recognize.

She approached him cautiously.

The man turned over one more card to reveal a single golden cup printed on the other side. "Good fortune," he announced to no one in particular. Without so much as glancing in Azra's direction, he muttered, "I take it the deed is done."

Azra looked up and let a cat-like grin blossom on her face. "Oh, it's done," she replied. "Would you like proof?"

He nodded.

She opened the leather bag that she wore slung over one shoulder and retrieved from it a hand that had been severed at the wrist. The damn thing stank, but she tossed it onto the table anyway, and her client nearly jumped back at the sight of it. It was the ring on the third finger that would truly interest him. Sal's ring. Really, she could have just brought that, but there was always the chance that her client might assume that she had simply taken the ring and left Sal alive.

"Well," the man said. "I suppose I should arrange payment."

"That would be much appreciated."

He looked up at her with hard, brown eyes. Azra had seen that stare before. It was the one people always put on when they were silently accusing you of something. She almost snorted in derision. So, this man was too good to get his own hands dirty with the bloody work of murder, but he would hire someone else to do the job and then sneer at them after the fact. "You didn't ask me why I wanted him dead."

Azra shrugged, then turned her head to look out the window. "Don't need to know," she said absently. "You're paying me. That's enough."

"Meet me here tomorrow," he said. "I have the money for you then."

The coward gasped when she sat down across from him. She leaned forward with her elbows on the table and offered a lascivious smile, the kind that usually beckoned a man into your bed. "That wasn't the deal," she purred. "Payment was due in full the instant you received confirmation of the target's demise."

A slight flush put some colour in the man's cheeks, and he narrowed his eyes to slits. "Don't threaten me, woman," he growled. "You'll get paid when I say you'll get paid."

"Hmm," Azra replied. "You know, I'd hate to have to refer this matter to my collection agency. Because, you see, I *am* my collection agency. And I have a policy of hunting down clients who don't pay and then skinning them alive. Personally, I think that's much too harsh. I told myself as much, but we both know there's no arguing with me when I've made up my mind about something. And between you and me, I can be a real bitch sometimes. Though, much as I hate to admit it, my methods *are* quite effective."

The client smiled, shaking with laughter, and then lifted one of his cards. The Fool. Perhaps that was what he thought of Azra. "You never even bothered to learn my name," he said. "I could be gone from Dry Gulch within the hour, and you would never see me again."

"You think I need a name to track you?"

"I think you're a desert rat," he said. "Perhaps you have something of a reputation out here in the middle of nowhere. But you wouldn't last two minutes in a civilized city."

Frowning, Azra looked down into her lap. "Perhaps you're right," she said, her brows drawn together with consternation. "I suppose I am outmatched."

She got up and turned away from him.

After two steps, she paused, retrieved a coin from her pocket and tossed it at the man. Like an idiot, he caught it without hesitation. "Now *you're* paying me?" he asked. "Well, at least you've learned your place."

Azra triggered the Force-Source.

His hand exploded in a spray of blood, gore spattering on the wall. For a second, he was utterly silent. And then he wailed like a babe screeching for his mother's teat. Tears streamed over his face, and he sank to his knees, clutching an arm that now ended in a bloody stump.

When Azra left the saloon, the blazing sun was high in the clear, blue sky. People had gathered in the street at the sound of the man's screaming: townsfolk who stared at her. They scattered as soon as they recognized her, running off in different directions, leaving only two men who both wore the blue uniform of a deputy. "Azra," one said, stepping forward.

He drew his pistol, and his companion followed suit a second later.

"Oh, please," Azra muttered.

She stretched her right hand toward them, palm out. Each finger bore at least one ring – simple bands of engraved iron – and she triggered the one on her middle finger, activating a Force-Source that would release kinetic energy in only one direction.

The two men were thrown backward, hurled to the ground. They grunted on impact, one dropping his gun and the other curling up on his side.

Azra triggered the Gravity-Source on her third finger.

Both pistols were pulled toward her, one flying right out of its owner's hand. The two deputies were dragged along the ground, but she killed the Source a second later. Azra caught one of the guns, allowing the other to land at her feet.

She shut her eyes and held the pistol up in front of her face, its barrel pointed skyward. She cocked the hammer. "Now, I don't suppose the sheriff will be along any time soon."

One of the deputies sat up.

"A pity."

Azra pointed the gun at him.

"Now, now, don't be hasty," a soft, feminine voice said behind her. Azra turned around to find a woman standing by the saloon's front window. No...Not a woman. This stranger was more like an apparition in a white dress that should have slid off her body the instant she moved. And yet the garment clung lovingly to her form.

She was a fair-skinned beauty with delicate features and soft, blue eyes. And her hair was like spun gold. "Death is so final, don't you think?" she mused. "Once they're gone, we can't have any more fun."

"Who are you?" Azra demanded.

Planting fists on her hips, the woman smiled and shook her head. "Most people call me the Weaver," she declared. "I've come with a...business proposal."

"What sort of proposal?"

The strange woman shrugged and then stepped down off the porch. Her laughter was like the tinkling of bells. "Nothing too onerous, I assure you," she said. "I want you to kill someone."

One of the deputies took this opportunity to stand up and rush Azra from behind. Azra spun around to face him, but she gasped when he seemed to run into an invisible wall, bouncing off of it and falling on his ass.

"Boys will be boys," the Weaver said.

Azra licked her lips. Perhaps the most shocking thing about this display of power was that she had felt nothing, no stirring in the Ether that would indicate the use of Field Binding.

Twisting around, Azra looked over her shoulder. "Why don't you do it yourself?" she asked, raising an eyebrow. "You seem more than capable."

The Weaver flowed toward her on feet that barely touched the ground. Her haughty smile sent shivers down Azra's spine. Whatever this creature was, she wasn't human. "Oh, I'm a very busy woman," the Weaver replied. "There are certain matters that require my attention. Besides, I think you'll find the rewards of my friendship most satisfying."

Without warning, the Weaver snapped her fingers.

And the world changed.

They were now standing in an alley between two red-bricked buildings that must have each been at least four stories high. The sky above was still a deep blue, but wispy clouds drifted lazily past. And the sun was lower than it had been just a few moments earlier. It was just shy of noon in Dry Gulch, but here, it was late afternoon.

Azra strode to the mouth of the alley and froze when she stepped out onto the street. The road was unlike any that she had ever seen before. Not dirt or cobblestones but some black material that sparkled in the sunlight.

There were more buildings across the way, and they all stood as tall as the ones on either side of her. Just as she was getting her bearings, a strange noise distracted her.

A bizarre metal contraption – a horseless buggy of some kind – came rolling toward her, and when it passed, it spat a cloud of dark smoke from a pipe. By the Almighty's left nut, what was this place?

Azra felt her jaw drop, the blood draining out of her face. She shook her head slowly. "Where have you taken me?" She tried to sound threatening, but she could not raise her voice above a whisper.

With a giggle, the Weaver stepped up beside her and stood on the edge of the stone walkway that bordered the road. "I'm sure you've heard of Aladar," she said. "I thought you might like to see it with your own eyes."

"The Aladri can Field Bind," Azra mumbled.

"Yes. I thought you might like a chance to learn their secrets."

Taking control of herself, Azra grimaced. She disarmed the pistol that she had stolen from the deputy and shoved it into her leather bag. Her holster was taken by the six-shooter she normally carried. "Who do you want me to kill?"

The Weaver chuckled. "Have you ever heard the name Desa Kincaid?"

A MERCILESS SUN beat down from a clear, blue sky, the sandy beach baking under its fury. Waves lapped at the shore, but even the water could do little to ease the heat. Eliza gazed out on the Strait of Avalas, on the island that called to her from ten miles away. She could just make out the metal ships that the Aladri kept in their harbour. Everyone said those boats should sink, but the Aladri kept them afloat with magic.

At night, their city glowed.

Sometimes, after her mother and father had gone to sleep, Eliza would sneak out of the village and come down to the beach just to see the distant lights of Aladar. They were beautiful. And bewitching.

At fifteen years old, Eliza was a twig of a girl in a gray dress and a white bonnet. She sat on a large rock with her legs curled up, hugging her knees. "I could swim it," she muttered to herself. She repeated that declaration often.

What would it be like to see Aladar? A city made of magic?

She noticed something strange. A fog rolling in off the water, hovering just a few inches above the waves and slowly seeping onto dry land. It was a hot summer afternoon. Not a cloud in the sky. That should have been impossible.

Aladri magic?

She gasped when the fog began to rise and coalesce into the shape of a woman. Seconds later, a creature that she could only describe as an angel stood there: a woman in a white dress with beautiful golden hair. "Hello, my dear," she said.

Eliza covered her eyes with both hands. "Not real, not real, not real," she panted.

"Oh, I assure you, I am quite real."

When she opened her eyes, the woman was still standing there and smiling in a way that set Eliza's mind at ease. "I have come to help your village," she said. "Perhaps you could take me to your elders?"

"Who are you?" Eliza stammered.

"They call me the Weaver."

Shivering, Eliza hugged herself and rubbed her arms for warmth. Summer or no summer, she was suddenly overcome with chills. "I...I'm not sure. If you're one of the Aladri, then I suppose I should take you to Mayor Hellman."

The woman glided through the sand, laughing softly. Her long, blonde hair was streaming in the wind. "I am *not* one of the Aladri," she insisted. "I am the one who can save you from them."

"Save us?" Eliza spluttered. "The-The Aladri have never harmed us. They trade some of their devices for fruits and vegetables."

The strange woman knelt before Eliza, unconcerned with any damage the sand might inflict upon her dress. Her face was grim, her eyes sympathetic. "They are liars, my dear," she said. "They deceive you with their tricks."

"I-"

"Please," the Weaver said, laying a hand on Eliza's cheek. "Trust me."

In the end, she did bring the Weaver to meet the mayor. Hollin was a small village about two miles from the shore. The houses were built out of lumber from a nearby forest, each with black tiles on its gabled roof.

Dozens of people strolled through the dirt streets: women in dresses that covered them from ankles to wrists, men in pale shirts and dark pants that they held up with suspenders. Most people wore either a bonnet or a straw hat.

The Weaver was smiling as she took in the sight. "What a beautiful village!" she exclaimed. "You must love it here!"

For some reason, Eliza was grinning as well. "I can't complain," she said with a shrug. "Mayor Hellman is right over there."

She pointed to a portly man in a pale-blue shirt who stood with his back turned, inspecting a sheep pen. He bent to scratch the head of a tiny lamb who came up to stick its nose out between two of the wooden slats.

"Thank you, my dear," Weaver said. "I can take it from here."

Eliza should have been unhappy – to bring a magnificent stranger like this into town only to be dismissed should have bothered her – but the only thing she felt was a calm serenity. Somehow, she knew that the Weaver would make everything all right.

"I don't see what you want me to do about it," Clarence Hellman protested. "The Aladri were living on that island long before we ever came to these lands. Sometimes, we see their ships sailing up the coast."

Clarence sat behind his desk in a small house with wooden walls, smoke rising from the bowl of his pipe. "They've never done us any harm," he added. "Their devices have made life easier for us on many occasions."

The woman who only called herself Weaver stood on the small, blue rug in front of his fireplace. She closed her eyes, breathing deeply as if to regather her patience, and then nodded. "I understand why you would feel that way, sir," she said. "But the Aladri dabble in sorcery. Surely you've seen the way their city lights up every night."

"I've seen it."

"That city tempts your children," the Weaver said. "I found Eliza on the beach with a look of longing on her face."

Trapping the pipe between two fingers, Clarence pulled it out of his mouth. "The young are always tempted by the unknown," he countered with a dismissive wave of his hand. "There isn't a soul in this village who hasn't gazed out on Aladar and wondered what it might be like to walk its streets. We grow out of it."

The Weaver frowned at him, and somehow, being the target of her disapproval left Clarence with a queasy feeling in his belly. "Sir," she began. "I know the Aladri. Given time, they will tempt your people to sin and vice."

"I don't-"

Clarence winced as a fit of coughing came over him. Pressing a fist to his mouth, he hunched over his desk and nearly hacked up a lung. His head ached. These fits had been growing worse and worse over the last few months.

It took a few moments for the coughing to subside.

When he looked up, he saw the Weaver through tear-blurred vision. She was standing over him with a look of concern. "Good sir," she said in a soothing voice. "The sickness troubles you, doesn't it?"

Wiping a tear away with the back of his hand, Clarence sniffed and shook his head. "The sickness comes for us all sooner or later," he barked. "My time just happens to be a little sooner than I would like."

"And if I took the sickness away?"

Clarence looked up at her. His mouth was tight with anxiety, and he felt a bead of sweat rolling down his forehead. "Even the Aladri couldn't manage that," he grated. "I begin to wonder if you might be a madwoman."

"Far from it," she assured him. "I am your saviour."

Despite himself, Clarence started laughing. Who did this fool think she was, strutting into his town with her bold proclamations? Whatever it was she was selling, good, honest folk like the people of Hollin would not be taken by-

His laughter cut off when she strode around the desk and crouched down next to him. Her smooth hand settled onto his chest. Even through his shirt, he could feel the warmth of her skin. "What are-"

"Shh..."

At first, Clarence thought that he might have imagined it, but within a few seconds, he knew that what he felt was real. The tightness in his chest began to fade. He could breathe easily.

Staring at her with his mouth agape, Clarence felt the

blood draining out of his face. "What are you?" he whispered. "What?"

"I am the woman who is going to save your people," she said. "The one who will lead you into a new golden age."

"How..."

"We must begin by purging sin from this world," she said. "How far to the nearest major city?"

Clarence sighed. There was a part of him that couldn't believe he was going along with any of this. It was all so surreal. "Vondranar is five days' ride from here...Why?"

"Because," the Weaver replied. "We are going to need men. Lots of men with guns."

7

Light spilled in from arch-shaped windows, falling on large, wooden tables. There were bookshelves to the left and the right, each one nearly filled to bursting with texts, some old, some new. Some bound in leather, others in wood.

Tommy strode through the library with a smile on his face. Just being here made him happy. Surrounded by so much knowledge. He could spend the rest of his natural life digging through these books, and he still wouldn't be able to read them all.

"What is it you wanted me to see?" Desa asked, walking behind him with her arms folded. Her sharp tone made Tommy anxious.

"Something that might help us," he promised. "I've spent three long days learning everything I could about your people's theology."

Desa stopped dead in the middle of the room, staring at him as if he had just started speaking gibberish. She arched an eyebrow. "How exactly is that going to help us bring down Adele?"

"Just trust me."

He found Dalen sitting at one of the big tables. The other man was bent over a tome of Aladri folklore, completely engrossed in what he was reading. He didn't even seem to notice when Tommy and Desa arrived.

Finally, Dalen looked up and blinked at them. "You got to come back with you!" he exclaimed. "Excellent! Excellent! It's a pleasure to meet you, Desa Nin Leean!"

Desa only nodded.

"Right then," Dalen began. "Well, I should start by giving credit where credit is due. We owe this discovery to Thomas. You know, he has the mind of a scholar. I think he would do very well at the University if we can persuade them to take a non-citizen. I must commend you on bringing him back with you, Desa Nin Leean. Perhaps you could speak to the Synod about…Time enough for that later, I suppose"

Dalen flipped through the pages until he found what he was looking for and then tapped the book with such force it made the table rattle. "It's right here!" He practically shouted the words and then clapped a hand over his mouth, his eyes flaring when he realized that he was much too loud for a library.

All the while, Tommy stood off to the side, hoping that Desa didn't notice him blushing. Ten minutes after meeting Dalen, Tommy knew that he was in the presence of a genius. Praise from him was no small matter.

"This could revolutionize the way we think about our history," Dalen said.

Desa stood over the table with her hands on her hips. One look at her, and Tommy could tell that she was running out of patience. That frown could have curdled milk. "I'm sure it's a wonderful discovery," she said. "Perhaps you could explain it to me before we discuss the larger implications."

"Yes! Yes!" Dalen all but shouted. "Thomas, why don't you take her through it?"

Dalen slid the book across the table, and Tommy found himself looking at a page of text written in the Aladri alphabet. He couldn't read a word of it, but Dalen had been willing to translate. They had several journals of notes spread out before them.

Tommy shut his eyes and then nodded once. "This," he said, gesturing to the page, "is the story of how your people came to this island. From what it says here, they made the journey over two thousand years ago."

"I am aware of this," Desa said.

Licking the tip of his finger, Tommy turned several pages until he found an illustration depicting a line of people walking through a forest. There were two women in front: one pale with long, red curls, the other dark with a round face and large eyes.

The redhead wore what he can only describe as armour and carried with her a large spear. The dark woman, on the other hand, wore a blue dress and a hooded cloak. "From what Dalen tells me, these are your goddesses."

"Mercy and Vengeance," Desa said.

"According to the text, they led your people here."

Desa eased herself into a wooden chair, crossing one leg over the other and staring up at him like a disapproving schoolhouse teacher. "The stories were never meant to be taken literally, Tommy," she said with forced patience. "This is mythology, not history."

"Oh, I'm sure they're heavily embellished in many places," he said. "But I believe that there really was a Mercy and Vengeance."

"And what, in your three days of scholarship, brought you to that conclusion?"

Tommy didn't answer her with words. Instead, he pawed through the books that they had left scattered on the table until he found the one that he was looking for. It was small, bound with leather, and if not for Dalen, it would still be collecting dust on a shelf that hadn't seen a human hand in years.

He turned pages with wild abandon until he found the illustration that he had seen last night. "Look!" he said, practically shoving the book in Desa's face. "Look!"

She went pale.

"I knew it!" Tommy jumped for joy, thrusting his fist into the air. "It matches the description you gave us perfectly."

Desa turned the book around to expose a drawing of a pyramid...A pyramid with a huge crystal on top. Every line was crisp and clear, the shading detailed and elaborate. The artist had taken great pains to faithfully reproduce what he had seen. "This," Desa whispered. "This is what I saw in the desert."

"It's the Temple of Mercy," Tommy said. "This book is a direct transcription of the *Vadir Scrolls*, the earliest writings that eventually became your *Tharan Vadria*. If what Dalen tells me is true, this book is a letter for letter reproduction of exactly what you will find in those scrolls."

"Oh, there can be no doubt," Dalen said from the other side of the table. His eyes lit up when he looked at Tommy. "Carn Von Tomlin was obsessed with the *Vadir Scrolls*. He studied them for years. His books were meant to give laypeople direct access to the scrolls. Normally, the Synod keeps them under lock and key. Carn believed that much of what we see in the *Tharan Vadria* is a bastardization of the stories found in the original scrolls. Naturally, this was considered heresy, but-"

Dalen cut off when he realized that Desa was glaring at him.

Tommy spun to face her, smiling like a dog with a bone. "It's the Temple of Mercy," he said. "The scroll says that Mercy built it to help people discover the other world."

"The other world?"

"Where the true nature of reality is revealed."

Drawing air through her open mouth, Desa shut her eyes. "The Ether..." she whispered. "That explains so much."

"What do you mean?"

"Something changed when I went to that abandoned city," she said. "It's much easier to find the Ether now. It was never difficult, not for me, but now it's almost instantaneous."

Tommy nodded. That all made perfect sense. If the crystal was designed to make it easier for people to find the Ether, then Desa's exposure to it would have amplified her abilities. He almost wished that he had been able to enter the city himself. "Whatever that thing that possessed Adele is," he said, "I think Mercy and Vengeance knew about it."

"What makes you say that?"

He flipped through the pages of Carn Von Tomlin's text until he came upon a drawing of two women standing side-by-side. One in robes, the other carrying something that looked like a spear. And they both faced a vaguely human-shaped shadow.

Desa frowned at the picture, then looked up to meet his gaze with skepticism in her eyes. "This could mean anything," she said. "Tommy, true scholarship requires years of dedication. You can't just make these intellectual leaps."

Shoving his hands into his coat pockets, Tommy backed away from her with his head down. "Maybe not," he muttered. "But it's something."

"It is indeed," Desa agreed. "At the very least, we learned more about that ancient city. You did well, Tommy."

He was blushing – why did he have to blush at times like this? – and he just couldn't keep the joy out of his voice. "Thank you…Mrs. Kincaid."

Sometime later, Tommy sat in the light that came in through the window, holding a toothpick between two fingers and musing on what he had discovered. Desa had been gone for about half an hour, leaving him with time to think. It was just a hunch, but something inside him kept insisting that the shadow represented whatever had taken over Adele.

On the other side of the table, Dalen stood with his chin clasped in one hand, inspecting the dozens of books that they had left in a haphazard pile. "You did very well indeed," he said. "Thomas, your reflections might spark a new debate on the early histories of my people."

Tommy slipped the toothpick into his mouth, gnawing on the end of it. "Well, at least, I'm good for something," he muttered. "First time for everything, I suppose."

"Why are you so hard on yourself?"

Tommy heaved out of breath, then shook his head in dismay. "You weren't with us on the journey that brought us here," he replied. "I was beyond useless."

Cocking his head, Dalen studied him intently. There was something in the way that the other man looked at him, something that put butterflies in Tommy's stomach. "I don't think that's true," Dalen said. "And I don't believe that Desa thinks it either."

Snatching up his hat from the table, Tommy put it over his face. If Dalen asked, he would say that his eyes needed a break from the light, but the truth was he didn't want the other man to see him blushing. "I appreciate the confidence," he said, his voice muffled.

"You have the mind of a scholar, my friend."

"Well, I certainly don't have the skill of a warrior."

Without realizing it, he slipped into the exercises that Desa had taught him. Simple meditation that should have opened his mind to the Ether. One...two...three...four...five. One...two...three...four...five. Dalen was saying something, but Tommy wasn't listening. Something about how impressed he was.

Why did the man insist on complimenting Tommy so much? It was downright awkward, and no doubt about that. No one spoke so fondly about anyone else. Well...Perhaps there were exceptions. He did recall some of the village girls fawning over his brother, endlessly babbling about how handsome Lenny was, repeating the same trite sentiments over and over. From the way he went on, you couldn't be blamed for thinking that Dalen was sweet on Tommy.

It hit him like a slap on the face.

Tommy felt a tightness in his chest, and those butterflies in his stomach tried to burst out of him. Almighty help him, was it possible? It seemed to defy all reason. Why would such a handsome, cultured man want a country bumpkin like Tommy Smith? It scared him to realize that he liked the idea.

But what about Miri?

Tommy was more than fond of her. In his idle moments, he sometimes imagined settling down with her. It was pure foolishness, of course. But could a man love two people at once? Maybe he could, and maybe he couldn't, but one thing was certain: Tommy was thrilled by the thought that Dalen might be falling for him.

In that moment of elation, he felt something.

He wasn't sure what it was, but when he reached for it, the world changed. The walls, the floor and the table all became clusters of tiny bits of matter, each one many times smaller than a grain of sand. Dalen had changed as well. When Tommy looked at him, he saw not a man but a galaxy of tiny, little flecks.

His second shock came when he realized that the hat was still covering his face. His eyes were closed, and yet he could see the world with perfect, vivid clarity. Not just the library, but the street outside as well.

"Are you all right?" Dalen asked.

"I think..." Tommy stammered. "I think I found the Ether."

Desa knocked on her mother's door. Everything Tommy had told her kept rattling around in her head. Was it all possible that her people had once known about the entity that had taken hold of Adele's body? And possibly her spirit as well.

She stood in the hallway, tapping her foot and watching the ray of light that came through the peephole. "Impossible," she muttered under her breath. "If there had been any record of it, I would know."

Just when she was about to leave, the door popped open to reveal her mother standing there in a blue dress. As usual, Leean wore her hair up in a bun. "Little one," she said. "How did teaching go?"

"Well enough, I suppose," Desa barked, entering the apartment. "I had forgotten just how dogmatic people can be."

Leean shut the door.

Desa sat down on the sofa with her knees together, folding her hands in her lap. "Sometimes I wonder if I could ever fit in here again," she said. "Have I changed too much? Am I still Aladri?"

The window was open, allowing warm, afternoon sunlight to enter the room along with the sounds of a bustling city outside. Desa still wasn't used to the rush of automobiles. Just ten years ago, they had been something of a rarity. But now...Now, everyone had a car and electric lights. Would Aladar even need Field Binders in a few years?

With a soft grunt, Leean lowered herself into the rocking chair. "Of course, you're Aladri. What kind of silly question is that?"

Desa bent forward with her elbows on her thighs, resting her chin atop laced fingers. "The question of a woman who finds herself unwelcome everywhere she goes in this city," she lamented. "I never knew our people had such disdain for the mainlanders."

"What happened?"

With a great deal of reluctance, Desa dragged the story out of herself. She started with Radavan's contempt for her foreign clothes and weapons, which led to a recounting of their match. She couldn't help but feel a little vindicated when Leean laughed at how thoroughly she had trounced Radavan.

Strangely, Desa found herself sharing Tommy's reflections on their history. They had been on her mind ever since she left the library. She wasn't entirely sure why. Maybe it bothered her to think that her understanding of history might have been flawed. Deep down inside, she wanted Tommy to be wrong, which was silly. She should pursue the truth wherever it led her, but perhaps such bias was only human nature.

"Will you seek out this temple again?" Leean asked.

Sitting back on the couch with her legs stretched out, Desa covered her mouth with one hand. She blinked as she thought it over. "I'm not sure," she admitted. "There is no reason to think that anything we might find there will help us against Adele."

Leean sat with hands gripping the armrests, a vacant expression on her face. "Maybe it isn't about what you might find," she murmured. "Maybe it's about what you might learn."

"What do you mean?"

"Perhaps the Ether is the key to defeating this Adele."

"Field Binding, you mean?"

"Perhaps." With a soft sigh, Leean got out of her chair and shuffled over to the kitchen. "Will you stay for dinner?"

"I'd love to."

Five minutes later, she was listening to the sound of bubbling water as her mother boiled potatoes in the kitchen. She could feel a slight stirring in the Ether. Leean was using a Heat-Source! Desa knew that her mother had learned Field Binding, but seeing it with her own eyes still filled her with pride.

Lost in thought, she found the Ether without trying. Now was as good a time as any to restore some of her tools. She began with a complex Infusion, transforming the buttons on her shirt into Force-Sinks that would only take energy from objects coming toward her. She did the same for the iron bracelet that she had purchased yesterday. In a world full of people with guns, you could never have too many Force-Sinks.

From there, she moved on to her belt buckle. She renewed its connection to the Ether, allowing it to sap even more gravitational energy. Her mind went to the gun that she still wore on her hip. She had been carrying it around like that all day.

On the mainland, no one would blink twice at the sight of someone – even a woman – with a gun, but here, the weapon earned her more disapproving stares than she would like. She would have to find a way to carry it more discreetly. She-

Something caught her attention.

A cluster of molecules in the shape of a woman was walking through the hallway outside the apartment. That in and of itself wasn't so unusual, but she could sense the woman's clothing. A poncho, leather boots and a holstered revolver. Those were accouterments that belonged on someone who lived in the desert. But that was only part of what caught Desa's eye.

This woman was carrying a veritable arsenal of Sinks and Sources. She had a ring on every finger, and every one of them had been Infused with a connection to the Ether. A desert-dweller who wasn't Kalia and who carried that many weapons? And now, she was right outside the door.

Desa felt it when the other woman found the Ether. But why...Of course...So she would know Desa's position.

The world snapped back to a place of solid objects. Desa threw herself to the floor half a second before a bullet burst through the wooden door and sped across the living room. Into the kitchen. "Mama!"

Coming up on her knees with one hand on the grip of her holstered pistol, Desa turned her head and squinted at the door. "Now, who are you?" Her voice grated, venom dripping from every syllable.

Leean poked her head out of the kitchen, blinking several times. Her forehead glistened with sweat. "What..." she stammered. "What was that?"

"Trouble."

Desa got up and ran to the wall next to the door. She pressed her shoulder against the plaster, gasping for breath. One thought, and she found the Ether once again.

The strange woman was still in the hallway outside, moving cautiously away from the apartment. Perhaps she thought her job was done. She would soon learn the depth of her mistake. The Ether fled once Desa released it.

She pushed the door open and stepped out into the hallway.

The stranger stood in the middle of the corridor with her feet apart, wrapped in that brown poncho. She was a pretty woman with creamy, pale skin and long, dark curls that framed her round face. "I was hoping it wouldn't be that easy," she said.

"Who are you?"

"Azra Vanya."

Pressing her lips into a thin line, Desa held the other woman's gaze. She nodded slowly, choosing her next words with care. "Why are you trying to kill me, Azra Vanya?"

It startled her when Azra chuckled. "It's nothing personal," she said with a shrug. "We have a mutual acquaintance who wants you dead."

"Adele."

"Is that her name?"

Grabbing a fistful of the poncho, Azra pulled the garment over her head and tossed it to the floor. Underneath, she wore a simple, sleeveless shirt that clung to her form. "Well," she said, drawing a knife from her belt. "This will be fun."

Desa was backing away from the other woman, a fat drop of sweat rolling down her forehead. "This is pointless," she said. "I don't want to fight you."

"You don't have a choice."

With astonishing speed, Azra closed the distance between them. Steel glittered as she brandished the knife. She slashed at Desa's throat.

Desa hopped back, the knife's blade coming within inches of her skin, the air whistling as it passed. Growling, the other woman raised her weapon high and brought it down in a swift, vertical arc.

Desa's hand shot up, catching her enemy's wrist. With her free hand, she delivered a punch to the nose, a blow that landed with a *crunch*. That should have ended things, but Azra clamped a hand onto Desa's throat and flung her sideways.

Desa went shoulder-first into the wall, grunting on impact. Without thinking, she backed away seconds before Azra's blade hit the spot where her head had been. She retreated through the corridor.

When she reached the wooden door at the end of the hallway, Desa kicked it open and backed out onto a fire-escape landing. The hot afternoon sun hit her hard. Her eyes needed a moment to adjust, but she could make out the dim shape of Azra striding through the corridor. "Fine," the other woman said. "We'll do this the hard way."

She tossed a coin through the door.

Instinctively, Desa triggered the Force-Sinks in her shirt buttons. A surge of kinetic energy washed over her, kicking up a wind, but she remained planted where she was on the landing. "Field Binding isn't going to help you."

"Don't be so sure," Azra replied.

Another coin came through the door, landing at Desa's feet. Frost spread out from it in a wave; the metal landing creaked, and the air became painfully frigid.

Throwing herself sideways, Desa tumbled down the

stairs. Each bump brought her a sharp burst of pain. The sudden drop in her body's temperature almost made her blackout, but she had gotten away in time. She settled to a stop on the next landing and forced herself to stand up.

Azra was at the top of the stairs, smiling like a wolf who had found a plump, tasty rabbit. The woman had a pistol in her right hand. She lifted it and cocked the hammer.

Thrusting her fist out toward the other woman, Desa triggered the Light-Source in her ring. Azra winced from the brightness, stumbling backward. That gave Desa the moment she needed.

Triggering her Gravity-Sink, she turned and leaped over the railing. Her jump propelled her across the narrow alley, toward the gray wall of the next building over. Desa planted her feet against it, then pushed off and upward.

She was soaring across the alley again.

Twisting around in midair, she rose up towards the landing where Azra stood with one hand shielding her eyes. Desa went right over the railing and then allowed gravity to reassert itself. Her feet hit the metal with a *clank*.

Azra rounded on her, swinging the pistol in a wide arc.

Quick as a cat, Desa surged forward and grabbed the other woman's wrist with both hands. With a quick twist, she forced Azra to drop the gun. "Nice try." She spun around and sent Azra careening into the railing.

The poor woman wheezed when the metal bar hit her chest. For half a second, she slumped over it. But then she was laughing. "You *are* a challenge!" she exclaimed. "I like that very much."

Azra turned around.

Desa kicked her in the chin.

Blood flew from the other woman's mouth as she collapsed against the railing. Recovering quickly, she leaped and flew right over Desa's head, held aloft by a Gravity-Sink. She landed next to the door that led into the building.

Red-cheeked and fuming, Desa hissed air through her teeth. "This ends now!" She strode forward.

Turning around to face her with a winning smile, Azra giggled. "I couldn't agree more!" She raised her right hand, palm out. Desa noticed the simple, copper ring on her third finger.

Suddenly, Desa was hurled backward as if by a powerful wind. Her back hit the railing, and she squeaked from the jolt of pain. Her thoughts were muddled; it was hard to concentrate.

Azra released another burst of kinetic energy.

This time, the railing gave way as Desa was slammed against it. She went tumbling backwards into the open air. Instinct took over, and she triggered her Gravity-Sink. But it would do little good. An object in motion stayed in motion unless acted on by an outside force. The lack of gravity would prevent her from accelerating, but she was already falling. Her hand stretched out, seeking anything to hold.

Her fingers closed around the edge of the landing directly beneath Azra. With no gravity, it was easy to pull herself up onto it. Desa got up on her knees, gasping for breath.

She drew her pistol, cocked the hammer and pointed upward. She fired, and a small hole appeared in the metal grating above her. And then another. And then another. Surely that vile woman was dead.

When she looked up through the gaps in the grating, Desa saw nothing but blue sky. The air was still chilly, though it was warming quickly. Where was Azra? She found no sign of the other woman.

Desa felt the blood draining out of her face. "Mama,"

she whispered. In a heartbeat, she was scrambling up stairs that were still slick with melted frost, metal groaning under her feet.

She ran through the open door and down the hallway toward her mother's apartment. Azra wasn't here, but several people poked their heads into the corridor to see what had caused the commotion. Some of them yelled at her. Their shouts didn't even register. Desa cared about only one thing.

She threw open the door to her mother's apartment and found the living room empty. Sunlight streamed in through the windows. The blankets on the sofa were a little rumpled, but other than that, there was nothing amiss.

A second later, Leean stepped out of the kitchen. Desa could see the fear in her mother's eyes. "What happened?" Leean demanded.

"She escaped," Desa said. "I couldn't catch her."

"So, what happens now?"

Crossing her arms, Desa leaned her shoulder against the door-frame. Her face twisted with the pain of words that she didn't want to speak. "I'm not sure," she admitted. "But one thing is certain: I have to leave Aladar again."

8

"An assassin in my city!"

Daresina Nin Drialla stood in the light that came in through her office window, staring out at her garden. She looked as if she wanted to put her fist through the glass, and her voice grated with barely-restrained fury.

Desa waited patiently with hands folded behind her back, her mouth tight with anxiety. When it became clear that the Prelate would say nothing further, she worked up the nerve to speak. "That's correct, ma'am. I suspect she's from the desert, the same place as Sheriff Troval."

Turning slightly, Daresina looked over her shoulder. The woman's raised eyebrow betrayed more than just skepticism. Desa would bet good money that the Prelate was thinking about throwing her into a cell again. "From the desert, you say," Daresina muttered. "How did she get here then?"

"That I can't answer," Desa admitted. "She certainly didn't come here with us."

"And yet she came here looking for you."

"There would appear to be the case," Desa agreed. "I can

be out of the city by tomorrow morning. If I leave, Azra will surely follow."

Once again, Daresina turned her back and gazed out the window. Desa could see the other woman's faint reflection in the glass. The Prelate was considering her offer. "And your friends? Will they be going with you?"

"I haven't asked them."

Daresina shook her head. "We just got you back." The Prelate turned on her heel and strode across the room at a brisk pace, practically shouldering Desa out of the way. She went to a small table opposite the window and poured herself some wine from a decanter.

Lifting her glass, Daresina inhaled the bouquet before downing it all in one long gulp. "I'm not inclined to lose you again," she said. "Your skills are invaluable."

Desa wasn't sure what to make of that. Aladar wasn't lacking Field Binders; from what she could tell, there were more active students of the craft now than there had been when she left ten years ago. "Why me?" When she realized that she had spoken her thoughts aloud, she decided to press the point. "Surely, there are others who can do what I do."

"You were virtuoso," Daresina said.

A blush put some colour in Desa's cheeks. She smiled despite herself. "With all due respect, ma'am," she began. "I don't think that's true. I'm good, but I'm not unique. So, what's the real reason?"

The Prelate held her empty glass in one hand and glowered at Desa through the lenses of her spectacles. "Very well," she said. "If you were to leave Aladar, would you teach our secrets to the mainlanders?"

"I don't believe Field Binding is our secret to keep."

"And that is why you cannot leave."

Desa marched across the room with fists clenched. By the eyes of Vengeance, she was angry enough to chew through metal! "Field Binding belongs to everyone," she insisted. "We have no right to hoard such knowledge."

It galled her when Daresina laughed at that. "I will never understand why you find those primitive fools so fascinating."

Craning her neck to meet the other woman's gaze, Desa narrowed her eyes. "We like to think of ourselves as enlightened, don't we?" she hissed. "But we carry all the same prejudices that we shun in others."

The Prelate turned her back and poured herself another drink. She took a moment to sip it before saying, "You may go now, Desa Nin Leean."

Tommy burst through the front door of Miri's townhouse to find the foyer empty. A set of wooden stairs led up to the second level, but the sound of a knife tapping a cutting board told him that Miri was in the kitchen.

He bounded through the hallway at full speed, yanking the hat off his head and tossing it aside. "I did it!" he exclaimed. "I did it!"

An open doorway led into the kitchen, and he found Miri standing with her back turned, chopping celery over the counter. She refused to even look at him. Something had changed after they came to Aladar, and he couldn't quite put his finger on what it was.

Standing in the doorway with his hands in the pockets of his trousers, Tommy frowned and looked down at the floor. "I did it," he said again with a hesitant step forward. "I found the Ether."

Miri stood up straight when she heard his declaration

and ventured a glance over her shoulder. "That's wonderful." She went back to chopping vegetables, and this time, the knife made an angry *thud* every time it hit the board.

"That's all you have to say?"

"I said it's wonderful."

Closing his eyes, Tommy tilted his head back and took a deep breath through his nose. "Miri, what's wrong?" he asked. "You've been angry with me ever since our first day in the city."

"I'm not angry."

Should he take her at her word? She certainly seemed angry, but he distinctly remembered moments when he had insisted that one of the village girls was mad at him – always after the girl made some biting comment – and he had learned that trying to make someone admit they were angry only made matters worse. Perhaps he should put her to the test.

Tommy shuffled up behind Miri and tried to wrap his arms around her belly. She flinched, pulling away from him, and he recoiled as if the touch of her skin might burn him. Definitely angry. "I'm sorry."

She said nothing.

Turning away from her, Tommy plodded back to the door. He paused and let out a sigh. "If you won't tell me what's wrong," he said, "how can I fix it?"

Maybe he should go find Marcus. The other man would be happy to learn of Tommy's success. After all, the ability to Field Bind meant that Tommy wasn't useless anymore. Marcus might be willing to teach him how to make a basic Infusion. He was halfway down the hallway when Miri called after him. "Are you staying for supper?"

Tommy shut his eyes tight, trembling with frustration.

He braced one hand against the wall to steady himself. "Do you *want* me to stay for supper?"

Of course, she didn't answer.

When he went back into the kitchen, Miri was leaning against the counter and glaring at him. "I suppose Dalen helped you with your little discovery."

Tommy felt intense heat in his face. He looked away, unable to meet her eyes. It wasn't as if Dalen had said anything or done anything to help him, but Tommy did wonder if he would have been able to find the Ether if he hadn't been so excited.

"I knew it," Miri spat.

"It's not like that," Tommy insisted.

"Are you in love with him?"

Tommy stood there with his mouth hanging open, shaking his head slowly. "I'm in love with you!" he shouted. "Don't you know that?"

Gripping the edge of the counter with both hands, Miri bent double. "No, I don't," she said. "For five days, that man was all you could talk about."

"Because we were helping Desa!"

"Oh, give over, Tommy!" She had used his real name. That was not a good sign. "We both know it was more than that!"

He sat down on one of the wooden chairs, hunched over and clutching the fabric of his trousers so hard his knuckles whitened. "I never wanted to hurt you." He knew that was a stupid thing to say the instant the words left his mouth, but what was said could not be unsaid; so, there was nothing to do but press on. "Yes, I feel something for Dalen. But I feel something for you too."

Miri strode forward and loomed over him. Her face was

haggard. "Then it looks like you're going to have to make a decision," she whispered. "I suggest you do it quickly."

He looked up at her with tears on his cheeks. "I'm sorry." His voice was weak, strained. "I...I'm sorry."

In the end, he didn't stay for supper. He had the distinct impression that Miri no longer wanted his company. Which left him with a conundrum. Where exactly was he supposed to sleep tonight? He thought about seeking out Marcus, but...No. That was a bad idea. The man wasn't likely to be sympathetic when he learned that Tommy had broken his sister's heart. Desa? No, she wouldn't want to deal with him. Still, he should probably tell her about his accomplishment. Without really thinking about it, he started walking in the direction of Leean's apartment.

When Desa returned home, she found Kalia sitting on her mother's sofa with a glass of wine cradled in both hands. The sheriff looked up at her and smiled. "You're back!" she exclaimed. "Your mother told me about everything that happened."

"I take it you will be joining us for dinner."

"If you don't mind..."

Crossing her arms, Desa paced across the living room. "I have no objection," she said with a shrug. "But I thought you were staying with Miri."

Kalia took a sip of her drink and grimaced. Not for the vintage, surely. Aladar made some of the best wine Desa had ever tasted. "She and Tommy are fighting," Kalia said. "I thought it best to give them some privacy."

Desa turned her back on the other woman, facing the window that looked out on the city. The sun had set, and the lamps were all glowing. Buildings across the way had lights in their windows.

"Do you know anything about the woman who attacked you?" Kalia asked.

"She called herself Azra Vanya."

The sound of glass shattering made Desa jump. She turned around to find Kalia standing in a puddle of wine. The woman's face was deathly pale. "Say that again," she whispered.

"Azra Vanya. Do you know her?"

"She's one of the most notorious criminals in Dry Gulch," the sheriff replied. "She has killed at least five of my deputies. And several others have gone missing."

Desa sat down on the windowsill, breathing deeply to calm herself. "I thought as much," she muttered. "I've faced some dangerous people, but this one...She knew how to fight and how to Field Bind."

Leean emerged from the kitchen and frowned at the sight of spilled wine on her floor. She did not comment, however, only glancing at Desa before she went to fetch a broom from the closet.

Desa sighed. More and more, she was starting to think that remaining in Aladar would only put the people she cared about at risk. In only a few short days, she had brought a ghost and an assassin into her mother's home. But she was certain that if she tried to leave, Daresina would send Elite Guardians to stop her.

Without a word of complaint, Leean began sweeping shards of glass into a dustpan. Kalia muttered an apology, but Leean told her not to fret about it. Accidents happened, after all.

Hugging herself, Kalia rubbed her arms for warmth. She took a few cautious steps toward the window. "Listen to me," she began. "If Azra's after you, she won't give up. She'll keep coming until you're dead."

Leean straightened with the dustpan in one hand and directed a flat stare at the sheriff's back. "Surely, the Elite Guard can stop her," she said. "We have dozens of Field Binders in this city, hundreds if you count those who are still learning."

"And Azra will kill every single one of them who gets in her way."

"What does she want with you, Desa?" Leean stammered.

Wiping sweat off her brow with the back of one fist, Desa shut her eyes. "She said that Adele sent her." This couldn't be allowed to continue. If Aladar's ancient texts did not provide a way to deal with Adele, a simple bullet would do the trick.

Their conversation was interrupted by a knock at the door.

Grumbling under her breath, Leean ambled across the room and pulled the door open to reveal Tommy standing in outside. The young man had a bright smile on his face. "Ladies," he said with a curt nod. "I have news."

He stepped into the apartment, doffed his hat and made a respectable bow to all of them. "Mrs. Kincaid," he said. "I found the Ether!"

Desa was on her feet before she even realized it, striding toward him with a grin that made her cheeks hurt. "That's wonderful!" she all but shouted. "I knew you could do it, Tommy!"

He went red, then pressed a fist to his mouth and coughed several times. "Yes, well," he mumbled. "Now that I've taken the first step, will you teach me how to make an Infusion?"

"Of course!" Desa replied. She noticed that Kalia was smiling as well, and it wasn't hard to understand why. There was nothing so satisfying as seeing someone experience the joy of communing with the Ether for the first time. "Meet us downstairs in an hour. I think Kalia might like to join us."

"Yes," the sheriff said. "I would."

Desa had chosen a small park near her mother's building for this lesson. It was nothing special. Just three curved benches positioned in a circle, surrounded by grass and trees. Of course, that wasn't what Tommy saw.

For him, the world was a tempest of molecules. That was the word Desa used for the tiny bits of stuff that made up everything, including his body. He could barely move, and that was a frustration. Somehow, communing with the Ether made it difficult to control his body.

Desa and Kalia were with him. He saw them both as figures composed of billions upon billions of molecules. But it was different than when he had looked upon Dalen while in the Ether's embrace. The women seemed to glow with radiance to rival the sun. They were both communing with the Ether as well.

Desa pulled upon something with her mind. Strands of the very same radiance that suffused her body. She fed them into the gaps between the molecules that made up a small, copper penny.

Tommy understood.

She was giving the penny a connection to the Ether, a connection attuned to kinetic energy. The coin would release a powerful blast when triggered. Or rather it would once the Infusion was complete. It took time to make a powerful Sink or Source.

Tommy reached for those strands of radiance with his thoughts. Nothing happened. For half a second, it seemed as if he felt...something. A brief fluctuation in the Ether. As if he had plucked it like a taut guitar string. But it lasted only a moment. He tried again with the same result. Every time it seemed as if he had control of the Ether, it would slip right out of his grasp.

Desa was still working on her infusion, but he could feel Kalia's eyes on him. Well, not her eyes. She was sitting slightly askew from his perspective, not looking at him, but he was aware of her attention. He had the distinct impression that she was trying to encourage him.

He tried once again, and this time the Ether responded. He gathered it into a thin strand and directed it toward the coin at his feet. He was so excited that he lost control, and the strand dissipated.

Frustration overwhelmed him.

The Ether fled, and then he was looking at two unremarkable women sitting on two benches in the middle of a grassy field. The nearby street lights provided enough illumination for him to make out their faces.

Kalia was sitting with her eyes closed, breathing deeply. She wasn't glowing any more. Tommy could sense something about her, something that told him she was still wrapped in the Ether's embrace, but he didn't *see* anything out of the ordinary.

Kalia opened her eyes, and then her face lit up with a smile. "You're doing very well, Tommy."

"Thank you, Sheriff," he muttered.

"I mean it!" Kalia insisted. "Finding the Ether is only the first step on a long road. Most people need at least several weeks of practice before they can make even the simplest of Infusions."

Desa finished her work, and the strange sensation that Tommy felt faded away. She stood up and faced him. "She's right, Tommy. True mastery of Field Binding takes time."

He closed his eyes, breathing deeply through his nose, and then nodded to both of them. "Thank you," he said. "Sheriff, might I have a moment alone with Mrs. Kincaid?"

"Yes," Kalia said. "I imagine you have a lot to talk about."

She was gone for almost five minutes before Tommy found the courage to speak, and in all that time, Desa made no attempt to break the silence. She was content to wait for him to say his piece.

"I'm sorry," Tommy began.

Cocking her head, Desa studied him with a quizzical expression. "I was unaware that you owed me an apology, Tommy," she said. "What exactly are you sorry for?"

"For being angry with you," he mumbled. "About Sebastian."

Desa sat down beside him, and he could see the tension in her face. "You had every right to be angry with me, Tommy," she said. "I wish I could tell you that I'm sure I did the right thing, but I can't."

"I think..." Tommy couldn't quite get the words out; his thoughts were all jumbled. Memories of Sebastian came bubbling to the surface of his mind, memories that brought with them an uncomfortable realization.

He no longer loved Sebastian.

It was the first time that Tommy had put that thought into words. When he remembered his former lover, he felt pity and sadness for the man that Sebastian might have been if he had only had the chance. But love? No, that was long gone. And its absence raised another troubling question. Had he *ever* loved Sebastian? If his affection could die so easily, was it ever real?

"I think," he said again, forcing himself to press on. "I think that, sooner or later, Sebastian would have tried to kill you. If Bendarian hadn't been there, he would have tried something else."

"Perhaps."

Tommy stood up with a huff, shaking his head as he paced through the grass. "Oh, there ain't no perhaps about it," he said. "He hated you, Desa. I never knew he had such malice in his heart."

"He showed no sign of it before you left your village?"

Tommy propped one foot up on the bench across from Desa, folding his arms and staring off into the distance. "He was angry sometimes," he said. "But who wouldn't be in his place? The world told him he was vile just because he was different."

A glance over his shoulder made him pause.

Desa was sitting with hands folded, and through the light was dim, he could see the tears on her cheeks. "Just the same," she muttered. "I'm sorry it ended the way it did."

"That means a lot, ma'am."

With a sigh, Desa stood up and nodded once. "Shall we go?" she asked. "It's getting late."

"Don't suppose you could spare enough for me to take a room at the hotel?" Tommy asked. "I reckon Miri doesn't want to see me right now. And I'm not exactly flush with Aladri cash."

"Come on then," Desa said. "Let's find you a place to sleep."

9

Gray clouds had settled into the skies above Aladar, threatening to loose a torrent of rain. Threatening but never making good on that promise. The air was still muggy and hot. Uncomfortably so, in Desa's estimation. Now, when had that happened? She had never minded the heat in her youth. Years of living in Northern Eradia with its forests of pine trees had changed her.

She walked with Tommy down a narrow street lined with white-bricked townhouses with dark shingles on their roofs. There was no one in sight, no people on the street, no cars driving past.

Tommy walked with his hands in the pockets of his duster, his mouth compressed into a frown. "You think..." He glanced over his shoulder with worry plain on his face. "You think she'll forgive me?"

"I wish I knew."

"But-"

Tossing her head back, Desa rolled her eyes. "Tommy, if you want to know about the Ether, I can answer your questions." How she wished he would focus on that instead.

Why did love turn people into idiots? "But in matters of the heart, I'm somewhat out of my depth."

Tommy shrugged. "Well, that about says it all, don't it?" He pulled the brim of his hat down over his eyes.

The walk to Miri's house took another five minutes. As one of the Ka'adri, she had a nice home with a small garden near her front door. There were roses in bloom. Someone else must have planted them. Miri would have been in Glad Meadows when the time was right for it.

As if the simple act of thinking of the woman summoned her, Miri emerged from the house in a long, dark coat. She looked up and sneered when she saw Tommy. "I have to report to my superiors. I don't have time to talk."

"You may as well hear him out," Desa urged.

Miri glared at her.

Perhaps involving herself in this lovers' quarrel was a bad idea. Best to keep quiet and avoid the hassle. She had enough problems already. Tommy opened his mouth to say something, but Miri silenced with one look. Ten seconds later, she was gone, stalking off down the street without another word.

Tommy yanked his hat off, threw it down on the sidewalk and then flattened it beneath his shoe. "Almighty have mercy!"

Desa stepped up beside him, shaking her head in dismay. "Maybe we should go to the library," she suggested. "Maybe we'll learn something useful."

"I'm not sure I want to go to the library," Tommy muttered. "Dalen..."

"Are you going to avoid him?"

Blushing hard, Tommy closed his eyes, and a tear slid over his cheek. "I don't know," he growled. "I just..."

Desa put a hand on his forearm, and some of the tension

drained out of him. "Then let me buy you some breakfast." A thought occurred to her, one that seemed to rush to the tip of her tongue. Her rational mind warned her that this was a bad idea, but she pushed on anyway. "You can tell me what happened with Miri, and maybe I can give you some advice."

Wiping the tear away, Tommy sniffled. "You sure you want to do that?" he asked. "I thought you said that it wasn't a subject you knew very much about."

"I'm sure."

They walked in silence for a while, making their way back to the city centre. Those dark clouds loomed overhead, but a gentle breeze took some of the heat away. Mercy be praised for that.

This neighbourhood reminded Desa of the one she had grown up in. Before fleeing the city, she had lived with her mother in a house very similar to the one that Miri now occupied. They had wanted for nothing in those days. People started talking about Desa's remarkable talent for Field Binding when she was only ten years old. She had been a child prodigy, her every need provided for.

That must have changed after she left.

The Academy would not continue to pay Leean's monthly stipend when her daughter was no longer an asset to the city. What would life have been like after that? She felt sick to her stomach at the thought of the hardships that she had inflicted on her mother. "It wasn't supposed to go this way."

"Mrs. Kincaid?"

Desa stopped dead in the middle of the sidewalk, her head hanging with the weight of her shame. "I was supposed to be gone for a few months," she mumbled. "Not for ten long years."

Tommy removed his damaged hat, and the wind ruffled his hair. "You know, I always wondered about that," he said. "You told me that you lost Bendarian's trail more than once. So, why didn't you go home after that?"

"I couldn't let him run loose."

Tommy looked at her, really looked at her, and there was something in his eyes. Something that made it clear he was putting the pieces together. Icy fingers squeezed Desa's heart. What would happen when he figured it out? He had only just forgiven her for Sebastian. Could their friendship endure another blow? "Not to argue with you, Desa," he began. "But there are lots of criminals out there, and if this Azra lady is any indication, some of them can Field Bind. What made Bendarian so special?"

"He was my responsibility."

"Why?"

"Because it was my fault!" she blurted out. "I'm the one who taught him how to commune with the Ether. Morley, Adele, the long line of corpses Bendarian left in his wake: none of it would have happened if not for me."

Tommy's eyebrows shot up, and then, of all things, he barked a laugh. "Well," he murmured. "Now, there's a story if ever I've heard one."

Desa leaned against a lamppost, closing her eyes and shuddering. "Radharal Bendarian came to us from the mainland," she said. "He was a young man then, not much older than you are now."

Tommy nodded.

"He claimed that his family died from the Strangler." Of all the ways to go, that was one of the worst. Desa had seen the effects of the infection first hand. Those who contracted it died gasping as their lungs filled with fluid. Based on her guess, it was bacterial, but she was no physician. And she had been five hundred miles away from Aladar at the time; there was no chance of procuring antibiotics. "He said that he had heard about the wonders of Aladri medicine. How we could cure even the most virulent infections. He wanted to know the secret. The Synod refused, of course, 'Our secrets are not for the mainlanders.'"

Tommy looked crestfallen as he stared down at his own shoes. "Nice to know your leaders hold us in such high regard."

"It's not entirely their fault," Desa explained. "Expeditions from the mainland have tried to take Aladar from us before. We kept them at bay with Field Binding. It was the only thing that allowed us to retain independence. So, you can see why the Synod would be reluctant to share any of our secrets."

"I can," Tommy agreed. "Still don't make it right."

Shutting her eyes tight, Desa stiffened. "Bendarian became obsessed with Field Binding," she said, starting up the sidewalk again. "I was only fifteen then. I took pity on him. The Synod forbade me from teaching him anything."

"But you did it anyway."

Rounding on him, Desa looked up at the young man. "Field Binding belongs to everyone!" she growled. "We have no right to hoard such knowledge!"

Tommy backed away from her with his hands raised defensively, his eyes wide with fright. Perhaps she had been a little too...emphatic. "I agree with you," he said. "I just wanted to get the facts straight."

"I'm sorry," Desa muttered.

"Don't be."

"When the Academy realized that Bendarian could find the Ether, they petitioned the Synod to let him stay on the island. I suspect they didn't want to let him out of their sight.

He was with us for several years; I became convinced that he was proof that the mainlanders were ready to learn our secrets.

"But then people started dying. At first, the police had no idea who to blame. People would just disappear without a trace. Several weeks later, someone would find a corpse. Always in a different place. Bendarian believed that he could Infuse people with a direct connection to the Ether."

"I thought that was impossible," Tommy said.

Desa turned her back on him, pacing up the sidewalk. "It is," she replied. "Not only can you not Infuse living things, you can't Infuse anything that has ever been alive. My leather belt, my cotton shirt: neither one will take an Infusion."

"Then why would Bendarian try?"

"He wanted to wield the power directly," Desa said. "Without the need to use objects as intermediaries. The Synod thought he was insane. They believed that he would never accomplish his goal."

"But, somehow Bendarian found a way. And now Adele has taken that power for herself."

They had come to an intersection at the edge of Miri's neighbourhood. A few cars rushed down a street lined with tall, box-like buildings made of red or white brick. Most had shops on the first floor, shops with large front windows that displayed everything from women's fashions to hunting equipment.

As usual, Tommy paused for a moment to admire the city. The sight of Aladar still filled him with wide-eyed wonder. "What I don't understand," he said. "This power that Bendarian found…What is it?"

"He called it the Nether."

"Sort of like an anti-Ether."

"I suppose."

Tommy rushed on ahead, then spun around to face her, walking backwards and gesticulating wildly. "See, this is why I think your people's history holds the key to defeating Adele," he said. "Mercy told your ancestors that the Ether is order. A tool that humanity can harness. She warned your ancestors that there were dark magics as well. Ones that offered incredible power at a terrible price."

Desa took a deep breath to calm herself. This was all new to Tommy. Patience was a must. "We've been over this," she said gently. "The stories were never meant to be taken literally."

Tommy was smiling and shaking his head. "You don't understand." He nearly backed into a woman who scooted out of the way at the last second. Did he even realize that she was there? "What do you know about my religion?"

"Very little," Desa admitted.

She breathed a sigh of relief when Tommy chose to halt and continue their conversation in front of the bakery. "The stories about the Almighty are all filled with impossibilities," he said. "Horses with wings, the sun zipping back-and-forth across the sky. Men who live to be a thousand years old. I have a hard time believing any of it."

"I see..."

"But," Tommy went on, "we have proof that at least some of your people's myths are based in fact. The pyramid, the crystal. Mercy warned your people about the dark power, and now we know that's real too! We've seen it!"

It made a kind of sense. The *Tharan Vadria* was more than just a collection of stories. Several chapters offered detailed instructions on how one might commune with the Ether. Even if the stories had been embellished, there might be a kernel of truth in them. Something they could use to stop Adele. "I think you've convinced me," she said.

"Good! Let's go to the library!"

She couldn't help but smile at his enthusiasm. "A sound plan," she said. "But what about your friend?"

Tommy tossed his arms up and then let them fall again. He was grinning so fiercely it almost made her laugh. "If you're willing to translate," he said, "then I don't need Dalen, do I?"

"I suppose not."

Something caught her eye. The dim reflection of a hooded figure was suddenly visible in the bakery's front window. A reflection cast by no object that Desa could see. She gasped.

"What?" Tommy asked.

Desa backed away from the window, one hand instinctively reaching for the pistol that she no longer wore on her hip. At first, she cursed her decision to leave it behind. But then what could a gun do against a ghost? "It's nothing," she stammered.

Tommy glanced into the window. "The ghost?" he asked. "I don't see anything."

The shadow slowly faded away, leaving only a transparent reflection of the buildings across the street. She could even see the baker boxing up a loaf of bread inside the store.

"Perhaps I'm going mad," Desa muttered.

Tommy was still staring into the window. If he kept that up, the baker would come out to shoo them away. "No, I don't think so," he said, shaking his head. "Kalia said that if you see that thing once, you'll keep seeing it for the rest of your life. There's a very real phenomenon at play here; we just don't understand it."

"You're growing wise, my friend."

"Well, it seems to me the best thing we can do is learn as much as we can."

"Yes," Desa agreed. "Yes, I think you're right."

MARCUS'S SHOE came down on upon the sand, kicking up a puff of dust. In dungarees and a white shirt with its top buttons undone, he walked along a beach where waves lapped at the land.

Off to his left, the eastern shore of Eradia stretched on with ten miles of water between them. Even with those clouds overhead, the air was still hot and damp. A good morning for a walk.

He paused to admire the view.

Marcus stood on the shoreline with his hands folded behind his back, squinting into the distance. "Your work is done," he told himself. "If Desa leaves again, you do not have to go with her."

But he knew he would.

Baring his teeth with a hiss, Marcus shook his head. "You're a foolish man, Marcus Von Tayros," he muttered. "A downright idiotic man."

He caught sight of something out on the water. Was that…Yes, that was a boat. The thing was barely big enough to hold two people, and he could just make out a pair of men paddling. They seemed to be coming his way. Odd, that. Eradian ships often sailed through the Strait of Avalas, but they usually steered clear of the island. Fear of Aladri magic kept them at bay. "Well, now," he said. "What's all this about?"

Mainlanders sometimes came to Aladar, but they always entered the city via the harbour. Going any other way might be interpreted as trespassing, and no one wanted to risk that. He decided to follow the beach to the place where they would make landfall.

It was a short walk to the spot where he would intercept them, and as he made his way along the shore, the boat grew larger and larger. He could see the faces of the two men. Both were pale and a little older than he was.

"Good morning, gentlemen!" he called out in Eradian.

They immediately turned their boat around, heading back toward the mainland. What *was* that about?

Marcus crossed his arms, scowling as he watched them go. "Eradians," he said, shaking his head. "An entire continent full of imbeciles."

As always, the library had that musty book smell, and Tommy was willing to bet that most of it came from the ancient text he held in his hands. He turned the old, yellow pages of a book that hadn't been opened in at least fifty years. Another commentary on the *Vadir Scrolls*. It was hard to focus; thoughts of Miri kept creeping into his head. Eventually, he located the crude drawing of a spear. "Look!"

He found Desa sitting in the light of a window. She blinked at the sound of his voice. "I'm sorry?" You might have thought she was the one dealing with matters of the heart.

He passed her the book.

"The Spear of Vengeance. What of it?"

Tommy spread his arms wide, smiling and shaking his head. "The weapon of a god," he said. "Let's operate under the assumption that this thing that took over Adele is of a similar nature as Mercy and Vengeance."

"A big leap," Desa replied. "But I'll humour you."

Tommy fell into the chair across from her, snatching a toothpick from his pocket and slipping it into his mouth. "Well," he began. "It seems to me that the weapon of a god can kill a god."

Desa was glowering at him with her brows drawn together. A heavy sigh escaped her. "Tommy," she said. "What did I tell you about making assumptions? First off, we don't even know that this weapon exists. Second, if it does, we don't know where to find it. And third, we don't know that it will do what you claim it will do."

Removing the toothpick with two fingers, Tommy felt his eyebrows rising. "You have a better idea?" he countered. "We've been hashing out plans for the last two hours. Name one idea we've had that doesn't rely on assumptions."

"I can't."

"My point exactly," Tommy said. "No matter what we do, we're going to be basing a lot of decisions on guesswork."

"I take your point," Desa whispered. "But let's try to refine it as much as possible."

"Of course."

"Are you all right?"

The question forced him to think about the painful emotions he had been ignoring. Emotions that, so far as his useless brain was concerned, felt very much like a punch to the chest. "I'll survive."

"I'm surprised you're still willing to talk to me."

Tommy sat up straight, blinking as he tried to puzzle out her meaning. "Why would I be unwilling to talk to you?"

Desa sat there with her eyes closed, breathing deeply. It was clear to him that she was trying to work up the nerve to speak. "Now that you know my secret," she muttered. "The depth of my crime."

In half a heartbeat, Tommy was out of his chair and

gaping at her from across the table. The depth of her crime? It dawned on him then that Desa was as much a victim of her upbringing as he had been of his. "Desa," he said. "You tried to help a man who lost his family. That's not a crime. And you aren't responsible for the things he did with the knowledge you gave him.

To his surprise, she smiled, and he was fairly certain that he could see a touch of crimson in her cheeks. "Thank you," Desa whispered. "But, just the same, I would prefer it if you kept my confession in the strictest confidence."

Tommy picked up the hat he had ruined, peering into it. "Well, you heard that," he said. "So, we're going to keep this between you and me, smashed hat."

Desa stood up, and then she bowed to him. A shallow bow but it still left him feeling embarrassed. "Thank you, Tommy," she said softly. "If you don't mind, I think I'll get some air. I need to clear my head."

10

Desa stepped out of the library, into the shade provided by the overhanging roof above the front entrance. Not that she needed much shade on a day like this; those thick clouds were still lingering. People were milling about on the street below, some walking past the park on the other side of the road, others looking into the windows of nearby shops. Gloomy weather didn't keep Aladri indoors. Not when the island was visited by a hurricane almost every year.

Bracing a hand on one of the massive, stone pillars, Desa paused to look out on her city. "The boy's smarter than he has any right to be," she muttered under her breath "Puts the fools in the Synod to shame."

She descended the steps at a quick trot, and before she was halfway to the bottom, she found herself grinning. "If he's so smart," she said, "maybe you should listen to him."

The plan to go searching for the Spear of Vengeance was sheer lunacy, but she had to admit that she had no better ideas. There had to be something they could use against Adele. Maybe Tommy was right; maybe the secret really was buried in Aladar's history. A visit to the clerics might be in order.

Desa started up the sidewalk with her head down. Her tan pants and thin, button-up shirt were a tad warm for summer in Aladar, but she had no local clothes, and she felt no inclination to purchase any. It was bad enough walking around without a gun on her hip.

Desa blinked.

Ten years ago, the prospect of openly carrying a weapon would have been unthinkable, and now, she felt naked without it. Her travels had changed her. And not necessarily for the better. Her shirt buttons were all Infused, though. As were her bracelet and belt buckle. She would not be totally helpless if trouble came her way.

A portly man who wore thick suspenders over his white shirt – his gray hair tucked under a billed cap – sneered as she passed him. She pretended not to see but then he called out, "You're Desa Nin Leean, aren't you?"

Turning abruptly, Desa faced him with her hands clasped behind herself. She tried to keep her face smooth. "I am," she admitted. "What business is that of yours?"

"Some people say you're a traitor."

Desa smiled, backing away from him. "Then some people have been wrong at least once in their lives." She turned to go, putting the fool out of her thoughts, but he was determined to be acknowledged.

"Bitch!" he called out behind her.

She looked back over her shoulder, watching him from the corner of her eye. "Tell me, friend," she said. "Have the citizens of Aladar become less courteous in my absence? I don't recall witnessing such uncouth behavior when I lived here, but those memories might be coloured by the innocence of youth."

The man's face went red, and he squinted at her. "You gave our secrets to the savages!" he snarled and took a bold step forward. "Everyone knows it!"

Desa stepped up to him, looking right into his eyes, never flinching, not even for a second. "Are you a Field Binder, friend?" she asked. "These secrets you covet, do you know them yourself?"

"What does that have to do with-"

"Do you know how to build cars?"

"No."

She gestured to the black automobile that was rolling past as they spoke. "I thought not," she said. "But I'm sure you've ridden in one. Benefitted from a piece of technology that you did not design."

The man was trembling with barely-restrained fury, the kind men seemed to display whenever you demonstrated that they weren't as intelligent as they liked to think they were. Perhaps she should have been frightened, but she wasn't. "You don't know me!" he spat.

"True," Desa conceded. "Perhaps I've underestimated you. Have you developed any vaccines? Or new antibiotics?"

"I-"

"But I'm sure you have accepted such medicine when you became ill," she said. "It seems that you draw a lot of benefit from other people's discoveries. Why should you object to others doing so?"

She left him to consider her words. For the moment, he was speechless, and she would rather end this conversation before he decided on his next rebuttal. Indulging fools only did so much good.

On the nearest street corner, she found a woman in a green dress running a small fruit-stand. There were plenty of items to choose from: plums, peaches, ripe oranges and bananas. The island offered ideal growing conditions for all, but she suspected some of those came from the mainland. Traded for Heat-Sinks that could keep food fresh or for Sources that could provide warmth on a rainy, winter night.

The young woman looked up at her with a bright smile. "Fresh fruit for you today, ma'am?" she asked. "We have delicious mangoes."

Desa approached the stand with hands in her pockets, inspecting the merchandise with her lips pursed. "A peach, perhaps," she replied. "It's been a long time since I've had one. How much?"

"Fifty cents for two."

So expensive! There was a time when you could get twice as much for half the price. Still, she paid it, fishing out one of the smaller bills from a wad that she kept rolled up in her pocket. Her account at the bank had been left to gather interest for ten years. While she certainly wasn't rich, it *was* a sizeable nest egg. The woman gave her several coins in change. She would Infuse them later.

Desa bit into the peach, juice running down her chin. With her free hand, she tossed a coin up and caught it. Time to head back to the library.

The fruit was sweeter than she remembered, but then she had been away for some time. The selection up north wasn't as good. Often, you were likely to get apples that were as hard as rocks.

The portly man was still there when she returned. He said nothing, though. Mercy be praised for that.

She saw a line of cars parked on the curb, blocking her view of the park across from the library. Were there really so many now? Aladar was changing. She-

Something was wrong.

Desa looked up to see Azra Vanya standing in the middle of the road with a pistol clutched in one hand. The woman wore a smile that could scare off a hungry wolf. She lifted her weapon.

Desa triggered her Force-Sinks an instant before the gun went off with a distinctive *CRACK!* A bullet jerked to a halt right in front of her and then fell to land at her feet.

Azra snarled, thrusting her hand out and triggering the Gravity-Source in her ring. The instant she did, Desa triggered the Sink in her belt. Azra flinched, startled when her attack had no effect. And then Desa threw the coin in her hand.

Azra tensed up, triggering Force-Sinks in anticipation of a powerful blast of kinetic energy. But it was just an ordinary coin. In that moment of distraction, Desa leaped.

Her Gravity-Sink carried her high into the air, and she soared right over the other woman's head. She killed the Sink. Dropping to the ground with a grunt, she landed right behind her enemy and spun around.

Azra rounded on her, shoving the gun in her face.

Desa ducked.

Once again, a thunderous roar filled the air. A bullet flew right over her head. Desa brought a hand up to strike the other woman's wrist, knocking the weapon away. She used the other to punch Azra's nose. The bitch was stunned.

Desa spun and back-kicked, driving her foot into her opponent's chest. Winded, Azra fell backward to land on the pavement. A snarl twisted her otherwise beautiful face.

Her hand lashed out like a striking snake, releasing a pulse of kinetic energy from her ring. The blast hit Desa at full force, throwing her backward. She landed near the curb and then collapsed against the side of a parked car. Her ears were ringing from the gunshot, and the world just kept spinning.

Azra curled up into a ball and then sprang off the ground, landing on her feet.

The woman took aim with her pistol, cocking her head and smiling viciously. She fired. Not at Desa, but a spot right next to her. A bullet drove itself into the ground. And then it unleashed enough heat to roast a duck.

Triggering her Gravity-Sink, Desa leaped into the middle of the road. She flew across the street with blinding speed, but even that wasn't fast enough. The heat singed her shirt. Desa didn't need to look to know that the skin on the right side of her body was badly burned.

But that wasn't the worst of it.

The wave of heat expanded to encompass the car, igniting the fuel in its tank and causing the damn thing to explode in a fireball that rose high into the air. Shards of metal flew off in all directions. People shrieked, but their howls were drowned out by the hissing and crackling of flames.

Azra gasped, backing away from the inferno with wide eyes. So, the explosion had not been her plan then. Of course not. She wouldn't even know what gasoline was much less what it would do when it was rapidly heated.

Even from across the street, Desa could feel the power of that blaze. She backed away with a hand up to shield her face, slowly climbing the library steps. The side of her arm was pink, but luckily, there were no blisters "You have to stop this!" she screamed. "You'll kill all these people!"

Azra answered that with the menacing grin. "That's your concern," she said. "Not mine." She lifted her gun again.

Desa triggered the Light-Sink in her necklace, submerging herself in darkness, and then threw herself down on her belly. She immediately rolled aside to avoid being where Azra had last seen her, but there was no sound of gunfire. Azra was waiting to make sure she had a clean shot.

Ripping the necklace off, Desa tossed it down on the steps. Her enemy might be able to estimate her position if the pocket of darkness remained centred on her. Desa kept rolling. She could still hear the flames across the street and smell the oily smoke.

Sure enough, a vicious *CRACK, CRACK* split the air.

Bullets hit the steps where she had been, kicking up chunks of stone, and then one unleashed a burst of kinetic energy. Desa was thrown sideways, hurled out of the darkness to land on the steps, sprawled out on her back.

With a quick pivot, Azra had her in her sights.

Desa lifted her forearm, triggering the Force-Sink in her bracelet. The growl of gunfire filled her ears, and a bullet came to a halt right in front of her. She let her arm drop, the bullet falling as well.

Azra lifted her weapon and pulled the trigger, producing nothing but an impotent *click*. The woman blinked, surprised by this turn of events, but then she realized that she had fired all six rounds. And she didn't have time to reload.

She threw her gun down on the road and drew her belt knife instead. Her cruel smile returned as she marched across the street. "It'll be more fun this way."

"Mercy protect me..." Desa forced herself to stand despite the pains in her body. "What demon gave birth to you?"

Azra broke into a sprint.

Desa turned and ran up the stairs. With the side of her leg burnt, every step was agony, but she forced herself to keep going. The sound of Azra's footfalls right behind her provided sufficient motivation.

Thick, stone pillars supported the roof above the library's front entrance. That would do. Yes, that would do.

Triggering her Gravity-Sink, Desa ran up one pillar and pushed off. She whirled around in midair and kicked Azra's face. The other woman stumbled, blood flying from her nostrils.

Desa released her hold on gravity and landed with her fists up in a fighting stance. "You want this over?" she hissed. "Fine. Let's end it."

Azra lunged at her, trying to stab her through the belly.

Pulling back, Desa caught the woman's wrist with both hands and gave a twist that made her enemy drop the knife. She lifted Azra's hand above her head, twirled under it and then yanked on Azra's arm so that the other woman was forced to bend double.

Desa kicked her in the stomach, expelling the wind from Azra's lungs. A second kick to the leg forced Azra down onto her knees.

Screaming, she pulled free of Desa's grip.

In a heartbeat, she was on her feet again, hissing like a cat as blood spilled over her mouth and stained teeth. She came forward without preamble, lashing out with a beastly high kick.

Desa ducked and felt a scuffed boot passing over her head. She backed away, but Azra spun for a back-kick.

Raising her hands up in front of her face, Desa intercepted the hit. A black boot struck her palms, leaving a sting in her burnt skin.

Azra rushed in for the kill.

Thrusting her fist out, Desa activated her ring and sent a beam of light into the other woman's face. Azra shut her eyes, stumbling.

Desa delivered a swift right-hook to the cheek, one that landed with devastating force. She jumped, using her Gravity-Sink for extra height, and twirled in the air, swinging her foot around for a brutal hook-kick.

Her heel connected with Azra's cheek.

The impact flung Azra down onto her side, and she groaned when her body hit the steps. Dazed, she rolled onto her back.

Desa straddled her, drew back her fist and pounded the other woman's face. Once, twice, three times. At that point, she realized that Azra was unconscious. So, she took control of her rage and forced herself to stop. She was a warrior, not a killer. Sebastian's laughter echoed in her head, but she ignored it.

Sirens wailed as police cars pulled up to the curb. Doors flew open, and then men in blue uniforms were scrambling up the steps. They were followed by half a dozen men and women in bright, yellow robes. One of them was Radavan.

He stood over Desa with his staff in hand, frowning and shaking his head. "We never had this much trouble until you returned."

Burnt and bruised, Desa shut her eyes and tried to control her breathing. "I do seem to have that effect," she rasped. "This one is exceedingly dangerous."

Radavan glanced over his shoulder, toward the car that was still belching fire and smoke into the air. "No doubt," he said. "What shall we do with her?"

"Strip her down," Desa panted. "Remove anything that might be a Sink or a Source and shove her in a cell. Have one of your people guarding her at all times. If she touches the Ether for even half a second, shoot her."

Radavan's mouth twisted in distaste. No doubt he still disapproved of guns. "Why not just kill her now?"

"Because," Desa growled. "I want to ask her some questions."

11

Lost in the Ether's caress, Desa could easily ignore the pain of her burns. She was safe in a quiet room one floor down from Prelate's office. It was all particles to her, not that there would be much to see if she were using her eyes instead of her mind. Just a wooden chair and a table with one window for light. She had ignored the chair, choosing instead to sit on the floor with her back against the wall.

She didn't try to Infuse anything; she just let the Ether bathe her mind in awareness. The sting in her arm and her leg, the burn on her cheek, bruised ribs and skinned knees: it was all there, and it was all fading. Slowly. Another hour, and she would be well enough to move around with only minor discomfort.

There wasn't much to do but sit here and wait; so, she let her mind wander. She felt Daresina on the floor above her. The Prelate was puttering about her office. No doubt she was upset about Desa's latest confrontation with Azra.

Daresina wouldn't like being spied on. Not that Desa had any compunctions about upsetting the other woman. But there wasn't much to see; so, she moved on.

They had Azra in a cell at the Third Street police station, but everything they had taken from her was locked in a vault in the second sub-basement. Three floors beneath Desa. Just on the edge of her awareness.

She focused on Azra's rings.

She could feel the strands of Ether forming a lattice between the molecules that make up each one. She couldn't trigger them, of course. They were bound to Azra, and the other woman could activate them even from miles away. Marcus had wanted to dispose of them all. To toss them into the ocean. A wise idea, but the Elite Guard wanted a look at Azra's Infusions. And Desa had to admit that her curiosity was piqued.

Such clever Field Binding.

It was possible to make a Sink that would only drain energy from one particular direction. Desa had done that with the Force-Sinks in her shirt and her bracelet. That was how she was able to stop bullets, to drain their kinetic energy, while she herself remained in motion. It was also possible to create Sources that would only release energy in one particular direction. Azra had done that with her rings. Each one had a stone so that it could be properly oriented on her finger.

One of those was a Gravity-Source that would pull on things from the side of the ring opposite the stone. Azra could use it to pull things into her hand. Another was a Force-Source that released kinetic energy from its stone. Dangerous, of course; if they ever got twisted around on her fingers, and if she failed to notice, they might harm Azra rather than serving her. Of course, it was also possible, albeit very difficult, to exempt yourself from a Sink or a Source's power. Marcus had done that with his Electric-Sources that spat lightning in every direction except at him.

She traced Azra's Infusions with her mind, looking for some indication that the assassin had done the same. She found nothing of the sort. Perhaps Azra didn't know that trick. That got her thinking.

All her life, Desa had believed that the Aladri were the only people to master Field Binding. But Kalia's people had been practicing the Great Art quietly for years. Maybe even decades. Their proximity to the ancient pyramid and its crystal certainly helped them in that regard. Still, what could she and Kalia discover if they sat down to compare notes? Once again, she cursed the Synod's policy of restricting such knowledge to their people alone. They would give Sinks and Sources to mainlanders who were willing to trade, but they would not teach those mainlanders how to make their own.

Her body was healing. She could feel the pain receding.

Under other circumstances, she might have been surprised when Kalia burst through the door, but Desa had felt the other woman coming for the better part of five minutes. "You're all right!" Kalia gasped.

Desa's severed contact with the Ether – it was all but impossible to move her body when her mind was in that trancelike state – and the collection of particles in front of her became a woman. Kalia shook her head. "Well, thank the Almighty for that."

Desa looked up at her, blinking several times to moisten her eyes. Sometimes, she forgot to do that when she was held in the Ether's embrace. "I am indeed," she said. "You needn't worry."

Kalia was smiling up at the ceiling, laughing softly for reasons that Desa couldn't even begin to imagine. "Do you know how many deputies have tried to bring in Azra

Vanya?" she asked. "And you do it just twenty-four hours after meeting the bitch!"

Desa shut her eyes, groaning as the aches throughout her body suddenly became sharp and clear again. She rolled her shoulders to relieve some of the pain in her upper back. "I hardly think that what I did is praiseworthy," she said. "Azra wreaked terrible destruction on that neighbourhood before I was able to subdue her. They're still putting out the fire."

"I see you have trouble taking a compliment."

"Like any other skill, it requires practice," Desa grumbled. "And I have had few opportunities to do so."

"Noted."

Wincing, Desa touched fingers to the side of her head. A wave of dizziness hit her like an oncoming train. "I'm sure the Synod will remand her to your custody once all of this is over," she said. "We can take her back to Dry Gulch together if you like. I'm eager to recover my horse."

Midnight must be worried sick about her. Not that there was much she could do. The desert was some thirteen hundred miles north-west of here.

"The stable hands are taking care of him, I'm sure," Kalia replied. "But that does raise an issue I have been avoiding. Desa, I can't stay here."

"I know."

Kalia took the wooden chair, sighing softly and watching Desa with the kind of frown that belonged on a schoolteacher. "Do you think they'll let me leave?" she asked. "Will they let you come with me?"

"Yes," Desa said. "And no. They will be more than eager to see your back, but the only way I'm getting out of this city is in the hold of the smuggler's ship."

"Well," Kalia muttered. "Then we'll have to come up with a plan."

"That would be ideal."

"Any ideas?"

"Not at the moment."

Tommy looked through a window with gray muntin at the destruction outside. The car across the street was now a smouldering lump of metal with police officers clustered around it. The Aladri fire team had finally doused the flames using Heat-Sinks and their remarkable running water.

The steps that led up to the library's front entrance were wide enough for seven men to walk abreast, but now, there was a big crater that people would have to avoid. He recognized it as the damage inflicted by a Force-Source.

Standing by the window with one hand on the glass, Tommy blinked as he took in the sight of it all. "Almighty..." He shut his eyes and turned his face away from the devastation. "It's a miracle no one died."

"Your friend seems to bring destruction in her wake," Dalen said behind him.

"This isn't Desa's fault."

Muttering under his breath, Dalen joined him at the window. He wrinkled his nose in distaste. "I didn't say that it was," he replied. "But things have been more...exciting since the lot of you came to town."

Tommy wet his lips and tried to come up with *something* to say. Something that would justify all this mayhem. "I'm sorry about that, I surely am," he began. "But we didn't intend to come here."

"So you said."

"It was Adele."

"The woman possessed by the entity you hope to defeat?"

Turning his back on the window, Tommy marched past the long, wooden table, trailing his fingers along its surface as he went. "She is more powerful than any Field Binder," he said. "Brought us here in the blink of an eye."

"How is that possible?"

Tommy looked up through the skylight, squinting as he considered the question. "Wish I knew," he said. "But I'm damn sure of two things, and one of them is that her power is pure evil."

"And the other?"

"Her power has limits. She *can* be defeated."

The sound of Dalen's quiet laughter made him feel like an idiot. At first, it did, anyway. But he realized, after a moment, that he didn't sense malice from the other man. "Has anyone ever told you that you're very brave?" Dalen asked.

Tommy sat on the edge of the table, hunched over with his hands on his knees. "Goodness help me," he said. "You *are* smitten, aren't you?"

Dalen came over to stand in front of him.

The other man wore a smile so bright it could turn night into day. "Is that really so surprising?" he asked. "You are quite handsome."

"No one's ever told me *that* before."

"Not even Miri?"

"Well, of course, Miri has," Tommy said with a shrug. "But Miri's crazier than a drunk weasel."

Dalen was smiling at him again. Tommy cleared his throat. He was suddenly painfully aware of the butterflies fluttering in his stomach. Why did the Almighty hate him?

Or Mercy? Or Vengeance? Or whoever it was that ran this benighted universe?

It was hard enough to keep his feelings straight with Miri yelling at him one moment and refusing to talk to him the next. Now, he had this handsome, intelligent man looking at him the way the village girls used to look at his brother. Tommy told himself that he would be a good partner, that he would stop talking to Dalen altogether. But when the other man got within five feet of him, his resolve melted away.

Maybe that wasn't such a bad thing. If his last few fights with Miri were any indication, she might not take him back even if he did choose her. A strong woman, that one. She had a will of iron and no tolerance for nonsense. Tommy admired that. All he had to do was think about her smile and…Bah! How could he be in love with two people at the same time?

Ruminating on it wouldn't do him any good; he had spent two days doing just that, and it had got him nowhere. No, the best thing he could do was focus on helping Desa.

He felt a little guilty for not coming to her aid when he heard the gunshots and explosions outside. But that was foolish. Tommy might not be a warrior, but at least he knew his limitations. Going outside would have only given that Azra woman a chance to use him as a hostage.

Hopefully, Desa wasn't angry.

He returned to his study of the ancient manuscripts and found nothing of value. Just the same stories he had read a hundred times now. Mercy leading the ancient Aladri across the face of the continent, Vengeance battling their enemies. But he kept reading because what else could he do? Dalen joined him, of course. He didn't have to ask; the other man just sat down at the table and began reading through the books they had assembled.

That was how Miri found him.

She came striding into the library, panting as if she had just run five miles. If she noticed Dalen's presence, she didn't react to it. "Mercy be praised!" she exclaimed. "You're all right!"

Tommy stood up.

Before he could say even one word, Miri seized his face with both hands and kissed him hard on the lips. "I was so afraid," she gasped. "That woman from the desert came after Desa again?"

"She did."

"And you were here?"

"I was here."

Miri fixed her gaze upon Dalen, and something changed. Her face became hard. "I see," she muttered. "Well, I'll leave you to it then."

Tommy backed away from her, crossing his arms and meeting her stare with one of his own. "He's only been here for the last half-hour," he said. "I started out working with Desa, but as you can see by the chaos outside…"

Miri turned away from him, covering her face with both hands. "I'm sorry," she mumbled. "I don't want to fight with you."

Dalen chose that moment to insert himself into the conversation. "Miri Nin Valia," he said. "I'm not trying to come between you and Thomas."

Fury boiled over inside Tommy. The scowl that he directed at the other man must have been fierce because Dalen recoiled. "Oh, you're not?" he spat. "Then what was the purpose of all those compliments?"

Dalen went beet-red, and sweat broke out on his forehead. He scrubbed it away with the heel of his hand. "I'm sorry," he stammered. "I didn't think..."

"Oh, you thought, all right," Miri snarled. "No one just blunders their way in between two people who love each other. *That* requires a plan."

"You really think he's a planner?" Tommy countered.

Miri turned her gaze upon him, and her dark eyes cut like razors. "Whose side are you on, anyway?"

"I'm not on anyone's side!" Tommy yelled. He knew that he was being far too loud for the library, but he didn't care. He was fed up. "The pair of you are like two children fighting over a rag doll, each grabbing one arm and pulling as hard as you can. You keep it up, and the damn thing will rip in half! Then neither of you will have what you want!"

He had expected them to ignore him – or maybe to argue with him – but it seemed his words had an effect. Miri averted her gaze and muttered something that might have been an apology. Dalen just stared numbly at the wall.

"I'm going for a walk," Tommy said, making his way toward the door. "The way things are going on here, I'll be safer out there even if Azra breaks loose and starts blowing things up again."

Two men in yellow robes stood on either side of a cell door. Desa could see Azra through the gaps between the thick, steel bars. They had put the other woman in an ugly, brown smock that covered her from shoulders to knees. Desa suspected that they had left her with nothing else on the off chance that she might have a Sink or a Source hidden somewhere on her person. Even her feet were bare.

Azra's cheek was bruised and swollen so that she had to keep one eye closed. Her nose was obviously broken. She looked up at Desa with raw hatred in her gaze, but she said nothing.

"Has anyone seen to her wounds?" Desa asked.

The Elite Guardians only glowered at her. One of them – a dark-skinned fellow with shoulder-length, black hair – snorted and said, "No doctor will go anywhere near her. Can you blame them?"

Desa stood before the door with arms folded, frowning down at herself. "We can't leave her like that," she murmured. "Can you find the Ether?"

Azra ignored her.

Stepping forward, Desa grabbed a bar in each hand and leaned in close to peer through the space between them. "I won't leave you with a concussion," she said. "If you can find the Ether, we can get you through the worst of it."

Her own body was still sore. The fabric of her shirt sometimes irritated the skin on her right arm, and her left side ached if she twisted the wrong way. Another hour or so in the Ether's embrace would do the trick for her.

The dark-skinned guard harrumphed. "You told us to shoot the bitch if she started trying to Infuse anything."

"I'll keep an eye on her," Desa said. "I'll know the instant she starts crafting an Infusion." Of course, to do that, she would have to commune with the Ether herself. But that would only hasten her own recovery. Two birds with one stone, as Tommy liked to say.

She backed up to the wall across from Azra's cell, then slid against it until her bottom hit the floor. Curling up her legs, she focused her mind.

The Ether came to her with remarkable speed. Azra gasped. Most people needed at least a minute to put themselves in the correct frame of mind. Desa was getting faster and faster. The crystal had changed her.

For a little while, the other woman was just a human-shaped cloud of molecules. Desa began to wonder if the pain was too great – finding the Ether required concentration – but just as she was about to give up, radiance erupted from Azra's body.

Ignoring her unease, Desa focused her thoughts on the task at hand. She would know if Azra began to Infuse one of the bars on the door or one of the bricks in the wall. Luckily, the other woman was wise enough not to try.

Minutes passed, stretching on while the two guards divided their attention between her and Azra. Before long, half an hour had passed.

Desa let go of the Ether. "That's enough," she said. "It's time to answer some questions."

The bruises on Azra's face were smaller, the swelling less severe. She opened her eyes and then smiled as if she had complete control of the situation. "What do you want to know?"

"Why did Adele send you to kill me?"

"Don't know," Azra replied. "Don't care."

"Why not just do it herself?"

Looking up at the ceiling with a triumphant smile, Azra giggled. "Now, that's the real question, isn't it?" she said. "That lady has power like I've never seen. Can't imagine why she would need me."

Tapping her lips with one finger, Desa closed her eyes and tried to work it out. "Nor can I," she muttered. "Unless... She's afraid of me, isn't she?"

Azra clapped her hands. "My, my, my," she cooed. "What a clever girl!"

"Why would she be afraid of me?"

Azra answered that with a shrug. "Can't say." She hopped to her feet and padded across the length of her cell.

"Thing is, whenever the big scary's scared of something, there's usually a reason."

Azra poked her face between two of the bars. "So, what's so special about you?"

"I wish I knew."

Turning away from her, Azra tittered as she shuffled back to her bench. "Don't be so modest, dear," she said. "Takes something special to beat me. Ooh... Can't wait for the rematch."

She looked over her shoulder and blew Desa a kiss.

12

"To be an effective fighter," Desa said, "you must develop many skills."

Rays of sunlight streaked through the forest. Desa had chosen a small clearing where rocks littered the hard-packed clay beneath their feet. Some were buried in the ground.

She had set up five large stones – each as big as a man's torso – in a ring around them, and she had painted a target on each one. That must have been a hassle; Tommy wondered whether training him was worth all this effort.

Desa stood in front of him with her back turned, inspecting her work. "Field Binding is a tool, Tommy." She spun around to face him. "One of many that you will master. But if you rely on it too much, you can become dependent."

He stood in the middle of the clearing with a pistol in his right hand, its barrel pointed down at the ground. Unable to look up, he nodded automatic agreement with everything that she was saying. "Is that why we're out here?"

"Azra became dependent on her power," Desa said. "Blowing holes in the ground, setting off Heat-Sources. And yet, I was able to best her without a gun or any offensive weaponry, Infused or otherwise. You must learn to outthink your enemies."

Tommy lifted the gun in his hand, frowning at it. "So, you brought me out here for target practice?" he asked. "I already know how to shoot, Desa."

"Do you know how to shoot with precision?"

Lifting his weapon in one hand, he targeted one of the rocks. He cocked the hammer and then squeezed the trigger. The recoil sent a jolt through his arm, and his ears were ringing.

The rock shattered into a dozen pieces, but he could see, on the largest one, that he had not hit the target.

"Not good enough," Desa said. "You must improve your aim."

"What difference does it make?" he protested. "I still destroyed the damn thing. Don't matter if I hit a man on the right side of his chest or the left. He's just as dead either way."

"Observe."

Desa stood with her pistol clutched in both hands, its barrel pointed downward. She lifted the weapon and squinted as she took aim.

CRACK!

One of the rocks crumbled as her bullet went right through the red dot that she had painted on its surface. She twisted with almost machine-like precision, lifted her gun and fired again.

Her bullet smashed the next stone into a dozen pieces, and it was clear that she had hit the target dead-centre. She did the same for the next two, destroying them both with deadly accuracy.

"All right," Tommy said. "You can shoot. But why is it necessary to be so accurate?"

Desa squatted and then popped open the cylinder of her pistol. She dumped the empty shell casings onto the ground and began loading it with fresh bullets. "Where you place a Gravity-Source matters," she said. "A few inches too far left or right, and a sharp object that you had expected to fly right past your partner goes through him instead."

"You did that to Martin, didn't you?"

Grinning from ear to ear, Desa looked up to meet his gaze. "I may have made a few...miscalculations on some of our first adventures."

She stood up.

Every trace of amusement vanished, and she became the disapproving teacher once again. "Now," she said, "you're going to practice."

"We're out of targets."

Turning slightly, Desa gestured to the narrow path that led out of the clearing. He followed it up a small hill, through the gap between two trees and down the other side. Tommy gasped when he saw what she had done.

There must have been two dozen big stones waiting for him, each with a target painted on its side. The smallest of them had to weigh at least a hundred pounds. How could she have...

"Gravity-Sinks," Desa said, coming up behind him. "It's easy to move rocks when they're weightless. Now...Time to get to work."

THE NEXT MORNING, a cloudy sky hung over the forest. The air was warm and damp, the ground soft from last night's rainfall. There were mud puddles all over the clearing, some ankle-deep, and yet Desa wanted to train anyway.

In gray pants and a sleeveless shirt, she stood before him with a wooden staff in hand. Her eyes cut him like daggers. "You must learn to focus," she said. "Not just to defend yourself, but you will have an easier time finding the Ether when you can clear your mind on command."

Tommy had his staff planted in the soft earth. He drew a slow breath through his nose. "You sure it's the best day for training?"

"There can be no better."

Desa rushed him, bringing her staff down in a swift vertical arc that would thump him on the head.

Tommy raised his weapon horizontally. Wood met wood with a loud, sharp *clack*. Desa swatted the side of his hip, and he yelped from the sting.

The end of her staff came down on his shoe. "Yeow!" he screamed. Then he was hopping on one foot. He barely even felt it when something struck the back of his knee and took his legs out from under him.

Tommy fell backward, landing in the muck, groaning on impact. "Well, that's just wonderful..." He sat up, pressing the heel of his hand to his forehead.

When he opened his eyes, the end of a staff was only two inches away from his nose. Desa was smiling down at him. "Again," she said.

"Throwing knives," Desa said.

Standing in the rays of sunlight that broke through the treetops, she tossed one up and caught its tip. That devilish grin of hers made him shiver. "Very useful in any number of situations."

Desa spun, turning her back on him, and flung the knife with a graceful flick of her wrist. It tumbled end over end through the air before burying itself in a tree trunk, the blade poking right through the red dot Desa had painted. "Now, you try."

With a shrug of his shoulders, Tommy stepped forward and sighed. "All right then…" He threw his knife.

The damn thing landed unceremoniously in some bushes, two feet wide of the tree. Well, at least he had managed to avoid cutting himself.

HE WAS thankful when Desa decided to take a break from combat training to focus on crafting Infusions. Time spent communing with the Ether healed some of the bruises that he had acquired sparring with Desa.

Every tree was a universe of tiny molecules, as was the air and the ground beneath him. Even the sunlight seemed to come in little packets, flowing one after another. He focused his mind on the bullet in front of him.

Desa sat cross legged across from him, glowing with power that suffused her body. She directed strands of the Ether between the molecules of a second bullet positioned only two inches away from the tip of her shoe.

Tommy tried to copy what she did, but every time he had the Ether in his grasp, it seemed to slip away. The lattice that Desa built inside her bullet was beautiful, a web of light that seemed to pulse. If only he could do the same.

Tommy concentrated.

He fumbled for the Ether and managed to get a hold of a thin strand of it. Success brought with it a surge of elation so strong he almost lost control again. But he managed to stay focused.

He fed that strand into the space between the molecules of his bullet and then added a dozen more just like it, copying Desa's pattern as best he could. At first, the web was composed of hair-thin threads, but they seemed to thicken with time. That was the key. The shape of the lattice determined what the Infusion would do, and the thickness of the strands determined how strong it would be.

For a long while, several minutes at least, Desa did nothing but wait while her threads thickened. Tommy did the same, but he felt impatience welling up inside of him. Sitting still for so long, focusing his mind on this one individual task, was difficult. When a surge of frustration made him lose the Ether, his strands were only half as thick as Desa's.

Tommy opened his eyes and became aware of the sweat coating his face. "Is it just me?" he panted, "or does the process actually slow down the longer it goes on?"

Desa broke contact with the Ether and laughed as she scooped up the Force-Source she had created. "Very good," she said. "I was wondering how long it would take you to notice."

"So, it's true?"

"The rate of Infusion isn't linear," she explained. "It takes about ten seconds to make a Force-Sink that will stop one bullet and a little under five minutes to make one that will stop six bullets. If you want one that will stop seven bullets, you'll be sitting there for the better part of half an hour."

He nodded.

Desa stood up, stretching as if she had just woken up from a refreshing nap. "There is a limit to how much any individual Sink can absorb," she said. "So, it's best to prevent your enemies from getting a clean shot at you in the first place. That's why we've been focusing on all these other skills."

The skies were clear on their fourth day of training, and the ground was blessedly dry. A light breeze blew leaves off the ends of branches and sent them tumbling to the forest floor.

Twirling his wooden staff in both hands, Tommy narrowed his eyes. "All right," he said. "I'm ready."

No more than twenty feet away, Desa stood before him with her weapon lowered, a sly smile on her face. A smile that beckoned him to make the first move. He had fallen for it before and regretted it every time. Of course, she might just stand there all day and wait for him to do something. Or she might launch into an attack at the very moment when he let his guard down.

With a quick step forward, Tommy swung at her ear.

Desa ducked, allowing his staff to pass over her head. She backed off and then poked him in the belly, forcing him to retreat.

Adapting in a heartbeat, Desa ran forward, raised her staff and tried to bring it down on his head.

Tommy lifted his weapon to parry, and they met with a sound like wood splitting in the blaze of a fire. He didn't just wait for Desa's next attack; he kicked her in the stomach while her midsection was exposed. "Good!" she said.

She swung at Tommy's legs.

He jumped and felt the staff passing under him. He was about to counterattack, but Desa reversed her swing and clipped him on the ear. "Ow! Damn it!" Her staff found its way behind his knee, as it so often did, and then Tommy was falling onto his backside.

Instead of remaining still, he rolled away over dried mud and roots. He got up on one knee a short distance away.

Desa came at him.

Tommy thrust out his hand and ordered his ring to emit a beam of radiance that hit her right in the face. Blinded by the light, Desa stumbled over an exposed root. She swore and nearly lost her balance.

Seizing the opportunity, Tommy stood up and used his staff to smack her short ribs, producing a yelp of pain. He was about to press his advantage, but Desa raised a hand to forestall him. "Good," she said. "Very good."

"Thank you," Tommy gasped.

"When did you learn to create Light-Sources?"

He couldn't help but smile. "Last night," he said. "I was... experimenting, and somehow, I just knew what to do."

Planting the end of her staff in the ground, Desa gave him a very dangerous look. "Well," she said. "If you're going to experiment, please limit yourself to light. Some of the more destructive forms of energy can be very dangerous if you don't know what you're doing."

"I promise."

"Good. Now, let's begin again."

AN HOUR LATER, Tommy was standing in the shade provided by several tall oaks, watching the leaves fluttering in the breeze. There was a red dot the size of his palm on the tree in front of him.

He tossed up his knife, caught the tip and grimaced as he estimated the distance. He threw it just as Desa had shown him.

An inch of steel sank into the tree trunk about a finger's width above the target. Tommy cursed. He thought he had it that time! Striding over to the towering oak, he yanked the blade free with a snarl.

"Don't be so hard on yourself."

He turned around to find Desa leaning against another tree and smiling at him. "You're getting better," she said. "It takes time."

"Yes, Mrs. Kincaid."

With a sigh, Desa got up and marched across the clearing to a pile of supplies that she had left by some rocks. Tommy had seen her setting up when he arrived this morning, but he had not asked what she had brought. "Here," she said. "Try this."

She stood up and turned toward him with a wooden bow in one hand and a full quiver in the other. "I strung it for you this morning. Had to borrow it from the Academy, but they didn't mind."

Tommy felt creases lining his brow. "Archery?" he stammered. "Begging your pardon, ma'am, but what's the point when we have guns?"

"Archery strengthens your arm and improves marksmanship."

He didn't think it would do much good in his case, but it was no more ludicrous than any of the other exercises Desa had put him through. He accepted the bow with thanks. What harm could it do?

Backing away from the target, Tommy pulled an arrow from his quiver. He nocked it and began a slow draw. The bowstring offered some resistance. His muscles burned from the effort, but he didn't mind. When he had his shot lined up, he loosed...and hit the target dead centre.

Tommy shrugged, his head hanging as chagrin set his face on fire. "Beginner's luck is all," he said. "Nothing to write home about."

"Try again," Desa urged.

With a deft hand, Tommy nocked another arrow. He

drew fletchings to cheek, muttered a prayer for luck and loosed.

The second arrow landed on top of the first one, dislodging it from the tree. Two perfect shots in two attempts. Tommy wasn't sure what to make of it.

Desa paced a circle around him with her chin clasped in one hand, sizing him up. "Hmm," she said. "Have you practiced with a bow and arrow before?"

He shut his eyes tight and then shook his head vigorously. "No, ma'am," Tommy insisted. "First time I've ever held one."

"One more time then."

Nock, draw and loose. His third arrow practically split the second one right down the middle. Tommy gasped. How was this possible? He had never been able to beat the other boys in an honest footrace, nor had he been strong enough to win a wrestling match. His aim with a rifle was mediocre at best.

"I think we've found your weapon of choice," Desa said.

"No offense, ma'am," Tommy interjected. "But a bow isn't much use against a gun."

"Perhaps not," Desa countered. "But imagine what you could do if you augmented your arrows with Field Binding."

Hearing that put a smile on his face. Several possibilities occurred to him. A Gravity-Source arrow that anchored his enemies to the ground. Or a Light-Sink that trapped them in darkness. "You're right!" he said. "Maybe this will-"

He cut off when he saw that Desa was staring intently into the trees. Her eyes were wide with fright, and her hand was reaching for the pistol that she wore on her hip. "What is it?" Tommy whispered. "The ghost?"

He tried to follow her gaze and saw nothing but a thicket with thin rays of sunlight shining down from above. A fat, brown squirrel looked up from his half-eaten nut. No doubt, the poor, little guy was wondering what had frightened these strange giants who had intruded on his privacy, but he soon lost interest and went back to his meal. "Desa?"

She heaved out a sigh of relief. "It's gone," she muttered. "But I swear that thing is getting more aggressive. It was coming right for us. Or...for me."

"Maybe we should head back to the city."

"No," Desa said. "It can find me anywhere I go. I'm no safer in the city than I would be right here. Let's continue the lesson."

THE SUN WAS a golden disk hovering above the horizon at the end of their fifth day of training. Tommy was exhausted; his muscles ached, and he felt as if he had shed three pounds in sweat alone.

He stood on a hilltop with his fists up, damp hair clinging to his forehead. "All right," he panted. "I'm ready for-"

Desa tried to punch him.

Leaning back, Tommy brought one hand up to swat her fist away. Another punch came at him, but he deflected that too. He felt his confidence swelling. Maybe he could win this match. Then the momentum changed.

Desa spun for a back-kick.

Her foot hit his stomach. Not hard enough to injure, but it did cause him some pain. Tommy folded up on himself. Her knee came up, stopping just half an inch away from his nose. Had she followed-through, he would be unconscious.

Straightening, Tommy wiped the sweat off his brow. He closed his eyes and nodded. "You win again."

Desa was smiling as she backed away from him. It

pleased him to see that her hair was just as damp, her shirt just as stained. "Don't be so hard on yourself," she said. "You *are* getting better."

Tommy leaned against an ash tree with a hand over his belly, breathing deeply as he looked up at the darkening sky. "Yeah, well..." he began. "I'm still making way too many mistakes."

"We've been at this five days."

"How long did it take you to become as skilled as you are?"

"Three years."

Tommy let himself slump against the tree trunk, grunting when his bottom hit the ground. He stretched his legs out and tried to ignore the pains that would make the walk home most unpleasant. "I'm not sure we have three years."

Desa turned her back on him, watching the sunset. She was only a silhouette to his eyes. "What do you mean?" she asked cautiously.

Mopping a hand over his face, Tommy groaned. He blinked several times, his eyes stinging from the sweat. "Adele," he said. "Or whatever she is. Seems she's fixing to end this world."

Desa said nothing.

Tommy frowned at her back. A single bead of sweat rolled down his forehead. "Be honest," he said, heart pounding. "Don't you sense it too?"

"I do."

"Then you need me to contribute now."

Turning around with a sigh, Desa shuffled over to him. She knelt before him, and he saw something in her dark eyes. Sympathy mixed with mild irritation, or so he figured. "You already contribute, Tommy."

"Marcus told me, when we were in Ofalla, that the best thing I could do for your cause was to leave and never come back."

"Marcus is an idiot."

They began the long trek home along a narrow path that followed rolling hills. The trees on either side of them were all shadows now. Some were thick enough to support a house in their branches; others were so thin he could almost close a fist around them, but they all seemed to loom ominously, branches reaching for him like grasping hands.

Desa triggered the Light-Source in her ring to illuminate the way. That made it easier to avoid tripping over roots. Sometimes Tommy wondered if it would be possible to harness this force the Aladri had discovered – they called it electricity – into a compact, hand-held device. Something that anyone could use, even if they didn't know the first thing about Field Binding. He dismissed the idea as soon as it occurred to him. Surely, if that were possible, it would have been done already.

"Have you spoken with Miri?" Desa asked.

He wrinkled his nose and then shook his head slowly. "Haven't talked to her or Dalen." Anger made him quicken his pace. "Right now, I don't want to hear two words out of either of them unless it's an apology."

Desa chuckled.

He spun around to face her, walking backwards. His cheeks were suddenly very hot. "Now, what's so funny about that?"

At first, the light from Desa's ring made his eyes smart, but she stopped dead and let her hand drop. With the ring pointed downward, there was just enough light for him to see that she was grinning. "I didn't mean to offend," she said. "It's just nice to see you gaining some confidence."

Tommy crossed his arms, heaving out a sigh. "I'm sorry," he said with a shrug. "I guess I'm just used to people…"

"Berating you and telling you that your opinions don't matter?"

"Something like that."

He half expected some nugget of wisdom from Desa, but she only started forward again, bringing the conversation to an abrupt end. There was nothing to do but follow her. It took another ten minutes before they could see the city lights in the distance, and by then, the last dregs of twilight were fading from the sky.

They walked for an hour in amicable silence. Tommy had come to realize that Desa was not one for idle chitchat. She wasn't taciturn either, but she only spoke when she had something relevant to say.

It wasn't long before they were back inside the city, walking down a street lined with tall, narrow townhouses. The electric lamps were all aglow, casting a warm, yellow light. He still marveled at the sight of them.

Desa paused at the corner of a street that would take her back toward her mother's apartment, nodded once and then left him without another word.

Smiling, Tommy waved goodbye. Then he turned on his heel and continued up the street that led to Miri's house. They had been fighting, yes, but she had been kind enough to let him stay there until the matter was sorted out.

He found her sitting on the front step with her hands on her knees, frowning into her lap. She looked up at the sound of his approach, and he could see the anguish in her face. Something was wrong. "We have to talk."

Only then did he notice that Dalen was present as well. The other man was puttering about in the shadow of a tree that grew in Miri's front yard. And he was mumbling to himself.

Miri stood up, towering over him from her position on the top step. "We can't go on like this," she said. "You're going to have to choose."

Dalen flinched at the sound of her voice and turned around. He seemed to have only just realized that Tommy had arrived. "Yes," he agreed. "You have to choose."

Crossing his arms, Tommy glanced from one to the other as the anger rose within him. "Oh, I have to choose right this second, do I?" The nerve of them, cornering him like this! "Very well. I choose neither."

Miri blinked.

Tommy stepped forward with his head down, exhaling roughly. He climbed the first step and then looked up at Miri. "I love you." It was the first time he had ever said it, and it surprised him to realize that he meant it. "But you blamed me simply for having a feeling, not for acting on it. You punished me for something I couldn't control, and you refused every attempt I made at reconciliation."

He turned to Dalen.

The other man jumped, bumping his head on one of the tree's low-hanging branches. "By the eyes of Vengeance..." he muttered.

"And you," Tommy went on. "You had to know that all of those compliments were out of line. And you'll both forgive me, but we have bigger concerns right now. Adele, the ghost, the bloody end of the world. Desa needs me at my best. So, I'm sorry, but my answer is, 'I choose neither of you.'"

He left them before they could protest.

Desa had given him enough money for another night at the hotel. He would stay there for now.

13

The Weaver looked out upon an expanse of small, white tents that covered a field of green grass. They were set up in neat, little rows so that people could easily move through the "streets" between them. Almost every man she saw wore the uniform of an Eradian soldier. Blue pants and a black coat with gold buttons. There were women present as well, tending cook fires, doing laundry. Every camp needed followers.

Her eyes fell upon a barrel-chested man who led his horse by the bridle through a lane between two rows of tents. Captain McCallum was an older fellow with curly, gray hair, a thick beard and eyes that seemed to call you a liar every time he looked at you.

And he was coming her way.

The Weaver had abandoned her filmy gown in exchange for a modest, red dress with a high collar that went all the way up to her chin. She wore pointed, leather boots as well, each one polished to a shine. Bits of lace poked out from her sleeves.

Her golden hair was pulled back in a long braid. She

had inspected it in the small mirror they had given her, noting that in such garments, she was almost indistinguishable from Adele Delarac.

Adele was a part of her, of course, but not the whole of her. Nor was she the raging mass of chaotic energy that Bendarian had called the Nether. That was present as well, but she was coming to realize that she was more than the sum of her parts.

"Ma'am," Captain McCallum said as she approached.

"Captain."

He shifted his weight from one foot to the other – the man always seemed to get flustered in her presence – and then cleared his throat with some force. "Another thirty men arrived this morning."

The Weaver nodded.

"Your doing?"

Soft laughter erupted from her throat as she clasped hands behind herself and strode past the man. "I did promise a miracle." Turning on her heel, she faced him again and tried to project sternness. "You will need all the soldiers you can get."

Pressing a fist to his forehead, McCallum scrubbed away the sweat. "Begging your pardon, ma'am," he began. "But is this attack on Aladar necessary?"

"You've seen what they can do."

"I've seen their incredible magic, aye," he replied. "And while I can't say that I ever felt comfortable in the presence of an Aladri, I never got the sense that any of them meant to do me harm."

"You have also seen what I can do," the Weaver said.

"That I have."

The Weaver needed only a little effort to make herself glow. A halo of golden light surrounded her from head to toe, and she smiled at the man. "And the miracles that you have witnessed first-hand," she said. "Are they not sufficient to earn your allegiance?"

The captain looked down at himself, muttering something under his breath. When he looked up again, his eyes were hard. "They're enough to make me think," he admitted. "But I'm hesitant to kill anyone unless I'm sure that it needs doing."

Allowing the halo to dissipate, the Weaver sighed. She nodded once in acquiescence. "Very well."

Without another word, she began a trek through the camp. There was nothing for McCallum to do but follow her. The man insisted on making his displeasure known. Idly, she toyed with the idea of killing him right then and there. Not out of anger. It was just refreshing to know that she could.

Of course, that would ruin the façade of the benevolent saviour that she had worked so hard to construct. She could endure a little aggravation. It was a small price to pay if it meant that one of these fool men put a bullet in Desa Kincaid. Better that than the risk posed by confronting the woman herself.

She led McCallum to the other side of the camp where several men whose loyalty she could trust were guarding a wooden crate. "You want proof?" she asked. "Then I shall provide. Open it."

One of the men looked up as if he couldn't quite believe what he was hearing, but when he realized that she was serious, he picked up a crowbar. With a growl, he used it to pry the crate open.

McCallum gasped.

The creature inside the crate was certainly shaped like a man – a tall and broad-shouldered man with arms like tree trunks – but it was covered in green scales from head to toe. Instead of a nose, it had only two small holes for nostrils, and its mouth was much too long.

When it opened its eyes, they were yellow with vertical slits for pupils. A forked tongue darted out of its mouth. The Weaver had to suppress a smile. Benny knew how to play his role well.

He leaped from the crate and began a mad dash toward McCallum.

The Weaver raised her hand.

Benny staggered to a halt, falling on his knees and clutching his head with both hands. He screamed as if someone had driven spikes into his skull. The Weaver had done nothing; there was no need to use her powers when Benny was perfectly obedient and followed the script to the letter.

She stepped forward and stood over him. "This is one of the demons the Aladri have created on their island." She laid a hand on Benny's scaly head. "This is what they would do to you with their magic."

McCallum stood there with his mouth agape, his face is pale as snow. "What..." He licked his lips and forced himself to speak. "What could create such a creature?"

"Devilry of the worst kind."

The captain drew his sidearm, cocking the hammer. Snarling, he pointed the gun at Benny. "Let's put it out of its misery."

Benny looked up at her, searching for some sign that she would put a stop to this, but he was wise enough to keep his mouth shut. She could see the question in his eyes. Would she let him die?

McCallum pulled the trigger.

His bullet became a puff of smoke right in front of

Benny's face. The captain fired again and again, drawing the attention of everyone in the camp, and every single round he unleashed transformed into harmless smoke.

"It will do no good, Captain," the Weaver said. "His magic protects him."

Sweat covered McCallum's flushed face. He closed his eyes and shuddered. "Then perhaps you can destroy this beast."

Crouching in front of Benny, the Weaver extended her hand and tilted his chin up with the tips of her fingers. "If only I could," she said softly. "I'm afraid that you must destroy the magic that created him."

"What magic?"

She stood up with her hands clasped demurely in front of herself, her head hanging as if she felt some terrible sadness. "Aladar," she said. "The Aladri have brought demons into this world. Kill them, and the demons will die."

It was ludicrous, of course; she noted that not one of the dozen or so people who had gathered around them asked *how* killing the Aladri would destroy the demons. Humans were so delightfully stupid.

"Then it'll be done, ma'am," McCallum said.

"Good. We attack tonight."

THE GOLDEN LIGHT of early evening came through the window, illuminating the bed in the small hotel room that Tommy had rented. He had been forced to borrow the money from Desa; she insisted that there was no need to repay it, but it still irked him.

Tommy sat cross legged with his hands on his knees, his eyes closed as he tried to concentrate. And oh, how he tried to concentrate. One, two, three, four, five. The Ether just wasn't coming today.

A knock at the door drew him out of his reverie.

He opened his eyes and then let out a breath. "It's open!" he called out.

A moment later, the door swung inward to reveal Desa standing in the hallway outside. She smiled when she saw him there. "You know," she said, stepping into the room. "There is such a thing as *too much* practice."

He looked at the bow that he had propped up against the wall and the quiver of arrows next to it. He had spent most of this morning training with Desa and hitting the target every time he launched an arrow. Usually right in the centre. It felt good to be proficient at something. He had asked when the Academy would expect him to return the bow, but according to Desa, they were in no hurry to recover it. Most of the Elite Guardians practiced archery to improve their marksmanship, but as the world marched on, it was becoming a forgotten art. "I wanted to make a few of those special arrows."

"And perhaps," Desa said, "to get your mind off things that she would rather not think about?"

He felt a burning in his cheeks, then shook his head ruefully. "You know me too well," he said. "Telling your prospective suitors that you refuse to choose between them is all well and good, but it still hurts to go home with nobody."

Desa sat on the edge of the bed, and he could tell by the way she hunched up her shoulders that she was nervous. "I'm going to see the Prelate," she said. "I was hoping you might come with me."

Tommy stood up, arching his back as he stretched, then

turned on his heel and paced over to the window. "Now, why would Miss Daresina ever want to talk to a savage like me?"

He peered through the glass at the street below, watching as a car drove past. There were people on the sidewalk as well: a young couple who walked hand-in-hand and an old man who led a boy – presumably his grandson – across the road.

"I'm going to ask her about the Spear of Vengeance," Desa explained.

Scratching his chin with three fingers, Tommy narrowed his eyes. "So, you've decided to go with my plan?" he asked. "Thought you said it was a big leap in logic. Or something like that."

He turned around.

Desa was staring into her lap. She looked positively crestfallen. "It's the best idea that we have, right now," she said. "If the Synod agrees to grant us access to the original *Vadir Scrolls,* we might at least be able to confirm if this weapon exists."

"Well, I suppose there's no harm in asking." He shuffled over to the wall and picked up the quiver. "Think you could help me Infuse a few of these before we go?"

"Of course."

He sat down on the floor again, closing his eyes and trying to focus. One, two, three, four, five. He couldn't feel the Ether no matter how hard he strained for it. It was almost as if he had lost the ability to sense it altogether.

"No, no," Desa said. "You're trying to force it. Just let it happen."

"If I do that, nothing happens at all."

He heard the slight squeak of the bedsprings as Desa got up and then the rustling sound of her sitting down across from him. "Just let your mind drift," she said. "We're in no hurry. The Ether will come when you're ready."

He did as she suggested, deliberately ignoring his frustration, forcing himself to think of anything *but* the task at hand. Of course, that brought his situation with Miri and Dalen to the front of his mind. He did *not* want to think about that. What was he going to do about those two?

He felt awful just thinking it, but a part of him wished that he could have them both. Now, if that wasn't proof of an oversized head, he didn't know what was. And it didn't matter anyway. He had chosen neither; he was stuck with neither. He-

The Ether washed over him.

"Good," Desa said softly. "Just relax...Let it come."

He was suddenly aware of everything: every scratch and the walls that surrounded him, every bump on the floor, the people in the hallway outside. It was glorious. Tommy immediately set to work, seizing threads of the Ether with his mind and feeding them into the gaps between the particles that made up his arrowheads.

By the time he was finished, he had an arsenal of specialty arrows at his command.

THIN CLOUDS FLOATED across the deep, blue sky as the sun sank toward the horizon. Marcus walked along a wide street that led down to the marina. There was still enough daylight for him to see the gray-bricked buildings on either side of the road, but the lamps would be coming on soon.

He noticed a few people milling about on the sidewalk. Most were probably on their way home, eager for a late dinner. He ignored the ones who gave him sidelong glances as he passed.

Marcus still wore dungarees and a duster, and he still carried a pistol on his hip. The wide-brimmed hat atop his head did him no favours either. Andriel had asked why he embraced mainland fashions even after coming home, and the simple truth was that he just didn't care enough to pick out a new wardrobe. And he would probably be leaving Aladar any day now. Besides, he wasn't interested in parting with his gun. The Elite Guardians could say what they wanted about primitive weapons, but the ability to kill at a distance without Field Binding was not to be underestimated.

At the end of the street, he could see boats in the harbour. Red sunlight reflected off the dark waters of the ocean like a thousand rubies spread out on a black tarp. It was a beautiful evening. He enjoyed the salty breeze.

Marcus plodded along with his hands in his coat pockets, his eyes downcast. "Well, now," he said with a shrug of his shoulders. "Another adventure won't be so bad."

He had no desire to visit the mainland again. Only a fool would willingly spend time with the primitive louts spread out across the Eradian continent – but Adele had to be stopped. One way or another.

Grinding his teeth, Marcus stiffened. "Send another in your stead," he muttered to himself. A sadistic thought occurred to him. "Perhaps Radavan would like the job."

But Miri would almost certainly go even if Tommy had decided that he was done with her. Marcus knew all about that, and he had made it a point to keep his nose out of it. His sister was an idealistic fool, but he was not going to leave her to face the savages on her own. Not when-

Something caught his eye.

A man in blue trousers and a black coat came around the corner from a neighbouring street. A tall man who carried a primitive rifle in both hands, who looked as if he was just itching to choose a target. Marcus recognized that uniform. What was the Eradian militia doing here? His mind flashed back to the boat that he had seen last week. Mainlanders trying to slip onto the island. Trying to slip onto the island from its *eastern* side? A clever plan, but surely someone should have seen them before now. How could they get past the fleet?

Marcus proceeded down the hill with a hand on his holstered weapon, his brows drawn together as he approached the stranger. "Ho there!" he called out. "You look lost."

The soldier flinched at the sound of his voice and did a quick about-face, pointing his rifle at Marcus.

"What are you-" Marcus shouted.

The soldier fired.

Thunder split the air, and then a very long bullet hovered about an inch away from Marcus's chest. Those rifles were much more powerful than a revolver! His Force-Sinks would only be able to absorb one more round like that. Of course, they also took longer to reload. The soldier worked the lever to eject the spent cartridge.

Drawing his pistol with a flourish, Marcus cocked the hammer extended his arm and then fired. No hesitation, no remorse.

Blood sprayed from the other man's chest before he could get his rifle up, and then he fell to the ground, sprawled out on the sidewalk. Another black-coated soldier came around the corner.

CRACK!

A bullet went through him before he could even raise his weapon.

Marcus stepped onto the road with teeth bared, hissing

like an angry cat. "Pathetic," he spat. Vengeance take these primitives. They thought they could invade his city? He would make them suffer for it.

Three more Eradians came into view from the adjoining street, each one carrying a rifle. They formed a line, dropped to one knee and tried to take aim.

Marcus angled his gun downward.

His bullet drove itself into the pavement in front of them. With a thought, he triggered the Force-Source that he had Infused into the metal, unleashing kinetic energy that sent all three men flying.

They were thrown backward like leaves kicked up by an angry wind. One man landed on the curb to Marcus's left, another on the sidewalk to his right. And the third was in the middle of the road.

One of them tried to sit up.

CRACK!

A shot went through his skull, splattering his brains on the concrete.

The one in the middle of the street had gotten up on all fours. He was pawing at the ground, searching for his lost rifle. Marcus ended him without a second thought. Only one more to go.

The third man was standing on the sidewalk and clutching a dislocated shoulder. His face was red, and tears streamed from his eyes. "No, no, no!" he pleaded. Begging did him no good.

A bullet hole appeared in his forehead.

Ignoring the *thump* his corpse made as it hit the ground, Marcus continued forward at a steady pace. He took fresh bullets from his bandolier and loaded them into his pistol. If more of these men thought to invade his home, he would cleanse them from Aladar's streets like a plague.

Marcus went around the corner, onto the street that bordered the marina. Wooden docks extended into the black water, and several boats were floating on the waves.

There were more Eradian soldiers on this road: half a dozen of them gathered together in a small cluster. One of them looked up and snarled when he saw Marcus. He tried to lift his rifle. The others followed suit.

Marcus pointed his gun at their feet.

He released a single bullet that landed in the middle of their group, and then he triggered the Electric-Source within it. Streaks of blazing, blue lightning shot up from the ground, a web of them that struck each man and scorched his body to a blackened husk of ruined flesh.

Cries of anguish echoed through the harbour.

Some of those men dropped dead after only a few seconds of exposure. One of them managed to back away, trying to outrun a tendril of electricity that clung to him with the tenacity of a leech. Eventually, he sank to his knees.

Marcus shot him to finish the job.

Another man was still kicking when the Electric-Source expended its last drop of energy. He was writhing on the pavement, smoke rising from his burning uniform. There were no words coming out of his mouth. Only screams and whimpers.

Marcus casually strolled up to him.

He planted one foot on the burned man's chest, pinning him. "Please!" the poor bastard cried, staring up at Marcus with horror in his eyes. "Please!"

The last thing that man saw was the barrel of a gun pointed right at his face.

14

Seated behind her desk, the Prelate looked up as Desa entered her office. Her face was pinched into an expression of rank disapproval. "Well," she said. "Let's get this over with. I'm a very busy woman."

The window behind her looked out on shadowy buildings under a twilight-blue sky. Desa was well aware of the late hour. Daresina said her schedule was packed to bursting and they were lucky to get a few minutes with her before she retired to her chambers for the evening. Well, a few minutes was better than nothing.

Desa strode up to the desk, stopping right in front of it, and regarded the other woman for a very long moment. "We have a request," she said. "We need to petition the Synod for access to the *Vadir Scrolls.*"

Removing his rumpled hat, Tommy stepped up beside her. He managed to project a sense of calm self-assuredness that amazed even Desa. Was this the same wide-eyed young man that she had taken from a backwater village only a few months ago? "If you please, ma'am," Tommy said. "It's very important."

"And why is that?"

"We're seeking information," Desa answered.

She saw lamplight reflected in the thin lenses of Daresina's spectacles. "On what topic?" The Prelate's eyebrows climbed higher and higher as if to say that no answer could possibly satisfy her.

Something told Desa to hold her tongue. She couldn't say why; it was just instinct. The Synod would not let them anywhere near those scrolls without a compelling reason – she would have to state their purpose eventually – but every fibre of her being told her not to trust Daresina. Tommy, however, felt no such reservation. "The Spear of Vengeance," he blurted out without a care in the world.

The Prelate gasped.

Leaning forward with her hands braced on the desk, Desa peered into the other woman's face. "You know about it," she whispered. "Wait…Are you saying this thing is real?"

"I've said nothing of the sort!" Daresina protested.

Desa straightened, backing away from the desk. She closed her eyes and let out a breath. "I've always suspected there were things the Synod kept from us. What do you know about this spear?"

The Prelate was on her feet in an instant, slamming a fist down on her desk. "It's a legend!" she snapped. "You wasted my time for this?"

"If this weapon is real," Desa said, "it may be the one thing that can destroy the entity inhabiting Adele."

"This again…"

Tommy stepped forward, setting his hat down on the desk and holding the Prelate's gaze. "Begging your pardon, ma'am," he cut in. "But you know very well that we aren't lying. Marcus and Miri confirmed it for you."

Daresina heaved out a sigh, her head drooping as if she

were suddenly overcome by a wave of fatigue. "Yes, I believe you," she admitted. "But the Spear of Vengeance won't help you defeat this thing."

"How do you know?" Desa asked.

"Trust me."

"Trust you?" Desa scoffed. "The very fact that you can say with any degree of confidence that the Spear will not help us betrays two things. One, the Spear is real. And two, you know what it does."

"Yes!" Daresina shouted. "Yes, I do!"

Desa narrowed her eyes as she studied the other woman. "And yet you expect us to trust you," she hissed. "What does the Spear do, Daresina?"

"That is not for you to know."

"What does it do?" Desa asked again.

A shrill, high-pitched scream outside was immediately followed by the sound of gunfire. Glass shattered somewhere, and then men were shouting in Eradian. By the eyes of Vengeance, what was going on?

Desa rushed to the window and looked out to find half a dozen men in blue pants and black coats on the street outside. Eradian soldiers? Here? One of them hoisted up a rifle and fired at someone that Desa couldn't see. "How did they get so deep into the city?" she wondered aloud.

"Miri!" Tommy squeaked.

Desa looked over her shoulder.

Her young companion was frantic, his face glistening with sweat. "I have to find her," he said, glancing this way and that. "I have to-"

"Go," Desa said.

Returning her attention to the window, Desa watched as three of the invaders scrambled up the front steps of the building. One began slamming his shoulder against the heavy, wooden door.

That door swung open, and men in red coats burst out of the building. The Prelate's security forces. Two of them died from rifle rounds before they even made it to the top step. More Eradians were gathering in the street.

Bent over with her hands on the windowsill, Desa shook her head. "They're coming to kill you, Prelate," she said. "Do you have a back way out of here?"

"I..." Daresina stammered.

"Hide," Desa barked. "I'll protect you."

She noticed a glass container filled with marbles on the table in the corner. They were purely decorative, but a trained Field Binder could make just about anything into a weapon.

She rushed over to the table, scooped up a handful of marbles and shoved them into her pocket. Then she opened herself to the Ether and began Infusing each one. Now, if the Prelate's men could just keep the invaders busy for a few minutes...

The last traces of twilight had faded from the sky, and the stars had come out. Black water lapped at the shore as the Weaver gazed out upon the distant lights of Aladar. From ten miles away, the city looked peaceful. You would never know that over a hundred enemy troops roamed its streets.

She stood upon the shoreline with hands folded over her stomach, pursing her lips as she stared into the distance. "Hurry now," she said gently. "No time to waste."

Another group of uniformed men surrounded her, each one clutching a rifle and glancing nervously toward the distant city. Ten at a time. That was as many as she could send in one trip.

The Weaver closed her eyes.

The men around her vanished. She had sent them to a street on the northern edge of the city. Each group landed in a different location. That would make it harder for the Aladri to respond and increase the likelihood that one of them would manage to put a bullet through Desa Kincaid.

The instant they were gone, another group of ten surrounded her. She sent those to the middle of the city, depositing them in front of the six-story building that the Aladri called the Academy. She could feel the Nether surging. Containing it was exhausting, a painful reminder that she was still trapped within a mortal body. The Nether could keep this up forever, but Adele would collapse if she didn't rest soon.

McCallum came up beside her. "Are you all right, ma'am?"

"I will endure," she mumbled.

He nodded.

Tucking his thumbs into his belt, McCallum looked out on the water. "If things were going well," he began, "the first teams would have stolen a boat and reported back by now."

"Your point?"

"We may need something stronger than rifles."

The Weaver opened her eyes. "No!" she snapped. "I will not use my powers on that city. Your men *will* do their jobs, Captain."

"But-"

"Leave me."

He turned away from her, sand crunching beneath his boots as he stalked off down the beach. As soon as he was gone, another group of soldiers approached. Brave men who were ready to be sent into battle.

A smile tugged at the corners of the Weaver's mouth. So, McCallum wanted something stronger than rifles? "You have all made me very proud," she murmured. "I am humbled by your courage and valour."

Their leader, a man with a thick, dark goatee, stepped forward and bowed his head. "Thank you, ma'am," he said.

"I have laid a terrible burden on your shoulders," she went on. "Honest men should not be sent to confront such dark magic with nothing but guns and knives."

"Ma'am?"

Turning to face them, the Weaver adopted a stately posture. She was a queen looking down on her subjects. "If I offered you the strength to defeat the Aladri," she said. "Would you accept it?"

The man with the goatee held her gaze for a long moment, and then he nodded slowly. "Of course, ma'am."

"Excellent."

She touched his forehead with two fingers, and he turned gray. His skin, his hair, even his clothing: all gray. Blackness filled his eyes from corner to corner, a dead stare that never wavered.

She changed the others with very little difficulty and sent them into the city.

THE ETHER FLED, and the world was once again a place of solid objects. Daresina was cowering in the corner, huddled up in the small space between the side of her bookshelf and a rather expensive-looking vase.

She was sniveling, tears staining her cheeks as her body

trembled. "What...?" she stammered. "What can you do against so many?"

Exhaling roughly, Desa bent over and brushed a lock of hair out of her face. "Well," she replied. "I'm going to need to borrow your ring."

The golden band on Daresina's third finger was marked by a fat ruby that sparkled in the lamplight. Much too gaudy for Desa's taste, but the Prelate seemed unwilling to part with it. "This? What do you want with this?"

"I've Infused it," Desa explained.

The Prelate yanked the thing off her finger and tossed it to the floor with a growl. She looked up, her eyes smoldering behind the lenses of her glasses. "You had no right!"

"Do you want to live?"

"Of course."

Striding across the room, Desa positioned herself in front of the other woman. "Then shut up and do what I tell you." She dropped to a crouch and picked up the ring. Luckily, it fit snugly on her index finger.

The sound of gunfire on the floor beneath them drove Desa's point home. Some of those Eradians had made it into the building. She had been keeping tabs on them while she was communing with the Ether. They would be here any moment.

Pressing her back against the wall, Daresina glanced toward the door. Her mouth was compressed into a line, her eyes wide with fright. "What...What should I do?"

Desa stood up and began a slow march to the door, pausing at the last second to look over her shoulder. "Stay here," she said. "Keep quiet."

She pushed the door open.

"What if they get past you?" Daresina asked.

"They won't."

Outside the Prelate's office, she found a huge lobby with red carpets that stretched from corner to corner. Two lines of pillars supported a vaulted ceiling, and the central aisle between them ran all the way to a set of double doors with ornate, golden handles.

Once again, Desa cursed herself for not bringing her gun. Not that she would have been allowed into the Prelate's office while armed. But a smarter woman would have learned her lesson after Azra. *Well,* she thought. *I'll just have to make do.*

There were four lamps on golden stands, one in each corner, and they all projected light up toward the ceiling. She had Infused every one of them. Not an easy task when she was in the other room; the further away you were from an object, the longer it took to create a stable connection to the Ether. The Sinks she had created were not very strong, but they would serve their purpose.

She heard footsteps in the hallway outside.

Fishing one marble out of her pocket, Desa squinted at it. "Tricks and tricks and even more tricks." She had exempted herself while crafting the Infusions. None of the marbles would affect her.

The double doors burst open to reveal eight men in black coats. They surged into the lobby like water through a burst dam. Every single one of them carried a revolver in his hand. They seemed to have abandoned their rifles, which made sense. Weapons like that weren't as useful in close quarters.

Desa threw the marble as hard as she could.

All eight men skidded to a stop, watching as the tiny bead of hardened glass flew over their heads and right through the door. Their leader, a tall man with a scar over his right eyebrow, stepped forward with a wolfish grin. "You missed."

"Did I?"

Spinning out of sight, Desa took cover behind the nearest pillar on her right. She pressed her back to it, waiting for the sound of gunfire. But there was nothing. She had to give them some credit; they didn't just waste ammo in a frenzy of bloodlust.

Retrieving more marbles from her pocket, Desa tossed them around the corner and let them scatter in the aisle between the pillars. A few men cursed, but nobody tripped. They were advancing slowly; she could hear the footsteps.

"Not gonna work, lady," one of them shouted.

Closing her eyes, Desa nodded once. She triggered the Force-Sinks that she had Infused into every one of those marbles, ordering them to feast on kinetic energy. None of them were strong enough to stop a man outright, but she didn't need to stop them. Only to slow them down.

She peeked around the corner and found several men trying to lift their pistols, moving lethargically as if they were trapped underwater. There were a couple of them in the back who were too far away to be affected by the marbles. Those two exchanged confused glances.

Desa slipped around her pillar on the side furthest from the aisle. Quick and quiet, she ducked around the corner again.

A man with bright, blue eyes stood there, rounding on her with excruciating slowness. He tried to raise his weapon, inch by agonizing inch. She killed the Sink nearest to him, and he snapped back into motion.

Desa kicked him in the stomach before he could aim, sending him careening toward his fellows. She killed the Sinks near them as well, allowing them to return to full speed just before Blue Eyes crashed into them. Three men dropped to the floor in a pile of bodies.

Desa moved on to the next pillar.

As she drew near, a man with a scraggly, gray beard stepped out from behind it, catching her by surprise. His fist slammed into her face before she could react. Hot tears blurred her vision, and she fell hard on her backside.

Before she knew it, Gray-Beard was on top of her, pawing at her, trying to get his hands around her neck. She seized his wrists, but the bastard was strong! It was all she could do just to keep him from choking her.

Desa turned onto her side and then hooked her leg around the back of his neck. With a quick twist of her body, she rolled him onto his back. Then she was on top of him.

She punched him in the face.

Dazed by the hit, he groaned and collapsed, blood spilling from his nostrils. One down and seven left. She could hear them moving. Footsteps behind her.

Drawing the unconscious man's belt knife, Desa flung it out behind herself without even looking. A high-pitched wail filled her ears. When she finally looked, she saw a bald man standing in the aisle with the knife sticking out of his right shoulder, his gun lying at his feet. Another second, and he would have shot her in the back of the head.

Three more men gathered behind her.

The marble that she had thrown into the hallway...

Desa triggered the Gravity-Source that she had infused into it. The men who tried to converge on her were suddenly yanked sideways toward the door. As was the bald fellow and his gun as well.

Even the man beneath her was dragged along the floor, carrying Desa with him. She rolled off of him and stood up, turning around with a grunt.

Several of her marbles were rolling toward the door.

It lasted only a few seconds before the Gravity-Source sputtered its last cough of energy. The whimpers of several men echoed through the lobby.

She ventured a glance and saw a pile of four bodies at the door. The bald man was clutching his shoulder and moaning. With any luck, they would stay down long enough for her to deal with the others.

Desa stepped into the aisle, turning her back on the four of them.

A man with a coarse, black beard leaped out from behind a pillar on her right. He drew his knife and came forward as if he meant to gut her. Desa noticed another discarded pistol on the floor.

The men by the door were rising; she could hear them. Given half a chance, they would come up behind her, and then she would be trapped. But her Gravity-Source had pulled all the marbles to that spot. She triggered every single one of them. Together, they were strong enough to sap the kinetic energy from all four men, freezing them in place.

Black-Beard gasped, his eyes widening when he saw that his companions were no longer moving. He recovered quickly, stepped forward and slashed at Desa's belly.

She hopped back.

Enraged, he came at her again.

Pulsing the Gravity-Sink in her belt buckle, Desa jumped and kicked him in the face. His head snapped backward, blood flying from his nose. There were two more men behind him. One was the leader with the scar above his eyebrow.

That discarded pistol was just sitting there in the middle of the aisle, begging her to reach for it. But she would have to go through a knife-wielding maniac first, and even if she got past him, the other two would be on her in a flash. Time to get creative.

With another brief pulse of her Gravity-Sink, Desa leaped to her right. She kicked one of the pillars, pushed off of it and launched herself toward Black-Beard.

He looked up just in time to see her coming.

Desa wrapped her legs around his neck, trapping his head between her knees. Toppling over, she pulled him down to the floor with her. They both landed with a *thump*. She immediately raised her left forearm and triggered the Force-Sink in her bracelet.

The growl of gunfire made her flinch.

A bullet hung in the air just three inches away from her head. Then it fell to the floor. The silence that followed was deafening. For a moment, nobody moved.

The man with the scar was standing at the end of the aisle with smoke rising from the barrel of his gun. His eyes flicked down to the bullet that had failed to kill her and then to the pistol that was right next to Desa.

Black-Beard struggled to free himself from the vise she had around his head. He clawed at Desa's legs, and she was forced to release him.

Worse yet, the marbles had drained all the energy that they could absorb, and the men by the door were starting to rise again. Seven against one. Not good odds.

Desa triggered the Electric-Sinks she had Infused into every lampstand.

The room was plunged into darkness as every bulb went out. She threw herself sideways – never be where your opponents had last seen you – and snatched up the fallen pistol. Those odds just got a lot better.

Several men cried out when the darkness came.

Someone lost his balance and fell to the floor. Someone else cursed, and the poor fool with the knife in his shoulder was screaming again.

She got up and took cover behind one of the pillars. The men were shouting at one another. She could hear them stomping around. Hopefully, they wouldn't get too close to the lamps. The Sinks she had created would gladly take electrical energy from a human body. And that could be fatal. "Where did she go?"

"I don't know."

"Where-"

The lights came back on. Her Sinks had been very weak, but it didn't matter. The game had changed, and it was time to teach these boys the new rules.

She peered around the pillar and found Mr. Scar standing in the aisle and aiming at the door. He must have caught the motion in the corner of his eye because he spun around to face Desa.

He tried to raise his pistol.

Desa fired first.

Her slug ripped through the man's body with a spray of blood, and he crumpled to the floor. Several more rounds whizzed past her, some scraping the marble off her pillar. Her ears were ringing. From the trajectory of their shots, she could say with confidence that most of them were gathered by the door. A little bravado would end this.

Stepping out into the open, Desa strode toward them. Her gaze never wavered, locked on them with deadly intent. "Go home," she said. "You'll find nothing in this city but pain."

Six men were huddled together by the door, including Black-Beard and Blue-Eyes. One of them stepped forward, lifted his pistol and pointed it right at her.

CRACK!

Her shirt buttons feasted on kinetic energy, forcing the bullet to stillness. It fell to land at her feet, and she stepped right over it, continuing her slow, inexorable march toward the pack of frightened fools. "Go home," Desa said again.

The one in front turned and ran, pushing his way through the others to get out the door. The rest followed him in a frenzy, abandoning their fallen comrades, leaving Desa alone in a quiet lobby.

She leaned against a pillar, her head lolling from a moment of fatigue. A deep breath exploded from her. "Done," she gasped.

But it wasn't.

Scar was bleeding out on the floor, but Gray-Beard was groaning as consciousness returned to him. He sat up with a hand against his forehead.

Desa faced him, gun in hand, scowling and shaking her head. "Your friends are gone," she said. "I strongly suggest that you go too. If you're still here in thirty seconds, I'll kill you."

He looked up at her, blinking, then stood up with a grunt. Quick as you please, he shambled out the door.

Now, she was alone. She checked on the Prelate and found Daresina crouching behind the vase. That vase must have tipped over at some point because there was a pile of dirt on the floor. And that wasn't all. Desa saw pens, sheets of paper and the Prelate's desk lamp strewn about on the red carpet. What could have...Of course. The Gravity-Source. This room would have been on the edge of its range, but that was still enough to do some damage. "Are they gone?" Daresina asked.

Exhausted, Desa braced one hand against the door-frame. "They're gone," she breathed. "Can you get somewhere safe?"

"I…"

"The city's under attack; I can't stay here to look after you. Leave the building as quietly as you can, and then find a safe place. A library. A warehouse. Anything!"

"Very well."

Once the Prelate was on her way, Desa took a few minutes to replenish her supplies. Scar had left her a second pistol and an entire bandolier of ammunition. She gathered them up, along with his holster and the marbles, and then she began Infusing new weapons.

Tommy ran.

The wide street lined with white-bricked buildings was illuminated by lamps that cast a yellow glow. Up ahead, he saw three Eradian men peering into shop windows, swinging their rifles about as if they expected demons to leap out of the nearest alley. Well, that was what the ignorant thought of Aladar. He himself had been much the same just a few short months ago.

He slipped into an alley, taking cover in the shadows, and stood with his eyes downcast. "You can do this," he whispered to himself. "You can do it. Just hold on a little longer."

The footsteps were getting closer.

Tommy pressed his back against the alley wall, wincing as his body trembled. *Don't see me! Don't see me!* he thought at the approaching men. *I'm not here.*

A figure appeared in the mouth of the alley, a man creeping past with his rifle pointed forward. He turned his head, but if he saw Tommy, he gave no indication. Tommy held his breath. The man was gone a second later. Others moved past him on the opposite side of the street.

"No good," Tommy whispered, shaking his head. "What's an idiot like you gonna do against hardened men like that?"

Well, there was something he could do, but he had to get back to his hotel room first. He could feel his Sinks and Sources; they were still where he had left them, Infused into the heads of his arrows. He would need them to have any chance against these soldiers, and he had to find Miri.

Because he loved her.

When the footsteps were gone, he darted out of the alley and resumed his sprint for the hotel. It was only a few blocks away. He would get his arrows and then...And then what? It wasn't as if he knew where to find Miri.

One problem at a time, he told himself. *Just keep going.*

LONG AFTER THE last group of Eradians had left, the Weaver stood on the shore, looking out on the Strait of Avalas and the distant city lights. The plan had seemed so good to her, but now something felt wrong.

She noticed something on the water. A ripple of motion. Extending her senses, she discovered that it was a small, wooden boat with four men in it. The first soldiers coming back to report?

She was patient. It took the better part of half an hour for them to haul their little boat onto the beach and get out. One fellow, an older gentleman with a scraggly, gray beard, bent over to knuckle his back.

The Weaver flowed toward him in her prim, red dress, her face stern. "Report, soldier," she said.

The man looked up with her with horror in his dark

eyes. He blinked a few times. She could see that his cheek was bruised, his nose broken. "Recommend a full retreat, ma'am," he said.

"Pardon me?"

"We tried to kill their Prelate like you told us." The Weaver had forgotten that this was the group she had sent on that particular mission. One human was very much like another. "They had a woman defending her."

"A woman."

"Aye, ma'am," Gray-Beard said. "Just one woman. Unarmed. She took us to pieces with their witchcraft. But... It wasn't just the magic. She fought like a trained soldier. Better than most men I've seen."

The Weaver's face darkened as she stared into his eyes. She tried her best not to shiver. "This woman," she said. "She was petite, with short, dark hair. Kind of an olive complexion."

"Yes, ma'am. You know her?"

Screeching like an angry cat, the Weaver backed away from him. Her hand came up before she even realized it, a stream of fire flying from her fingers. Flames that enveloped Gray-Beard from head to foot, reducing him to ash.

The other men looked on in wide-eyed horror. A second later, they turned and ran along the beach, no doubt hoping to find safety with their commanders.

The Weaver stretched her hand out toward one, releasing a lightning that streaked toward him and punched right through his body. He fell face-down in the sand, smoke rising from his corpse.

The other two were still running.

With a flick of her wrist, the Weaver sent a fireball after one, watching as it sizzled through the air and exploded on contact with his body. She dragged the other one back to her with carefully applied kinetic energy. He was kicking and thrashing as she pulled him through the sand.

"Benny!" she screamed.

The snake-man emerged from the shadows, standing silently and awaiting her instructions. His loyalty did little to soothe the Weaver's ire. "These idiots aren't going to destroy her!" the Weaver spat. "She's too strong for them."

Benny only nodded.

Spinning around to face him with an impish grin, the Weaver strode forward. "We will just have to come up with something better." She caressed Benny's scaly face with a gloved hand. "Won't we?"

"I will destroy her for you, Mistress."

The Weaver tittered, then stood up on her toes to kiss him on the cheek. "You can't Field Bind anymore, Benny," she said. "You gave up that power to embrace the strength I gave you."

He growled. Perhaps the loss troubled him more than he let on. Poor Benny. He had truly believed that he would be the vessel to contain the Nether. "Your enhanced strength and speed might make you a match for an ordinary Field Binder," the Weaver added. "But not for Desa Kincaid."

"What shall we do, Mistress?"

Without warning, the Weaver kissed him on his scaly lips. A slow, tender kiss. When she pulled away from him, black smoke flowed out of her mouth and into his. His eyes popped open, and then they turned black.

"A portion of my power," she said. "Now, I'm gonna want that back, Benny."

"Yes, Mistress."

"Good. Now, be on your way."

Benny disappeared without further comment, and she knew that he had transported himself to the island. She could feel him through the connection they shared. How fitting. For ten years, Radharal Bendarian had wanted to kill Desa Kincaid. Now, he would get his chance.

She turned around to find the soldier she had captured lying in the sand and sobbing with his face hidden behind his hand. He looked up at her, his red cheeks stained with tears, and groaned.

The Weaver clicked her tongue.

Squatting before him, she smiled and shook her head. In a way, it was a relief to no longer have to play the role of the prim and proper goddess. Even if only for a little while. "Well, now," she said. "Let's see what y'all look like from the inside."

She began removing his skin strip by strip.

15

Miri scrambled up the library stairs.

The windows that she saw through the gaps between the pillars were still lit up. Which meant there might be people inside. She couldn't see anything specific though. The sound of a gunshot made her freeze.

Off to her left, several Aladri police officers were sticking their heads out from the alleys between the gray-bricked buildings and firing at the Eradian soldiers who clustered together further up the street. The Eradians clearly weren't used to urban warfare. But then could you expect anything else? For half a second, Miri thought to go and help her countrymen, but her priority was Tommy. And if he was anywhere, it would be the library. She suppressed a surge of jealousy.

Sprinting up the steps with her duster trailing out behind her in the wind, Miri snarled and shook her head. "Bloody fool of a man," she spat. "I don't know why I go to this much trouble for him."

She threw her shoulder against the wooden door.

It swung inward with some resistance, and then she

found herself in the lobby. The reception desk was unoccupied, and she saw no signs of life. Perhaps everyone had fled. Or maybe-

A hand popped up from behind the desk, clutching a revolver. Before she could say one word, the gun went off with a *CRACK! CRACK! CRACK!* Bullets flew past on her right and her left, pounding the walls and burrowing into them. Not one of them hit her.

"Whoever you are," the shooter cried, "I'm armed!"

Well...obviously.

Miri strode forward with her teeth bared, stuffing the anger back down into the pit of her stomach. "Dalen?" she asked. "Is that you?"

His head poked up from behind the desk, and he blinked when he saw her. "Oh," he mumbled. "Oh! I thought you were one of those horrible militiamen."

Miri planted fists on her hips, glowering at him with all the disapproval she could muster. "Well, if I was," she said. "You'd be dead."

"Now, that's a hasty judgement, don't you think?"

"Your aim is truly atrocious."

Dalen's face reddened, and he averted his eyes, no doubt hoping that she wouldn't notice. "Well, um..." He scrubbed a hand through his hair. "Are you...Are you looking for Thomas?"

"Is he here?"

"No," Dalen stammered. "I thought he might be with you."

Heaving out a sigh, Miri let her head hang. She slapped a palm against her brow and groaned. "Of course..." she muttered. "Why should anything be easy?"

She was startled by the sound of footsteps on the stairs

outside, and then men were shouting, "In there!" By the eyes of Vengeance! Her luck was sour tonight.

"They heard your gunshots," she mouthed to Dalen.

He ducked behind the desk again.

Miri turned and ran to the corner.

Spinning around to face the door, she pulled open her coat and drew throwing knives from sheaths on her belt. She had a pistol as well, but discretion might be preferable.

The door burst open, and two men in black coats stood in the entryway, each with a rifle pointed at the desk. They exchanged glances, no doubt wondering who had fired those shots.

Miri threw her first knife. It tumbled end over end and then buried itself in the thigh of the man nearest to her. He cried out, falling on his knees.

Her second knife went into the other soldier's neck, and that man stumbled sideways, collapsing against the doorframe. Blood fountained from the wound. Then he fell to the floor, dead.

Miri ran for them.

Dropping to her knees, she slid past the first man, grabbed his gun and wrenched it out of his grip. She was on her feet again in an instant, twisting around to face the door.

A third soldier stepped through.

Miri fired.

Her bullet went through the man's chest with enough momentum to throw him to the floor. He landed on his back and slid across the polished tiles, leaving a trail of blood in his wake. A fourth man stuck his head through the door, looked around to see what had happened and gasped when he saw Miri.

She worked the rifle's lever, ejecting the spent shell, then choked up on the weapon and fired again. Her next round took the poor fool right between the eyes and left a spray of red on the wooden door.

"I'm armed! I'm armed!" Dalen shouted from behind the desk.

Miri shook her head.

Ejecting another spent shell, she targeted the man who was on his knees and put him down quickly. "They're dead," she barked at Dalen. "And we should go."

He scooted out from behind the desk, then stood up and tried to recover some semblance of dignity by clearing his throat and saying, "Well done. Yes, I suppose it is time to be gone."

Getting out the door required them to maneuver around the fallen bodies, and the sight of the carnage she had wreaked pushed bile to the tip of Miri's tongue. She could kill if she had to, but she had no love for it.

Together, she and Dalen descended the steps. The street was eerily quiet. She scanned the park on the other side of the road for any sign that enemy soldiers might be hiding in the trees. So far as she could tell, she and Dalen were alone.

A low, growling sound caught her attention.

When she looked around, she saw a man shuffling along the empty road. A man who was entirely gray. Even his clothing lacked the smallest trace of colour. His growl was echoed by several others, and then six more of them were plodding up the steps.

"What...What's going on?" Dalen asked.

Miri lowered her rifle and drew in a shuddering breath. "Well," she answered. "Our problems just got a whole lot worse."

. . .

Tall buildings stood on either side of the street outside the Prelate's office. One was five stories high with arch-shaped windows on every floor. It had been constructed in the last ten years, and from what Desa had been told, it was used primarily by the Banking Guild. Another, slightly shorter tower was home to the electric company.

She still heard gunshots in the distance, though they were much less frequent now. She had been walking for about five minutes, and in all that time, she had not had even one encounter with another group of soldiers.

Desa had a holstered pistol on her hip and a bandolier of ammo across her chest. She walked along the middle of the road, heedless of any cars that might come her way. She was fairly certain that no one would be driving tonight.

That left her with a question: what exactly should she do next? Should she find her friends and try to protect them? Or should she locate a group of Elite Guardians and try to join their ranks. She was quite concerned about Tommy. Her young protege had made admirable progress in the last few days, but he was still very much an amateur. Hopefully, he had managed to find Miri.

Desa wondered where Marcus would be in all of this chaos. Fighting Eradians, no doubt. Knowing him, Marcus would take this invasion as a personal insult. Well, as long as he didn't go too far-

A strange noise drew her out of her reverie.

Reacting by instinct, she turned to her left and found a strange figure on the sidewalk. A man who had once possessed a neatly-trimmed, golden beard. Only now, that beard was as gray as the rest of his face. His eyes were black and feral. "Of course," she muttered. "Always the same old tricks, huh, Adele?"

The gray man charged toward Desa.

Twirling her pistol in one hand, she extended her arm to point it at him. She cocked the hammer and fired.

A slug went through the man's chest, but he didn't stop. He seemed to only be momentarily dazed before resuming his headlong charge. The bullet had driven itself into the wall behind him.

Desa triggered the Force-Source she had Infused into it.

The surge of kinetic energy hit the man from behind and sent him stumbling forward. Right into her trap.

Desa jumped with a high snap-kick, striking his chin with the tip of her shoe. The man staggered, arms flailing. She landed with a hiss, then raised her weapon and shot the man's thigh, forcing him down onto his knees.

Stepping forward, Desa stood over him. She pointed her gun at the man's head and fired a single shot.

A hole appeared in his forehead. He toppled over, black ichor pooling on the pavement. That seemed to do the trick. Whatever these things were, they were still bound by human anatomy to some degree. They might be able to ignore pain; they might be able to shrug off a pierced lung, but without a brain, whatever force animated them couldn't do much.

A gurgling sound behind her.

Without looking, Desa thrust her gun out behind herself and fired. The gurgle became a squeal, and then she stepped aside so that another gray man could stumble past her and collapse on top of the first one. Her shot had gone through his knee.

Desa pointed her gun at the back of his head.

She fired, and that poor bastard spasmed once as black blood sprayed onto the ground. He fell on top of his companion.

Two more gray people were rushing out of nearby alleys:

one with dark skin and a thick beard, the other pale and clean-shaven. The dark man was closest. He leaped and flew toward Desa.

Taking one step backward, she raised her left forearm and triggered the Force-Sink in her bracelet. Stripped of kinetic energy, the bearded man hung suspended in midair. She let him drop to the ground, but the instant he landed, he kicked the gun out of her hand.

Desa jumped and wrapped her legs around his waist, using her own momentum to throw him down onto his back. Perched on top of him, she punched him in the face once, twice, three times. He didn't even notice.

His hand shot up to grab her throat.

Drawing the belt knife that she had stolen, Desa plunged hard into the dead man's forehead. He flailed uncontrollably beneath her and then went still.

The other one was coming up behind her.

Twisting around, Desa released a stream of electricity from Daresina's ring, a jagged bolt of lightning that hit her enemy square in the chest and flung him across the street.

He landed with a wheeze, smoke rising from his blackened flesh. His legs kicked a few times, and then he tried to sit up.

Desa walked over to him, pointed her gun at his head and ended it quickly. When he stopped thrashing, she took a few moments to reload. If the city was overrun with these creatures, she would need every single bullet, every single Sink and every single Source. None of this should have surprised her. Adele would stop at nothing to see her dead. She-

The sound of hands clapping made her freeze.

"Well done," a raspy voice said. "Truly impressive."

. . .

MIRI STOOD with her back against a pillar, the rifle held tightly in both hands. Her teeth were clenched, and she hissed air through them. "All right," she said softly. "We make our stand on three."

Dalen was huddled against the next pillar over, waving his pistol about in a way that didn't exactly inspire confidence. His face was glistening with sweat. "What do you mean 'make our stand?'"

"Start shooting. One...Two...Three, now!"

Miri aimed around the pillar, lifting her rifle to find a bald, gray man on the third step. He paused when he noticed her, then began a mad scramble to close the distance. Miri fired a round through his chest, throwing him down onto his back.

More grays were coming up the stairs: a lanky man who couldn't be much older than Tommy, and a portly fellow who might have been his grandfather. Both came running for her.

Working the lever, Miri ejected the shell and then took aim again. She fired a second shot through the portly one's head, and down he went. The skinny one leaped over the bald man's body and ducked between the pillars.

He rounded on Dalen.

CRACK!

A bullet erupted from the skinny man's back and grazed Miri's arm hard enough to make her yelp. Dalen, the idiot, didn't realize that bullets didn't stop just because they hit their targets.

Worse yet, the dead man ignored the shot to his chest and advanced on Dalen, choking him with both hands. Squealing and wheezing, Dalen struggled to get free. It did him no good.

Miri drew another throwing knife, tossed it up and

caught the tip of the blade. She flung it at the man and watched it land in the back of his head. He thrashed once, then released Dalen and fell to the ground.

More enemies were charging up the stairs.

Another six men in colourless, Eradian uniforms trampled over their fallen companions as they raced toward Miri like a pack of feral beasts. She braced herself for the fight.

An arrow landed on the fifth step.

"Get clear!"

Miri did as she was told, taking cover behind a pillar and gripping it tightly. She risked a peek and saw half a dozen bodies being tossed up into the air. Then the wave of kinetic force hit the pillar and made it rumble. She had to fight to hold on lest she be thrown backward.

When it was over, she peered around the pillar and saw her Tommy standing on the sidewalk with a bow in hand, his next arrow already drawn. Some of the men that he had knocked down were already rising.

Three of them began a mad dash for the man she loved.

Tommy turned on his heel, aiming for one of them, and then he loosed. A gray man with thick, dark hair went down when an arrow pierced his forehead. He fell flat on his face and went still.

The other two were nearly down the stairs.

With a quick step backward, Tommy drew another arrow, targeted the next one and loosed. That man staggered when the shaft went through his chest, and then he exploded in a cloud of black goo.

The kinetic force expanded, throwing the third one sideways. There were even more of them running up the street. Miri saw at least a dozen of those abominations trying to converge on the library.

Turning his back on her, Tommy pulled another arrow

from his quiver and aimed for a spot on the building next to the park. "You might want to hold onto something," he shouted.

His arrow drove itself into the wooden frame of a third-story window.

Then the gray hoard was being lifted off the ground, pulled upward and flattened against the front wall of the building. Miri felt the tug of gravity. It was weak at this distance, but she clung to the pillar anyway.

One by one, Tommy targeted them, drawing arrows with incredible speed and planting each one in the head of a dead man. They all stopped thrashing, and then, without warning, they fell to the ground, landing in a pile. A pile of motionless, colourless bodies.

Miri proceeded down the steps at a quick trot, gasping for breath. "Thank you." She stopped in front of Tommy and nodded to him. "How did you find us?"

Tommy was smiling down at himself, his face flushed with chagrin. His answer was a shrug. "I reckoned you'd be looking for me," he said. "So, I figured you'd be where you expected me to be."

"Good thinking."

"My word, Thomas," Dalen said, coming down the stairs. "You certainly have become proficient with that bow."

Tommy looked up at him with a serious expression. His face hardened even further. "Thanks," he said. "But that's beside the point right now. Give me a moment to recover my arrows, and then we'll be out of here."

"Killing the dead," the raspy voice hissed. "A painfully easy task."

Desa whirled around to find a shadow striding out from

an alley on the left side of the street. When the figure stepped into the light, she saw that it was tall, well-muscled and covered in scales from head to toe. Yellow eyes with vertical slits for pupils watched her. No... It couldn't be.

Covering her mouth with one hand, Desa felt her eyebrows rising. "Bendarian," she gasped. "I should have known I hadn't seen the last of you. My luck isn't that good."

He replied with a serpentine smile, a forked tongue darting out to lick his nose. "Thought you were free of me, did you?" He stepped into the middle of the road and stood before her.

"A girl can dream."

Without warning, Bendarian dropped to a crouch, seized a man-hole cover with one hand and ripped it free of its mountings. Impossible! No one was that strong. He stood up and hurled the thing at her.

Desa pulsed her Gravity-Sink and leaped, flipping through the air as the metal disc flew past beneath her. She landed with her fists up. "So, you learned some new tricks."

"You have no idea."

In a blur of motion, he turned and ran to the right side of the road. He bent his knees, squatting to grab a bench on the sidewalk. Metal groaned as the screws popped, and then he was holding the bench above his head.

He rounded on Desa and threw it.

She drove forward, somersaulting over the pavement and coming up on one knee. With incredible reflexes, she drew her pistol, cocked the hammer and pointed it at him.

CRACK!

Bendarian's hand snapped up to catch the bullet. It took a moment for her to recognize the soft wheezing sound as his laughter. "You didn't think that would work, did you?"

He leaped with incredible power, flying through the air

with his arms spread wide, passing right over Desa's head. The crunching sound of cracking the pavement marked his landing right behind her. She spun around to face him.

Bendarian seized a fistful of her shirt and then lifted her off the ground. With a growl, he threw her and sent her flying backward toward a building.

Desa thrust her left hand out behind herself, triggering her Force-Sink bracelet. Technically, it was meant to drain kinetic energy from objects that were coming toward her. But motion was relative. When the object in question was stationary while she herself was in flight, the bracelet slowed her down instead.

Desa landed on the sidewalk.

She looked up to find a blur of green coming toward her. She had only two seconds to react. Instinct took over, and she used the bracelet again, draining the kinetic energy from Bendarian, stilling him. He was taller than she remembered, his limbs thicker, and those green scales almost reflected the lamplight.

Desa let her arm drop.

Bendarian blinked in confusion.

She kicked him in the belly with enough power to make him double over. She punched him in the face, and he stumbled, black blood dripping from the corner of his mouth.

Pulsing her Gravity-Sink, Desa jumped over his head. She landed on the sidewalk behind him and then took off across the road.

When she turned around, he was rubbing a smarting mouth with a scaly hand. "You always were cagey." His voice was like a crumpling paper. "But my mistress has given me the tools I need to end you."

His eyes turned black. Pure black from corner to corner, like two small pits into the depths of the Abyss itself.

He raised a green hand, and a fireball sparked into existence above his open palm. Drawing back his arm, he threw it at Desa.

She ran toward the oncoming projectile, then dropped to her knees at the last second, allowing the fireball to rush past overhead. It struck the building behind her with a small explosion that sent chunks of stone flying.

"My turn!" Desa said.

She thrust her fist out toward Bendarian and triggered the Electric-Source that she had Infused into Daresina's ring. A single bolt of lightning erupted from the ruby, zipped across the street and struck Bendarian's chest hard enough to propel him backward. He slammed into the building behind him, sparks flashing over his body.

Desa raised her gun in one hand, aiming for a spot above his head. She fired a single bullet into the building's front wall and then triggered the Force-Source within it. Chunks of stone rained down upon Bendarian.

He raised his hands, and then they stopped, hanging suspended in midair. He flung those hands out toward Desa, and the stones followed suit, bearing down on her like a swarm of angry bees.

She threw herself sideways and rolled out of the way. Bits of stone hit the ground where she had just been.

"I'm not the only one who learned new tricks!" Bendarian yelled.

Once again, the snake-man had a fireball balanced above each of his palms. He threw them at Desa, one after the other.

Desperately, she rolled aside.

One fireball struck the road, and then the other followed

less than half a second later, each one spraying pieces of asphalt into the air. The stink of melted tar filled her nose. By the eyes of Vengeance! He was just too powerful!

The lightning should have killed him – it would have done in any normal human being – but the Nether sustained him somehow. That shouldn't have surprised her. She had seen him recover from bullet wounds to the chest. If only she could cut him off from it…

Bendarian stamped a foot down on the sidewalk.

The quake that followed made the city groan. The ground trembled beneath Desa. She couldn't fight this. Not even with Field Binding. She had tried to kill him in that pyramid, and she had failed then too.

With his quiver refilled with slightly-used arrows, Tommy ran down the street. There were no more enemies in sight, no signs of trouble. "First, we find Desa," he said. "She will know what to do."

Miri was on his left and running hard. She glanced toward him, and her scowl betrayed what she thought of that plan. "How do you expect to find anyone in this chaos?" she asked. "She could be anywhere in the city."

"I found you, didn't I?"

On his right, Dalen was huffing and puffing, trying desperately to keep up. The man's face was red. "I'm all for finding reinforcements," he said. "But perhaps Miri is right."

Tommy shook his head forcefully. "I left Desa at the Prelate's office," he said. "If we head back in that direction, we'll probably find her."

"What about my brother?" Miri asked.

"If you have some idea of where he might be," Tommy replied. "I'm happy to look. But-"

He cut off when a troop of black-coated men came running into view from an intersecting street. They didn't stop to give Tommy and his friends any trouble; they just kept running until they were out of sight. Seconds later, men in yellow robes leaped from a nearby rooftop and sailed effortlessly across the street. Tommy could feel their Gravity-Sinks. Well, at least the Elite Guard was out in force.

Craning his neck, Tommy watched them go. "Maybe that's our best bet," he said. "If the city has organized any kind of resistance, they'll know about it. Come on."

He ran around the corner in pursuit of the Eradian men. They were half a block in front of him and running like horses who feared the whip. Not one of them looked back to see what might be coming up behind them.

A man in yellow descended from the rooftops with his metal staff in hand. He landed in the middle of the street, extended his hand and released a stream of lightning from his ring. A jagged, blue lance that struck the rear-most Eradian and threw him to the ground.

Tommy felt his jaw drop. He blinked and then gave his head a shake as if that would dispel the image of what he had just witnessed. "Just like that?" he asked. "He didn't even try to take them alive!"

Dalen stumbled up beside him, wiping sweat from his brow. "It's no more than they deserve," he said. "They're foreign invaders."

"They're people!"

The Elite Guardian leaped, held aloft by his Gravity-Sink, and then landed in the group of Eradian soldiers. Tommy couldn't see what was happening, but he watched as one black-coated man went sprawling onto the sidewalk.

Another took a staff hit to the belly, and a Force-Source

propelled him backward through the window of a flower shop.

Tommy recognized the Elite Guardian. It was the one who had insulted Desa's gun and then challenged her to duel. What was his name again? Oh, yes. Radavan.

One of the Eradians tried to sneak up behind him with a knife in hand.

Radavan spun on him, his staff whirling around in a blur to strike the man's cheek. The Eradian stumbled, and then Radavan shoved the end of his staff into his belly. The poor man bent forward with a hand on his stomach.

Moving like a ghost on the wind, Radavan drew a knife from his belt and plunged it into his enemy's shoulder. He kicked the other man hard enough to send him stumbling all the way to the sidewalk. Tommy felt a Heat-Source being triggered. And then the Eradian soldier was screaming, flailing about as his skin turned red and then black.

"That's enough!" Tommy shouted. "They're beaten! You need to offer them the chance to surrender!"

Standing in the light of a nearby street lamp, Radavan turned around with a smirk on his face. "This is no concern of yours, outlander," he said. "Leave now lest you incur the wrath of the Elite Guard."

"The Abyss claim me if I will!" Tommy yelled, striding forward. "You're straight-up murdering people, and I won't stand for it!"

"What will you do to stop it?"

"Whatever I have to."

"Tommy..." Miri broke in. "Are you sure this is wise?"

He ignored her and continued his inexorable march toward the man in yellow. The grip of his bow felt good in his hand. A reminder that he could defend himself if he had to. *If* he had to.

Scoffing at him, Radavan extended his hand and unleashed a burst of kinetic energy that hit Tommy like an oncoming train. He was thrown backward, landing on his bottom with a whimper.

"This is the grandest city in the world," Radavan said. "I am charged with its protection, and I will not fail in my duty." He turned his back on Tommy and resumed his pursuit of the soldiers who were now limping away.

Tommy forced himself to stand.

With a snarl, he took an arrow, nocked it and drew fletchings to cheek. He aimed directly at the other man's back. "Radavan," he growled. "You have *failed* this city!"

His enemy spun around.

Tommy released his arrow and watched it zip through the air. It stopped right in front of Radavan, held aloft by the other man's Force-Sink. Chuckling maliciously, Radavan let it fall to land at his feet. "Very well, stranger," he said. "If you are really so eager to die..."

He stretched a hand out, and Tommy felt a stirring in the Ether. He knew what would happen next; so, he triggered the Electric-Sink in his pendant half a second before lightning flew from Radavan's fingertips.

A streak of crackling electricity tried to scorch Tommy to ash and winked out of existence mere inches away from him. A moment later, Radavan lowered his hand. His eyes widened in shock.

In a blur of motion, Tommy retrieved another arrow, nocked it and drew back the bowstring. He let it fly and drove the shaft into the pavement, well to Radavan's left.

The other man laughed...

...Until Tommy triggered the Force-Source in the arrowhead. Kinetic energy sent pieces of asphalt into the air and threw Radavan sideways. He slammed into the front wall of the building, wheezing on impact, and then fell to land on the sidewalk.

Tommy nocked another arrow, aimed his bow upward and loosed. His next bolt struck the building's facade, and he released another blast of kinetic force the instant it made contact. Red bricks exploded out in all directions.

Some of them almost fell on Radavan.

The other man raised his left hand and used a Force-Sink to prevent those bricks from pummelling him. He walked out from under them and let them fall to the ground behind him with a crash like thunder. "Desa Nin Leean has made you dangerous, boy."

Radavan leaped in a wide arc.

Before Tommy could react, the other man kicked him in the chest. His lungs felt as if they had been beaten with a sledgehammer. He thought he might collapse from the pain. It was all he could do to stay on his feet.

Radavan landed in front of him and strode forward with a murderous glint in his eyes. His staff whistled through the air as it clipped Tommy's chin.

Dazed by the hit, Tommy fell onto his backside. His head was swimming, but he was very much aware of his opponent standing over him. Radavan drew another knife, crouched down and tried to ram it through Tommy's throat.

Tommy's hands shot up to catch the other man's wrist.

By the Almighty, this bastard was strong. The knife blade inched closer and closer to its target. There had to be something he could do.

An arrow on the ground.

It must have slid out of Tommy's quiver when he fell. He snatched it up and jammed it into Radavan's shoulder, eliciting a cry of pain. His adversary stood up and backed away.

Tommy yanked his gun out of its holster, pointed it at

the other man's chest and cocked the hammer. He fired several times, but every bullet stopped short of its target floating in the air for a few seconds before it fell to the ground.

Radavan was grinning as he came forward to stand over Tommy. "Did you think it would be so easy, boy? Did you-"

CRACK!

Another bullet jerked to a halt in front of Radavan, but Tommy hadn't shot it. *Miri,* he realized. She seemed to have gotten Radavan's attention. "Go away," he said. "You're nothing but a buzzing fly."

He flung his hand out toward her, and Tommy felt it when he triggered his Force-Source ring. Miri's yelp and the *thump* of a body hitting the ground told him that she was out of the fight. *His Force-Sinks.* Tommy noted that they were Infused into several stones on his necklace. If they were anything like Desa's, then they would only take energy from objects that were coming directly toward Radavan.

Tommy sat up and pressed his gun to the side of Radavan's thigh. And then he pulled the trigger. The bullet went through one leg and then right through the other, causing Radavan to fall on top of him.

Tommy pushed him away.

Radavan landed on the pavement, blood fountaining from his wounds. His face was already gray and covered in sweat. And his eyes...Tommy had never seen such horror in another man's eyes before.

The enormity of what he had just done settled onto him. There was no way they could get him to a physician in time. Radavan was going to bleed out here in the street. Which meant that Tommy had just taken his first life.

. . .

THE EARTH GROANED beneath Desa as Bendarian stood on the sidewalk and cackled with delight. She tried to stand, but the quake took her legs out from under her. Falling flat on her face, she hissed. When the shaking finally subsided, she looked up to see Bendarian readying another fireball.

A gunshot rang out through the air.

A bullet chewed through Bendarian's chest with a burst of black blood. Not her bullet. The snake-man collapsed against the building behind him, but then his wound began to close itself.

Kalia stood at the mouth of an alley with a pistol in one hand, smoke rising from its barrel. "I think that's quite enough," she said, marching forward. She fired again and again and again.

Each round made Bendarian spasm as it punched through his body, but none of them were enough to put him down for good. He tittered and then tossed a fireball at Kalia.

She shot it.

The fireball vanished in a puff of smoke as her bullet passed through it. A Heat-Sink. An instant later, her shot struck the wall behind Bendarian, and frost spread out from the hole that it made.

Bendarian's eyes were frantic; his mouth was open, and venom dripped from his fangs. "I was toying with Desa."

He stretched a hand out toward Kalia.

She floated off the ground, legs kicking. Her hands clawed at something invisible around her neck as she rose higher and higher into the air. Desa could see it in her face. The poor woman was choking. "But you," Bendarian hissed. "You, I will kill."

Desa felt her heart pounding.

There had to be something she could do! Something! If

only...If only she could see the force that gave Bendarian his power. Maybe then something would occur to her. She had never reached for the Ether in the middle of battle before – even if she found it, it would only leave her helpless – but the crystal atop the ancient pyramid had changed her. There were times when it almost felt as if the Ether came unbidden.

She let it in.

The world transformed before her eyes: pavement and lampposts and buildings all splitting apart into storms of dancing particles. Her hand was now a cluster of tiny bits of matter with the Ether exploding from the gaps between them as brilliant, glorious light. She expected to see something similar when she looked at Bendarian, but she could not have been more wrong.

There was no light emanating from his body. The Ether was in every stone, every grain of sand, every blade of grass. It was everywhere, in everything. Everywhere except Bendarian. When she probed his body with her mind, she found only a profound emptiness. A nothingness that seemed to drink in the light. Just the thought of it made her feel cold inside. If the emptiness could be filled...

She forced the Ether into the gap.

Bendarian cried out in shock, and Kalia fell to land on her knees in the middle of the road. Desa broke contact with the Ether and found the other woman wheezing as she tried to breathe.

Bendarian was on the opposite sidewalk, clutching his head and moaning in pain. His yellow eyes fluttered open. Yellow...They turned black when he was drawing on the Nether. Maybe that meant...

Standing up, Desa extended her arm to point her gun at

him. She fired once, then twice, then three times, thunder splitting the air as the recoil sent a jolt through her body.

Bendarian flinched as the first round went through him; his limbs twitched when the second shot pierced his flesh, and he collapsed against the building after the third bullet left a hole in his chest. A hole that wasn't closing on its own.

Baring her teeth, Desa growled as she paced across the road. Her face was on fire. "That's it, isn't it?" she said, shaking her head. "That's the secret."

Bendarian slumped against the wall, leaving a trail of black slime in his wake. He whimpered when his body hit the ground, and pressed a hand against his chest in a vain attempt to hold his guts inside his body.

Desa stepped right up to him, pointing her gun directly at his head. "That's why Adele won't face me herself," she barked. "Because she knows that I can take her power away."

Bendarian tried to say something, but the only sound that came out of his mouth was an unintelligible croak.

"Good to know."

She fired one more shot that went right through his skull and splattered his brains all over the wall behind him.

PART II

16

Azra sat with her back against the brick wall, her eyes closed as she listened to the commotion. Another gunshot somewhere nearby. She wasn't sure what was happening outside, but at least it was entertaining.

She heard something else – a minute stirring in the air – and when she opened her eyes, the golden-haired woman stood before her. Azra's first instinct was to kill her, but she waited.

"Well?" the Weaver said. "Are you coming?"

Azra raised an eyebrow.

Her two guards appeared on the other side of the cell door, each staring in shock at the woman who had somehow slipped past him. One raised his hand, and Azra knew that he would loose a stream of lightning.

"Field Binders," the Weaver said, rolling her eyes.

Bricks flew out of the wall across from the cell door, pummeling the two yellow-clad men from behind. They cried out in pain, but the onslaught did not stop until they were down on their knees.

The Weaver's face was flushed, her brow glistening with

sweat. It was almost as if...as if she were straining herself. "Will you hurry up?" she snarled. "I have no desire to remain in this city."

Azra stood up, stretching as she took a deep breath. Then she punched the other woman right in the nose. The Weaver shrieked, recoiling, falling back against the bars. "How dare you?"

Seizing the other woman's pretty, red dress, Azra pulled her close. She bared her teeth as she whispered in the Weaver's ear. "As far as I'm concerned, you're the reason I am stuck in this cell!"

A fist to the stomach made the Weaver fold up and groan. "So," Azra went on, "you can rot. I'm not going anywhere with you."

The decision was taken from her when her surroundings changed without warning and she found herself standing on a beach where dark waves licked the shore. Stars twinkled in the night sky, and she was very much aware of the muggy heat. The prison's stone walls had shielded her from it.

The Weaver was there as well, bent over with a hand on her stomach. Her face was twisted in pain. "Fool woman," she wheezed. "You'd rather stay in that cell? At least this way, you can kill Desa Kincaid."

Azra kicked her.

The Weaver toppled over onto her back, then rolled onto her side, writhing in the sand. "Insolence!" she hissed. "I saved-"

Azra squatted next to her, smiling impishly. She trailed a finger along the other woman's jawline. "I'm not killing anyone for you," she purred. "You want Kincaid dead, do it yourself."

Standing up, she turned her back on her would-be benefactor and sauntered away down the beach. Barefoot, clad only in a rough, gray smock, she felt more dignified than she would have in silk. There was something glorious in claiming your independence.

"Very well," The Weaver said behind her. "I suppose you aren't up to the task."

Azra paused, looking back over her shoulder, waves of brown hair falling over one eye. "Well, now that you mention it," she said. "I *do* enjoy a challenge."

DESA WATCHED as Bendarian's corpse finally went still. He was sitting there with his back against the wall, his legs stretched out on the sidewalk. His face was a ruin; she was about to look away, but something caught her eye.

Black smoke rose from Bendarian's mouth, clumping together in a floating blob that hovered above the sidewalk. It almost seemed to be aware of her, and the thought of it made her skin crawl. It lingered for only a moment before shooting off into the sky, heading westward. *Back to its master,* she realized. *That was the Nether.*

Behind her, Kalia moaned.

Desa turned around, gasping, and then ran to the sheriff. She knelt next to Kalia. "It's all right," she said. "I'm here."

Rolling onto her back, Kalia blinked at her. The woman closed a hand over her own throat. "Hurts..." she croaked. "You killed him?"

Desa felt a fat tear sliding down her cheek. "At long last," she said. Shouldn't she be relieved? Her duty was finally done – the monster that she had created would never harm another soul – but the weight in her chest was still there. The guilt that gnawed at her had not abated. Would it ever?

At least Martin could rest in peace. "We'll get you to a doctor."

"I'll be all right," Kalia muttered, though her voice rasped as badly as Bendarian's had. "An hour with the Ether, and I'll be happy as a plump cactus."

Desert slang? Desa didn't ask. "You know," she said. "The last time someone came to my rescue, she betrayed me."

Such grief in the sheriff's eyes. Desa could not figure out why. It wasn't Kalia who had naively ignored her instincts. It wasn't Kalia who had let that evil into the world. It wasn't Kalia who failed. "Anyway," Desa went on. "Thank you for-"

Kalia sat up with a grunt, laying a hand on Desa's cheek. She kissed Desa's lips softly, tenderly. And when she pulled away, she was smiling.

Blushing, Desa looked away. She brushed a lock of hair away. "Um, well..." she stammered. "Thank you for...What you did was very brave."

"I'm sorry if I was too forward."

"We..." Desa had no idea what to say. It had never occurred to her that Kalia might feel that way about her. And love was the last thing on her mind; she had no time for it. Not when the world needed her to be sharp. But she didn't want to hurt the other woman. Eventually, she managed to blurt out, "We should find the others."

And that was the end of that.

***

Radavan's body was lying in a pool of its own blood. The man's face was pallid, his eyes glazed over and staring at Tommy in silent condemnation. Amazing how quickly the change came. This was death. This was what it looked like. He tried to take it all in, to burn it into his brain.

Tommy stood over the corpse with his head down,

gasping for breath. "We should..." The words came out of him with some resistance. "We should bury him."

Miri came up beside him, clapping a hand on his shoulder. "Are you mad?" she whispered in his ear. "We need to leave. Now. Before anyone sees what you did here."

"I want to confess."

Miri slapped him.

Tommy winced, turning his face away from her. The sting in his cheek was something his mind could focus on. He clung to it like a lifeline. "I can't leave. I have to take responsibility."

Positioning herself in front of him, Miri crossed her arms and held his gaze until he wanted to wilt under her stare. "You do that," she began, "and they will put you to death. You can't just walk into a police station and tell them you killed one of the Elite Guard."

Tommy felt his shoulders slump. He couldn't find the strength to look up. "Maybe I deserve to die," he mumbled. "I just..."

"Well, whatever you deserve," Miri cut in, "*I* just committed treason for you. You confess, and there will be questions. They're going to wonder how I was involved in all this. They'll confiscate your weapons, and it won't take them long to deduce that there are four bullets on the ground, and you only fired three."

He couldn't listen to this! Treason, investigations, the police looking for someone to blame. He would go to the gallows if that would pay for his sin, but if his crime put Miri's neck in a noose? No, he couldn't bear that. And what about Dalen? The other man was right behind Tommy, breathing hard.

"What do we do?" Tommy asked.

Turning her back on him, Miri paced to the sidewalk,

bent low and picked up one of his fallen arrows. "Retrieve all of these," she barked. "*All* of them, mind. We make it look like one of the Eradians shot him."

"Through the legs?" Dalen mumbled.

Miri froze, looking back over her shoulder. Her eyes cut like daggers. "Everyone knew that Radavan liked to gloat," she said coldly. "Grab one of those corpses. Bring it over here."

Numb and exhausted, Tommy did as she said. He and Dalen chose one of the black-coated men – there were at least half a dozen bodies strewn about this block – and dragged him over to lie beside Radavan. He had selected one who appeared to have died from a stab wound. It seemed to him that any investigator who found Radavan's body would have a harder time believing that one of these soldiers had killed him if that soldier had also been burned to a crisp. It was possible, Tommy supposed; maybe the soldier got off a lucky shot and Radavan had scorched him with his dying breath. But that seemed less plausible.

They put Tommy's pistol in the dead man's hand and made sure to remove a fourth bullet from its cylinder. That would align with the evidence on the ground. It had to be an Aladri pistol. The weapon had to match the ammunition; no one would believe that you could fire Aladri bullets from an Eradian gun.

That, of course, begged the question of how this nameless soldier had gotten his hands on an Aladri firearm, but Tommy supposed that there were suitable explanations. Perhaps he had stolen it from a fallen policeman. There were plenty of those all over the place. By the time they were finished, the story had coalesced in Tommy's mind.

Like the stuffed-up popinjay that he was, Radavan had paused to gloat over the hapless Eradian he had just defeated. That gave the man a few seconds to grab the nearest weapon to hand and fire off a clever shot. Of course, that tale hinged on the soldier knowing the intricacies of how Force-Sinks worked, but it wasn't impossible. The man might have been able to figure out the basics by seeing Radavan in action. Or it could have been a lucky guess that just happened to pay off.

Their work finished, the three of them fled before anyone could stumble on the scene and deduce what they had done.

The deep-blue twilight of early morning filled the skies, but Desa had not been able to find a bed. She had spent most of the night trying to locate Daresina and make sure that the Prelate was unharmed. A thankless job if ever she had done one.

She now stood in an examination room in the hospital basement. Bendarian's body was stretched out on a steel table, his scales shining under the light of a naked bulb that hung from the ceiling.

Daresina stood in the corner with hands folded over her belly, her face frozen in an expression of horror. "It's all real," she whispered. "All of it."

The doctor, a man who wore a white apron over his button-up shirt, stroked his chin as he examined the corpse. "I'm not sure what his creature is," he said. "I don't think it's natural. How something like this could have evolved..."

Approaching the table with her fists clenched, Desa snarled at the corpse. Even dead, Bendarian could stoke her fury. "It was once a man," she said. "But he was...changed by magic...somehow."

The doctor grunted.

"They were all men once," Daresina mumbled.

"Of course." Desa whirled around to face the Prelate. "You know something about this. I should have expected as much."

Daresina leaned her shoulder against the tiled wall, a heavy sigh exploding from her. There were dark circles under her eyes. "It is part of the secret histories," she said. "Records known only to the Synod."

"And what do they say?"

The doctor paused his study of the corpse to eye the Prelate. Daresina was aware of his scrutiny, and she hesitated before speaking. Perhaps she was regretting her decision to say anything, but it was too late to back out now. Rumors flew on wings made of half-truths and innuendos. Once revealed, a secret could not be contained again. Better to divulge the entire truth than to let people fill in the missing bits with flights of fancy.

"These...snake-men..." Daresina said. "They are the servants of an entity that the *Vadir Scrolls* name *Hanak Tuvar*. The Unmaker. They were all men once, drawn in by the promise of power and made thralls to *Hanak Tuvar*. Slaves to its will."

"The thing that's possessing Adele."

Daresina looked solemn, but she nodded slowly. "In time," she said, "it will discard her as well. When she has outlived her usefulness."

Covering her face with one hand, Desa massaged her tired eyes. "Forgive me if I'm less than sympathetic," she muttered. "So, now that we finally agree that this thing exists, how do we kill it?"

"You cannot kill *Hanak Tuvar*."

"Yes, but I'd like to try anyway."

Daresina gestured to the door, and Desa had no choice

but to go with her. They walked side by side down a long hallway where dim bulbs bathed the walls in ugly, yellow light. They passed wooden door after wooden door, each with a polished, brass handle, but other than that, there was nothing to see. Desa ignored the scent of chemicals in the air. "All right," she said. "We're alone. Talk."

"The Spear of Vengeance," Daresina said. "You asked me about it. It was a weapon that Vengeance forged in the war against *Hanak Tuvar*."

"What does it do?"

"The scrolls say it has the power to kill a god."

Desa stopped, resting one hand against the wall, her head hanging with fatigue. "Find the spear," she said. "And stab Adele."

Daresina used one finger to slide her glasses back up her nose. She blinked and then cleared her throat. "Do not be so glib," she admonished. "Even if you can find the spear – which is no easy task – I doubt that it will be a simple matter of stabbing this Adele."

"Where is it?"

"In the Temple of Vengeance, of course."

Desa looked up at the ceiling, rolling her eyes. "Of course," she said, nodding. "How silly of me. I found a pyramid in the desert that Tommy claims is actually the Temple of Mercy."

"No!" the Prelate snapped. "You will find nothing of value there."

Desa arched an eyebrow.

Backing away across the width of the corridor, Daresina spread her hands. "That place is a tomb of empty promises," she insisted. "My advice is to never go back under any circumstances."

That was an oddly vehement reaction. Common sense

would suggest that the Temple of Mercy was the more hospitable of the two, but Daresina almost seemed to fear it. But then, the abandoned city had its own dangers. The answer hit Desa like a smack in the face. "You know about the ghost, don't you?"

"The ghost?"

A chill ran down Desa's spine, and she shook her head. "An entity that haunts the pyramid," she explained. "And the city surrounding it. I don't know where it comes from or what it wants."

Daresina's eyes widened. "No," she mumbled. "No, I know of no ghost."

Strange. If the ghost wasn't the source of Daresina's apprehension, then what was? She put the thought out of her head for now. It was a question that she could deal with another time. "All right," Desa said. "Where is the Temple of Vengeance?"

"Ithanar."

Hissing air through her teeth, Desa shut her eyes. "Ithanar." She paced back and forth across the hallway. "You mean the continent that everyone thinks is cursed because almost no one who goes there ever returns."

"And those that do," Daresina said, "will not speak of what they saw."

"I knew you wanted me dead, Prelate," Desa said. "I never knew how badly."

"Don't take that tone with me. I told you that recovering the spear would not be an easy task."

"All right," Desa said. "Then I guess I'm going to Ithanar."

. . .

Tommy sat in his hotel room with his back against the wall, hugging his knees and trying to keep his breathing steady. He had killed a man. He had *killed* a man. There were a few truisms that a mediocre person could use to assure himself that he wasn't totally worthless, and one such was, "At least, I haven't killed anyone."

So much for that.

He sniffled and then scrubbed at his eyes. "Keep your head, Tommy," he whispered. "Desa needs you at your best."

A knock at the door made him jump. Was it the police come to arrest him? The room was utterly dark except for a thin crack of light spilling in. "Thomas?" Dalen said, his voice muffled by the wood. "May I come in?"

"Yes," Tommy replied.

The door swung inward, admitting light that made Tommy's eyes smart. "I thought..." Dalen began with a tentative step forward. "I thought you could use a friend."

Crestfallen, Tommy stared dejectedly at nothing in particular. His only response to that was a small shrug. "I'm not sure I deserve a friend, right now."

"Nonsense," Dalen said.

He shut the door gently so that the latch only made the softest click and then shuffled over to stand by Tommy. It was too dark to see the man's face, but Tommy heard sympathy in his voice. "What you did was necessary. That man...That man was out of control."

"Didn't you say that the Eradians were foreign invaders?" Tommy countered. "That they were getting what they deserve?"

"And I was wrong about that."

Squeezing his eyes shut, Tommy banged the back of his head against the wall. "Yeah, well," he muttered. "That doesn't change the fact that I'm a murderer."

Dalen knelt in front of him, reaching out to lay a hand on Tommy's shoulder. "You are nothing of the sort," he said with steel in his voice. "Thomas, I was there. I saw it all. Radavan would have killed you."

"Only because I started a fight with him."

"After trying to reason with him."

For some reason, hearing that only made things worse. The crack in the dam burst. All the emotions that Tommy was trying to contain came pouring out of him. He sobbed. Almighty forgive him, how he sobbed. His resolve melted, and once the tears started, he made no effort to stop them.

Dalen said nothing. He just wrapped his arms around Tommy and held him close. And for a little while, that was enough.

DARESINA REMAINED in the hallway for several minutes after Desa was gone. Thinking about the...*beast*...that she had seen lying on the table made her stomach turn. All the legends were true. As Prelate, she was more than just the head of government; she was also the face of the Aladri religion. But she had never really believed any of it. Tall tales and foolish superstitions: that was all you would find in the scrolls that had given birth to the *Tharan Vadria*. The holy book itself was nothing but a compilation of old stories, and half of those had been declared as uncanonical. Her people were marching toward the future, not some ancient, forgotten past.

But now she had proof that the ancient stories were true. How many of the horrors detailed in the *Vadir Scrolls* – and in the *Tharan Vadria* after them – were based on real events? If the nightmares were true, so were the wonders. And that presented her with an opportunity.

Eventually, she heard the creak of a closet door opening and the scuff of a man's shoes as he stepped out of the darkness.

"You heard?" Daresina asked.

"I heard."

She closed her eyes, trembling as a chill went through her body. "Very good," she whispered. "Then you know what you have to do."

A lengthy silence made her question that assessment. Was her agent daft? Or was he simply reluctant to do what must be done? Finally, he said, "You can count on me."

Excellent.

The pieces were all coming together.

17

"So, there you have it," Desa said, concluding the summary of everything that Daresina had told her. "We go after the spear. We use it on Adele. I trust that you will all be coming with me."

Tommy and Marcus sat on her mother's sofa, each with eyes that looked ready to fall out of their heads. Their stunned silence lasted so long, Desa began to wonder if she had been speaking gibberish the whole time.

Kalia was in a wooden chair with one leg crossed over the other. Something about her made Desa think of a hunted rabbit. It was clear that the sheriff would rather be anywhere else.

That left Miri.

She stood by the wall, idly studying her nails, effecting a facade of casual indifference. "You realize," she said, breaking the silence, "that this is an insane plan. Please tell me you realize that."

Marcus was on his feet in an instant, scowling at Desa as if she had just proposed taking all of her money and setting it on fire. "Beyond insane," he added. "I would place our odds of survival at ten to one."

Tommy just stared numbly out the window, lost in his own thoughts. Something was wrong there, something deeper than troubles of the heart; Desa would have to ask her protegé when she got a moment.

She sat on the wooden table with her hands on her knees, matching Marcus's glare with one of her own. "Aladar has suffered one of the worst incursions in its long history," she countered. "You saw the kind of power that Adele can unleash."

"Still," Marcus said. "There has to be another way."

"I wish there were," Desa replied. "But all of the signs point us in this direction. Tommy's research suggests that the Spear of Vengeance is a powerful weapon, and the Prelate has confirmed as much."

Desa stood up, breathing deeply, and let her gaze linger on each one of them for a moment. "I will go alone if I must," she said. "I won't ask any of you to put your lives at risk."

"Not alone," Tommy mumbled. "I'm going."

"I as well," Kalia insisted.

Desa couldn't even begin to articulate how much of a relief it was to hear the sheriff say that. Perhaps she was a bit smitten – best not to think on that – but she did not want to say goodbye. Not after…Everything.

From the corner of her eye, she saw her mother standing in the doorway that led to the kitchen, wearing a frown that broke Desa's heart. She knew what her mother would do. Leean would put on a brave face and tell her that what she was doing was right and necessary. And then she would cry herself to sleep in private.

Desa wished that there was something she could say.

More than anything, she wanted to stay, to spare Leean the pain of losing her daughter a second time. But she had created a monster, and then, in trying to rectify that mistake, she had allowed something much worse into the world. Desa Kincaid had no right to embrace a simple life while others suffered for her sins.

And what more could she say? Marcus was right. The odds of any of them coming back were not good.

With a loud harrumph, Marcus stepped forward and then nodded to her. "If this is what we must do," he said. "Then, of course, I will come."

"What about Dalen?" Tommy asked.

"What about him?" Desa replied.

When Tommy looked at her, his blue eyes were as hard as diamonds. "Dalen has spent years studying your people's ancient history and religion," he said. "We know how this story goes. My mother must have read me a dozen different versions of it when I was a boy. The pyramid will have traps. Or riddles. Or something that requires some obscure bit of knowledge. Dalen might have the answers we need."

Miri was leaning against the wall and watching him with a dangerous glint in her eye. "The man's a walking disaster," she said. "Nearly got me killed twice. Sweet Mercy, I *would* be dead if he wasn't such a terrible shot. And you want to take him to the most dangerous place on this planet?"

"It's not about what I want," Tommy said.

"Isn't it?"

Desa raised a hand for silence and, wonder of wonders, the pair of them shut up. "Make the offer," she said. "Tell him we'd appreciate his help. If he wants to come, tell him he can meet us at the pier at two this afternoon. If not, well...That's his prerogative."

That put paid to any further discussion on the matter.

And a good thing too. Now was not the time for a lover's spat. "Gather your things," Desa said. "Say your goodbyes. We leave in six hours."

Ten minutes later, the five of them were gone, leaving Desa alone with her mother. Leean said nothing about her plan; instead, she started cleaning the kitchen as if this were an ordinary, summer morning.

Desa stood in the doorway, unable to lift her eyes from the floor. "I'm sorry," she said. "For leaving you again."

Her mother was bent over the stove and scrubbing it with a cloth. "I'm not angry with you, Little One," she replied. "Not at all."

"I think you are."

Her mother turned, and Desa immediately regretted her words. What she saw in Leean's eyes was not anger but grief. "Too much responsibility has been forced upon you, my dear."

Leaning her shoulder against the door-frame, Desa sniffed as a single tear rolled down her cheek. "You saw what Adele did," she whispered. "How she rallied innocent men to her cause. How she deceived them. She would enslave the entire world."

Leean stood before the stove with hands gripping the fabric of her dress, nodding along with every point. "I'm not saying the job doesn't need doing," she muttered. "I'm not saying you shouldn't be the one to do it. But it's not fair."

"You know I'm not coming back."

"Let's not be fatalistic."

"It's not fatalistic to acknowledge the truth," Desa said, turning away and marching back into the living room. She began straightening the cushions on the couch. It felt good to keep her hands busy. "Few people return from Ithanar."

"A low probability of success is not a certainty of failure,"

Leean shot back. "Any woman who expects to die will find a way to make it happen."

Well…There was no arguing with that. Desa feared that she had pushed her luck too far already, tempting fate more times than she could count. But there was no need to trouble her mother with such somber thoughts. Their last hours together should be happy.

As if sensing her thoughts, Leean stepped into the living room with a smile on her face. "Come," she said. "Let's speak no more of unhappy things. You have ten years of adventures to share with me, and we've barely scratched the surface."

"You want me to go to Ithanar?"

Dalen approached the wooden table with a stack of heavy books in his arms, setting them down with a loud *thud*. He straightened and then knuckled his back. "I'm afraid that Miri's assessment of my ineptitude may be correct. What use could I be to you on this adventure?"

Tommy was standing between two of the arch-shaped windows, leaning against the wall and chewing on a toothpick. "You know a lot about your people's ancient history," he said. "I reckon that'll come in handy."

Looking over his shoulder, Dalen answered him with a raised eyebrow. Almighty but the man was handsome. Those smoldering, brown eyes… "If I go with you," he began, "I'll likely prick myself on a poisonous thorn or fall into some quicksand or anger one of the natives with my bumbling. I'm nothing but a liability to you, Thomas. Try again."

Tommy shut his eyes tight, tossed his head back and drew in a sharp breath. "All right!" he snapped. "I asked you to come because I don't want to say goodbye. There! Is that what you wanted to hear?"

"Actually, yes."

Blushing, Tommy smiled and then looked down at his own feet. "Well," he said. "So long as my babbling entertains you."

"And Miri?"

"She's coming too, of course." Tommy didn't want to think about how having both of them along for this trip would make for some very awkward moments. And he didn't want to think about Miri at all. The guilt was still plaguing him, and Miri's decision to hide what he had done somehow made it worse. Strange that he would feel that way. She had done it to help him – Tommy knew that – but the resentment still left a bitter taste in his mouth. "The old gang back together for another adventure."

"Possibly the last adventure," Dalen muttered.

Tommy shuffled over to the table with his hands in his coat pockets. "Thanks for the reminder," he said. "Look, if you don't want to come..."

It shocked him when the other man started laughing. "Who says I don't want to come?" Dalen asked. "I just like to catalogue the full extent of my stupidity before I indulge it."

"But you were pretty adamant about the danger. What made you change your mind?"

Dalen put his hands on Tommy's shoulders, then leaned forward to kiss his lips. A soft kiss, but one that got Tommy's heart racing. It was all he could do not to slam Dalen against the wall and-

He put those thoughts out of his mind. The library was no place for such things. Besides, any contemplation of his own happiness brought with it the inevitable realization that he did not deserve it. And then Radavan's face floated in his mind. Dead eyes staring at him.

Breathless, Tommy pulled away and blinked several times. "Yeah..." he mumbled, nodding. "You know how I feel."

Dalen wore a sheepish grin. "I do," he agreed. "I have for some time now. Perhaps Miri should know too."

Tommy had to suppress a groan. That was *not* the right thing to say. The last thing he wanted to think about was this absurd situation the three of them had stumbled into. Of course, running from that reality only named him a selfish fool. Tommy Smith: the man who couldn't make up his mind.

He sat on the table, folding hands in his lap, and let out a sigh. "So, you'll come with us?" he asked. "Frankly, we could use another man to even the scales."

"Yes," Dalen said. "I'll come. Now, tell me about this Adele Delarac. If I'm going to help you destroy her, I had best learn all I can."

"Not much to tell, really," Tommy replied. "She was a snoot-nose aristocrat from Ofalla. Looked down on all of us except Desa, whom she claimed was her soulmate. Or some such nonsense. I never liked her. Not sure how she learned about the Nether, but taking it for herself was her plan from the start."

A strange look passed over Dalen's face, and then he smiled. Not the lascivious smile that promised more kisses. No, this was the smile he got whenever he solved a puzzle. A sliver of fear wormed its way into Tommy's belly. He was coming to recognize the other man's many expressions; that suggested more than simple infatuation. "Perhaps," Dalen said, "a visit to the Ofalla library is in order."

"What for?"

Dalen replied with a small shrug. "As you said, Adele had to learn about the Nether *somewhere.*" The pieces came together in Tommy's mind. "Now, you said that she was an aristocrat; so, it's not a stretch to believe she was well-traveled. But I am fairly certain she never came to Aladar, which means..."

"There are records of the Nether elsewhere in the world," Tommy finished.

"Exactly."

Peering up through the skylight, Tommy squinted as he considered the implications. "Just when I thought it was getting easier," he muttered, shaking his head. Then another thought occurred to him. "I suppose she could have learned about it from Bendarian. She knew who he was, though she never claimed to have met him."

"Yes, but how did *he* learn about it?"

"Good point."

"Well, how about that?" Dalen said. "It seems I *do* have something to contribute."

Desa found her friends waiting on the dock.

Marcus, in dungarees and a long, dark coat, stood with hands on his hips, looking out on a marina where boats floated on the water. There were wooden sailboats and metal trading ships and even small craft that could only fit two people. She also noticed a few people swimming to escape the summer heat.

Miri wore a sleeveless shirt and kept her dark hair tied in a braided tail. She tossed up one of her throwing knives and caught it with a practiced hand. Her bag of supplies was propped up against a wooden post.

Kalia stepped forward when she saw Desa coming,

nodding once in respect. Then she offered a cheeky grin. "I guess going home can wait," she said. "The mayor can't fault me when I'm off saving the world."

Tommy and Dalen had their heads together as they scanned the pages of a leather-bound book. The newest addition to their merry band was gesturing exuberantly and relaying his reflections on the nature of the goddesses.

In tan pants, a purple shirt and a wide-brimmed hat, Desa stepped onto the dock. She frowned at the lot of them, but that frown soon became outright laughter. "You're all a bunch of lunatics."

They all paused and gave her their attention.

"But," Desa continued, "I wouldn't want to be going on this mission with anybody else. Thank you."

No sooner did she finish her terse speech than Daresina came striding onto the dock, trailed by all eight members of the Synod. They were an august procession: men in well-tailored suits, women in gowns that were suitable for any ball. Desa suspected that this lavishness was some attempt to honour her plucky, little band.

Daresina confirmed that suspicion by drawing herself up and forcing a smile. Or at least making a decent attempt at it. The Prelate's smiles were colder than a blizzard in High Falls. "We come to see you off," she intoned. "And to offer what little we can in gratitude for the service you have done our people."

She gestured.

A small truck came puttering along the road that bordered the marina, settling to a stop behind the assembled dignitaries. In its bed were several burlap sacks. Desa was about to inquire as to their contents, but labourers began unloading them before she could get one word out.

"Food and ammunition," Daresina explained.

"Thank you."

"For centuries, knowledge of the Spear of Vengeance was a secret guarded closely by the Synod and the Clerics." The Prelate stiffened as if the revelation of that secret sickened her. Or perhaps Desa was misreading her intent. "The prophecies say that it is the birthright of our people and that one day, we will venture forth to bring it home. That day has come."

Prophecies?

Desa had never heard of any such prophecies. What was Daresina playing at? She had a sick feeling in her stomach that said she wasn't being told everything she needed to know. But what could she do except suffer the pomp and circumstance with as much dignity as she could muster and then carry on with the mission?

"Arvin Von Normon will take you to the mainland."

The man who stepped forward was tall with dark-brown skin and a neatly-trimmed beard. "Do you know where you wish to go?"

"If memory serves," Desa answered, "the town of Pallin is about thirty miles north of here. It's a decent-sized fishing village and trading port. We can catch a train there that will take us along the southern coast to Hedrovan."

The Eradian Railway Company had a network of tracks that covered most of the southern half of the continent. They were still expanding northward to major cities like High Falls and Ofalla. But while the former city was more than eager for a new source of commerce, the Ofallans had built their town to monopolize river trade. Trains could threaten that.

But whatever problems they might have caused for backward-thinking northerners, Desa blessed the geniuses who had given birth to the railroad. Trains would make the first leg of their journey much easier.

"Very well," Arvin said. "If we leave now, you'll be in Pallin before dinner time."

Despite his misgivings about being noticed by mainlanders, Arvin dropped them off at a spot on the coast just two miles south of Pallin. That certainly made carrying all those sacks of fruits, vegetables, salted meats, bread and cheese a little easier. And ammunition. There was a sack full of bullets that Kalia hauled without complaint. The Synod had been kind enough to provide them with Heat-Sinks to keep the food fresh as long as possible, but Desa would have to make more later.

The train ride to Hedrovan would take the better part of three days, and meals would be provided. After that, they would probably spend at least one night in the city before setting off on their long journey south. Time enough to procure some horses. But every delay made the Prelate's gift less and less valuable. Some of the food they carried would have spoiled by the time they needed it. Still, better to have and not want than to want and not have.

Pallin was bigger than Desa remembered. Ten long years had passed since she had last visited the sea-side town. The trail they followed through a dense woodland soon became a dirt road that cut through the centre of town. Gray-brick houses with tiled roofs stood on either side of the street, each with an unlit lantern above its front porch.

A horse-drawn cart came rolling toward them. The man in the driver's seat – a tall fellow in a straw hat – took a long look as he passed. Desa held her breath but nothing came of it. Some of the men who had attacked Aladar not one day earlier had probably come from this village. She and her friends all wore Eradian fashions – even Dalen had managed to find a pair of old, brown pants that he kept up with suspenders – but there was always the possibility that any one of them would be recognized.

They took rooms at a small beach-side inn called *The Water's Edge* and stowed their belongings away. With nothing to do but while away the evening, Desa took a little time to herself and watched the wooden sailing ships drifting through the Strait of Avalas. They were antiquated but still beautiful to her.

The island that she called home beckoned to her. Aladar was located on its southern tip; this far north, there was nothing to see but forested hills. That didn't lessen the urge to dive into the water and swim all twelve miles. The strait was a little wider here.

When boat-watching ceased to amuse, she took a walk to clear her head. There were some beautiful hiking trails just beyond the edge of town. That was where she found Tommy and Dalen.

The two young men were standing in a small glade with rays of sunlight streaking down through the treetops. They were both engrossed in one of Dalen's books, chatting quietly with one another. Desa's first instinct was to give them some privacy, but she decided it was time to straighten out something that had been on her mind all day.

Tommy looked up when he heard her footsteps and offered a wan smile. "Desa," he said. "Lovely evening, isn't it?"

"Indeed it is," she said. "Dalen, might I have a word with my apprentice?"

The young librarian looked surprised, but he did not protest. "Of course." He patted Tommy on the shoulder, then strode past Desa, twigs snapping beneath his feet as he went.

Tommy looked like a cornered rabbit. She half thought he might bolt at any second. "What is it?" he asked.

Desa leaned against a tree trunk, sighing softly as she gazed up toward the heavens. "Perhaps you should tell me," she said. "Something is upsetting you. Out with it."

"I don't know what you mean."

"Tommy..."

He backed away from her with his hands up in a placating gesture. "All right!" he snapped. "Yes. I admit it. I'm still troubled by all this tomfoolery between myself and Miri and-"

"No," Desa cut in. "That's not it. Try again."

The poor boy went pale and then glanced at the trail as if he thought he might be able to outrun her. She could see the calculation in his eyes; there was something that he did not want to share.

The distant blare of a train whistle made Tommy jump. He took control of himself and then took shelter under a tree on the other side of the glade. "I killed Radavan."

Desa gasped.

Her protégé stiffened as tears spilled over his cheeks. "It wasn't something I wanted to do," he said. "But he would have killed me."

Bit by bit, the story came out of Tommy. Watching Radavan slaughter the Eradians, challenging him, losing and using a desperate trick to survive. By the end of the tale, Tommy was weeping.

"I'm so sorry this happened to you," Desa said.

Tommy scrubbed a tear off his cheek with the back of his hand. It was clear that he was shocked by her response.

"You're sorry this happened to *me?*" he rasped. "Desa, I killed a man."

Tilting her head back, Desa closed her eyes and let the warm sunlight fall upon her face. She breathed deeply through her nose. "I don't know if what you did was the right thing," she replied. "But it *was* the necessary thing."

"I didn't have to challenge him."

"Perhaps not," Desa said. "But I would have done the same in your place. We have power, Tommy, and with it comes an obligation not to misuse it. I fought eight men in the Prelate's office. I let seven of them flee. Your instincts were correct. Radavan was a small man with an inflated sense of his own superiority. What he was doing was nothing short of an atrocity."

"Does that make it right to kill him?"

"Did you try to reason with him first?" she asked. "Did you give him a chance to back down?"

Tommy shuddered and fell back against the tree. "Of course, I did," he said. "But he refused."

"And would he have killed you?"

"There is no doubt in my mind."

Desa sighed, marching across the glade and placing herself right in front of him. "Then you did all that you could," she said. "Now, you must learn to live with what you have done."

"So, I just forgive myself?"

"Of course not. Doing the necessary thing should never be easy, Tommy. The guilt prevents it from being so. It's horrible, at first, I know. But in time, you learn to manage it."

Tommy licked his lips, then glanced up the dirt path as if he expected someone to intrude on their privacy at any moment. "Miri and I made it look like one of the Eradians killed Radavan," he said. "I wanted to confess, but she forbade me from doing so."

"I can't say I'm unhappy about that."

"Well, I am!" Tommy insisted. "I feel like I should have accepted responsibility for my crime."

"My people would have executed you, Tommy."

Making a fist, he slammed it against the tree trunk and then hissed from the sting it brought him. There were shallow cuts on the side of his hand. "Maybe, so," he said. "But isn't that what I deserve?"

Desa took a step back and then shook her head slowly. "I don't believe so," she answered. "The right thing isn't always the necessary thing. You acted to defend people who could not defend themselves."

"People who attacked your city."

"And *why* did they do that?" Desa countered. "Because they are evil? Savage? Or because Adele tricked them into fighting a battle they couldn't win? I've traveled this world for many long years, Tommy. I've learned that the borders of nations are just lines on a map. People are people wherever you go. Most are good. Some are not."

He nodded.

"Come," Desa said. "It's getting late. We have a train to catch tomorrow."

Marcus waited for the sound of their footsteps to recede and then stepped out into the open when he knew they were gone. It had been sheer happenstance that put him on this trail at the right moment to hear Tommy's confession. At first, he had been filled with rage. The boy had sided with Eradians against one of the Elite Guard? He deserved to die! But Desa's words gave him pause.

She had called Radavan's actions an atrocity. If that was true, what did it say about Marcus? He had killed Eradians without remourse. He had taken pleasure in their deaths. The question did not sit well with him.

No, it did not sit well at all.

18

Trees rushed past in the train's window, sliding away before Tommy could get a good look at them. The first leg of their journey took them south as they followed the curve of the coastline. Soon, they would be heading west.

He should have been excited – he had always wanted to ride a train – but the guilt kept gnawing at him. There were fleeting moments where it left his thoughts, but it always returned. A part of him wished that Miri could be here; she always took such pleasure in seeing him experience something new. But he wasn't up for company. He had chosen a car populated with strangers so that he could be alone.

Tommy sat on one of the wooden benches with hands clasped in his lap. He should have been smiling, but all he could do was stare out the window.

Across the aisle from him, a man was slouching in his seat with his hat over his face, snoring softly. A woman in a lavender dress kept fanning herself despite the fact that an open window provided more than enough of a breeze to keep things cool.

The whoosh of the car door opening made him sit up.

He twisted to look over his shoulder and found Miri standing at the end of the aisle. She smiled, then motioned for him to follow. Without waiting to see if he would, she went back through the door.

Tommy sighed.

He wasn't interested in conversation, but Desa was right. All he could do was learn to live with what he had done, and he couldn't put off Miri forever. Sitting around and moping would only make it that much harder to do his duty when the time came.

There were no benches in the next car, only small, round tables where men in coats played cards. A few looked up when Tommy came in, but they quickly went back to their games. It was going to be a long three days.

Miri was standing by the window with her arms folded, gazing out at the scenery that went rushing by. "I thought we should talk," she said as he drew near. "I wanted...I want to apologize."

"For what?"

She cast a few furtive glances at the men who might overhear and then whispered. "You know what."

Ah.

She was apologizing for making it look as if Radavan had died by the hand of some random soldier. For stopping Tommy from confessing. Truth was he wasn't entirely sure how he felt about that. Desa's words from the night before stayed with him. He wasn't proud of what he had done, but he didn't deserve to die for it.

Tommy braced one hand against the window, sighing as he watched the trees go by. "I forgive you," he murmured. "It was probably for the best."

"So, now you think it was right?"

"I don't know if it was right," he replied. "But it *was* necessary."

Miri nodded.

She claimed a chair at one of the empty tables, crossed one leg over the other and gave him that look that dared him to kiss her. "There's more," she said. "I thought we should talk about us."

Tommy sat down across from her, folding his hands on the table and leaning forward to stare at her. "Us?" he asked, his eyebrows rising. "You mean you still want to be with me?"

"Feelings don't go away just because we had a fight."

He closed his eyes, breathing slowly to calm himself. "No, they don't," he whispered. "But mine are complicated."

Miri sat back, pinching her chin with thumb and forefinger, studying him like a puzzle she intended to solve. "Still can't choose, huh?" she said. "Well, I suppose I should feel flattered that I'm still in the race."

"This isn't a race."

"No," Miri agreed. "In a race, somebody wins."

Tommy stood up, heaving out a breath, and then backed away from the table. "I wish you two would just get to know each other," he said. "Then maybe you wouldn't be at each other's throats."

He left her to chew on that, making his way toward the sleeping cars near the back of the train. He had left a book in his bunk, and right then, keeping his mind busy seemed like a good idea.

A well-dressed couple in the dining car looked up as he passed, and the gray-haired woman sniffed. Everywhere he went, it was the same thing; the uncultured, country oaf drew the eyes – and the disdain – of his social betters. He was growing weary of it. Quite weary indeed.

He passed Desa and Kalia as they shared a light breakfast. They offered him a seat, but he politely declined. The two of them deserved a little privacy, and it was about time that his mentor found someone worthy of her affections. He was still furious over what Adele had done to Desa. To all of them.

Marcus was puttering about in an empty car, pacing back and forth through the aisle between the wooden benches and mumbling to himself. At first, Tommy was afraid to draw the other man's attention; so, he waited patiently. When it became clear that Marcus wasn't going to stop ruminating anytime soon, he cleared his throat.

Marcus jumped.

The man spun around, one hand settling onto his holstered pistol, and then sneered at Tommy. "What are you doing, boy?" he demanded. "Have you no better use for your time than sneaking up on me?"

"Sorry!" Tommy said. "I thought I should get your attention before I came charging through."

"How long *have* you been standing there?"

Tommy eased himself onto one of the benches, choosing his words with care. "Long enough to know that you're quite put out," he answered. "Perhaps you might like to talk about it. What's troubling you?"

Baring his teeth with a throaty growl, Marcus shook his head. "That is none of your concern, boy!" he snapped. "I don't know what gods I must have offended to be cursed with you and your endless questions!"

"Sorry!"

"Sorry," Marcus spat. "That's all you're good for, isn't it?

Whimpering and crying and moaning about how sorry you are! The worst mistake Desa ever made was taking you out of your little village. She should have left you to die there."

It took some effort, but Tommy forced himself to rise and stand toe-to-toe with the other man. He kept his face smooth, his gaze never wavering. "You know, it occurs to me that we have three Field Binders on this mission already."

Marcus stiffened.

"Why don't you get off at the next station?" Tommy went on. "Catch a train back to Pallin and go home?"

He shouldered his way passed Marcus, who grunted at the indignity of being shoved aside. Terribly rude, but he was livid, and his patience had been stretched to its limit. He was two steps from the door at the back of the car when Marcus hissed behind him.

"You arrogant, little speck of bile," the other man snarled. "You really have gotten above yourself, haven't you?"

Tommy left without further comment.

The instant that he was alone, the fury he had been suppressing came rushing to the surface, and he had to fight the urge to put his fist through the window. The nerve of that man! Marcus had always been gruff, but this was beyond the pale!

He found Dalen in the sleeping car. The other man was pawing through one of his books with a gusto that Tommy would have found endearing if he wasn't in such a vile mood. Bloody Marcus!

"Hello!" Dalen said. "You look-"

"If you're thinking of paying me a compliment," Tommy cut in. "I would advise against it."

Dalen looked as if someone had slapped him, but he

quickly took control of himself and nodded. "Very well," he said. "Is there anything I *can* do for you?"

"No." A thought occurred to him, and he corrected himself. "Yes. Spend some time with Miri. Maybe get to know her a little."

Dalen blinked.

"I would really appreciate it," Tommy said, "if you two got along."

THE CONSTANT RUMBLING of the train was almost soothing. One thing was certain: Desa would sleep well tonight. How long had it been since she had last traveled by rail? She and Martin had taken a train once in pursuit of a man who had killed five girls in three different villages.

Desa was bent over a table in the dining car and peering into her cup of tea, watching as the dark liquid danced. She lifted it with both hands and inhaled the tangy aroma. Best to enjoy the simple pleasures now, while she still could.

Kalia was sitting across from her with hands folded over her stomach. The sheriff wore the kind of satisfied smile that only a good meal could elicit. "You know," she began. "You're going to have to do something about those three."

"What three?"

"Tommy and Miri and Dalen."

Watching the other woman over the rim of her cup, Desa calculated the many ways this conversation might go wrong. She was the last person in the world who ought to be giving anyone else advice about matters of the heart. "That's their business," she said. "I say we leave them to it."

"Those three are a pile of kindling just waiting for a spark," Kalia muttered. "Best douse them in some water now."

Desa didn't argue.

"You really don't want to, do you?"

Desa slurped as she sipped her tea. It was quite delicious. Fruity with a delicate aftertaste. "What would you have me say? Any advice I might give would only incense them."

Kalia pursed her lips as she considered the question. "I would have you speak with Tommy," she said at last. "The boy is your apprentice; he'll listen to you. Tell him that he had better make up his mind soon. The longer he strings them along, the worse it will be when one of them finally decides they've had enough."

It was good advice, but Desa was hardly the one to give it. Besides, young people had a tendency to get prickly when you tried to push them away from one partner or toward another. Even the simple suggestion that it might be time for Tommy to knuckle down and choose one could produce a heated argument that she wanted no part of. "Tommy listens to me when I give him advice about Field Binding," she replied. "I doubt he wants my opinion on this."

She deliberately avoided mentioning that Tommy had asked for her opinion a few weeks ago. The lad would probably listen if she decided to speak up, but it was even odds if he would prosper from taking her advice.

"I suppose we ought to sort out our own feelings," Kalia said, "before presuming to lecture anyone else on such things."

"I'm sorry?"

The other woman blushed and then glanced out the window in a desperate attempt to avoid looking at Desa. "You know what I'm talking about," she mumbled. "The kiss we shared…"

"It was nice."

"Is that all it was?"

Setting her cup down on the table, Desa sat up straight and gave the other woman a flat stare. "It's not going to work," she said, shaking her head. "You, me...I can't give you the kind of life that you deserve."

It startled her when Kalia smiled and looked down at her empty plate. "You know, dear," she replied. "For someone with such a dim view of men, you do a remarkable job of sounding just like one."

"That's hardly-"

Motion in the corner of her eye.

When she looked, she saw a dark, hooded figure standing in the middle of the dining car. A phantom wrapped in a burial shroud as black as a moonless night. The hood made it impossible to see the creature's face, but Desa knew that it was watching her. Only her. It seemed as oblivious to everybody else as they were to it.

Two tables away, an older man and his wife were chatting happily over plates of bacon and fried eggs. Across from them, a dark-skinned fellow sipped his tea and never so much as glanced at the ghost even though it stood right in front of him.

"What is it?" Kalia asked. She cringed as the answer came to her. "You're seeing it right now, aren't you? It's right here, in this very train car."

Desa nodded.

The ghost took one step forward.

And then it vanished. It didn't fade away or dissolve; it just disappeared. One moment, it was there, and the next, it wasn't.

Kalia leaned over the table and peered into Desa's face. "How many times?" she demanded. "How many times have you seen it?"

"Five...Maybe six."

"No, no, no," Kalia whispered. "Oh, this is not good."

"What?"

"People who encounter that thing keep seeing it even if they never return to the abandoned city," Kalia said. "But in every case I've heard of, months or even years can pass between successive visits. You've seen it more times in a month than most people do in a lifetime."

Now, it was Desa who shivered.

"Whatever this thing is, Desa, it's fixated on you."

Miri stood on the back platform of the caboose, gripping the metal railing as she watched the landscape fly by. Trees receded into the distance on either side of the track. The sky was clear with only a few clouds, but a nice breeze kept the heat at bay.

How had she gotten herself into this mess? She had never been the sort of woman to toss her heart into a man's lap. And Lommy...Tommy...was supposed to have been an easy mark. She remembered seeing him that first time in Glad Meadows, sitting there like a hunted deer, afraid to budge lest he bring the predators down on him. Her task had been so simple.

Marcus had wanted information on what Desa had been up to. And there was this boy that she could fleece with a few quick words. Talk fast and talk often: that was one strategy she had learned. Make the boy's head spin, and he would tell you everything you needed to know. She had never planned on falling for him.

The door opened behind her.

"Here you are!"

Pressing her lips together, Miri squinted into the

distance. "Yes, here I am," she said, nodding. "What do you want, Dalen?"

When she turned around, the young man stood in the doorway with a frantic look about him, his eyes darting back and forth as if searching for an escape. He could just go back inside and leave her alone. "I thought we should talk."

Miri leaned against the railing, gripping the metal bar and glaring at him. "You want to talk," she said. "What exactly do we have to talk about?"

"Thomas wants us to get to know each other."

"Oh, he does, does he?"

Dalen stepped up beside her with hands folded behind his back, frowning as he took in the scenery. "I admit that you have no reason to like me," he began. "But I have always admired the Ka'adri."

"Is that so?"

"I thought of becoming one myself."

Covering a smile with one hand, Miri chuckled. "You'll have to forgive me," she said when she caught him looking. "The thought of you trying to throw knives or shoot a gun is just…"

His cheeks went red, and she regretted her words. "Yes, well," he growled. "I *did* realize that I was better suited to other professions."

"I'm sorry," Miri mumbled. "That was cruel."

"Yes, it was."

With a heavy sigh, Miri turned her face up to the heavens and blinked. "Not one to ever give an inch, are you?" she asked, shaking her head. "Well, I suppose I do owe you some thanks. We all do. Without your translations, we never would have learned about the spear."

"And without you," Dalen said, "Thomas wouldn't even

be alive. He told me about what you did in Thrasa. Those gray men..."

Miri shivered.

They stood in silence for a little while, watching the trees slide past. There wasn't all that much to see as they rounded the southeastern tip of the Eradian continent. Just thick forests on either side of them. The awkwardness was hard to ignore. Finally, Miri forced herself to say *something*. "Why do you call him Thomas?"

"Why do *you* call him Lommy?"

"Because Tommy is such a dumb name," they both said in unison. And then, they were laughing. For the first time, she found herself enjoying Dalen's company. Maybe he wasn't so bad after all.

IT WAS WELL past midnight on the second night of their journey, but Desa couldn't sleep. She was lying in her bunk with hands folded over her chest, staring vacantly at the ceiling. Finding sleep was becoming more and more difficult for her. Every time she started to drift off, the thought that she might wake up to find the ghost standing over her set her pulse racing. She could handle Field Binders and assassins, but ghosts?

She kept the shade on her window up to stave off total darkness, but there was very little moonlight. Even if there had been, there would be nothing to see outside but flat grasslands. They were now headed westward across the Plains of Haleem, following the curve of the coastline. A light drizzle had started an hour ago, but it did nothing to ease Desa's mind.

"You can't sleep, can you?" Kalia murmured.

Desa rolled onto her side, blinking. "I'm sorry," she whispered. "Was I keeping you awake?"

There was a soft *thump* as Kalia dropped down from the top bunk to land in a crouch. The other woman straightened. Somehow, there was just enough light for Desa to make out the shape of her silhouette: the long, flowing hair spilling over her back, the soft curves of her body hidden under cotton shorts and a thin undershirt. "Of course not," she said. "Not directly, anyway."

"What do you mean?"

Kalia twisted around to face her, and somehow Desa knew that she was smiling. "Well," she said, "I *do* worry about you."

Rolling onto her back, Desa suddenly felt the need to pull the blankets up to her shoulders. "The…The ghost," she stammered. "Has it ever hurt anyone?"

"Not to my knowledge."

Shutting her eyes tight, Desa sucked in a hissing breath. "Well," she whispered. "At least we have that."

Kalia knelt next to the bunk and rested her hand and Desa's arm. "You'll be all right," she said softly. "I believe that."

"How many times have I faced death," Desa grumbled. "And now, *this* unnerves me."

For a moment, Kalia was silent, but Desa was very much aware of the other woman's fingers caressing her arm. "It's not just about death," Kalia said. "Death by a bullet or a knife or even an infection is horrible, but it's something you can understand. The ghost is terrifying precisely because you *don't* understand what it is. What does its existence say about the larger universe? Does it mean that some part of us endures after we're dead? And if so, what is that existence like?"

"Ah," Desa teased. "I'll sleep like a baby now."

"Well, I had two ideas for how I might take your mind off your troubles. This seemed the safest."

"What was the other?"

Kalia crawled into the bed, laying a hand on Desa's cheek. Their lips met, and Desa gave in despite the little voice in her head that urged her to be cautious. No...She didn't just give in; she melted into Kalia's embrace.

Moving almost of their own accord, her fingers grabbed the hem of Kalia's undershirt and practically ripped the garment off of her. Then she was trailing soft kisses over the other woman's neck.

Coherent thought flew out of her mind, and instinct took over. Nothing mattered except this glorious creature in her arms. And she was blessedly unafraid.

Finally, when the haze of delight passed, Desa found herself curled up with her head on Kalia's chest while Kalia ran fingers through her hair. "You were wonderful," the sheriff murmured.

Desa smiled and nuzzled her lover. "So were you."

Sleep came easily then. Blissful, peaceful sleep.

LYING in her bunk with her hands folded behind her head, Azra smiled and listened to the constant chugging of the train's engine. The crew were starting to think of her as a recluse because she so seldom left her cabin, but she couldn't risk running into Desa or one of her friends.

It had been a stroke of good luck that put her in Pallin on the very day that their group passed through. She had been dreaming up a way to sneak back into Aladar so that she could finish the job – not out of any loyalty to the Weaver; that bitch could rot – but trying to kill someone and failing vexed her. As a matter of pride, Azra *had* to kill Desa Kincaid.

Two days in this bloody coffin, sneaking out only to steal scraps from the dining car or to relieve herself. Still, patience had rewarded her with some juicy tidbits of knowledge.

It seemed that the golden-haired boy was having trouble choosing between a man and a woman who had both thrown their hearts at his feet. She had learned that much by listening at Tommy's door before he and his bunkmate went to sleep. A risky move, but worth it.

The rest came from what little the waiters in the dining car managed to overhear. She had paid two of them a considerable sum of money to eavesdrop and report back to her. And to keep quiet. Ensuring the last had required a bit of subtle intimidation on her part. She was not well acquainted with subtlety, but in this case, a soft touch was necessary. Directly threatening them could see her thrown off the train, but without a little fear, they might decide to report her presence to Desa in exchange for a better offer.

She had lured one of those waiters to her cabin for a little fun, making sure to leave her weapons on display the whole time. The other one had come in to find her sharpening a knife that she playfully flourished before slamming it back into its sheath. Good boys, both of them. They shared with her whatever scraps they could.

So, Desa had encountered the creature in the abandoned city. Fascinating. Azra had thought to go there herself if only to see the thing with her own eyes, but she had never gotten around to it. It wasn't fear that held her back; death by vengeful spirit was one of the more interesting ways to go, but days spent roaming around the desert were days not spent applying her trade.

And it was time she got back to doing that.

They would be arriving in Hedrovan tomorrow afternoon; she would have to make her move before then. She would have done so on the very first day, but curiosity had stayed her hand. There was never any harm in taking some time to know your enemy. But the game was over now.

Time to play her last card.

19

Desa woke up in the warmth of Kalia's embrace. The other woman was wrapped up in her arms, sound asleep with her head on Desa's shoulder. The bunk they shared was barely big enough for the both of them, but it may as well have been the nicest bed in the finest hotel. For a little while, she was content to just lie there, to listen to the rain pattering on the window. They would not be arriving for another few hours; there was no rush to get out of bed.

Without even realizing it, she dozed off again, and when she woke up, Kalia was raining kisses on her face. She smiled upon realizing that Desa was awake. "Well, good morning," she murmured.

Desa reached up to lay a hand on the other woman's cheek. She sat up and brushed Kalia's lips with hers. "Good morning."

Any thought of conversation was squelched by a ferocious kiss that had her grabbing a handful of Kalia's hair. They rolled over so that Kalia was on her back, and then it was Desa who trailed kisses over her body. Over every delicious inch of her.

Desa lost track of time as they made love again, but she was in no hurry. It was slow and tender at first, gradually building to a furious flame. And when it was over, they were both breathless.

Touching their noses together, they shared a smile. Desa brushed a lock of hair off Kalia's cheek and tucked it behind her ear. "You are so beautiful," she whispered.

"So are you."

Kalia rolled onto her back, crossing her arms as she stared up at the ceiling. "So, I guess we should talk about…"

"You want this to be more than one night of passion."

Kalia nodded.

Holding the blankets to her chest, Desa sat up and bumped her head on the bunk above her. "Damn it!" she growled, rubbing her forehead with the heel of her hand. The anger melted away in an instant.

Kalia was looking up at her with those dark, tilted eyes, waiting for an answer but not asking for one. It nearly broke Desa's heart to see it. "So do I," she murmured, leaning in to kiss her lover's lips. "I want that very much."

"Good."

They cuddled for a while, kissing and talking and laughing. Shooing Tommy away when he knocked on their door and asked if they were coming to breakfast. Eventually, Desa realized that it was mid-morning. "We should probably get up."

"If you insist."

A blush singed Desa's cheeks, and she grinned as she shook her head. "I'd much rather stay here," she lamented. "But we *do* have a quest to finish. Duty and destiny and all that."

"They might still have some breakfast in the dining car."

"Would you mind if I met you there in say...half an hour? I'd like to take a walk, clear my head."

"Of course."

Getting dressed almost seemed like a tragedy, but she forced herself to put on a pair of gray pants, a black shirt and her duster. The air was chilly with a deluge coming down outside.

She wandered aimlessly for a little while, making her way forward to the front of the train. She had no destination in mind; her legs just wanted to move. So many thoughts kept tumbling through her head. Kalia. What a life with her might be like. Would they travel the world as Desa had for so many years? Or settle down in Dry Gulch, keeping the peace in that little, frontier town? Desa couldn't see herself as a deputy.

Perhaps they could return to Aladar. Kalia might like it there. If nothing else, the climate was more hospitable than her desert home. All of this was moot, of course.

It was very unlikely that they would survive this mission.

That put a lump of sadness in Desa's belly. She realized that her resistance to opening her heart again – to letting someone else in – was due in no small part to the fact that she expected to die. What was the point of starting a relationship if you had no future to look forward to?

Well, pointless or not, she had made a commitment to Kalia, and she would honour it. Desa Nin Leean was many things, but a heartbreaker was not one of them.

She eventually found an empty car and chose to stay there for a little while. It was just like all the other passenger cars: a narrow aisle divided two sets of wooden benches, each pointing toward the front of the train. She chose the front-most bench on the left-hand side and sat down to watch the scenery go by.

The only thing to see in the window was a blur of green with droplets of water streaking over the glass. They were traveling through another patch of woodland. Which, if she knew her geography, meant they would be arriving at Hedrovan in a little under two hours.

Desa had never been to the great city on Eradia's southern border, but she knew it well by reputation. It was one of the few places on the continent where slavery was still legal. There was a very good chance that Sebastian would have ended up there if Desa hadn't rescued him. *Instead, he's dead. Not much of a trade.*

She put the guilt out of her mind. Sebastian's fate was as much of his own making as it was of hers. And Tommy was probably better for his absence. Hopefully, there would be opportunities to continue his training on their long journey.

She was truly impressed with how far he had come. The poor lad was probably still beside himself over Radavan's death. Well, what needed doing needed doing. And while the taking of any life was tragic, Desa would not shed a tear over this one. She-

"So, here you are."

That voice.

Desa knew that voice.

Twisting around in her seat, she found Azra Vanya standing just inside the car's back door. The woman wore black – ripped pants and a sleeveless shirt – and carried a pistol in her hand. "I thought we should be alone for this."

Azra lifted her weapon, cocking the hammer, and giggled as she took aim. There was murder in her eyes.

Desa threw herself to the floor.

A hole appeared in the bench as Azra's first shot punched through it, sending wood chips flying. The bullet went right on through the wall. Possibly into the next car where it might kill some innocent passenger.

With a thought, Desa ordered her necklace to drink in light energy, bathing her end of the train car in darkness. She made a quick sideways roll across the aisle and took cover behind another bench on the other side. More gunshots rang out.

Desa's first instinct was to reach for her pistol, but a gunfight in these close quarters was dangerous. Bullets went through walls. Someone else might get hurt. She had to disarm the other woman.

She popped up, killing her Light-Sink.

Azra tried to adjust her aim.

Thrusting her fist out, Desa released a hair-thin tendril of electricity from her ring, a lightning bolt that streaked over the benches and struck Azra's gun. The other woman shrieked as a jolt went through her body, and her weapon fell to the floor.

Azra took a desperate step backward, arms flailing to keep her balance. She quickly righted herself, and her dark eyes promised pain. "Oh, clever, clever girl."

With her belt buckle draining gravitational energy, Desa hopped up and skipped over the benches, taking them two at a time until she reached the back row. She leaped and kicked Azra in the chest.

Her opponent was slammed against the door, wheezing as the air fled her lungs. This time would be the last time. She wouldn't let Azra escape just to wreak havoc again.

Desa landed with her fists up in a fighting stance.

She charged in and threw a punch, but Azra's hand came up to casually deflect the blow. A beringed fist hit her right between the eyes, and her head rang. Sliver stars filled her vision.

Desa hardly even felt the boot that landed in her stomach. Thrown backward by the hit, she collapsed against a bench in the last row. Her eyesight returned just in time for her to see Azra striding forward.

The other woman lifted a knife and tried to plunge it through Desa's neck.

Desa's hands shot up to seize her wrist, holding the blade at bay. Barely. Her arms trembled with the effort. She brought a knee up to hit Azra's stomach, forcing the bitch to back off. But Desa didn't let go.

She wriggled away and then twisted around, keeping one hand on Azra's wrist and placing the other on her elbow. Growling like a feral dog, Desa bent her enemy over the back bench.

A fist to Azra's skull made her groan. A second punch to the kidneys produced a satisfying squeal. Desa reached for her belt knife.

Azra flung an elbow into her nose.

Desa stumbled.

In that moment of confusion, Azra spun around to face her. The woman thrust out her open palm and triggered a Force-Source in one of her rings.

A wave of kinetic energy hit Desa before she could react, lifting her off the floor and propelling her backward until she hit the door. She landed with a gasp, her body aching and begging for a reprieve.

Azra stooped to recover her pistol.

Time for a change of venue.

Quickly, Desa opened a door and slipped into the cramped space between train cars. She immediately began climbing the ladder up to the roof. Rain began pelting her, and it occurred to her that this might not be a good idea.

Atop the train, the wind was fierce. Trees rushed by on

either side of her, and the driving rain created a slick surface beneath her feet. The roar of the engine made it hard to hear anything else. Why, oh why did she think that this was a good idea? *Because there are no innocent bystanders up here.*

Well…That was a good reason.

Azra's head popped up over the edge of the train car, and she grinned when she saw Desa. She quickly ascended the last few rungs and then stood up on the roof. Rain drenched her long, wavy hair and soaked through her clothing. "Yes," she purred. "This is a much better place to settle things."

"I couldn't agree more."

Desa's hand was a blur as it snatched a throwing knife from her belt and tossed it up to catch the tip. She hurled the knife at her adversary and watched it tumble through the air.

Azra leaned to her left, steel whistling past her ear. She straightened and chuckled. "Terrible aim, don't you think?" She came forward, shaking her head in dismay. "Oh, I had expected better."

Azra began a high kick.

Mere fractions of a second before her boot connected with Desa's ear, Desa triggered the Gravity-Source that she had Infused into the knife. The other woman was yanked backward.

Azra landed on her bottom, legs kicking as she slid across the wet train roof. Only a momentary burst of gravity. Anything more might have knickknacks in the car below clinging to the ceiling. There were no people in range. She hoped.

Drawing her belt dagger from its sheath, Desa fell upon her enemy like a wolf on the hunt. She straddled Azra and tried to stab her.

Azra caught her wrist, baring her teeth and hissing as

she struggled to prevent the steel from sinking into her flesh. Turnabout. Hardly fair play in Desa's estimation, but all that mattered now was ending this.

Azra rolled her over.

Now, Desa was on her back, and somehow the knife was descending toward *her*. A snarling face filled her vision, and she could smell the other woman's breath. Onions. It was vile.

With a quick twist of her hips, Desa flipped them over so that she was on top once again. But now, they were practically hanging off the side of the train. She tried to drive her blade home.

Azra shoved her sideways…over the edge.

In a last, desperate grab, Desa caught the lip of the train car's roof and hung on for dear life. The ground was a blur beneath her dangling feet. Trees flew past behind her, some with long branches that tried to claw her back. She triggered her Gravity-Sink, and the fight to hold on was suddenly a little easier.

Azra stepped into view, standing on the edge and smiling down at her. "Good bye." She raised one leg as if to slam her boot down on Desa's fingers.

Grabbing the edge with both hands, Desa pushed herself upward and rose like an arrow loosed from a bow. She kicked Azra's face as she passed and sent the woman stumbling across the width of the train car.

Desa flipped through the air, killed her Sink and landed with a *thud*. Her fists came up in a defensive posture.

Azra tried to rush her.

Desa spun for a back-kick, driving a foot into the other woman's chest with enough force to push her right off the side of the car. She felt a momentary stirring in the Ether that indicated the use of a Gravity-Sink.

Azra drew her pistol, pointed it out behind herself and fired several shots to propel herself back onto the train. She landed with a grunt.

Backing away, Desa tried to gulp air into her lungs. Her heart was pounding. Azra was catching her breath as well, wiping moisture off her brow with the back of one hand. "This isn't working," she said. "You just refuse to die."

Desa stood with her feet apart, one hand hovering over her holstered pistol. Tiny droplets slid over her forehead. "Let's do this as they do in the frontier towns," she said. "No tricks. She who draws first survives."

Slamming her gun back into its holster, Azra stepped forward and nodded once. "Agreed," she said. "Whenever you're ready."

"I'm ready."

Azra's fingers twitched.

Desa narrowed her eyes.

Each woman drew her weapon.

CRACK-CRACK!

One bullet hung in front of Desa and the other in front of Azra who flung her head back and laughed like a banshee. "You didn't really think I'd abide by that silly rule, did you?" she exclaimed. "No, I'm pleased to see you didn't!"

Azra strode forward, raising her pistol in one hand and firing. The muzzle of her gun flashed twice. Two more slugs stopped dead in front of Desa's shirt, stilled by the Force-Sinks in her buttons.

Azra kept squeezing the trigger, but she had fired every round in her cylinder. The only thing she got for her trouble was a pitiful clicking sound. Realizing her predicament, she tossed the gun aside and began a mad dash for Desa.

Throwing herself down onto her belly, Desa extended

her hand and fired a clean, precise shot that skimmed a bullet along the rain-slick roof.

And she triggered the Heat-Sink within it.

Water flash froze to ice beneath Azra's feet. The woman slipped, arms flailing, and fell onto her backside. She was writhing and whimpering, clutching a bruised hip.

Grumbling, Desa got up on her knees. She fished copper penny out of her pocket and tossed it. When the coin landed next to Azra, she ordered it to release a powerful burst of kinetic energy.

Azra was hurled into the air, off the train and into the forest. Branches snapped as she crashed through them. Her screams were like the tortured wailing of the damned. Desa shivered, and it had nothing to do with the ice she knelt on.

Crawling back to the ladder was...difficult...to say the least. She refused to stand up lest she slip and fall, and the ice was frigid beneath her knees and palms. Every part of her ached. She would need to spend some time communing with the Ether.

Back in the car where this fight had begun, she found the conductor himself inspecting the damage. He was a tall fellow with a neat, gray beard and hard eyes. "What happened here?" he demanded. "Did *you* do this?"

"Not me."

"I heard gunshots. The passengers are frightened."

Desa leaned her shoulder against the wall, shivering. She was drenched from head to toe, which would leave the man with questions she did not want to answer. "There was a woman," she said. "She attacked me, tried to shoot me. Tried to throw me off the train. I hung on, and she left."

"Left?"

"Almost like she could fly...She just hung in the air and

then flew off into the woods. I think she was using some kind of magic."

A snarl twisted the conductor's face. "Aladri witchcraft!" he spat. "I've seen it myself a time or two. Are you all right?"

Desa sat on one of the benches, hugging herself and rubbing her arms for warmth. She nodded vigorously. "I'm fine." Her teeth chattered, but she made no attempt to stop it. Anything that made her look more like a victim would only work to her advantage. "But it was horrible!"

Lying in this way made bile rise up in her stomach, but if the conductor suspected that she had killed Azra, it might go very badly for her. He might decide to contact the authorities in Hedrovan. They might toss Desa into a cell. Perhaps that was what she deserved, but the fate of the world itself depended on this mission; she didn't have time to languish in prison. The right thing and the necessary thing: they weren't always the same.

The conductor gathered all of the passengers and any crew who weren't currently running the train to interrogate them on what they had seen and heard. The sound of gunshots had caused no small amount of commotion, but luckily, it seemed that there were no witnesses to her fight.

Kalia looked as if she were torn between relief and guilt. Knowing her, she would have wanted to fight beside Desa, and she would see her failure to do so as some kind of lapse. Not that she could have done much against Azra. She might not have even known that anything was amiss. The dining car was far enough away that she might not have heard the shots over the constant roaring of the engine. Many of the passengers gasped when the conductor told them what had happened. One woman almost fainted. They had been oblivious to the danger; that much was certain.

Eventually, two waiters came forward to confess that

Azra had paid them to spy on Desa. The descriptions of what they had seen in Azra's cabin lent credence to Desa's story. When a woman openly brandished knives and guns, people were more than willing to believe that she was a killer. The revelation that she had employed Aladri magics only cemented that impression.

So, Azra had been spying on her.

That could be a problem.

She went back to her cabin to change into dry clothes. And then she joined her friends at a small table. Marcus was livid about the conductor slandering Aladar's reputation – and about Desa's refusal to defend her homeland – but thankfully, he didn't make too much of a fuss about it.

By the time they arrived in Hedrovan, they were all in a somber mood.

Azra was stretched out on a mucky slope, groaning and shivering. The trees that rose up all around her did little to keep the rain at bay. She was cold, and she suspected that it had little to do with the temperature.

Movement was next to impossible; her body was broken, battered. Very likely, she was suffering from internal bleeding. So, this was how she died. At least it was at the hand of a worthy adversary.

She was only vaguely aware of the sound of mud squishing under someone's feet. The simple act of turning her head was exhausting – pain shot through her as muscles contracted – but curiosity got the better of her. She had to know who had come to be with her in her final moments.

The Weaver cursed as she lifted her skirts to step over a fallen log. Her eyes settled onto Azra, and the disapproval there was unmistakable. "So," she began. "You tried to go off on your own, and it didn't work out so well, I see."

Azra moaned.

The Weaver crouched beside her. Somehow, the woman was completely dry. The rain just seemed to swerve around her. "Finding you was no easy task," she went on. "In truth, I wasn't even looking. I had expected to find Desa and her friends somewhere near Aladar. What could make them come out this way?"

Azra wished she had an answer. She suspected that it had something to do with the ghost of the abandoned city. Hedrovan was one possible stop on a route that would eventually take them back to the desert. But whatever the reason, Azra wouldn't speculate even if she could. She had no interest in helping this woman.

"Looks like you're dying," the Weaver said.

Azra nodded.

"You know that's something I can't undo, right?" The Weaver grimaced as if acknowledging that limitation pained her. "Oh, I can reanimate your body. But the essence of you...Whatever it is that makes you you...That's gone."

To the Abyss, no doubt. Azra wanted to laugh but that only set her insides on fire with another wave of pain. Yes, the Abyss would take her. And within six months, she would be running the place.

"Do you want to die?"

What kind of question was that?

"It's not too late," the Weaver murmured. "I can save you. But you should know that my healing comes with a price."

Azra hesitated.

The Weaver lifted her delicate hand, and darkness filled her eyes from corner to corner. "So," she said. "What's it going to be?"

20

Hedrovan was an ugly city. Not majestic like Aladar or functional like Ofalla. It was a place where square, stone buildings lined each side of muddy streets, spaced apart at haphazard intervals. The roads weren't even paved. Horse-drawn carriages kicked up a spray of muck as they passed.

Tommy plodded along with a burlap sack cradled in one arm, a suitcase full of clothes in his opposite hand. His mouth dropped open when he looked upon the city.

The rain had stopped – and thank the Almighty for that – but the streets were still a mess. Sometimes, barefoot people in ratty clothes would dash out from an alley, and sometimes, they would pause to eye Tommy and his friends. Tommy could see the calculations in those stares. Were these six strangers who carried travel bags and sacks full of food worth the trouble it would take to rob them?

So, far, no one had made the attempt, which was no surprise. Dalen was the only member of their group who *didn't* openly display a weapon on his person. Five armed foreigners, one of whom carried a bow and quiver in addition to his gun? A wise man would just keep walking.

But the poverty...

Tommy had never seen such deprivation. It would have been unthinkable in his little village. What would these poor people do come winter? He suspected that they were too far south for snow, but cold rains could be just as deadly.

Twice now, Tommy had tried to offer a vagabond an orange or grapefruit from his sack, and each time, Marcus stopped him, offering a cuff across the head on his second attempt. That put a fire in Tommy's belly. He opened his mouth, but Desa spoke first.

Walking slowly with her arms wrapped around her sack, a bag of clothes slung over her shoulder, she gave Marcus a look that could peel the skin off his back. "Touch my apprentice again," she said. "And you and I will have words that you won't enjoy."

"The boy's an idiot!" Marcus snapped. "Feed one of these wretches, and the rest will swarm us before we can find an inn."

An idea occurred to Tommy.

If giving away food was off limits, he would settle for handing out the coins and crumpled-up dollar bills that he had been carrying since Thrasa. He pressed one silver mark into the hand of an urchin with a mop of black hair. "I don't have much to give," he said. "But I won't need money where I'm going."

"Yes, boy," Marcus grated. "It's not as if we'll need that coin to purchase horses."

And that was how it went for most of the long walk from the train station to the inn by the waterfront that Marcus claimed would offer a decent room. It seemed that he and Miri had passed through Hedrovan on their way north to find Desa. Which made sense. Four days on a northbound train would bring them to New Beloran, and from there, it was an easy ride to Ofalla. With a good horse, you would only have to sleep rough twice.

The inn was called *The Golden Sunset.* The saloon on its first floor was a bit posher than what Tommy had been expecting. More of a tavern, really, if one geared toward a certain class of clientele.

Long windows in the crimson walls allowed plenty of sunlight into the room. The square tables were made of polished mahogany, and each one had a candle burning in a small, glass jar. And that was only what he could see from the mudroom.

The innkeeper was a stout woman with more than a few threads of silver in her golden hair who stood in the doorway, blocking their path. "Slippers," she said. "You'll not be tracking that filth over my floor."

Fortunately, she had many pairs to spare. Miri claimed that it was common practice in many of Hedrovan's finer establishments. Some guests brought their own slippers; others availed themselves of what the proprietor had to offer.

"Sirilla Althari," the innkeeper said as she ushered them through the door. "I own *The Golden Sunset*. It's a pleasure to see you again, Marcus Von Tayros."

He nodded to her and then reached up to tip his hat. "And you as well, mistress," he said. "I see that business is still good."

There were at least a dozen well-dressed people in the tavern. Men in finely-tailored suits, women in colourful dresses who wore their hair in ringlets. Like many of the other big cities, they were a cosmopolitan bunch, some light, some dark, some with delicate features like Kalia's.

Gliding across the floor like a swan on the water, Sirilla paused to look back over her shoulder. "Come," she said.

"We have some nice roast chicken for dinner. By the time you get settled into your rooms, I'll have plates ready for you."

They gave Tommy, Dalen and Marcus a room on the second floor. Unwed women slept on the third, Sirilla insisted. No exceptions. It wasn't a lavish room. Certainly not compared to the hotel he had visited in Aladar. In fact, it was a little cramped. There were only two beds. He and Dalen would have to share. He knew right away that neither one of them would want to sleep next to Marcus. Well, it was only for one night. They would be leaving as soon as Marcus could procure horses.

After stowing their bags in a small closet, they went back downstairs to find the dinner that Sirilla had promised laid out on one of the larger tables.

Tommy sat down in a wooden chair, heaving out a sigh. The walk from the train station hadn't been *that* long; why was he so tired? "And so ends the easiest leg of our journey," he said.

Desa sat across from him with her fork in hand, frowning at her plate. She stabbed a carrot and then popped it into her mouth. "The trip across the Halitha should only take about seven days. After that…"

Eradia was connected to Ithanar by a narrow land bridge that spanned the Sapphire Sea. Well, narrow was a matter of perspective. The damn thing was about a hundred miles wide and nearly twice as long. Hedrovan was located right at its northern tip.

Wiping his mouth with a napkin, Marcus grunted. "Might want to stock up on ammo," he said. "No telling what we'll find down there."

"I thought Daresina gave us plenty of ammunition," Dalen said.

"My advice remains the same."

Chewing thoroughly, Desa shook her head. She gave Marcus a sidelong glance. "Horses first," she said. "We'll need at least one packhorse."

Marcus sat back with his arms folded, glowering at Tommy as if this were all his fault somehow. "Had to deplete my bank accounts in Aladar and convert the funds to Eradian currency. Seven horses…That will be expensive."

"I had to dip into my savings as well," Desa lamented. "But it's not like it's going to matter. We're not the sort of folk who live long lives."

Kalia and Dalen exchanged glances.

Tommy suspected that this was another complaint about his decision to feed Hedrovan's poor. He was about to say something, but a woman in a filmy, blue dress cut him off. And "filmy" didn't even begin to describe it. The damn thing was practically see-through!

She was a lovely girl: pale with red hair that she wore tied back. Her eyes were a striking shade of green. The only thing that marred her beauty was a mark on her cheek. Tommy almost hissed when he saw it. He knew that mark well; it was the same one that had been branded onto Sebastian's face.

This young woman was a slave.

She bent to slowly fill each of their cups with red wine, then straightened and stood before them with a beatific smile. "Is there anything else I can get you?"

"No, thank you," Desa said.

The girl left them without another word.

When she was gone, Tommy leaned forward with his hands on the table. "You're just going to accept this?" he spluttered. "How can you let her serve you?"

"This is the way of things in Hedrovan," Marcus replied.

"The way of things!" Tommy all but shouted.

Miri paused with her cup halfway to her mouth and watched him from the corner of her eye. "I don't like it either," she said. "But if we start a fight here, we'll all end up with a rope around our necks."

"The laws here are harsh," Dalen agreed.

Kalia sat there with her mouth agape, shaking her head slowly. "Harsh or not," she began. "Right is right and wrong is wrong. We should do something about this."

"Under other circumstances, I might agree with you," Desa said. "But even with Field Binding, the six of us cannot take on the entire City Watch. And if we don't recover the Spear of Vengeance, this world is doomed."

Grumbling to herself, Kalia bent over her plate to shovel several buttered carrots into her mouth. Well, at least she had said *something*.

Bare-chested men in skirts as thin as the slave girl's dress entered the room to clear empty plates. Each one was lean and muscular, an exemplar of the male form. One was as pale as Tommy, another olive-skinned like Desa. And they all had brands on their cheeks.

Tommy stiffened.

There had to be something he could do.

Desa gave him a look that told him to squelch whatever idea had come into his mind. His teacher knew him too well.

When dinner was over, Miri went to the beach to watch a sun setting. The clouds had finally parted, and the skies were clear. Waves out of the Sapphire Sea lapped at the shore. The waters had earned their name. Even in the waning light, Miri could see that they were a brilliant shade of blue.

She stood on the wet sand with hands shoved into her back pockets, gazing off toward the southern horizon. Somewhere, beyond those waters, the northern coast of Ithanar was waiting. She couldn't see it, but it was there. Waiting.

Off to her right, maybe twenty miles away, the land curved sharply southward. By this time tomorrow, they would be well into their journey across the Halitha. A one-way trip if everything she heard was correct.

Was she willing to die for this cause?

Marcus often talked about the glory of their Aladri heritage, but the truth was that barely a century ago, their great grandparents had come to Aladar as refugees. Back then, the Synod had been willing to take in anyone who came in peace, anyone who wanted to escape the wars that raged across the Eradian continent. That had changed when Miri's mother was a young woman. Aladar had closed its borders shortly after discovering the petroleum reserves on the northern side of the island. So, was she willing to die for her people? Did it matter? She wouldn't be doing it just for her people, but for everyone.

"I thought I might find you here."

Miri flinched at the sound of Dalen's voice. He should *not* have been able to sneak up on her.

She turned around to find him standing on the beach and gazing off toward the horizon just as she had done a few moments ago. "You seemed troubled at dinner," he said. "I thought you might like to talk."

So, he could be observant when he had a mind to try. Well, perhaps she wasn't giving him enough credit. He had been able to sweep Tommy off his feet. That required a certain amount of finesse.

"My head agrees with Marcus." She wasn't sure why she was confessing this to *Dalen* of all people, but the words were coming out of her, and there was no stopping them. She did not want to. "But my heart agrees with T...Lommy. I realize that we have an important task ahead of us, but a part of me wants to kill the guards outside the slave quarters and set them all free."

"I understand."

"Do you?"

Dalen stepped forward, sand squishing under his boots, and held her gaze for a moment before speaking. Such penetrating, dark eyes. She had never realized that he was so handsome. Perhaps because she had been committed to disliking him. "You're a good person with a kind soul," he said. "Of course, it bothers you."

Miri blushed, looking away so he wouldn't see. Perhaps the fading daylight would be enough to hide her chagrin. Perhaps not. "Thank you," she muttered.

"I want to let them out too."

"Are you going to tell me why we shouldn't?"

"There's no need of that," Dalen said. "You already know why we shouldn't. You said as much at the table."

Miri felt her mouth tighten as the anger welled up inside her. "Well, maybe I was wrong," she said coldly. "How do you keep going when there are no good choices, only degrees of evil?"

She was surprised when Dalen hugged her and downright shocked when she returned the embrace. "Maybe," he muttered, "when this is all over, we can come back and lead a revolution."

She couldn't help the burst of laughter that escaped her. "You *are* a fool, aren't you?"

"I would have thought that much was obvious."

. . .

Alone in his room and kneeling on the floor, Tommy floated in the Ether's embrace. He could sense everything around him, including Miri and Dalen walking along the beach. It pleased him to see that they were getting along. Even if he wasn't there to enjoy the moment with them.

Leaving them, he focused on a slave on the first floor, a tall man who left by the back door and followed a stone path behind the inn. Where exactly was he going? The stable? No, that wasn't it. The man was headed to one of the two outbuildings on either side of the inn. Was that…Yes.

Tommy's mind slipped through the wall with ease, and though the barracks was on the edge of his range, he could sense half a dozen men inside. All slaves. So, that was where they slept when they weren't on duty. The other building must have been for the women. Good to know.

He shifted his focus, returning his attention to his room and the collection of stones that he had left on the floor. They were all collections of molecules to his eyes, as were the floorboards and the bedsheets. The Ether hummed all around him. He should clear his mind by practicing the Infusions Desa had taught him; he had gathered the stones for that purpose. He had Infused almost every arrow in his quiver, and there were only so many Force-Sources and Heat-Sinks he could create before the whole thing became redundant.

But what to do with the rocks?

He could make one into a Gravity-Sink, carry it around in his pocket, but he already had one of those in a clover-shaped pendant that he wore around his neck. Desa claimed that the best place for a Gravity-Sink was somewhere near your centre of mass. For men, that was the shoulders.

He had been reluctant to experiment with it. His first attempt had seen him clinging to the ceiling of his hotel room, afraid to kill the Sink. Eventually, he had maneuvered himself to a spot above the bed and used that to cushion the impact.

Tommy already had one Gravity-Sink; he had no desire to make another, and even if the need arose, he could do it in his sleep. They were just basic Infusions. There was no need to exempt yourself or apply directional restrictions. Now, a Force-Sink, on the other hand – one that didn't leave you immobilized while it drained energy from incoming bullets – *that* took some doing. Tommy had one in a second pendant, this one shaped like a star. He had created it under Desa's supervision, and he wasn't sure that he could repeat the process without her guidance. Not yet.

He kept wondering if he had truly seen the limits of what Field Binding could do. Heat, light, kinetic force, gravity and electricity: those were the five basic forms of energy, or so the Aladri claimed. But surely there had to be more. Surely there were other forms of energy in this world. Why should Field Binding be limited to those five?

He let his mind drift, let instinct take over. A lattice took shape in his thoughts. He applied it to the molecules of one stone, building the pattern strand by strand, waiting for them to thicken. A Source for a new kind of energy. He was eager to test it, but before he did, he Infused one of the other stones, creating a perfect inversion of the lattice he had just completed. A Sink to balance the Source. If anything went wrong, he could trigger both at the same time, and they would cancel each other out. He hoped.

Tommy severed contact with the Ether.

Kneeling on the wooden floor with hands folded in his lap, he opened his eyes. "Well," he muttered. "Here goes nothing."

He triggered the new Source.

Nothing happened.

Well, he was painfully aware of his own heartbeat, but that was just fear. He looked around the room for some sign of what he had done, but nothing was amiss. The two beds were there, made neat and tidy. The oil lamp was burning on the small table. Nothing was floating. Or on fire. So far as he could tell, the new Source had no effect whatsoever. Why *was* his heart thundering in his ears?

Tommy let out a breath.

That brief exhalation was like the crashing of a waterfall. Come to think of it, his heartbeat wasn't the only thing he heard. The hiss of the oil lamp was louder than it should have been. "Oh, dear..."

Clapping his hands over his ears, Tommy shut his eyes tight. What should have been a soft murmur came out like a scream. He immediately killed the Source. And just in time, too.

Someone pounded on the wall from a neighbouring room. "Keep it down in there!"

Sound.

The Source amplified sound energy. Which meant that the Sink...He triggered it and found himself in a world of total silence. No breath, no heartbeat. No hissing from the lamp.

Cautiously, he stood up and stamped his foot down on the floor. Nothing. This must have been what it was like to be deaf. Tommy jumped up and down as hard as he could over and over again. That should have created enough of a racket to bring the innkeeper down on him, but after several minutes of stomping around, no one came.

Tommy stood between the beds with his hands on his hips, smiling triumphantly. "Oh, wow." He should have expected it, but it was still quite a shock to speak and hear nothing. "The things I could do with this."

He killed the Sink.

Knock, knock, knock.

He jumped, stumbling backward with a hand over his mouth. Whoever was at his door seemed rather insistent to get in. Maybe he should have been more careful. Maybe the Sink didn't work as well as he thought.

He opened the door, expecting a tirade from the innkeeper, and found Desa standing in the hallway instead. "What did you do?" she asked, striding into the room without invitation.

"Did you hear me jumping around?"

"What? No!" Desa stood over the rocks that he had left on the floor. "I felt a stirring in the Ether unlike anything I have ever sensed before, and when I came to investigate, I couldn't hear anything. Not even my own knocking. What did you do?"

Blushing, Tommy bowed his head and clamped a hand over the back of his neck. "Well," he said, stepping forward. "I created a new kind of Source…and Sink."

"A new kind of Sink?"

"A Sonic-Sink," he suggested. That seemed as good a name as any. "It drains sound energy. And the Source-"

"Amplifies it," Desa cut in. She rounded on him, and the look on her face was a mix of pride and fear and anger. "Tommy…You promised me that you would resist the inclination to experiment."

"I know, but-"

"If this had been something dangerous, it could have killed you. Can you imagine what might have happened if something heavy had fallen on the floor while the Source was active?"

"Yes, but-"

Desa's face softened; a smile replaced the stern glare that she had given him only moments earlier. "But," she said, clapping him on the shoulder. "This is a remarkable accomplishment. Aladri Field Binders have tried for centuries to manipulate a new kind of energy. I knew taking you on as a student was a good idea!"

"Thank you. And I promise...no more experimenting."

Desa sat on the foot of his bed, nodding curtly as if that settled matters. "You'll have to show me how to make one on our journey south," she said. "The ability to move silently will be very useful indeed."

They talked for a little while longer. Desa was quite eager to know what had prompted him to attempt a new type of Infusion. He told her everything he could, that it was mainly a reaction to her insistence that there were only five types of energy the Ether could manipulate.

"Is that all?" Desa asked.

She knew.

Somehow, she could see through him.

"No," Tommy whispered. "No, it's not. I was thinking that if I could move silently, it would be easier to free the slaves."

He expected to see condemnation or disapproval in Desa's eyes, but he found nothing but sympathy there. "Tommy," she murmured. "You have a good heart."

"We can't just leave them like this!"

With a heavy sigh, Desa stood up and reached out to lay a hand on his cheek. "I have come to realize that you are a cautious man. Most of the time, anyway." He couldn't argue with that. "I suspect your plan was to do it in the dead of night."

Tommy nodded.

"The slave quarters will be guarded," Desa said. "A high-end establishment like this will hire men to stand watch during the night. Are you prepared to kill anyone who would stand in your way?"

His heart twisted at the thought of it. More killing. The last thing he wanted. Even still, he had spent his whole life backing down when he knew he was right. And he was done with that. "You don't think I could do it?" he spat.

"Oh, I *know* you could do it," Desa replied. "Your skill with a bow is formidable and your knowledge of Field Binding more than sufficient to deal with a few lightly-armed men. The question is 'could you do it without bringing the entire City Watch down on us?'"

"Arrows make very little noise."

"They do indeed," Desa agreed. "And they leave wounds that look very different from those inflicted by bullets, even to the untrained eye. Tomorrow morning, when Sirilla Althari finds her guards dead and the slaves gone, who do you think she will suspect?"

"Then I'll use my gun! I'm not such a bad shot!"

His eyes widened when Desa clamped a hand over his mouth. Only then did he realize that he had been speaking much too loudly. "You're more than competent with a pistol," Desa conceded. "But can you guarantee that your new Sonic-Sink will muffle the gunshots? Most likely, there will be two guards in front of each barracks, which means that you will have to fire four shots. That's a lot of sound energy for one Sink to absorb."

Tommy was getting flustered. It was supposed to have been such a simple plan: sneak out in the middle of the night and set the slaves free. He hadn't anticipated the presence of guards. The truth was he didn't know if he could kill anyone. "All right," he panted. "Then we set them free, and we leave in the middle of the night. Before anybody has a chance to call the Watch."

Desa's raised eyebrow told him what she thought of that plan. "Without horses?" she asked. "Carrying our supplies on our backs? How far do you think we'll get?"

"We can't just do nothing in the face of this injustice."

"We won't," Desa assured him. "When this is over, when we've recovered the spear, you and I will come back here. And we will set these people free."

Tommy closed his eyes, breathing deeply to quell his anger. "I guess," he said, "that will have to do."

21

Just shy of noon the next day, they left the city in a procession of six horses. Only six. Marcus had visited two stables the night before and three more this morning. In the end, he had spent every penny they had to spare, but even that had been insufficient. The mounts he had procured were less than ideal. Most were past their prime. With one beast relegated to the role of packhorse, Desa and Kalia had to double up. They were the smallest, and so it made sense for them to share a saddle.

The sheriff didn't mind, and truth be told, Desa had no complaints either. Having Kalia's arms around her waist as she guided her roan mare through the muddy streets of Hedrovan was reassuring. She was about to undertake a very dangerous journey, but at least, she wasn't going alone.

Tommy was right in front of them on a brown gelding with a white spot on his rump. The poor lad kept glancing to the side of the street where beggars sat in the shade of tall buildings, thrusting clay bowls out to whoever passed within arm's reach. Every now and then, someone dropped a coin into one of those bowls, but for the most part, people pretended not to see the squalor right under their noses.

Tommy sighed.

Desa's heart broke for him. Sometimes, she thought it might have been best to leave him in Aladar. He was a clever lad; she had no doubt that her apprentice could find some form of productive work and settle into a comfortable life. But no. Tommy would have been offended by the suggestion that he stay behind. And he was a foreigner.

Perhaps she was imagining it, but Desa couldn't escape the feeling that her people had grown more distrustful of outsiders in the years she was away. Or perhaps the distrust had always been there and she, as a young woman, had simply failed to notice.

Kalia pulled her close and nuzzled the back of Desa's neck. "You're growing somber," she murmured.

Desa felt her mouth tighten as she studied Tommy's back. "Just wondering if I bring heartbreak everywhere I go."

"What kind of fool's talk is that?"

Chuckling softly, Desa reached up to pull the brim of her hat down over her eyes. The clouds had parted, and the city was baking under the summer sun. "Have you met me?" she asked. "If there is a way to blame myself for something, I'll find it."

Kalia kissed the side of her neck. "That's because you see only the heartbreak, my love," she said. "And never the good you do."

It took the better part of an hour to reach the edge of town, and then they followed a narrow dirt road up the slope of a gentle hill. From the crest, Desa could see distant train tracks extending north through green fields. And to the south, the sparkling waters of the Sapphire Sea.

There were peach trees on the hilltop.

Miri drew rein and hopped out of the saddle, landing with a grunt. She led her dappled gray by its bridle. "May as well stock up," she said. "No telling when we'll get another chance."

She began plucking peaches off the branches. Tommy decided to assist her, guiding the packhorse into the shade of the trees and filling the sacks it carried with as much fruit as they could hold. The animal decided to start grazing, stretching its long neck to munch on the grass.

Marcus sat his saddle with a curious expression, gazing wistfully toward the land bridge that would carry them to Ithanar. He almost looked sad. Odd that. Marcus could be gruff at the best of times, but over the last few days, he had been downright surly. Even cruel. Perhaps it would be wise to inquire as to what was troubling him.

Perhaps not...

Knowing Marcus, he would be just as likely to snap at her as he would to divulge anything useful. Some people had to face their problems on their own.

A distant whinny drew her out of her reverie.

Desa felt her jaw drop, then shook her head slowly. "It can't be..." She jumped out of the saddle, landing hard in the grass.

The others called out to her, but Desa ignored them as she scrambled down the hillside. Was she just imagining it? Surely, it was impossible. She was half-convinced that she was mad when another whinny pierced the air, louder than before.

A majestic, black stallion crested a nearby hill and reared when he reached the summit, his legs kicking as he let out another high-pitched cry. "Midnight!" Desa shouted as she ran up to meet him.

The horse nuzzled her and licked her forehead, causing Desa to recoil. "Gah!" She wiped saliva off her brow. "How did you do it? How did you find us?"

The answer came to her in a sudden flash of understanding. For Midnight to have come all this way, he would have had to have set out from Dry Gulch almost immediately after they were separated. But how could he know where she would be weeks ahead of time? There was only one possibility. "You can sense me," Desa whispered. "You know where I am."

In response, the stallion licked her again.

That was the only thing that made sense. Midnight hadn't been trying to reach Hedrovan. He had been trying to reach Aladar, traveling south and east across the face of the continent. When he sensed Desa heading westward on the train, he changed course to rendezvous with her here.

She didn't have to guide Midnight back to the others; he just followed her to the peach trees.

Her friends were all standing on the hilltop, watching her disbelief on their faces. Well, except Tommy; he was smiling like a toddler at his first festival. "I'm happy you found us, my friend," he said, stepping forward.

Midnight nuzzled him.

After that, things went a little easier. They used the roan as a second packhorse while she and Kalia rode Midnight. Having her steed back lifted Desa's spirits considerably. For the first time since leaving Aladar, she felt optimistic about this journey. It wouldn't last – she knew that – but you had to celebrate the small victories when they presented themselves.

Most of the first afternoon was spent following a narrow, dirt road that cut through the rolling hills. There was nothing to see: just water on their left and a vast expanse of grassland on their right. Desa was sure that they would encounter other travelers – farmers on their way to market or lawmen bringing a prisoner to face justice in Hedrovan – but there was no one.

Come to think of it, she saw no farms or settlements of any kind, and that unnerved her. Hamlets usually sprung up within a day's ride of a major city. But not out here. The land was so desolate it was almost bleak. Marcus claimed it was because people feared the Halitha. Ithanar was cursed, you see. Which meant that nobody in their right mind wanted to live near the land bridge that connected to it. There were settlements east and north of Hedrovan, but to the west? Nothing.

Afternoon was fading to evening when the land curved southward, but they didn't begin their trek at the earliest opportunity. Instead, they followed the dirt road for another mile or so. The eastern shore of the Halitha was a sandy beach. The horses would find better footing on grassy plains further inland.

By the time they were ready to cross, the shadows were growing long. Tommy, Kalia and Miri all suggested that they stop for supper and sleep by the roadside, and Marcus did not protest. No one wanted to begin the journey without the sun overhead to give them courage.

They dined on fruit and salted meat. Desa encouraged them to eat the preserves that Daresina had offered five days ago now. The peaches they had collected would keep a little longer. Heat-Sinks in the form of small coins kept the food fresh. Desa renewed their connections to the Ether before turning in.

She slept well with Kalia snuggled up in her bedroll and Midnight lying down only a few feet away from her.

Morning dawned bright and early with Marcus, who

had taken last watch, nudging them with his foot to rouse them all. They ate a quick breakfast, mostly tough, chewy bread and fruit, gathered their supplies and left within half an hour of rising.

So began their journey to Ithanar.

Despite its reputation, the Halitha was entirely unremarkable. Beautiful but utterly mundane. Green fields stretched on to the southern horizon with only a few lonely trees dotting the landscape here and there. The sun was halfway to its zenith when they paused at the top of a particularly high hill. From up here, Desa could see for miles in every direction.

The lush grasslands seemed to go on forever. When she looked to her right, there was no sign of the western shore, but to her left – barely a mile away – the ground sloped down to a gorgeous beach where the crystal-blue waters lapped at the sand. Perhaps she could go swimming when they stopped for the night. She was already feeling the grime of a day's ride in the hot sun. A month in Aladar had spoiled her. She had grown used to bathing every day.

Desa stared into the distance while the wind ruffled her hair. "It's breathtaking," she murmured. "How could anyone think this land is cursed?"

Kalia giggled behind her.

Not far ahead, at the edge of the hilltop, Marcus sat atop his red gelding. He looked back over his shoulder and sneered at them. "Are we going to dawdle here all day?" he barked. "That damn spear isn't going to find itself."

Tommy rode up beside her and favoured Desa with a sympathetic glance. "I'm sorry," he mouthed as if Marcus's cantankerous disposition were his fault.

So, they pressed on.

The second day of their journey was mostly uneventful,

but Desa noticed Miri and Dalen chatting amicably. That was good, she supposed, but she wondered how Tommy would react when he saw just how well those two were getting along. *Not my business,* she insisted. That sentence had become a mantra she recited whenever she caught herself thinking about her three young friends.

Kalia took every opportunity to cuddle up and squeeze her tight, and for a wonder, Desa was happy to receive such affection. Not so long ago, Adele had been sitting behind her in Midnight's saddle, doing much the same thing.

Maybe, just maybe, there was hope that things might go differently this time.

"Good!" Kalia said.

She was on her knees with hands folded in her lap, her face bathed in the glow of a small coin that she had Infused when they stopped for dinner. Miri had wanted to start a campfire, but on a hot night like this, no one else shared that sentiment.

Across from the sheriff, Tommy sat crosslegged with his eyes closed. Desa could feel the Ether surging within him. Or perhaps it was more accurate to say that the Ether emanated *from* him. Neither one was entirely correct; the Ether was everywhere. In all things, at all times. However, it seemed to intensify in one spot whenever someone communed with it.

Miri was a shadow at the edge of their camp, gazing off at the last sliver of twilight on the western horizon. Sometimes Desa wondered what the young woman was thinking. Miri could be quite reserved.

Dalen was sitting in the grass with his back to the glowing ring, using its light to read a leather-bound book.

Desa wasn't sure what to make of him either. Reserved or not, Miri, at least, was a known quantity. Any misgivings that Desa once had about her had long since evaporated. The woman had proved herself many times over.

But Dalen...

She sensed no deceit from Dalen; the boy *was* honest. A little too honest, in her estimation. But she sometimes had the sense that he wasn't fully aware of what he had gotten himself into. Just a love-sick puppy who had followed Tommy into the wilderness.

Kalia became one with the Ether and held onto it for about five seconds before she severed contact. Just long enough to check on Tommy. "Excellent," she said. "Hold the lattice in that pattern."

Curious, Desa reached for the Ether herself, and her world became a tempest of particles. She traced the Infusion that Tommy was crafting with her mind. When he was finished, it would be a powerful Force-Sink with appropriate directional modifiers. It was the modifiers that gave him trouble. Most beginners struggled with them.

Basic Infusions – those that would take energy from or release energy to anything that was within range – were easy. But useful tools often required at least one modifier.

Marcus sat on a fallen log with his knees apart, staring intently at the ring. He blinked as if noticing Tommy for the first time and muttered something under his breath.

Desa ignored him.

With an exasperated sigh, Marcus got up and stomped over to her. "Do you truly think this is right?" he asked. "Sharing our secrets with outsiders?"

"They aren't our secrets to keep," Desa countered. "Perhaps you didn't notice, but Kalia's people learned Field Binding without any help from Aladar."

Spinning around to face Tommy, Marcus shook his head in disgust. "Yes," he whispered. "Something will have to be done about that."

"What is *that* supposed to mean?"

Marcus didn't answer her; he just stalked off into the night, pausing to stand beside his sister for maybe ten seconds before continuing on his way. If he said anything to Miri, it was too soft for Desa to catch it, but the other woman's shoulders slumped.

Not good.

ANOTHER DAY in the saddle brought with it more aches and pains and sweat and grime. And boredom. Desa had endured more than her fill of that. There were only so many conversations you could have while traveling through the desolate wilderness. The highlight of their afternoon had been spotting a group of rabbits scampering through the grass. Tommy had promptly shot two with well-placed arrows, and Desa had cooked them with a Heat-Source coin.

They ate well that evening.

It would be another hour or two before full-dark came, but they had all silently agreed that they would go no further today. The idea that had been rattling around in Desa's head for two days became irresistible, and she decided to go for a swim. Summers were even hotter this far south than what she was used to in Aladar.

The sinking sun cast golden light upon the beach as waves washed over the shore. A few palm trees sprouted from the sand with broad leaves that fluttered in the wind. The scent of salt hung in the air.

Standing on the shore with hands clasped behind her back, Desa stared off into the distance. A warm breeze caressed her face. "Well," she muttered, "you always wanted to see the world. And now you've seen more of it than any person has a right to."

The conifer forests of northern Eradia, the sun-scorched clay of the Gatharan Desert, the tropical paradise that spread out before her: she had seen them all. And she had met so many people along the way. Sometimes, they confirmed her worst suspicions, but often, they surprised her.

Thrasa had been just another backwater town. She had expected them to fear and loathe her power as so many others did, but not only did the locals show an interest in Field Binding, they also hailed Desa and her friends as heroes.

A scuffing sound got her attention.

When she turned around, she found Kalia walking barefoot through the sand, carrying her boots in one hand. The other woman's long hair was streaming in the wind. A few strands whipped across her face, but that didn't hide her smile. "The others are all sharing scary stories around a glowing coin," she said. "I thought I'd come join you."

Chuckling softly, Desa bowed her head to the other woman. "That sounds lovely," she said, stepping forward. "Have I told you how wonderful you are?"

"Not nearly enough."

Five minutes later, they were neck-deep in water that was so warm it could have done for a bath. Kalia was so beautiful, floating there and smiling at her like a goddess. "What?" she asked when she caught Desa looking.

"Just admiring you."

Kalia splashed her.

The water hit Desa right in the face, and she winced.

She spat some of it out of her mouth and then shook her head forcefully. "Not nice!"

Her own splash had the other woman squealing and retreating to get away. "All right, all right!" Kalia shouted, raising hands up to shield herself. "I yield."

"I accept your surrender."

A smile blossomed on Kalia's face, and she giggled. "Well, it was hardly a fair fight," she said. "I'm a desert dweller, remember? I'm somewhat out of my element."

A fair point.

Desa submerged herself completely to cool off. Her head broke through the surface a moment later, and she reached up with both hands to thread fingers through her wet hair. "Curious," she said. "How exactly did you learn to swim?"

"There *is* an oasis near my town."

"Ah, yes."

"So…You seem a little happier."

Crossing her arms, Desa pursed her lips as she looked up toward the darkening sky. "Happier?" she said, her eyebrows rising. "Perhaps. But I think I've just decided to enjoy the time I have left while I have it."

A sudden grimace was Kalia's answer. "Still convinced that we're going to die, I see," she murmured. "Well, I suppose a sunny disposition is better than a dour one."

"Some of us *are* going to die."

"You don't know that."

Desa narrowed her eyes as she studied the other woman. "Need I remind you that almost no one who goes to Ithanar ever returns?" she asked. "The odds of all of us making it back to Aladar are slim."

Cocking her head, Kalia blinked as if a thought had just occurred to her. "Is that why you were afraid to get close?" she inquired. "You were afraid that I might die?"

"Just the opposite," Desa countered. "I was afraid that *I* might die...And then you would have to endure the grief. Better that I should pass as a strange woman you hardly knew than as someone you loved."

In the dim light, she could see the other woman's scowl, and she knew that she had said the wrong thing. It was something of a talent that she had developed over the years. "I am not a child," Kalia said in a dangerous voice. "I don't need you to protect me from heartbreak."

"I'm sorry."

Kalia turned away and swam back to the shore. At first, Desa was tempted to go after her, but if the other woman had decided to end the conversation, trying to press the point would not win her any sympathy. Desa sighed. *This was why no one should come to her for advice on matters of the heart.*

"So, you think I'm doing well," Tommy asked.

Gently holding his horse's bridle, he guided the animal down the shallow slope of a grassy hill. They were all walking to let the horses rest. Four days of traveling had taken them nearly halfway across the Halitha, or so Marcus claimed. With any luck, the second half of the journey would be just as uneventful as the first.

He had a sinking feeling that wish would not come true.

So far, the terrain had been nothing but open grasslands with the odd stream or fresh-water pond, but he could see a forest looming in the distance, perhaps a mile away. Crossing through that might be difficult. He supposed that they could go down to the beach and bypass the forest entirely, but walking on sand would force the horses to work harder, and many of them were not in the best shape.

There didn't seem to be a good answer. Tommy was just glad that he wasn't the one who had to make the decision. Let Marcus be the one to carry that burden. The other man would only snap at him if he dared to offer a suggestion.

Tommy was in his shirtsleeves, and those were rolled up to his elbows. His hat was pulled down over his eyes, but his cheeks were still sunburnt. He had taken to walking with his head down, and that put a crick in his neck.

Sheriff Troval was at his side, walking with her arms swinging and smiling pleasantly at the scenery all around them. She didn't seem to mind the heat. "I think that you are doing *quite* well," she said with a curt nod. "When it comes to Field Binding, no two people learn at the same rate, but you are still faster than many I've seen."

"Well, that's good to know."

Not far ahead, Marcus was leading his red around the towering trunk of a palm tree, and of course, he seemed to be unaffected by the sun's relentless onslaught. Tommy wished he knew the other man's secret.

He slipped a toothpick into his mouth and gnawed on it to ease his frustration. "Oh, hey!" he said when a thought occurred to him. "Would you like me to show you how to make a Sonic-Sink? Desa said she wanted to learn, but we haven't had an opportunity to sit down and practice."

"After dinner," Kalia said. "I'm eager to learn."

"Where *is* Desa?"

The sheriff paused to look back over her shoulder and frowned as if she thought that Desa might be up to no good. "Bringing up the rear," Kalia answered. "She needed a little time to herself. Time to think."

Tommy had no idea what that was about, and he felt no inclination to ask. He was happy for Desa – and for Kalia as well – but if the two of them had had a fight, there was little he could do about it. Not when he could barely sort out his own feelings.

Miri and Dalen had taken to riding and walking side by side. They spent most days chatting quietly with an almost secretive air about them. Tommy was glad that they were getting along, but sometimes it seemed as though they had both forgotten that he existed. He wasn't a fool; he recognized the signs of budding infatuation when he saw them.

Well, maybe it was for the best.

Tommy Smith had been unable to choose, and so fate had chosen for him. Poetic justice, he supposed: the two lovers he had spurned found comfort with each other.

It wasn't long before they reached the edge of the forest. Tall trees with branches covered in thick, green leaves strained for the sky. There didn't seem to be a clear path through the brush, which was not unexpected. Roads were hammered into the earth by constant foot traffic. If no one traveled these lands, well…

Clasping his chin in one hand, Marcus narrowed his eyes as he studied the trees. "No easy way through," he said. "I suppose I'll have to scout."

Kalia stepped forward, removing her hat with a flourish and bowing to him. "Why don't you leave that to us?" she said upon rising. "Thomas and I will reconnoiter the area. He could use the practice."

Tommy blinked.

"Are you ready?" Kalia asked.

"For what?"

In response, she turned her back and triggered a Gravity-Sink. She jumped and soared right up to the treetops, grabbing a branch to steady herself. "Come join me! It's beautiful up here!"

Well…What else could he do?

Shutting his eyes, Tommy took a deep breath. He nodded once and triggered the Gravity-Sink in his pendant. The feeling of weightlessness washed over him.

He jumped and shot straight up, nearly crashing through several hanging branches that barred his path. He managed to grab one and plant his feet against the tree trunk. Holding on was easy; his arms didn't ache from the effort. Grunting and cursing, Tommy pulled himself up.

Kalia was perched on a nearby branch and staring southward. Her mouth was a thin line. "Oh, dear..."

When his head broke through the leafy canopy, Tommy saw what was troubling her. The forest went on for miles! Just a sea of trees with no end in sight! No wonder so few people came this way! This little patch of woodland would make an all but impenetrable barrier. They would have been better off taking a ship. Not that they could find one. Few sailors were willing to drop anchor on Ithanar's shores.

"Come on," Kalia said.

She began skipping over the treetops, hopping from branch to branch without a care in the world. Tommy was hesitant to follow; he hated heights. His Gravity-Sink would endure for the better part of an hour – he knew that – and yet he still felt as though he might fall to his death at any moment. Still, Kalia had promised the others that they would find a clear path, and if Tommy didn't make good on that, he would hear no end of complaining from Marcus.

Steeling his nerves, he took off after his friend. "Wait for me!"

WAVES CRASHED over the shore as they finally made camp on the beach. Perhaps an hour of daylight remained to them. The evenings were coming sooner as summer drew to a close. Up north, the leaves would start changing colour in a few weeks. But down here, well...Tommy suspected that they would remain lush and green for a while yet.

He and Kalia had scouted the forest until their Gravity-Sinks were all but exhausted, and they had found nothing they could use to get through. The humans could maneuver around trees and muck-filled ditches, but the animals would be helpless in there. Traveling along the beach was their only option, and it wasn't a good one. Horses could not graze on sand, and the forest might go on for days for all they knew. Maps of the Haliha weren't exactly reliable.

Tommy sat on a large rock, restringing his bow and frowning thoughtfully as he considered their predicament. "We should send someone out to fetch water," he said. "We saw several streams running through the forest."

Marcus stood at the water's edge with his back turned. He nodded, but it seemed to Tommy that he wasn't really listening.

A short way down the beach, Desa and Kalia were standing together, holding hands and gazing into each other's eyes. They ought to be a part of this discussion, but Tommy didn't want to interrupt their private moment.

Miri was lying on her back with a throwing knife balanced between the tips of her two index fingers, using her folded-up duster as a pillow. "I suppose I can go," she said.

"Want me to go with you?" Tommy asked.

She smiled and turned her head so that her cheek was pressed against the fabric of her coat, watching him with those gorgeous, dark eyes. "I'll be fine," she replied. "They *do* teach us a thing or two about foraging before they send us into the wild."

Tommy winced but nodded slowly in acquiescence. It

wasn't that he didn't trust Miri to take care of herself, but her refusal to let him come along meant that she was not eager for his company. "Good luck."

With a soft sigh, Miri stood up and dusted off the back of her shirt. She shot a glance toward Dalen. "Coming?"

Tommy opened his mouth to protest and then snapped it shut again.

Closing his book with a *thump,* Dalen returned it to his saddlebag and gave his dun mare a gentle pat. The horse snorted in appreciation. "This shouldn't take very long," he announced for anyone who might be listening. "We'll be back soon."

"But..." Tommy protested.

Miri arched an eyebrow.

"Wouldn't you rather have a Field Binder along with you?" he blurted out. It was the first thing that came to mind. "It can get dark in there at sundown."

Miri held up a hand to display the simple, iron band on her third finger. She gave it two quick twists, and the ring burst alight with a powerful glow that made Tommy's eyes water. "Marcus made it for me," she explained.

Well...So much for *that* excuse.

They were gone before he could think of another objection; so, Tommy went back to checking his bowstring. Good and taut. Ready for battle. He chuckled at the realization that just six months ago, he would never have imagined himself going into battle.

A horse's whicker and the sound of hooves in sand got his attention. When he looked up, Midnight stood over him. The black stallion bent his long neck to lick and nuzzle Tommy's forehead. It tickled!

Tommy closed his eyes, shaking with laughter. "All right, all right," he said. "At least someone here is on my side."

Midnight tossed his head with a powerful neigh, and Tommy took that as a yes.

The towering trees cast shadows over the uneven ground. There were so many that Miri could only see the sinking sun as a brief flare of golden light in the gaps between them. It was decidedly cooler in here. Not chilly, but the drop in temperature was hard to ignore. The air almost seemed to quiver.

Craning her neck, Miri squinted at the treetops. "This forest is old," she whispered, shaking her head. "And I don't think it wants us in here."

Dalen stood on a flat rock with one hand pressed against a tree trunk. "Pointless superstition," he said. "Trees can't think, and forests don't want anything."

A sudden breeze made leaves rustle on branches, and Miri jumped as a chill ran down her spine. She hunched up her shoulders and shuddered. "Did anyone ever tell you you're an arrogant bastard?"

"All the time."

"Ever think about doing something to change that?"

Hopping off of his rock, Dalen sauntered through the space between two trees. "I don't know." He found a small gully and crouched there, inspecting the babbling waters of a stream. "Do you ever think about changing that passive-aggressive streak?"

"Excuse me?"

Dalen met her gaze, and his face lit up with a grin. "Come on," he said. "Inviting me along after Thomas expressed a desire to go with you? Don't tell me that wasn't an attempt to make him jealous."

Miri stood under a branch with her hands in her coat

pockets, struggling to think up a response to that. "Did it ever occur to you," she said at last, "that I might *want* to spend time with you, and never mind what Lommy says about it?"

"Well, then I consider myself blessed."

She blushed.

Dipping his canteen into the water, Dalen lifted it up to examine its contents. "Doesn't look too dirty," he said. "A good boiling should make it safe."

Miri leaned against a tree trunk, heaving out a deep breath. "Well, let's fill up the bottles, then," she muttered. "The important people must be getting thirsty."

"You don't consider yourself to be one of the important people?"

"Look around you, Dalen," she snapped. "This isn't our story. Lommy, Desa, my brother: they're the Field Binders. They're the ones who are going to find the spear and put a stop to whatever that monster inside Adele is."

"So, only Field Binding makes one important?"

Blowing air through puckered lips, Miri looked up at the sky. "Abstract philosophy is *your* forte," she said. "I'm just a patriot, charged with the duty of keeping a close watch on Aladar's many enemies."

She kicked a stone and sent it skittering along the ground until it hit the base of a nearby tree. "Sometimes I don't know why I came along for this fool's quest. Lommy doesn't need me. Not anymore."

Dalen strode toward her with a look in his eyes that she could only call hungry. "Then he's a fool," he said. "A fool who cannot see what he is losing."

He laid a hand on Miri's cheek, and she closed her eyes, leaning into his touch. "I thought you only liked boys."

"Did I say that I only like boys?"

"Well, no-"

His lips came down on hers, and she was surprised to realize that she was kissing him back. Her fingers seized a clump of his hair. Her body melted against, and for a few blessed minutes, she stopped thinking.

Miri and Dalen returned with water as the last traces of daylight were fading, and the group sat down to a late dinner. Desa used several Heat-Source coins to boil the water they brought back, and then she refilled the canteens. That would last them another day or two. Hopefully, there were more grasslands on the other side of this forest. Maybe a nice pond. Marcus had purchased fodder for the horses, but that would not last long if they had to walk another four days along a beach.

They had gone through most of their preserves from Aladar and many of the peaches that Miri had picked up at the start of their journey. They would have to find another source of food soon. Desa thought about taking Tommy into the forest. There were bound to be small animals in there, and he could use the practice.

For now, though, what she wanted was sleep.

The stars were twinkling overhead, but the moon had not come out yet. The sound of the nearby waves soothed her nerves, but that was nothing compared to the feeling of Kalia's arm around her stomach. They had made up earlier that evening, and now, the other woman was curled up with her head on Desa's chest. Everything was just right.

With her head resting on two folded coats, Desa closed her eyes and let herself drift off. She had done her turn at watch last night – which meant that she could sleep until morning – and the sand beneath her body was enough of a cushion to let her rest easy. Her last thoughts as she slipped into unconsciousness were that Kalia made her feel perfectly safe.

A blood-curdling scream pierced the air.

Desa sat bolt upright.

Kalia scrambled off of her and brushed the hair out of her face. "What? What?"

Years of training kicked in, and Desa assessed the situation. It was still dark, but a quarter moon was now high in the sky. Which meant that several hours had passed at least. It was probably close to dawn.

The others were rising from their bedrolls, looking around in confusion. Miri was down on one knee with her pistol drawn. The horses were panicking. Marcus had tied them to trees on the outskirts of the forest, and now they were struggling to get away. Only Midnight remained untethered, and he stood silently, watching.

Tommy was ten feet away with a glowing ring pointed at the treeline. He had been assigned second watch, which meant that much of the night had indeed passed. "It came from in there," he said.

Another inhuman shriek made him flinch.

Then something rose out of the forest. A winged creature, black against the night, and much too big to be a bat. Desa had only a brief glimpse of it as it passed in front of the moon, but if she had to guess, she would say that it was about the size of a tall man. And she thought she saw two green eyes.

It took off over the Sapphire Sea, stirring up quite a wind. At the rate it was going, it would traverse a hundred miles in an hour. No animal could fly that fast! She tracked it for as long as she could, but within a minute, it was just a black speck in the night sky. And then it was gone.

"What was that?" Dalen panted. "What was that?"

Kalia was gasping for breath.

"Stay calm," Desa told them.

Tommy stepped up to the water's edge, shining his Light-Source ring into the heavens. Of course, there was nothing to see. Just the night sky and the twinkling stars.

"Tommy!" Desa barked. "Stop that!"

The boy twisted around to face her, and she could see the question in his eyes.

Desa forced herself to rise slowly and paced over to him. "The creature might not have noticed us," she said, patting her apprentice on the arm. "Let's try not to attract its attention."

His ring went dark a second later.

"What do we do?" Marcus asked, stomping through the sand. That he was willing to defer to her on this meant that he was truly frightened. The man styled himself as the de-facto leader of their group, always taking point, always behaving as if his opinion should be the final word on any issue.

"If it hunts by air, we'll be easy prey on the beach," Miri said. "Should we go into the forest?"

Desa shuffled back to her bedroll, shaking her head. "I think the forest is the last place we want to be right now," she said. "For the moment, we should wait to see-"

Another ear-piercing screech silenced her, reverberating off the water. She scanned the eastern horizon, but nothing stood out to her. Just darkness. Stars. Waves crashing. By the time she noticed the black spot that kept growing larger and larger, it was too late.

The creature came barreling toward them, wings flapping, green eyes glowing with inscrutable menace. It flew right over them, so close that Desa could have touched its belly if she had reached up in time, then slipped between two trees and vanished into the forest. Given its speed, it should have crashed through branches, but there was nothing. Not a sound except the frantic whinnies of the horses.

"Tommy, Kalia, Marcus," Desa said.

She drew her pistol, cocking the hammer, and then took off in a sprint, sand puffing under her feet as she raced toward the treeline. With a thought, she triggered the Light-Source in her ring. The creature knew they were here; there was no longer any point in hiding.

The others were right behind her.

Desa stepped between two trees, shining her light this way and that. She saw tall, twisted trunks, roots growing through the soft, red clay and bushes with long, thin leaves. But no man-bat.

The others joined her, each casting their light about in different directions. Together, they provided more illumination than the forest would see under the noonday sun, But the creature was nowhere to be found. Worse yet, there was no sign of its passing. No snapped branches, no claw marks in bark, no strange footprints. It might never have been there for all that Desa could tell.

"It doesn't make sense," she growled. "Something that big cannot move that fast through a forest this dense and not leave a mark!"

Marcus had his teeth bared in a snarl. "Perhaps," he said, "it would be wise to get out into the open."

Desa nodded.

They found Miri and Dalen waiting for them on the beach, standing side by side in wide-eyed horror. "Did you..." Miri swallowed visibly and then forced herself to go on. "Did you find it?"

"No."

There was no going back to sleep. Not after that. Desa untied the horses one by one and gently guided them away from the trees. Kalia had suggested that she be the one to perform that task, but Desa wasn't willing to put anyone else at risk. Not when the man-bat might leap out from the shadows at any moment.

Instead, Kalia and Tommy soothed each of the horses to make sure they wouldn't bolt. Midnight played a hand in that as well. Seeing one of their own standing calm and quiet had an effect on the others.

Everyone wanted to be as far away from that spot as possible, but they had to wait until they were sure the animals had settled down. Eventually, they decided to walk their horses along the beach with Desa and Marcus in front, using their rings for light.

The deep-blue of twilight crept into the eastern sky, and with it, the tightness in Desa's chest began to fade. She was beginning to think that the man-bat had lost interest in them; perhaps they weren't the sort of food that it preferred.

Then they heard it.

A terrible scratching sound like claws digging into tree bark. It came from just inside the forest. The horses started to spook, but with Midnight herding them, they stayed together.

The scratching went on for a minute or two and then ended abruptly. When it was gone, the silence that followed felt ominous. The only sound was the gentle splashing of the waves.

Desa shut her eyes, a rasping breath escaping her. "We need to find out what that was," she said. "Kalia, Marcus, you're with me."

Miri was guiding her mare by the bridle and peering

into the forest with a tight frown. "Are you sure?" she asked. "If that thing is in there…"

"If it's following us, we need to know it."

With pistols drawn and rings glowing, the three of them began their search. Once again, they found nothing amiss, but Desa was determined to know for sure; so, they probed a little deeper

Five minutes later, they came upon a fat tree with strange markings carved into its bark. A sharp, jagged script that seemed all too familiar to Desa. "Is that what I think it is?" she asked in a breathy voice.

Marcus nodded. "Ancient Aladri."

"Dalen," she said. "We need him."

The young librarian was reluctant to go with them; Desa and Marcus practically had to herd him toward the marked tree, and when he saw the characters that had been carved into its trunk, he gasped.

"What does it say?" Desa demanded.

"Um…"

"Dalen," she snapped. "What does it say?"

Scrunching his eyes tight, Dalen trembled. "It says, 'Go no further,'" he mumbled. "'Death awaits.'"

22

The rest of their journey across the Halitha passed in somber silence. Late in the afternoon on the day following their encounter with the man-bat, the forest began to curve away from the beach, veering off to the southwest. They found more grasslands, which offered many opportunities for grazing the horses. Streams and fresh-water ponds allowed them to refill their canteens; they even found citrus-fruit trees. Desa liked the oranges best, though the grapefruits were larger. How did Tommy put it? More food for less effort.

Their journey was much easier after they left the forest behind, though any vestige of the optimism she had felt was gone. There were no more evening swims, and they now had two people on watch at all times while they slept.

They never saw the man-bat again, nor any sign of its existence. Whatever, it was, it seemed to have lost interest in them. The unanswered questions were what kept Desa awake at night. What was that thing? What kind of animal could move at such speed and leave no trace of its passing? Was the creature responsible for the markings they had found on that tree? If so, it was intelligent and *aware* of who they were.

She shivered.

Three days after their encounter, the beach began to curve eastward. They had reached the northern shores of Ithanar. The maps in Dalen's books were centuries old, which meant there was every chance that they might be useless. The land might have changed considerably in all that time, and cartographers from that period were less than accurate. Nevertheless, their course was clear.

They had to travel southeast for another three hundred and fifty miles. And then, if the maps were to be believed, they would reach the edge of the Borathorin Forest. The Temple of Vengeance was supposed to be located somewhere deep within those woods.

At first, Ithanar was rather unremarkable: lush, green fields with trees dotting the landscape here and there. Not so different from southern Eradia. The days were warm and the nights muggy.

They traveled east along the coast for a few days and then veered south. A week passed without incident. The only thing that troubled Desa was that in all that time, not once did she see any signs of civilization. People *did* live in Ithanar – she was sure of it – but they seemed to stay clear of the coast.

In time, they came to the banks of the Norondra, a wide river that flowed north into the Sapphire Sea, and followed it for several days. Desa was about ready to say that there was nothing of interest in Ithanar, but then she saw something she didn't expect.

Windmills.

Several dozen of them spread out in a field about a mile west of the Norondra. And they weren't like any windmills she had ever seen before. They were taller, with blades made of some thin metal.

Tilting her head back, Desa squinted at one. She shook her head slowly. "Well," she muttered. "We were looking for signs of habitation."

Marcus was right next to her with the reins of his horse in hand, and by the look on his face, he was expecting marauders to jump out from behind any one of those towering structures. "The Synod claimed that Ithanar was populated by savages."

"The Synod was wrong about something," Desa said. "What a shock!"

"We should avoid whoever lives here."

"Or," Miri said, riding up on her gray mare. "Just a thought. Perhaps we introduce ourselves? Maybe purchase some supplies?"

"We have no currency they will take," Marcus spat.

Desa answered that with a shrug of her shoulders. "We have Field Binding," she said, urging Midnight forward with a gentle squeeze of her thighs. "You'd be surprised what people will trade for a well-crafted Infusion."

They rode through the field of windmills, ever watchful for some sign of the people who had built them. At first, there was nothing, but it wasn't long before they reached a pair of flat-top boulders with a wide gap between them. Each one was about as high as a tall man's chest, which made them the perfect spot for an ambush. Desa felt herself growing tense.

A flicker of motion caught her eye.

Someone was crouching behind the rock on her right, staying low so that only the top of his gray hood was visible. His garments were a perfect camouflage. Desa almost missed him.

She brought Midnight to a halt.

Swinging her leg over the stallion's flanks, she dropped to the ground and landed with a *thump*. "Hello there!" she said, reaching up to tip her hat to whoever was hiding back there. "Do you live nearby?"

Two men popped up from behind the boulder on her right and two more from behind the boulder on her left. Every one of them had his face hidden under a hood, and they all carried some kind of crescent-shaped device.

Desa stepped forward with her hands up in a mollifying gesture, forcing herself to smile. "Are these your lands?" she asked. "We mean no disrespect. We're just peaceful travelers passing through."

Dalen came up beside her, frowning as he studied the hooded figures. "They might not understand you," he said. "Few people on this continent speak Eradian. *Toth nadro y alla kensho.*"

"What did you say?" Desa muttered.

"A greeting in Talmahri."

One of the hooded men lifted his crescent-shaped weapon, holding it like a pistol. He pulled what appeared to be a trigger, and the device emitted a thin stream of blue lightning that rushed over the ground and struck Dalen in the chest. Sparks flashed over his body as he toppled over.

One of the others pointed his gun at Desa.

By instinct, she raised her right forearm and triggered the Electric-Sink she had Infused into a new bracelet. When the lightning came for her, it winked out a few inches away from her body.

The hooded men gasped and recoiled.

They were surprised.

Running forward, Tommy nocked an arrow, drew back his bowstring and loosed. The shaft went over the boulder on her left and landed in the grass on the other side. The two men behind that rock were suddenly shrouded in a pocket of darkness. "Now!" Tommy bellowed.

Extending his hand, Marcus pointed his gun at the other boulder. He fired once, his barrel flashing, and released a single bullet. As it passed, he pulsed a Gravity-Source that pulled the other two men off their feet.

Desa took the opportunity he had provided.

She darted through the grass, breathing hard, and ordered her belt buckle to make her weightless. In a single bound, she leaped right over the boulder, killed the Gravity-Sink and landed on the other side.

The two men that Marcus had knocked down were rising. One came at her, trying to point his weapon.

Desa surged forward, grabbed his wrist with both hands and twisted so that he was forced to drop the lightning-gun. A palm-strike to the face made his head snap backward, and he stumbled away.

The other one was right behind her.

She whirled around, extending her fist, and used her ring to shine a light into his hood. The poor fellow shut his eyes, raising his hands to shield himself.

Slipping past him, Desa kicked the side of his leg and forced him down onto his knees. Her elbow slammed into the back of his head, and that was enough to leave him face-down in the grass.

Tommy ran through the grass, bow in hand, and hissed air through his teeth. The patch of darkness was right there on the other side of the boulder, and he could hear the two men shuffling around inside it.

With a single thought, he ordered his pendant to drink

in gravitational energy. He leaped, soaring high into the air, and pulled an arrow from his quiver as he dropped into the gloom.

Tommy killed the Light-Sink.

He had landed between the two men.

Turning on his heel, Tommy nocked, drew and loosed in one smooth motion. His arrow struck one man's lightning-gun, tearing it out of his grip before he could aim.

Thrusting his right hand out behind himself, Tommy triggered the Force-Sink in his bracelet and used it to stop whatever the other one was doing. Only for an instant. Just long enough for him to turn around.

He found the second man halfway through the motion of lifting his strange pistol. The fellow blinked, confused by what must have seemed to him like an opponent who moved with inhuman speed.

Tommy kicked him in the belly, shoving the poor fool away, knocking him down onto his backside.

Someone came up behind him.

An arm wrapped itself around Tommy's throat, putting pressure on his windpipe. He was pulled tight against the hooded man's body, held firmly, unable to escape. Desa's training told him what to do.

Squeezing his eyes shut, Tommy threw his head backward and smashed the other man's nose with the back of his skull. It hurt, but it gave him the wiggle room that he desperately needed.

Crouching down, Tommy flung an elbow into his captor's stomach. His hand snapped up to smack the man's nose with the back of his fist, producing a sharp *crunch* that was followed by the thump of a body hitting the ground.

And then he was free.

Any thought of celebrating died when he looked into the

distance and saw a dozen more hooded figures coming this way. He and his friends were badly outnumbered.

Marcus ran through the gap between the boulders.

Perhaps thirty yards away, another group of hooded warriors was charging toward him, and every single one of them had one of those crescent-shaped weapons. Not good. He could tell that those guns drew upon the Ether, but the people wielding them did not seem to be Field Binders. They had displayed no other powers. Perhaps that gave Marcus an edge.

He twirled his gun around his index finger, caught the grip and then extended his hand to aim for a spot ten feet in front of the advancing platoon. He fired, and his bullet drove itself into the earth.

The instant the first hooded figure stepped over it, Marcus triggered the Force-Source that he had Infused into the metal.

The ground exploded with a spray of dirt, tossing bodies into the air. Not all of them, unfortunately. Some of the others in the back of that group crouched down and took aim with their peculiar weapons.

Raising his hand to shield himself, Marcus triggered the Electric-Sink in his ring half a second before several thin bolts of lightning came his way. It must have seemed to his enemies that he was catching every jagged, blue lance. If only they knew that his Sink had absorbed almost all that it could handle.

He raised his pistol once again.

"Don't kill them!" Desa shouted.

Vengeance burn that woman!

The hooded men were jabbering at each other,

wondering what to do now that their weapons had proved ineffective.

Marcus aimed his pistol and fired three rounds over their heads. The third was another Gravity-Source. He triggered it, and the hooded men were thrown to the ground, dragged through the grass.

They were kicking and flailing as the bullet pulled them away. Within seconds, it was too far away to do any good, but the men were still down. He could finish them all with a few well-placed shots before they recovered. But Desa wouldn't have that. No. She had to do everything the hard way.

Marcus strode forward.

"Aniaaak!"

The strange howl came from a man in a blue cloak who rose up from the tall grass a short distance away. He pulled back his cowl to reveal an olive-skinned face with a cleft chin. His short, black hair was marked by a few flecks of gray. *"Halidokh…Noral eliago vin toron shen."*

The two men on either side of Desa were still groaning, but they made no further attempts to rise. She took stock of her friends and saw that Tommy was standing by the other boulder and warily watching the pair that he had disarmed. Good for him! Her young apprentice had come a long way.

The man in blue strode forward with grim resolve on his face, his eyes fixed on Desa as if he knew that she was the leader of her group. "You wear Eradian clothing," he said. "You carry Eradian weapons, but you command powers that no Eradian has ever possessed." Kalia grumbled under her breath at that. "Who are you?"

Removing her hat, Desa held it over her chest and

bowed to the man. "I am Desa Nin Leean of Aladar," she said. "And despite what appearances might have you believe, I come in peace."

The man hissed, baring his teeth. "Aladri," he spat. By the sound of it, he would have been happier if they were Eradians. "What business do you have in our lands?"

"We have no business in your lands," Desa replied. "We are simply passing through."

"I must have an answer."

Desa set the hat back on her head and then nodded once. "And you *will* have an answer," she promised. "But first, why don't you tell me why you attacked one of my people when we did nothing to threaten you?"

"He is young; his heart is strong. The blast he took will have only stunned him."

"That doesn't answer my question."

All around her, the other hooded warriors were starting to rise. Her first thought was to reach for a weapon, but they did not seem to be making any threatening gestures. Instead, they just gathered together around their leader.

The blue-clad man studied her with a tight frown. "We do not allow Eradians on our land," he said. "Their ships have come to our shores and taken too many of our people as slaves. No one lives near the coast anymore."

"Who are you?" Marcus demanded.

"I am Rojan Von Aldono." Placing a hand over his heart in imitation of what Desa had done, he bowed to them. "And we are the *Al a Nari,* the People of Mercy."

An Aladri name?

Curious.

"Now," Rojan pressed. "Your business in our lands?"

Marcus holstered his pistol with a loud harrumph and then stepped forward to lock eyes with the other man. "Our business is our own," he growled. "Now, step aside, and we will be on our-"

"We seek the Spear of Vengeance," Desa said.

Marcus turned his glare upon her.

Rojan shuddered as if someone had just dumped a bucket of cold water over his head. "The Spear of Vengeance," he gasped. "So, the time has finally come. This must be brought before the Council. Come with me."

"But-" Desa protested.

In an instant, every one of the hooded warriors had his lightning-gun up and pointed at her. "Come with me," Rojan said again.

Well, there was no arguing with that.

THE WEAVER MATERIALIZED on the roof of a stone building and looked out on the city of Hedrovan. It was a depressing sight; wide, muddy streets were laid out in a grid pattern. No artistry. No flare. Perhaps those were Adele's sensibilities, but they mattered nonetheless.

Stepping up to the edge in a sleeveless, black dress, she frowned and shook her head. "Where are you?" She knew from what little she had pulled out of Azra that Desa and her friends had come here. Headed north to Ofalla, she assumed. But she had visited Bevington, the next city on the north-bound line, and asked anyone who would speak with her. No one had seen anyone who fit Desa's description. Nor any of her friends. It was of no consequence. The Weaver would find them eventually.

It was only a matter of time.

23

The town that the *Al a Nari* lived in was nothing short of beautiful. Small houses made of brick and, each with a large front window, looked out on a paved street lined with metal lampposts. Desa could see that every one of those lamps had an electric bulb. When Rojan caught her looking, he said, "What do you think the windmills are for?"

It was a short ride to the town square, where perhaps a dozen fruit and flower carts surrounded a fountain that was shaped like a hooded woman pouring water into the basin. Desa recognized her as well; she had seen depictions of Mercy in the *Tharan Vadria*. These people truly revered her.

From what she could tell, the *Al a Nari* were a happy bunch. Most wore colourful clothing – pants and loose-fitting shirts – and at first glance, you might have thought they were Aladri. Every man, woman and child she saw had an olive complexion with dark eyes and hair to match.

Granted, Aladar had become a more cosmopolitan city over the last two hundred years, but that change had come as a result of the Synod's decision to take in Eradian refugees. The old-stock Aladri, those who came from bloodlines that went back to the city's founding, looked very much like Desa.

The gray-stone buildings that surrounded the town square were packed close together without an inch of space between them. Through shop windows, she saw what appeared to be a seamstress making a beautiful red dress and a butcher chopping meat behind a wooden counter.

As they rounded the fountain, Desa found herself confronted by a white building with an arched entryway and a domed roof.

A few quick gestures from Rojan had the hooded warriors dispersing in all directions. Some appeared to be returning to their posts on the outskirts of the city. You never knew who might show up.

Desa and the others waited patiently.

Rojan turned to them with a warm smile. "Remain here," he said, nodding. "I will inform the Council of your presence."

He spun around and trotted up the stone steps, opening the front door and ducking into the building. Strange that he had left them alone. No matter how many dirty looks Marcus cast toward the locals, Desa would make sure that no one in her group caused any trouble. But Rojan had no way of knowing that.

Marcus stood with his horse's lead gripped tightly in one hand, his teeth gritted in defiance. Defiance of what, she could not say. "We should go," he whispered. "Leave now before they have a chance to decide what they want to do with us."

His sister was glaring daggers at his back and patting her mare's neck to keep the animal from dancing. "Brilliant," Miri said. "Let's just leave now and confirm their worst suspicions about us. Surely they won't try to chase us down."

Tommy was on the bottom step with his thumbs hooked around his belt, examining the building. "Don't know about you," he began. "But I'm of a mind to stay."

"Of course, you are," Marcus growled.

"These people obviously know a thing or two about Field Binding," Tommy went on as if the other man hadn't spoken. "Might behoove us to learn what they know."

Folding his arms over his chest, Marcus took a step forward and shook his head. "Twenty minutes ago, they were shooting at us," he grumbled. "We stay here, who's to say we don't end up in a prison cell?"

"I don't think these people are hostile," Kalia interjected.

"Perhaps not," Dalen said. "But they *are* interested in the Spear of Vengeance. Which means they might be reluctant to let us leave. I say-"

Desa held up her hand for silence.

All eyes turned on her, but she said nothing. Only a fool spoke before they knew what they wanted to say, and managing this pack of wild dogs was no task for a fool. She ran through the scenarios in her mind.

Rojan had said something about the time coming at last when she told him that they were after the Spear of Vengeance. That sounded almost prophetic. Clearly, his people were *expecting* someone to come along and take the spear. And if that was something they wanted to stop, they probably would have attacked Desa and her friends. "I think that we are safe here," Desa said.

"What makes you say that?" Marcus grumbled.

Before she had a chance to answer, the door opened, and Rojan came out of the domed building. He descended the steps two at a time with a smile on his face. "The Council is willing to see you."

"We'll need to stable our horses," Marcus said. "And-"

"Just her," Rojan clarified. He was pointing right at Desa, which made her feel more than a little uneasy. Still, she would probably have an easier time making a good impression without the others arguing and sniping at each other.

Up the stairs and through the door.

The instant she stepped into the building that housed the *Al a Nari's* governing body, she was amazed by how much it reminded her of the Hall of the Synod back in Aladar. A long hallway with a vaulted ceiling stretched on to what appeared to be some kind of reception area. There were paintings in ornate, golden frames on each wall. The only real difference was that instead of red carpets, this place had blue.

Rojan led her deeper into the building.

Desa walked through the hallway, turning her head to inspect the paintings. "Quite impressive," she said, her eyebrows climbing. "Your people have made some beautiful artwork."

One depicted a waterfall spilling over high cliffs. Another was a picture of a field of tall grass under an open sky. Reverence for Mercy was a common theme. In one painting, she was leading people along a path through the forest. Another one had her presiding over what was presumably the founding of this city.

At the end of the hallway, she found a lobby where four stone pillars supported the high ceiling. A bubbling fountain in the middle of the room sprayed water into the air. Desa noted the arch-shaped door in the back wall.

Rojan took two steps forward, then paused and looked back. "I will announce you," he said. "Wait here."

Moving quickly around the fountain, he went to the door and knocked once. It popped open just a crack, and Rojan spoke to whoever was on the other side. Desa couldn't hear what was said, and she suspected that she wouldn't understand in any event.

After a moment, Rojan turned back to her and smiled, motioning her forward. "Come! Come! They will see you!"

Desa removed her pistol from its holster, then crouched down to lay it on the floor. She took off her duster and hat as well, leaving them in a small pile. In gray pants and a sleeveless shirt, she stood up to accept his invitation.

Rojan observed her with a raised eyebrow.

Grinning bashfully, Desa felt a burning in her cheeks. She bowed her head in respect. "Best not to greet a head of state with deadly weapons on your person," she explained. "And removing one's hat is just custom."

She strode across the lobby.

She wasn't sure what she would find on the other side of that door; part of her expected a windowless room where lights shone down on hooded figures, but the truth was far more mundane.

It was just a simple room with a long, wooden table.

Oh, the walls were painted with stunning murals of farmers reaping barley or small children dancing or people sharing a meal together. The carpet was thick under her feet, and a skylight provided ample illumination. But all in all, it was just a room with a table.

The eight people who sat behind that table all wore blue. That colour seemed to denote authority among the *Al a Nari*. Four men and four women. Just like the Synod. Curious. Did these people have a Prelate as well?

The eldest of the women – a matron with a round face

and curly, gray hair that she wore tied back – stood up and greeted Desa with a smile. *"Tanael. Shaoh Vandra Nin Salaya."*

"She is Vandra Nin Salaya," Rojan translated.

"Ni shaka tasso Te'Alon."

"She bids you welcome to Te'Alon."

Unsure of what to do, Desa dropped to one knee and kept her eyes on the floor. "I thank you for your kindness and hospitality," she said. "Your city is remarkable."

"You may rise, young one," Vandra said.

Shocked to her core, Desa looked up and blinked. "You…"

The old woman stood on the other side of the table with her hands clasped in front of herself, her head bowed as if she were the one who was expected to show deference. "Yes," Vandra went on. "I know your language."

"Well, it's good to meet you," Desa said. "I take it Rojan told you why we are passing through your lands."

"You seek the Spear of Vengeance."

"Are you willing to help us in that endeavour?"

Vandra sat down, folding her hands on the table. It was clear to Desa that she was deep in thought. The other councilors were all exchanging glances. Did they all speak Eradian? "Well," Vandra replied at last. "That depends."

"On what, if I may ask?"

"Whom do you serve? Mercy or Vengeance?"

Desa opened her mouth and then snapped it shut again. How was she supposed to answer *that?* Obviously, the other woman wanted her to say Mercy, but why would a servant of Mercy be searching for the Spear of Vengeance? "I serve humanity," Desa said.

"And how will humanity be served by your possessing the Spear of Vengeance?"

"Hanak Tuvar has returned." Several councilors gasped,

and one of them actually shivered. They may not have all understood Desa, but they knew that phrase. That much was certain. "I tried to prevent it, but I failed. The legends say that the spear is the only thing that can defeat *Hanak Tuvar*."

Vandra regarded her until the silence became awkward. Desa felt very much like a worm that had caught the attention of a hungry bird. "One more thing remains," the other woman said at last.

Desa was about to ask for clarification when she felt the Ether surging within Vandra. The other councilors reached for it as well, and within seconds, all eight of them were wrapped in Ether's embrace.

Were they watching her? Was this a test of some kind? Desa wasn't sure what they expected to see except the particles that made up her body. Should she embrace the Ether as well? Its siren song called to her, whispering in the back of her mind.

She gave in to that temptation and found herself confronted by eight human bodies that radiated light. Only then did it occur to her that every one of these councilors knew how to commune with the Ether. Could they all Field Bind as well? That was one thing that set them apart from their Aladri counterparts. When last she had checked, only two members of the Synod could craft Infusions.

One by one, the lights that emanated from each councilor went out. Desa severed contact with the Ether as well.

Vandra opened her eyes, and a warm smile grew on her face. "You *do* serve Mercy," she said. "We will tell you all that we know."

Desa breathed a sigh of relief and then nodded slowly in thanks. "I'm very grateful for that," she replied. "When do we begin?"

"First, you must rest," Vandra said in a tone that made it clear she would suffer no arguments on this point. "Your people have traveled a long way, and you are tired. We will prepare a banquet in your honour."

THE *AL A NARI,* it seemed, could be quite generous once they decided that they liked you. They had given Desa and her friends rooms at a small hostel that they used to house visitors from neighbouring towns, which brought to mind a whole new set of questions. Neighbouring towns? Until today, Desa had seen no signs of civilization anywhere on this continent. She had thought that this was just a remote settlement, but apparently, the *Al a Nari* were spread throughout this region. They just stayed far away from the coast.

The room that she shared with Miri and Kalia was cheerful with bright, yellow walls. Electric lights provided plenty of illumination, and the window looked out on a small garden where daisies grew. There were two sets of bunk beds and wooden cabinets to store their things.

Their hosts had been most generous. Desa tried to refuse the garments that she was offered, but there was just no arguing with these people. She had very little room in her saddlebags as it was; she couldn't possibly take anything more than what she absolutely needed. Still, it was nice to wear clean clothes.

Evening had come when she emerged from the hostel in a thin, white dress with short sleeves. She would have preferred a good pair of trousers, but the *Al a Nari* woman who had taken her clothes to be laundered insisted that she would want to wear something nice to dinner.

She found Kalia standing in the garden in a sleeveless,

blue dress with a skirt that flared. The sheriff's long hair was tied up in a braid, and she smelled faintly of perfume. One look at her, and Desa gasped.

When Kalia turned around, she was wearing a smile that could light up a moonless night. "Hello there," she said.

Before she could get one more word out, Desa rushed forward, seized the woman's face with both hands and kissed her hard on the lips. It lasted for only a few seconds – she knew that – but the moment seemed to linger as if time itself had slowed down. "You are so beautiful," she panted when they finally broke contact.

"So are you," Kalia whispered.

The sound of Marcus clearing his throat startled her – leave it to a man to ruin a tender moment – and Desa forced herself to step out of her lover's embrace. The very last thing she wanted was to endure one of Marcus's disapproving stares.

He now wore gray pants and a white, button-up shirt with an open collar. His hat was gone, exposing dark hair that he wore in a short ponytail. "Perhaps," he began, "such open displays of affection should be avoided until we are certain that they will not offend local sensibilities."

Kalia stuck out her tongue.

Desa wanted to kiss her again.

Tommy was in similar garments when he came through the door. Of course, he was blushing as though he had been given an honour that he didn't deserve.

"You look very handsome," Desa told him.

"I feel foolish."

Approaching him with her arms crossed, Desa smiled and shook her head. "I would imagine that is a common occurrence," she said. "For a man."

Tommy looked up to meet her gaze and then narrowed

his eyes. His face softened after only a second, and he broke out laughing. "Shut up!"

"Perhaps," Marcus said, "we shouldn't keep our hosts waiting."

"Shut up!" they all said in unison.

With a soft sigh, Dalen stepped out into the open and then braced a hand against the side of the building. He still looked a little woozy. The jolt he had taken had only left him unconscious for about ten minutes, but it was still hard on the human body.

"Are you all right?" Desa asked.

He nodded.

Miri was the last to appear, and Desa had to admit that she was quite breathtaking in her short, yellow dress. She smiled when Tommy and Dalen both murmured their approval and made a passable curtsy.

The walk to the banquet hall took them along paved streets with more of the small houses they had seen earlier. There was also a large, square building with rectangular windows. Desa assumed that it was a school. She saw what looked like a bookkeeper's office on a nearby street corner; so, that confirmed that these people did use some form of currency. They were just very generous.

When she peered into the front window of a bookshop, she saw dozens and dozens of cloth-bound books on the wooden shelves. What she wouldn't give to read some of those! Granted, they were probably written in a language that she couldn't understand, but Dalen might be able to translate. Any one of those texts might give her some insight into the history of the *Al a Nari*.

The banquet hall was another white building with a domed roof, though it was notably smaller than the one that the Council used. At least fifty people were gathered together in front, all chatting with one another. They went silent as soon as Desa and her friends arrived.

Rojan stepped forward, now dressed in a flowing, blue robe. He placed a hand over his heart and bowed to Desa. "You are welcome here, friend."

"Thank you," Desa said.

"I'm told that dinner will be another hour or so," he said. "But the cooks do good work on short notice."

That gave Desa some time to mingle with the townsfolk. The first man she met was a clerk in the Council Building. Dalen had to translate most of what the poor fellow said, but it seemed that his job was to monitor local agriculture. There were several dozen farms within two days' ride of the village, most spread out to the south and west. A few were nestled against the banks of the Norondra.

It was hard to get much in the way of details – the *Al a Nari* could be remarkably tight-lipped – but what little she could learn painted a picture that was very different from what years of Eradian prejudice had led her to believe about Ithanar. There were as many as twenty *Al a Nari* cities of varying size spread across this region of the continent. This one, which the locals called Te'Alon, was just the northernmost outpost.

They were a peaceful society that harnessed the energies of wind and water along with the power of Field Binding. Some of the larger settlements even had small vehicles that were quite similar to cars, except these were powered by electricity. Desa would be very interested to learn how they did that.

In time, when the sun was sinking and the sky was a deep, twilight-blue, they were ushered into a large room with round tables covered in white, linen tablecloths. The eight members of the Council were waiting for them there.

Dinner consisted of goat meat in a tangy sauce along with fresh vegetables. Broccoli, carrots and peppers. It was quite good, but after three weeks on the road, Desa would praise any food that she didn't have to cook with a Heat-Source.

As the meal drew to a close, Vandra stood up at the head table with a glass of wine in hand. She smiled as she looked out on the assembled guests. And then she began a speech in Talmahri.

Dalen was kind enough to translate.

"Dear friends. Our forebearers knew, when Mercy brought us to these lands, that one day our distant cousins would return and claim the legacy of Vengeance. We have been taught to fear and hope for this day. Those who claim the spear must do so with pure hearts. In the hands of one who serves Mercy, it will be a light to lead all people out of darkness. But in the hands of one who serves Vengeance, it will bring the ruination of humankind."

Desa felt a chill as she listened. What was all this about? Rojan had indicated that the Spear of Vengeance featured prominently in *Al a Nari* folklore, but this almost made it sound as if taking the weapon would usher in the End Times. For the first time since leaving Aladar, she wondered if this quest was a good idea.

As opposed to the alternative?

Without the spear, she couldn't think of a way to stop Adele. And if Adele wasn't a harbinger of the End Times, she didn't know what was.

"We welcome our guests," Vandra went on. "True servants of Mercy. Tomorrow, they will set out for the Borathorin Forest and meet their destiny. We will give them as much food as we can spare, and some of our best soldiers will travel with them for a time to see them to the borders of the forest."

Kalia was staring into her wine glass with her lips pressed together in a thoughtful frown. "Now, why don't I like the sound of that?" she muttered.

Desa wasn't thrilled about it either.

All eight members of the Council stood up along with a gray-bearded man that Desa could only assume was the *Al a Nari* equivalent of a Prelate. What *was* this about? Did the *Al a Nari* want to take the spear for themselves?

That didn't fit with what she had seen of their temperament.

"Tonight!" Vandra exclaimed. "We celebrate!"

Musicians began to play string instruments that Desa had never seen before. One was almost like a cello but with five strings instead of four. Another was almost like a violin, but the sound it produced was ever so slightly different.

When the music started, the assembled guests rose from their tables and began dancing. Desa had no intention of joining in. She had never learned how to dance as a young woman, and ten years in the wild had not provided her with an opportunity to rectify that situation.

Kalia, however, was more than happy to take part. She grabbed Desa's hand and practically pulled her onto the dance floor. Any misgivings she might have had seemed to have melted away.

Desa would not have expected someone who grew up in the desert to be so skilled on her feet, but the sheriff danced with all the grace of an Ofallan aristocrat. At first, they kept to the basic forms – Desa was terrified of stepping on the other woman's toes – but it wasn't long before Kalia started twirling in ways that made her skirts flare out.

Those guests who had remained seated watched them

with a keen interest and clapped whenever Kalia did something fancy. They seemed to have no objection to seeing two women together; in fact, as Desa scanned the crowd, she saw a pair of men sitting in the back who held each other's hands.

Miri took a turn with Tommy and then one with Dalen. Both young men nearly tripped over their own feet, though Dalen seemed to enjoy it with casual confidence while Tommy got flustered. At one point, Desa suggested that the two boys share a dance, but neither one was interested in that idea. It wasn't fear of judgement, they assured her when she gestured to the pair of men she had seen earlier. Those two were now swaying to the music and gazing into each other's eyes. No, it wasn't fear of what the *Al a Nari* might think if they saw Tommy and Dalen together. Rather, her young apprentice and his would-be lover were afraid that they might make fools of themselves. Desa resisted the urge to tell them that it was a little too late to be worrying about that.

Still, it was a pleasant evening. She had never really been to a banquet before, and she was glad that she could experience it for the first time with Kalia at her side.

She was just starting to relax when something caught her eye.

A hooded figure stood on the far side of the dancefloor, watching her with malicious intent. No one else seemed to notice it. Several people walked right by it without a second glance. It lingered for only a moment and then vanished.

Desa shivered.

Their trip across the Halitha had given her a reprieve. She had not seen the creature even once during the journey. Maybe that was because other threats were lurking on that stretch of land. Maybe those supernatural creatures respected each other's territory. Whatever the reason, her reprieve was over.

The ghost was back.

As the evening wore on, Miri found herself standing on the small patio outside the banquet hall, listening to the wind sighing as it passed through the branches of nearby trees. The streetlamps were all glowing bright and she could see what looked like a park across the way.

For the hundredth time since leaving Aladar, she wondered why she had come along on this journey. Which was silly. She came because she wanted to help; she knew that. The real question was what could she possibly contribute to this mission?

She wasn't a Field Binder like her brother or Desa or Kalia. Dalen also lacked that particular talent, but he had demonstrated his worth by translating the *Al a Nari's* language. No doubt those skills would prove valuable when they reached the Temple of Vengeance.

So, why was Miri Nin Valia here?

Not so long ago, she would have insisted that Tommy needed her protection, but that was no longer the case. And she had no reason to think that he wanted her protection. Not anymore. Her superiors back home might be interested to know about the *Al a Nari*, but the Ka'adri existed to protect Aladar from threats. And these people hardly qualified. If Adele showed up, it was highly unlikely that a well-placed throwing knife would do her in. Miri had nothing to offer the others. She was just...luggage.

Her ears perked up at the soft scuff of footsteps.

Turning around brought her face to face with Tommy and Dalen. The two of them might have been twins, both standing there and refusing to look at her, though Tommy couldn't take his eyes off his shoes and Dalen was fascinated by the plants in the garden.

"Yes?" she said.

"We have a problem," Dalen muttered.

Miri held his gaze just long enough to make him squirm and then nodded slowly. "I daresay we do," she agreed. "I have developed feelings for both of you."

"And I feel the same," Dalen insisted.

Tommy blinked as if this were all news to him – more fool him; he should have been able to see what was happening right under his nose – and then a strange look came over his face. Miri recognized that vacant stare. Her Tommy was working something out in his head.

Dalen backed away with his hands in his pockets, shutting his eyes tight and taking a deep breath through his nose. "Well, then it seems we're in a bit of a quandary," he said softly. "Perhaps it would be best if we all gave each other a wide-"

"Hold on," Tommy cut in. "What's the problem?"

"I should think it would be obvious," Dalen replied.

"No, think about it!" Tommy insisted. He turned to Dalen. "You like her, and you like me." And then to Miri. "And you're smitten with both of us. And I'm smitten with both of you...Why should any of us have to choose? Why don't we just...*be* together? All three of us."

Miri closed her eyes as she thought it over, exhaling through her nose. "Isn't that a bit...unorthodox?" she asked. "I would imagine that it conflicts with the values you were raised with, Lommy."

His only response to that was a shrug. "I've pursued a relationship with another man," Tommy said. "I've practiced 'witchcraft.' Or at least, that's what my people would say if they knew. If you were to ask the reverend back home, he would tell you that my soul is already damned three times over. May as well have a little fun on my way to the Abyss."

Miri paused to consider it.

"Come on," Tommy pressed. "Surely a goddess like you wouldn't object to having *two* men showering her with the love and attention that she deserves."

Hearing that put a smile on Miri's face. "You make a *very* compelling argument."

"He does indeed," Dalen agreed.

Miri took both of them by the hand and pulled them toward the street. "Come on, boys!" she said. "This party's over, and I can think of several ways that we can have a lot more fun!"

24

After many long days of riding, Desa found herself at the western edge of the Borathorin Forest. Trees unlike any that she had ever seen before ran north and south to the distant horizon: trees with broad, flat green leaves. There were a few palms in there, but much of the flora was strange to her.

Rojan and a dozen of his best people had come with them from Te'Alon. Together, they traveled south and east in a caravan, making their way toward the very heart of Ithanar. Ten long days in the saddle, living off the food the *Al a Nari* had provided. Their route had taken them close enough to the city of Ludinata to resupply, but they still had to ration their food carefully. At least there was plenty of grass for the horses.

Yes, plenty of grass.

Somedays, that was all they saw: rolling, green hills under blue skies with fat clouds or soggy fields that had been drenched by persistent rainfall. Once or twice, they crossed over a river – and there was that day they spent traversing a patch of woodland – but for the most part, it was grass.

Desa was almost relieved when the Borathorin finally came into view; then she had a chance to contemplate the enormity of that forest. Even from a distant hilltop, she could see that it was bigger than she could have possibly imagined. A woman could get lost in there and wander aimlessly until she starved.

Desa sat in Midnight's saddle with the reins in hand, chewing her lip as she stared up at the treetops. "Well," she whispered. "You *did* say it was big."

Rojan was beside her on a white gelding who flicked his ear. The man had pulled back his blue hood, and his face had lost some of its colour. "Yes," he murmured. "I did."

His warnings aside, it was clear that Rojan had not understood just how huge the forest was until he saw it with his own eyes. Old maps and logbooks from long-dead explorers were one thing; actually being here was quite another.

Marcus rode up on her other side, glancing over his shoulder to sneer at her. "Well," he said, jerking his head toward the treeline. "Our destiny awaits."

Death awaits.

The words that had been carved into the tree on the Halitha were suddenly there in Desa's mind. She had a sinking feeling that this was what they had been referring to. But how could the man-bat have known where they were going? Assuming, of course, that it had been the one who carved those symbols into the tree.

Closing her eyes, Desa took a deep breath and then nodded. "We should be on our way," she agreed in a tight voice. "The sooner we find that spear, the sooner we can be away from this place."

"You will not be able to take your horses in there," Rojan

said. "The forest is too dense. The animals can remain here with us. We will see to it that they are cared for."

"You're not coming with us?"

Rojan shook his head. "This challenge is not ours to undertake." He slid out of the saddle to land in the grass with a grunt. "My people and I will remain here as long as we can. If you survive this journey, you will need food and water. Your horses will be safe with us. Remember the dangers I warned you about. If you should encounter any brightly-coloured frogs-"

"Avoid them," Desa said, dropping out of Midnight's saddle. She pulled her poncho a little tighter despite the heat. "Some excrete a compound that will cause us to hallucinate. Others carry a deadly toxin."

"Snakes with red and black scales-"

"Are highly venomous," Marcus growled. He was stomping toward the trees with his head down, his eyes shaded by the brim of his hat. "However, most will not bite unless directly threatened."

With his horse's lead gripped tightly in one hand, Rojan studied them both. "Those are the dangers that you will encounter in the outermost layer," he explained. "What you will find beyond that, I cannot say. Borathorin means 'realm of the dead' in the language of our ancestors. It is said that those who go too deeply into this forest never return."

Well, Desa had heard much the same about Ithanar, but so far, the continent had failed to live up to its reputation. Nevertheless, the man-bat's warning was gnawing at her. Something about this place just felt...wrong.

They put up as much food and water as they could carry into knapsacks and canteens and began the final leg of their journey. Marcus took the lead, as he so often did, and Miri was right behind him. Tommy and Dalen followed her while Desa and Kalia brought up the rear.

At first, their trek was more of a nuisance than anything else. Muddy paths ran through the gaps between trees with branches that hung so low even Desa had to stoop to get under them. How Marcus managed it was beyond her. Roots popped out of the ground everywhere she looked, and the constant chittering of insects annoyed her.

The air was so hot and sticky that Desa was forced to remove her poncho. At one point, she found Marcus resting with his hand on a tree trunk, his head hanging as he tried to catch his breath. The man's shirt was soaked with sweat.

Tommy had undone his top two buttons, but his face still glistened. "Forgive my impertinence," he began, "but do we have any idea how long it will take us to reach this temple?"

Dalen was leaning against a tree and gazing up at the sky with anxiety clearly visible on his face. "The annotations of Carn Von Tomlin were quite clear," he said. "The Temple of Vengeance is hidden within this forest. But it will take us several days to reach it."

On the other side of the narrow path, Marcus was caressing the grip of his pistol and hissing. "Several days!" he snapped. "Have you seen how large this place is? What if we're twenty miles too far north or twenty too far south? We could wander for months and *never* find the temple."

"It doesn't work that way," Dalen panted. "The *Vadir Scrolls* are very clear on this point. All paths in the Borathorin inevitably lead to the temple. Geometry here is... folded somehow."

"Folded?"

Raising his hands defensively, Dalen shook his head. "Don't ask me to explain it," he said. "I know only what the scrolls say. Mercy wanted to give humankind knowledge, but Vengeance insisted on making sure that we earn it. The forest is a test of will. Those who survive it reap the reward."

"And those who prove unworthy?" Miri inquired.

"Are cursed to wander these woods forever."

Kalia was fanning herself with her straw hat. The look she gave Dalen called him an idiot. "Glorious," she said. "Thank you for informing us *before* we entered the crazy goddess's death trap."

"We're in it now," Dalen said. "There is no going back. If you try, well...You probably won't like the result."

"Well, that's just brilliant."

Desa held up a hand for silence, and every one of them clamped their mouth shut. Five sets of eyes turned upon her, all waiting for some little nugget of wisdom that would give them the courage to press on. She had none to give. The simple truth would have to suffice. "We all knew there was a good chance we wouldn't be coming back from this mission," she said. "Nothing has changed. We carry on. It seems to me that Vengeance is the kind of goddess who loathes cowardice. So, standing around and complaining strikes me as a very bad idea."

With that, they were on their way again.

The hours passed as the sun rose to its zenith and then began to sink again. The terrain became rougher with steeper hills, bigger ditches and more roots sticking up out of the ground. More than once, they had to wade through ankle-deep puddles.

Perhaps it was Desa's imagination, but the trees almost seemed to crowd in on her. The gaps between them were narrower, the branches barring her path thicker. A test of will indeed!

She saw some of the frogs that Rojan had mentioned

when they skirted around the edge of a pond. Blue frogs with black spots, red frogs with white stripes. They were quite beautiful, actually, but that didn't stop Desa from staying well out of leaping distance. One touch could be lethal from some breeds, and she wasn't sure she remembered which were which.

Marcus began hacking at some of the low-hanging vines and branches with a short sword he had gotten from one of the *Al a Nari* rangers. It was called a machete. Every time he did, the forest seemed to groan.

Rays of golden sunlight were slanting in from the west when they finally chose a spot to camp overnight. Darkness would soon be upon them; they could go no further today. There was too much of a chance that someone might trip over a root and break a bone or step into a bog and run afoul of one of those frogs. Even Light-Sources couldn't eliminate that danger.

Kalia used an Infused coin for illumination while they ate a light dinner of juicy cantaloupe and pork jerky. The fruit helped to alleviate some of the saltiness. They were rationing their water as much as possible. The odds of finding anything that was safe to drink in this place were... not good.

Desa went to sleep with Kalia's head on her chest, gently stroking the other woman's hair.

THE NEXT MORNING, they were on their way again, splashing through brown puddles, scrambling over roots and rocks, ducking under branches that tried to swat them in the face. One thing Desa could say for this forest: it was lush and green. Full of life. That was why she felt so uneasy when she saw a dead tree standing next to the path.

That shouldn't have bothered her. Trees died all the time, didn't they? But something about it just felt...off.

She couldn't say what species it was; every leaf had been stripped away long ago. Its bark was now a dull, grayish-brown, and rotting branches hung off its carcass. Some looked like they were ready to snap and fall on anyone who got too close. Needless to say, they carefully maneuvered around *that* obstacle.

The sight of it left them feeling dismayed. For a while, they walked in silence, but it wasn't long before Dalen started chattering about his books while Miri made playful comments and Tommy laughed. Desa was glad to see that those three had found a kind of equilibrium.

Five minutes later, Marcus called a halt. It seemed they had encountered yet another obstacle. "Another pond," he said. "Looks big."

"Let me have a look," Desa muttered.

Stooping low, she ducked under a branch. The twigs left scratches on her back, and she cursed when she finally had enough room to stand up straight. Marcus wasn't lying; the pond *was* big.

Silver rays of sunlight streaked through the treetops and shimmered on the surface of the brown water. It looked as if it might be a mile long; they would have to go around. Trying to go through was out of the question. Not with all the frogs...

Desa froze.

Where were the frogs?

The last pond had been teeming with life. But this one? No turtles. No snakes. Come to think of it, she no longer heard the buzzing of insects. When had that happened? Desa had been ignoring the constant background noise since yesterday morning. At some point, it had just stopped, and she had failed to notice.

When she turned, Marcus was standing under a tree branch and frowning at the surface of the water. She could see it in his face. He knew that something was amiss. "We'll have to go around," he said again.

"Come on."

They followed the edge of the pond with considerable difficulty. There was no simple path they could follow. Instead, they shuffled around trees. The soft, slippery mud under their boots made it hard to find good footing. But that wasn't the worst of it.

Desa saw another dead tree, and then another, each in the same atrocious state as that first one. She had to hold onto one for support, and the branch she grabbed snapped right off. If not for Dalen catching her, she would have fallen flat on her face.

The sun was almost at its peak by the time they made their way around the pond. Desa was feeling nervous, but there was nothing to do but press on. All roads led to the temple, or so the legend said.

Thankfully, they found a clear path and followed it up a shallow hill. Everything looked normal, but Desa was painfully aware of the silence. No birds, no crickets. By the Eyes of Vengeance! A forest was supposed to make noise!

They hadn't been on the path five minutes when she spotted another dead tree. Ten minutes after that, the dead ones began to outnumber the living. "We should turn back," Dalen said behind her.

Miri paused, twisting around to face him with a scowl that ought to have frightened him more than the rotting forest. "But you said-"

"I know what I said!" Dalen snapped. "I was wrong. This is the wrong way. We should turn back!"

Squeezing her eyes shut. Desa trembled as she stuffed the irritation down into the pit of her stomach. "We're not turning back!" she growled. "This is a test, remember? I have no intention of failing!"

That earned her a few blessed minutes of silence. Just a few. Dalen decided to pipe up again when it became clear that the situation was growing dire. "Look around you!" he said. "This can't be the right way!" Desa didn't have to look; she knew what she would find.

They were surrounded by death.

All around them, withered, gray husks reached for a cloudless, blue sky. Every branch was bare. Every last one. Without the leaves overhead, there was nothing to shield them from the heat. Desa's eyes smarted. After a day in the shade, she wasn't used to such bright light.

If any animal had ever lived here, no sign of it remained. There should have been dried leaves strewn about on the mucky ground, but those were gone too. As if this forest had been left to rot for centuries.

Death awaits.

The man-bat's warning made perfect sense to her now. This place was a graveyard, and if she wasn't careful, her bones would spend eternity wasting away here. "We should turn back," Dalen said.

Licking her lips. Desa nodded slowly. "Perhaps you're right," she whispered. "But first let's get a sense of just how far this phenomenon extends. Maybe, in a couple miles, we'll find living trees again."

She triggered the Gravity-Sink in her belt buckle, making herself weightless. Then she bent her knees and jumped, shooting up into the air with incredible speed.

A branch loomed overhead.

Desa grabbed it with both hands, pulled herself up and perched upon it. She still had about a hundred feet to go before she reached the treetops, but a queasy feeling was already settling into her belly.

The branch might have broken under the weight of a full-grown woman, but without gravity, it held. That was until Desa jumped off of it; then it snapped and plummeted to the earth below. "Get clear!" she screamed.

Her leap propelled her higher and higher until she was soaring through the open air, floating above the forest. Her worst fears were confirmed then.

An ocean of dead trees expanded in every direction, to every horizon. Endless, unbroken death as far as the eye could see. There was no temple anywhere in that mess, but that wasn't what concerned her.

Less than half an hour ago, they had been making their way around the pond, and there had been plenty of living vegetation then. They couldn't have traveled more than a mile since. Not in a dense woodland like this. She should have seen green leaves nearby, but there were none.

In fact, at this height, she should have been able to see the borders of the forest. But there were no borders. It went on forever. No way out.

She lessened her belt buckle's hold on gravity just enough to let herself float gracefully down to the ground. When she landed, the others were all waiting for her. No wanted to be the first to ask, but they all wanted to know.

Desa shut her eyes and shook her head. "There's no getting out of here," she said. "The forest goes on forever."

Pale-faced and shivering, Tommy stood before her with his mouth working soundlessly. "What do you mean?" he finally asked, jerking his thumb back over his shoulder.

"There were living trees back that way. We walk for ten minutes, and we should be able to find them."

"They're gone."

"How can they be gone? We *just* saw them."

Dalen stepped forward to put a hand on Tommy's arm. "Geometry is folded here, remember?" he said. "We aren't getting out unless the forest allows it."

Miri was shifting her weight from one foot to the other, clutching a knife in one hand. "What do we do?" she mumbled. "If this place is cursed like they say…I don't want to die here."

"We go forward," Desa declared. "This is a test, remember? Let's pass it and get what we came here for."

She could tell that her words had failed to inspire the others, but they still followed when she started down the path in the same direction they had been going earlier. And why not? If the forest went on forever, forward was as good as backward.

The hours wore on with nothing but dried-up branches crunching underfoot and oppressive heat beaming down from above. Desa hoped to see some change in the landscape – some indication that they were making progress – but they might have been going in circles for all that she could tell.

The sun began to sink behind them, which meant that they were still heading east. But they came no closer to the temple. If there was a temple. Perhaps that was the lie. It was a thought that she did not want to entertain, but Desa had to acknowledge the possibility that this was all an elaborate trap to lure in unwary treasure hunters. How many of the legends surrounding Ithanar traced their origins to this place?

Go no further. Death awaits.

Had the man-bat been trying to warn them? If so, why had it begun by terrorizing them? Desa forced herself to stop thinking about it. If there was an intelligence behind those fierce, green eyes, it was utterly inhuman.

Still, she couldn't let the others see her growing doubt. Dalen said this was a test of will. If so, maybe the best way to pass was to carry on in spite of adversity. It was quite the gamble, but what did they have to lose? Turning back would do them no good.

When evening came, they made camp in a small glade, surrounded by the corpses of trees that stood nearly two hundred feet tall. She and Tommy both Infused coins with fresh connections to the Ether, giving each one a physical trigger so that anyone could activate them. They made two for each member of their group and handed them out. In a place like this, keeping the darkness at bay was crucial.

The last traces of blue were fading from the sky as she curled up in her bedroll. A glowing coin in the middle of the glade cast a soft, steady light that allowed her to see all of her friends. Most of them were settling down to sleep.

Tommy, who had taken first watch, sat on a log with his knees apart and watched the coin. Desa could sense his fear – and she wanted to say something – but words failed her. She was responsible for bringing him along on this fool's errand. If Tommy died here, it would be her fault. And the same was true for Kalia and the others.

Just as she was about to close her eyes, she noticed a hooded figure standing in the shadows, almost beyond the range of Tommy's light. Of course, the ghost would follow her here. When it noticed her looking, it stretched a hand out toward her as if...as if it were trying to beckon her. And then it vanished.

There was no longer any doubt about it: they were all

going to die here. With those unpleasant thoughts plaguing her, she fell into a fitful sleep.

When she woke up, dawn had come, and a thick ceiling of gray clouds filled the sky. The air was colder than it should have been. Cold and damp like a morning in late autumn, which made no sense. She was in the middle of a tropical rainforest; surely, the temperature couldn't have dropped that quickly. Under other circumstances, Desa would have been very concerned. But at the moment, she had bigger problems.

Her friends were gone. As were their bedrolls and their supplies and the coin that Tommy had left in the middle of the glade.

She was completely alone.

25

So far as Desa could tell, she was in the same place where she had gone to sleep. But her friends were gone. Quickly, she ran through a list of scenarios in her head. Even in her most cynical moments, she wasn't capable of believing that they would just sneak off and leave her behind. That only left one possibility: Something had taken them. But why had it left Desa behind?

She stood up with some effort.

Blinking slowly, Desa turned her head to examine her surroundings. "Hello?" she called out to anyone who might be listening. "Kalia? Tommy? Marcus?"

A skittering sound behind her made her jump.

She spun around and found...nothing but dead trees. That noise must have been the scampering of a small animal, but there were none nearby. Sweet Mercy, it was cold! Not quite freezing, but definitely chilly.

Desa crouched down next to her meager possessions and began folding up her bedroll. Instinctively, she checked her pistol and breathed a soft sigh of relief when she realized that it was still in its holster.

She packed her things into her knapsack, slung that over her shoulders and began a long trek through the woods. There was nothing to do but go forward. If she died here, well…At least she had tried.

Distant laughter made the hair stand on the back of her neck.

Drawing her pistol, Desa cocked the hammer and turned in a tight circle, swinging the gun back and forth. Once again, there was nothing that she could call a viable target – just rotting trees all around her – but there was no mistaking it this time. That had been an old woman's cackle.

Clenching her teeth, Desa seethed with rage and frustration. "Whoever you are," she barked. "This game no longer amuses. Show yourself!"

No one answered her.

Carefully, she crept down a gentle slope to a muddy stream about a foot wide. She paused there, searching for some indication of where she ought to go next. The clouds overhead seemed even darker than before.

Desa hopped over the stream and continued on her way with her gun in hand. She didn't dare go unarmed. Not in this place.

Her boots sank into the soft ground with every step, and pulling them free required some effort. A damp breeze cut right through her shirt and ripped the warmth from her body. She thought about taking the poncho out of her knapsack, but such garments could be restrictive, and she wanted to be able to line up a clean shot in the blink of an eye.

Step by step, she climbed to the top of a small hill only to discover…more of the same. Why should she have expected anything different? The forest was endless.

"Desa…" someone cooed behind her.

She whirled around.

There was no one there, of course, but now she knew that she wasn't alone. "Desa," the voice called again, louder than before. And somehow, it was still coming from behind her. Enough of this! If something was pursuing her, she would let it catch up.

And then she would teach it some manners.

Tommy woke up in the glade to find himself alone. It was morning, but clouds blotted out the sun, and the air was dreadfully cold. He scanned the campsite and saw no sign of his friends. Even their things were gone, but somehow, his remained. The coin that he had left glowing when Miri relieved him was still there, but it was burnt out now.

Tommy shut his eyes, breathing deeply, and focused his mind. He reached for the Ether, slipping into the exercises that Desa had taught him. One, two, three, four, five. One, two three, four, five. It came to him with a little effort, but something was off. The Ether was agitated in some way. As if it were recoiling from a wrongness that surrounded him.

Everything else looked as it should; the trees and the air and the ground beneath him were all clusters of molecules. He Infused the coin with a fresh connection to the Ether. He didn't bother giving it a physical trigger. If he was going to be the one using it, a thought would do.

When he was finished, he took a moment to check his bowstring. There was no telling what he might find in here. He wanted to be ready.

That done, he gathered his belongings – coat, coins, bow and quiver – and set off in the same direction he had been going yesterday. East, or so he hoped.

Five minutes of plodding along brought him to a gentle slope that he descended with care. At the base of the hill, he came across a narrow stream of muddy water. It couldn't have been more than a foot wide. Easy to hop over, which, he did.

"Tommy..."

He flinched at the sound of his name and frantically pulled an arrow from his quiver. In a second, he had it nocked and drawn. But there was nothing to shoot.

"I'm here, Tommy."

Shutting his eyes tight, he trembled as the rage welled up inside of him. He knew that voice all too well. He would never forget that voice. "Radavan!" he hissed.

When he turned around, the dead man was standing there in his flowing, yellow robes, looking much as he had in life. "Hello, Tommy," he said. "I thought we should chat."

Miri had been wandering through the woods for hours, long enough to witness the dawn and the gray sky that it revealed. Something had changed – that much was certain – and she had been the only one awake to witness it.

It had happened about an hour after she relieved Tommy and took her turn at watch. She had been sitting on a fallen log, peering out into the darkness. Even with the glowing coin behind her, it was hard to see anything specific. Nevertheless, the light it cast was a comfort to her. Marcus had complained that it would be hard to sleep, but a watchwoman who couldn't see was useless. And in this place, safety took precedence over anything else.

The night passed without incident until she heard something skittering through the trees behind her. A rodent, she suspected. Normally, that wouldn't have bothered her, but this place was supposed to be devoid of life.

Yanking her gun out of its holster, Miri stood up. She

cocked the hammer and then silently maneuvered around the tree at the edge of their campsite. She found no sign of an animal, but the instant she stepped outside the glade, everything changed.

The air dropped in temperature, and the light from the coin went out, leaving her stranded in the pitch-black of a starless night. She fished the penny that Tommy had given her out of her pocket and ran her thumb along its surface to make it glow.

When she returned to the glade, the others were gone. Even their belongings were missing, although Miri's bedroll and knapsack remained. The first coin had vanished as well, which explained the sudden darkness.

What could have taken them?

First, she searched the immediate area, and when she found no indication that her friends had ever been there, she began to expand outward. The sudden chill felt wrong to her. Not only was it weather that was atypical for this part of the planet, but it also left her with a very unsettling question. What if it wasn't her friends who had been taken? What if it was her? Something Dalen said kept nagging her. *Geometry is folded here.*

When the sun came up, she carried on even though all she really wanted was to bundle herself up in her coat and lie down.

Miri shuffled along a dirt path with her gun in hand, her eyes flicking back and forth as she scanned the nearby trees. "This is a test," she muttered. "Which means there is a way to pass."

A twig snapped under her boot.

Stopping between two trees, Miri heaved out a breath. "So, how do you pass a test?" she said. "You learn the rules on which you are graded, and you conform to them."

This place had rules; it had to! If she could figure out what they were, she might be able to get out of here.

"I'm sorry, darling. You don't understand."

Miri gasped and twisted around, nearly shooting the person who had spoken. She was glad that she didn't.

The woman who stood before was just shy of average height with a stately air about her. She wore a red dress with sleeves that went down to her wrists and a gold necklace with an emerald. Black hair in a multitude of braids framed a face of soft, chocolate-brown skin. Miri knew this woman well.

It was Valia Nin Vaeda.

Her mother.

Cautiously, Miri lowered the gun and took a step back. "Who are you really?" she demanded. "This is a trick."

Valia smiled, shaking her head in dismay. "It's no trick, dear," she said. "I'm afraid you misunderstand your situation. This isn't a test. You're here to suffer for your sins."

"Desa…"

She felt it: that unmistakable tension at the base of her neck, the kind you only got when someone was standing right behind you. She waited until the very last second, and then she turned.

Of all the phantoms that she might have encountered, she would not have expected it to be a tall and gangly young man with pasty, pale skin and black hair that he wore parted in the middle. The beginnings of a pitiful mustache clung to his upper lip, and the brand on his cheek marked him as a slave.

Lifting her chin as she studied him, Desa sniffed. "Sebastian," she said, backing off to put some distance between them. "You mean to tell me that the Abyss couldn't cough up anything more formidable?"

He spread his arms wide, smiling, and then bowed to her. "Well, I wanted the first crack at you," he said. "You know. Since you *killed* me. Bet you never thought I'd come back, huh?"

With a growl, Desa raised her weapon and squinted. "I can rectify that situation!" Thunder rang out through the forest when she squeezed the trigger.

Her bullet went right through Sebastian as if he wasn't even there; he didn't even seem to notice. Wheezing with laughter, he shook his head as he advanced on her. "Oh, I'm afraid it's not that simple."

"Clearly."

"You see, I'm..." He dragged a finger across his throat and then laughed again. "Quite dead. So, shooting me? A bit anticlimactic, don't you think?"

"What do you want?"

He shrugged and began pacing a circle around her. "Well, an apology, for one thing. You see, you just-" He snapped his fingers. "Shot me dead right there. Didn't even give me a chance to find redemption. Aren't you hero types supposed to try to save my soul?"

As he paced, Desa turned so that she was always facing him. Her jaw tightened. "I gave you *plenty* of chances!" she spat. "More than a miserable wretch like you deserved."

Sebastian waggled a finger at her, chuckling softly. "Keep telling yourself that, my dear," he said. "Maybe one day you'll believe it."

If this was supposed to frighten her, she wasn't impressed. She had hunted dozens of bounties over the years, and some of those resulted in her putting a man in the ground. Any one of those would have scared her more than this fool.

Desa slammed her pistol back into its holster and then stepped forward with her head held high. "So, you're here to haunt me," she said. "If you're expecting me to feel some kind of guilt—"

"Guilt? No, I wouldn't expect that from you."

"Then kindly go back where you came from."

She stalked off through the forest, down a narrow winding path that skirted the base of a hill. Without warning, Sebastian leaped out from behind a tree on her left and planted himself right in front of her. "Oh, I'm afraid not."

Desa punched his face.

Or rather, she tried to. Her fist went through his head and out the other side, causing Sebastian to giggle. His malicious grin made her very uneasy. "Still struggling with the concept, are we?" he mocked. "Well, I suppose that I should clarify one little loophole in the rules. You can't hurt me..."

He flicked a finger at her.

Desa was hurled backward like a stone kicked up by a whirlwind. Her spine hit the rough surface of a tree trunk, and then she dropped to the ground, landing on her knees. Dizziness made her want to empty her stomach.

Her hand came down on something, and she yelped at a sudden sting. The tip of her finger was bleeding. Clearing away the mud revealed one of Miri's throwing knives on the ground. Her friends were still here! Somewhere...

Sebastian giggled. "But I can hurt you!"

"You were supposed to take care of him."

Miri stomped along a narrow path with her fists

clenched so hard her nails were digging into her palms. "I'm not listening to this," she snarled. "Leave me alone."

Valia poked her head out from behind a tree and smiled the smile that had always made Miri feel better when she was a little girl. "It was the one thing I asked you to do, and you let me down," she said. "Have you seen what's become of him?"

Rounding on her mother, Miri shoved a finger in the other woman's face. "I was a child!" she screamed. "That was too much weight to put on any girl's shoulders!"

Valia stood there with hands on her hips, thrusting out her chin with a disdainful snort. "A dutiful daughter would have put her family first," she said. "But you...and your boys. The whore of Aladar: isn't that what they called you?"

"Shut up!"

"Three years in the Academy, and you never learned to touch the Ether." Covering her mouth with one hand, Valia giggled. "But then it's not like you really tried, is it? Meditation wasn't for you. You never had your brother's discipline."

Miri backed up until her body was pressed against a tree. She pounded the trunk with her elbow. The sharp sting told her that she had broken the skin. "Well, If you love Marcus so much, why don't you go haunt him?"

"Drinking and debauchery," Valia continued as if Miri hadn't said a word. "That was the legacy that my daughter left me. I told you...I *begged* you to take care of him. But look at your brother, Miri. Look what they did to my sweet, special boy!"

Miri was weeping, tears streaming over her face. She bent double and trembled as each sob tore its way out of her body. "I was the youngest!" she whimpered. "He was supposed to take care of *me!*"

"You disgust me."

Just like that, the tears shut off like water from a faucet. There were some things that a parent should never say to their child. Her rage was like an inferno that scorched her sadness to ash. "*I* disgust you?" Miri whispered. "After everything you've done? Don't ever speak to me again, you horrible, vindictive *bitch!*"

Without thinking, Miri drew one of her throwing knives and tossed it. The blade tumbled end over end for two full turns before it passed through her mother's head. Valia didn't seem to have been harmed in any way, but the attempt made her furious. She lashed out with a wave of her hand.

Something struck Miri across the cheek hard enough to turn her head. A little harder, and it would have snapped her neck. She spat blood onto the ground.

Another flick of Valia's wrist was followed by a second blow that left Miri dizzy and disoriented. "How dare you!" Valia snapped. "Show your mother some respect!"

"Don't walk away from me, Sheriff!"

Kalia did everything in her power to ignore the ghost that had been following her for the past twenty minutes. She continued down a muddy path, refusing to look back no matter what. Deny the spectre's existence, and you rendered it powerless. She had heard that somewhere.

She gasped when the man who should have been right behind her stepped out from behind a withered tree and barred her path. Billy was tall, thin and pale with dirty-blonde hair and face that belonged on a boy five years his junior. He had worn that deputy's star on his uniform for all of three weeks before a bullet claimed him. "Why weren't you there with us, Sheriff?"

Gaping at the lad, Kalia shook her head. "It wasn't..." She winced, shuddering as she drew in a breath. "You aren't real!"

Turning on her heel, she left him.

She had gone no more than five steps when he once again popped out from behind a tree and put himself in front of her. "Who was it you were chasing that day?" he asked. "Oh yes! A horse thief! Pursued him halfway to Fool's Edge, didn't you?"

"Billy, stop this."

"So, you weren't there when Azra came to town."

Shutting her eyes, Kalia felt a single tear on her cheek. She sniffled and tried to push the grief away. "I couldn't have known," she protested. "I couldn't have known!"

Billy strode forward at a slow, steady pace, his gaze fixed on her with deadly intent. "She tore right through us like dry kindling, Sheriff," he said. "For fun! Because she was bored! None of us could Field Bind."

"It wasn't my fault."

"But you can," Billy went on. "You could have stopped her, Sheriff...If you had been there."

"That's it, son."

Marcus was down on his knees, trembling, the barrel of his pistol pressed against the side of his head. His breath misted in the cold air. Frigid rain pelted him, mixing with his tears.

His finger curled around the trigger.

"The shock will only last a moment," his father said. "And then you'll be at peace."

A heavyset man in a fine, gray suit, Tayros Von Amand paced a circle around his son. Somehow, his shoes left no mark on the soft earth, and the rain never touched him. Marcus had always believed that when a man died, he was just gone. Nothing remained, no spark of consciousness. He had been sure that he would never have to endure his father's disapproving stare again.

He had been wrong.

Tayros was a distinguished gentleman with salt-and-pepper hair that was thinning on top. "Just an instant of pain and fear," he promised. "Then you will be with us again. Your mother misses you so."

Gritting his teeth, Marcus sucked the air into his lungs. He folded up on himself, unable to put the gun down. "I can't!" he pleaded. "Aladar needs me!"

Halting right in front of Marcus, Tayros paused to check his pocket watch with a frown of disapproval. "Son," he said. "We both know what happens if you don't pull that trigger."

"The future isn't written yet!" Marcus screamed. "I won't let it happen!"

"You won't be able to stop it."

"You don't know that!"

With a soft sigh, his father turned away and began pacing toward a crooked tree that loomed in the distance. "A man cannot deny his nature!" Tayros declared for all the forest to hear. "You are what you are, Marcus: a killer."

He paused and looked over his shoulder with eyes that cut Marcus to the bone. "Now, do the world a favour by removing yourself from it."

Marcus felt his grip tighten on the pistol. His finger itched, eager to pull that trigger, eager to be done with it. Maybe it was for the best. He had known, when he agreed to go on this journey, what would be expected of him. A man did his duty. Even when it cost him everything…

He allowed himself one last look at his father and froze

when Tayros stepped aside. There was something carved into the bark of that crooked tree. Eradian script. Marcus was certain of it.

He got up on shaky legs.

"What are you doing?" Tayros demanded.

Ignoring the ghost, Marcus ran for the tree. He nearly lost his balance twice, slipping and sliding in the mud, but managed to stay upright. Tossing his gun away, he cursed when he got close enough to read the message. It was written in Eradian characters.

"Get away from that!" Tayros bellowed.

Marcus felt the hairs stand on the back of his neck.

He threw himself to the ground half a second before a lightning bolt blasted the tree and sent chunks of wood flying. The rest of it went up in a crackling blaze.

Somersaulting through the muck, Marcus came up on one knee. He rose slowly and turned around to face the ghost. The tree was gone, but Marcus had read enough of the message to know what he had to do. "You are not my father," he said.

RADAVAN STOOD beneath a drooping branch with his arms spread wide. The smile on his face promised agony. "It was a dishonorable move," he said. "Killing me the way you did."

Tommy wasn't listening.

Backing away from the other man, he pulled an arrow from his quiver, nocked it and drew. Those gray clouds that filled the sky kept threatening to unleash a downpour, but so far, no rain had come. His weapon would be useless otherwise.

He loosed.

The arrow went effortlessly through Radavan's chest and

drove itself into the tree behind him. Well, what else should Tommy have expected? You couldn't kill what was already dead. "It won't work," Radavan said as if that wasn't painfully obvious. "But this might."

He thrust a hand out, lightning flying from his fingertips. A jagged, blue lance that streaked through the air and winked out of existence half an inch away from Tommy's chest, absorbed by the Electric-Sink in one of his pendants.

Radavan stiffened.

Grinning, Tommy felt a sudden warmth in his face. He looked down at himself and then offered a shrug. "Gave it a physical trigger," he explained. "Figured I might not be able to react in time if one of the *Al a Nari* decided to blast me with his ray gun. So, the Sink activates if a powerful burst of electrical energy comes my way."

"You should have never been taught the Great Art," Radavan spat.

"Bothers you, doesn't it?"

"Impudent mongrel!"

His hand flew out toward Tommy again.

Bending his knees, Tommy triggered his Gravity-Sink and leaped. He shot up toward the treetops just before another lightning bolt flashed beneath him. This one hit a large rock and blasted it to pieces.

As he rose above the forest, Tommy drew his pistol, cocked the hammer and aimed for a spot on the distant horizon. He fired four times, and he recoil sent him soaring backward through the air.

Twisting around in mid-flight, he watched the trees scrolling past beneath him. All dead, all rotting. And they seemed to go on forever. What was it that Dalen had said about this place? Something about being folded? Was the forest truly infinite, or did it simply loop back on itself?

When he was sure that he had put sufficient distance between himself and the ghost, Tommy allowed gravity to reassert a tiny fraction of its power – just for a second – and began a slow descent to the ground.

He landed in a part of the forest that was indistinguishable from any other section he had visited. There was nothing to do but keep moving until he encountered another ghost, but something caught his eye.

A fat tree with a crooked stump.

It wasn't so different than any of the others, but he was sure...Yes. Those were letters carved into the trunk, and the fact that he could read them meant that it had to be a message from one of the others.

Heedless of any danger, he ran through the muck with his bow in one hand and his gun in the other. When he got within five feet of the thing, he saw that his suspicions were correct. It was indeed a message.

The ghosts aren't real.
Don't listen to them.
Stay strong
I'm coming for you

-D.K.

D.K.

Desa Kincaid.

Tommy felt hope swelling within him. Desa was here, and she was coming to save them. If anyone could figure out what was going on and put a stop to it, she could. Still, he couldn't help but wonder why he had not encountered any of the others. When had Desa marked that tree?

Soft laughter nearby made him shiver. Radavan was closing in on him. Well, if he couldn't fight, then he had only one option. Run and hope that he survived long enough for Desa to get him out of this mess.

Sebastian's ghost was ranting about something, but Desa barely even noticed. She was fascinated by the knife in her hand. It was definitely one of Miri's but the blade was covered in so much rust it must have been lying there for a year at least. Probably longer. Something about that tugged at her.

"Are you listening?"

She looked up to find Sebastian coming toward her. His face was red, and his teeth were bared in a vicious snarl. Like every other self-absorbed man she had met, he hated being ignored. "If words aren't sufficient to hold your attention," he growled, "Perhaps this will!"

He flung a hand out toward her.

By instinct, Desa raised her left arm up to shield herself and triggered the Force-Sink in her bracelet. She felt the kinetic energy that should have flattened her draining away into the Ether. "Interesting," she mumbled.

"What is?"

Desa stood up to face him with all the dignity she could muster. "Infused tools work against you," she said. "Which means that what you are doing isn't some form of magic. It's a physical phenomenon."

Sebastian froze, his jaw tightening as if he hadn't expected her to reach that conclusion. Fury replaced surprise an instant later. "You always thought you were so smart," he said. "So much smarter than us country bumpkins."

Clapping her hands, Desa strode away from the tree and shook her head. "I must commend you," she said. "You imitate him quite well. But we both know that you are not Sebastian. Why don't you show me who you *really* are?"

He crooked a finger.

A sudden twist of gravity had Desa stumbling toward the young man. She triggered the Sink in her belt buckle and leaped, sailing right over Sebastian's head. When she was clear, she let herself fall to the ground and took off at full speed.

She was bobbing and weaving around trees, ducking under branches and skidding through the mud. She had no direction in mind; every one of these wooden husks looked identical to her, and there was no getting out of this place until she passed whatever the test was.

Were the others all right?

Miri's knife proved that they had to be here somewhere, but why couldn't she find them? And how could the steel have rusted so quickly? What was it that Dalen had said yesterday? Geometry is folded here.

"What do you know about geometry?" Desa panted as she ran. "Geometry...The shortest distance between two points is a straight line. Parallel lines never intersect. The universe has four dimensions. Three of space..."

Desa slid to a stop.

Bent over with her hands on her knees, she drew the air into her lungs. "Three of space," she repeated. "And one of time. That's it!"

She turned around...

...And found herself face to face with an imposing figure in a black hood that swallowed the light. The ghost from the abandoned city was standing right in front of her. At this distance, she should have seen a face in that cowl, but there was nothing.

It reached for her with gloved fingers.

Without thinking, Desa slapped its hand away.

The ghost flinched as if she had caused it pain, and Desa squeaked as well. *That* should not have happened. "You're solid," she whispered. "You're not an apparition like Sebastian. You're real!"

Desa reached out with her feelings and made herself one with the Ether. The world changed before her eyes, dead trees becoming clusters of spinning particles. She expected to see much the same when she looked at the ghost, but she could not have been more wrong.

The hooded phantom was gone, replaced by a stately woman in a blue dress who radiated light and warmth. She was beautiful: just over average height with dark skin and flowing, black hair. Her face had a motherly quality, and when she looked at you, you just knew that everything would be all right.

Mercy...

"Finally, child," the goddess said. "I didn't know what else I could do to get your attention. You are a stubborn one."

Desa was about to sever contact with the Ether – she could barely stand, much less speak in this state – but Mercy raised a hand to forestall her. "No, Desa, you mustn't let go. You won't be able to comprehend my words without the ability to perceive the true nature of reality, and we haven't much time. Think your questions. I will understand."

Time for what?

"Time before I am yanked back to my prison. And then I must build up the strength to contact you again. Listen carefully, Desa. You will find nothing of value in my sister's temple. Return to me. I will teach you what you need to know."

But I am trapped within this forest.

She felt a little better when Mercy smiled. "You are a clever girl, Desa," the goddess said. "Simply remember who you are dealing with, and you will find your way out. I cannot remain here any longer. Come back to the desert. Find me."

And then she was gone.

Releasing the Ether, Desa exhaled and fell back against a tree. She brushed damp hair out of her face. "Remember who I'm dealing with," she muttered. "Who exactly am I dealing with?"

She heard Sebastian's grating laughter somewhere nearby.

Turning on her heel, she took off again, running as fast as she could. She scrambled up a shallow hill and then down the other side.

The mud gave way beneath her feet, and she slid the last few paces, arms flailing to keep herself upright. When she regained her balance, she noticed something. A fat tree with a crooked stump in the middle of a small grove.

Where were the others?

Frantically, she tried to reconstruct her thoughts from the moment before Mercy had appeared. Geometry. Three dimensions of space. One of time. Miri's knife suggested that the other woman was somewhere in this forest, but Desa couldn't find her. Or more accurately, Miri had been in this forest a long time ago. Long enough for the knife to have rusted. "Of course," Desa whispered. "We're all here. Same place. Different time."

But where was she in the sequence of events? Near the

beginning or the end? Miri had been here before her – that much was certain – but what about the others. *Think, Desa!* Had she seen any indication of Tommy's presence? A discarded arrow? What about Marcus? Or Kalia? As she ran through her memories of the last few hours, Desa realized that she had not seen any sign of her friends. Perhaps that meant that she was fairly early in the timeline. Well, it didn't matter because she was putting an end to this. Once and for all.

The others would be enduring tests of their own.

There had to be something that she could do to help them.

Drawing her own belt knife, Desa ran to the crooked tree and began carving a message into its bark. The first thing she could think of. It wasn't much, but she could hear Sebastian's footsteps. She didn't have much time.

When she finished, she turned and ran to meet him. If Sebastian saw the tree, he might destroy it. And her effort would be undone.

She found him on a narrow path that descended a sloping hill. When he noticed her, Sebastian froze in mid-step and studied her with a wolfish grin. "Well, well, well," he said. "Time to finish this, don't you think?"

"Yes indeed," Desa replied. "But first show me your true face…Vengeance."

The young man opened his mouth to speak, but any words he might have said were swallowed as he began to fade away. Bit by bit, he grew more and more transparent until he was gone.

Desa felt herself growing tense.

An old woman's cackling filled her ears.

When she turned around, a crone in tattered rags was hobbling along the path with shaky steps, leaning her weight on a wooden cane. This goddess might have been lovely once, but hollow cheeks and a bone-white complexion had ended that. Thin hair clung to her scalp in wispy, silver strands. And her eyes…Desa had never imagined that she would see such hatred in another woman's gaze.

"Figured it out, did you?" Vengeance croaked. "Well, it's about time somebody did. You humans provide such poor amusement."

Desa shut her eyes and then nodded slowly. "We do indeed," she agreed. "Perhaps then you should let us go."

Vengeance threw her head back, and her laughter was like the sound of rocks grinding together. "Think it's that easy, hmm?" she mocked. "No, no, no! You wandered into my woods. Now, I get to play."

Desa strode forward with the knife gripped tightly in one hand, refusing to look away. "To what end?" she asked, raising an eyebrow. "Just to satisfy your sadism? Or is this a test of some kind?"

"Most people speak to a goddess with more respect."

"You're no goddess," Desa scoffed. "Mercy said that she has been imprisoned in the abandoned city. Well, I have a hard time imagining that anyone could imprison a god. No, you're not divine. You're just a form of life that we don't understand."

She knew she had the right of it when she saw the fear on Vengeance's face. It was hard not to gloat. The stupid humans weren't supposed to see through the curtain. Desa took a great deal of pleasure in disabusing this crone of her preconceived notions. "I could flatten you in an instant," Vengeance hissed.

"So, do it."

Vengeance hesitated.

A smile tugged at the corners of Desa's mouth. "As I thought," she said, bowing her head. "I would imagine that it gets very tedious here, alone in the forest with nothing to do."

Vengeance waved her hand.

Some unseen force sheared a branch off a nearby tree, and it began to fall.

Desa thrust her fist into the air, triggering her bracelet, and the branch hung suspended above her head. She stepped out of its path and let it fall to the ground behind her. "How it must vex you," she went on, "seeing us measly humans defend ourselves with the power you gave us."

Vengeance was hunched over with one hand on her cane, smiling and shaking her head. "I find ways to occupy my time," she said. "With proper discipline, you can keep a human on the verge of death for *years*."

"Did you create Ether?" Desa asked. "Or did you merely exploit it for your own ends?"

"Your bravado is rather transparent, girl."

"And yet, for all your power, I'm still standing here."

Desa turned her back on the old woman, pacing up the path to the top of the hill. She slid her knife back into its sheath and gazed out on the ruined landscape. "It must have taken quite some work, creating this twisted reflection of the forest."

She nearly jumped when Vengeance suddenly materialized right beside her. The haggard, old woman wore a vicious smile. "Reflection," she mumbled. "You still don't understand. This is no reflection. This is the real thing."

"I've seen the Borathorin," Desa countered. "The place is teeming with life."

"*Was* teeming with life," Vengeance said. "No longer."

Something about that did not sit well with Desa. Was

the other woman claiming to have wiped out every living thing within a hundred miles? Vengeance would have to be powerful to call herself a god, but to do that much damage in such little time… "What do you mean?" Desa asked.

A wheezing cackle was the old woman's first reply. "Don't you like the future, Desa?" she said. "Thirty thousand of your years have passed since the day you entered the forest. This world is now a wasteland of ice."

"That's impossible."

"Impossible?" Vengeance exclaimed. "I am a god, you impudent, little primate. That word has no meaning for me."

Sucking air through her gaping mouth, Desa closed her eyes. A shiver went through her. "How…" she stammered. "How did it happen?"

Vengeance chuckled and poked the ground with her cane. *"Hanak Tuvar* played her part," she said. "Your people harnessed her power, and you built weapons. Terrible weapons. You wiped yourselves out. A fitting end for sinners who deserve every last drop of suffering that I could inflict on them."

"Send me back," Desa pleaded. "I can prevent this."

"Why would I want to prevent it?"

"The scrolls say you came to this world to teach us."

Once again, Vengeance laughed, and at this time there was glee and it. She whacked Desa with the cane. "I care nothing for your benighted, little species. Your misery amuses me."

Desa sighed. Appealing to the other woman's better nature was not going to work. There had to be something. Something she could offer. Maybe to persuade Vengeance, she had to see the truth about Vengeance.

She made herself one with the Ether.

The crone before her did not suddenly become a beautiful goddess. Instead, she appeared much as she had to Desa's human eyes. Old, withered. But there was something more. Strands of the Ether connected to Vengeance like the threads of a spider's web, each one stretching off to infinity. Desa instinctively knew that this was why the Ether was so chaotic in this place.

With her mind, she gently tugged on one of those strands, and Vengeance flinched. It took the utmost delicacy, but she managed to cut that thread and let it snap back into the other woman's body.

"What are you doing?"

This place is your prison, Desa thought. *I'm setting you free.*

One by one, she sliced the threads. She couldn't say how she knew it, but they weren't just strands of the Ether; they were parts of Vengeance's very essence, ties that anchored her to this place. Every time Desa cut one, the other woman seemed to absorb it back into her body. In time, her appearance began to change, and light spilled forth from her as it had with Mercy.

Finally, Desa severed the last one and let the Ether go.

The creature that stood before her was nothing like the hag she had been only moments before.

Desa was now in the presence of a breathtaking woman who would tower over most men, a queen in resplendent, golden armour that shimmered despite the lack of sunlight. Her pale face was framed by ringlets of dark, red hair that fell past her shoulders, and her eyes – a fierce, vibrant green – almost seemed to glow.

"Thank you," Vengeance said, raising a hand. "Now, burn."

Desa winced, preparing herself.

When no fire came, she forced herself to open her eyes

and saw Vengeance standing there with confusion on her face. "Why?" the goddess asked. "Why would you do this for me?"

"How do you defeat vengeance?" Desa whispered. "With mercy."

Vengeance lowered her hand with an exasperated sigh. "Oh, very well," she said, rolling her eyes. "It seems one of you apes is capable of learning."

She snapped her fingers, and the forest changed.

The gray sky was suddenly blue, the air muggy and warm. Dead trees were now covered with lush, green leaves. Birds chirped, and insects buzzed all around her. The Borathorin was once again what it should have been: a haven for plant and animal life.

Best of all, she was no longer alone!

Marcus stumbled out of the brush, waving his hat to shake the leaves off of it. "I see you made good on the promise," he said. "The one you carved into that tree."

A few seconds later, Tommy came out into the open with his bow in hand, looking back as if he expected something to follow him. "Is it...Is it done then?" he asked. "We passed?"

Kalia's shirt was drenched with sweat as she hopped through the gap between two trees. "Oh, Mercy..."

"Wrong goddess," Vengeance muttered.

Miri was next, backing away from something and pointing her gun at whatever it was. She cast a few furtive glances around and breathed a sigh of relief when she saw her friends.

"Where's Dalen?" Desa asked.

Vengeance gestured to a tree where the young librarian was lying with his back against the trunk, his legs stretched out before him. "He slept through it," she said. "Irritating man. I had such fun planned for him."

"Be that as it may, ma'am," Tommy said. "My question remains. Did we pass your test?"

"You passed," Vengeance assured him. *"All* of you passed. You will find what you need in that clearing."

Desa turned around and gasped when she saw what appeared to be a massive, black pyramid. There were trees in the way – she couldn't be certain – but except for the colour of the stone, it looked very much like the one in the abandoned city.

Vengeance stepped forward, armour clinking, and thrust her chin out toward the distant structure. "Take care," she said. "The weapon of a god is a force of incredible, destructive power. But as you have just learned, the ability to inflict destruction may not be the solution to your problems."

Desa nodded.

"And now," Vengeance went on. "I must leave you. My work is done. My time on this planet is finally over."

The goddess spread her arms wide, and radiance exploded from her body. Her arms and legs retracted until she was a ball of light hovering five feet above the forest floor, tendrils of white fire streaming off of her.

She shot up toward the heavens and vanished in a final twinkle.

Kalia was dumbstruck, blinking slowly as if she couldn't believe her eyes. "Remind me to change religions," she muttered. "So...What next?"

"We go to the pyramid," Desa said. "And claim what we came for."

26

They followed a narrow path through the trees for about five minutes before arriving at a clearing where the sun shone brightly overhead. The dark structure that Desa had seen was indeed Vengeance's temple.

It looked very much like the one she had seen in the abandoned city, except that pyramid had been made of pale stone while this one was as black as night. The crystal on its flat roof was also different. Instead of a perfect teardrop, this one was shaped like a grasping claw with jagged fingers pointed skyward.

It had the same effect though.

Desa could feel the Ether pulsing, calling out to her, singing in her mind. She had to resist the urge to make herself one with it and glory in its embrace.

Craning her neck to study the massive structure with lips pursed, Desa blinked once. "Well," she muttered. "We're here."

Tommy stood beside her with his eyes as wide as teacups. "What is it?" he asked. "I feel strange...As if...As if..."

"As if the Ether is begging you to commune with it?"

He nodded.

Marcus stepped forward to join them with his pistol in hand. There were mud stains on his knees, and his hat was a little rumpled: all of which combined to make his sneer that much more intimidating. "You aren't the only one," he grumbled. "I feel it as well."

"I don't," Miri said.

"I suspect you have to touch the Ether at least once on your own," Desa explained. "But once you do…"

Tommy looked up at the crystal with wonder on his face. "This thing makes it so much easier," he whispered. "I always had the concentrate, but now I feel like…like…I could do it with just a thought."

Kalia was sitting on a rock and fanning herself with her hat. "So," she said. "What we do now?"

"We go inside."

Pressing a fist to his mouth to stifle a yawn, Dalen came shuffling out of the forest. "Are you sure that's wise?" he asked in a sleepy voice. "Won't there be traps?"

"Perhaps," Desa conceded. "But I'm not inclined to think so. There were no traps in the last one, and I suspect that we have passed all of Vengeance's tests."

With that, they began a slow, reluctant march towards the end of their journey. Wide, stone steps led up to an entrance in the pyramid's front wall. As she climbed them, Desa became aware of the aches and pains that she had been ignoring.

On the landing, Desa paused to peer into the dark passageway that led down into the shadowy depths. A musty smell confronted her, and she waved her hand in front of her nose to dispel it.

"Should we all go in?" Dalen asked behind her.

Trailing her fingers over the stone wall, Desa shook her head. "No," she said. "I don't think there's any danger, but if Vengeance did leave booby-traps, a smaller party will have less chance of triggering them."

"How many then?" Miri asked. "Do you plan to go in alone?"

"Two people should be sufficient."

With a heavy sigh, Marcus removed his hat and stood at the entrance to the tunnel. "I volunteer," he said. "You and I have the most experience with Field Binding. It makes sense that it should be us."

Desa turned around to see if the other four had any objections and found that they were all just standing there, waiting for her to take charge. Well, Marcus seemed as good a choice as any. Though she could see the irritation in Kalia's eyes. The sheriff had been practicing the Great Art for the better part of ten years. To have Marcus dismiss that experience so easily would have annoyed Desa as well.

She and Marcus began their descent.

It was much cooler once she was out of the sunlight, and she had to use her ring to keep the darkness at bay. The passage was very narrow, forcing her to walk two steps ahead of Marcus.

When the slope leveled off, she could see well enough to extinguish the glow in her ring. A hole in the ceiling allowed sunlight to filter in through the bottom of the crystal, casting sparkling patterns on the walls.

In the centre of the room, a raised floor stood about five feet high with unlit torches on all four corners. Aside from the colour of the stone, this chamber was identical to its twin in Mercy's temple.

The only other difference was the spear.

At first glance, it appeared to be one piece of solid metal, though she couldn't say what kind. The whole thing was reflective with delicate runes etched into the haft. It was driven point-first into the stone directly under the glittering crystal.

Marcus halted at the mouth of the tunnel, scratching his chin with three fingers. "Is it that easy?" he asked. "Do we just...take it?"

Leaning her shoulder against the wall, Desa folded her arms. A frown tightened her mouth. "I doubt it," she said. "We may have passed the test, but I doubt that thing will just come free for any hand that grasps it."

"I suppose there's nothing to do but try."

Marcus walked over to the base of the raised floor. Triggering his Gravity-Sinks, he jumped and landed on top of it. Desa felt her heart racing as he went to the spear and then closed his hands around it.

He gave one quick tug.

Nothing happened.

Spinning around to face her, Marcus threw his hands up. "Well, you were right," he said. "It won't come free for just anyone."

"Perhaps I should try."

"Be my guest."

With a quick pulse of her Gravity-Sink, she joined him up there. Refracted light fell upon her, bringing with it uncomfortable heat. The spear drank it in. She could see her distorted reflection in the metal. Surely, if Marcus couldn't draw it out, she would fail as well. Still, she had to try.

Desa took hold of the haft.

With very little effort, she pulled it free of the stone... and gasped as new awareness blossomed in her mind. Little bundles of sensations that she instantly recognized as the signatures of Infused tools. "What is it?" Marcus asked.

Twirling the spear, Desa thrust it at the wall and released a stream of electricity from the tip, a lightning bolt that pounded the stone and sent fragments flying. "So, it's an Electric-Source," Marcus grumbled.

"Not just an Electric-Source."

Desa strode forward, then slammed the end of the spear down on the floor. Some of the rocks she had blasted came flying toward her. She waited until they were just about to pummel her, then raised the spear defensively.

Every one of those rocks came to a halt in the air. She left them like that for a moment, then allowed them to fall. "A Gravity-Source," she said. "A Force-Sink. Every single type of Infusion combined within a single object."

"That's impossible!"

It certainly should have been. The spear contradicted everything they knew about Field Binding. Practitioners had tried for centuries to create multiple Infusions within the same object; no one had ever succeeded. The general consensus was that it could not be done. Except Vengeance had managed it somehow.

"It must be studied," Marcus said behind her.

Holding the spear delicately in both hands, Desa frowned as she examined it. "Yes," she agreed. "It must."

On a whim, she made herself one with the Ether and traced the weapon with her mind. There were indeed multiple lattices between the molecules. So many that she could not track them. It was like trying to follow an individual thread in a tangled-up ball of yarn. But she could say one thing with absolute certainty:

She had used the Electric-Source, Gravity-Source and Force-Sink Infusions, draining them of some of their power.

And yet the strands of Ether that corresponded to those particular lattices were already starting to thicken. The spear was Reinfusing itself!

Desa released the Ether.

"Do you realize what this means?" she whispered. "If we can figure out how to duplicate this technology, it could provide us with limitless, free energy! It could-"

She cut off when a jolt of electricity went through her body, trapping her in a fit of convulsions and turning her muscles to jelly. Her legs gave out, and she landed face-down on the stone. The last thing she heard before blacking out was the clatter of the spear falling from her grip.

Desa was stretched out before him, unconscious on the floor with the spear slowly rolling away from her. The sight of her like that left him with a queasy feeling that he just could not ignore. The things he did for his people.

Marcus stood with one fist thrust out, sunlight glinting off the ring that he wore on his third finger. "For what it's worth," he said. "I'm sorry."

He strode across the raised floor, then stooped to retrieve the spear. The instant he touched it, he felt a new awareness of its power. It seemed that the spear would bond to anyone who held it.

Marcus straightened, then held the weapon up in front of his face, scowling as he inspected it. "Such a curious thing," he mumbled. "Is it truly worth all this pain?"

That question was not his to answer. His Prelate had given him a mission, and he would see it done. For Aladar. Now, what to do with the others? They would have questions when he emerged from the pyramid without Desa at his side. Perhaps he could stun them as well. Tommy and

Kalia might make that difficult; he suspected that they each possessed Electric-Sinks of their own. Tommy certainly did. But the librarian was no threat to him. And his sister...

He would have to leave them all behind. If the spear was as powerful as he believed, he might be able to just sail over the trees until he reached the edge of the Forest. After that... Well, perhaps he could steal some supplies from the *Al a Nari* before beginning his long journey home.

"Marcus!"

A chill went through him at the sharp crack in his sister's voice. He turned to find her standing at the mouth of the tunnel with a pistol in hand, a pistol that she pointed at him. He had seen that look in her eyes before; it was the one she got just before she killed an enemy. "What did you do?" Miri demanded.

"Step aside, Sister."

"Vengeance spit on me if I will!"

Marcus paced to the edge of the raised floor, shaking his head in dismay. "She'll wake up," he promised. "The blast I hit her with was only enough to incapacitate her, not to kill. The five of you can make your way back to the *Al a Nari*."

"You attacked her," Miri mumbled.

"I did what was necessary." Marcus hopped down, landing hard, and then drew himself up in front of his sister. "The spear belongs to Aladar, Miri. To Aladar and no one else. It is our birthright."

Miri lowered her weapon and then backed off into the darkness of the tunnel. He could barely see her, but her breath rasped in his ears. "Birthright," Miri whispered. "Marcus, what in blazes are you talking about?"

"The Spear of Vengeance."

"What of it?"

Try as he might, Marcus couldn't suppress a sigh. "Do

you mean to tell me that you still haven't figured it out?" he asked. "Even after Te'Alon? One would have thought that you would notice the parallels."

Miri was just a silhouette to his eyes, but he could tell that she was cocking her head and studying him. His sister was a brilliant woman, but sometimes she did not see what she did not want to see. "What parallels?"

"The *Al a Nari*," he said. "An idyllic society at the edge of the world – hidden from everyone – and yet they are so very like us. Their names, their government, their mastery of Field Binding: almost mirror images of what we see in Aladar. Use that clever mind of yours, Miri; put the pieces together. If they are the People of Mercy, then who are we?"

"No," she whimpered.

"*Al a Dri,*" Marcus said, pronouncing every syllable. "The People of Vengeance." He exhaled, working up the courage to speak the words that would cost him his sister's respect. "Daresina sent me on this mission because she knew that Desa's bleeding heart would prevent her from doing what was necessary. The spear belongs to Aladar. It is the weapon that we will use to break the nations of this world and forge an empire that will endure for a thousand years."

"Marcus, you can't do this."

He raised a hand, closing his fingers into a fist and pointing his ring at her. "Step aside, Miri," he warned. "I won't ask again."

In the darkness, he could see that she had raised her pistol again. "I won't," she insisted. "You're not going to hurt me, Marcus. I know you better than that."

"Then I will simply find another way out of this pyramid."

He turned and ran.

. . .

"By the eyes of Vengeance," Miri cursed, slamming her pistol back into its holster. She ran out of the tunnel and chased her brother around the raised floor. He vanished around a corner, but she could still hear his footsteps. There was still a chance that she could set matters right. If she could just talk some sense into him before he made matters worse. Desa would forgive him; she knew it.

On the opposite side of the central chamber, she found another corridor that led deeper into the pyramid. She could see her brother clearly; there were bricks in the walls that glowed with fierce, orange light. Under any other circumstances, she would have marveled at that, but at the moment, she had larger concerns.

Miri pursued him into the tunnel.

Glancing back over his shoulder, Marcus growled. He slipped into a doorway on his left. With any luck, that was a dead end, but even if it wasn't, rushing in would be most unwise.

Miri drew one of the many throwing knives that she wore on her belt and crept through the narrow passageway.

Pressing her back to the wall, she shuffled the last few paces and then peered around the corner. She pulled back just in time, half a second before a hair-thin streak of electricity shot through the door and struck the wall across from her.

"I won't be dissuaded!" Marcus bellowed.

The brief glimpse she had of her brother was enough for her to get a sense of his surroundings; he was in the middle of a room with four stone pillars that supported the ceiling. So far as she could tell, there was no other way out, but there were plenty of opportunities for an ambush.

She had to get that spear away from him. If she could just make him sit down and listen, she knew that she could get through to him. Unfortunately, she had fought Field Binders before. Even with the best tactics, the odds of winning weren't good. Her only hope was to overwhelm him before he had a chance to use one of his tricks. Which meant...Which meant she couldn't hold back.

Miri spun around the corner and threw her knife.

Standing between the nearest two pillars, her brother raised the spear and did something that rendered her attack useless. Her weapon slowed to a stop as if the air had thickened around it.

In that moment of distraction, Miri broke into a sprint. She leaped and tried to kick Marcus, but whatever power had captured the knife did the same to her, leaving her floating in the air.

Marcus flicked the spear toward the wall.

Miri was thrown sideways, sent shoulder-first into the stone. She groaned on impact and then dropped to land on shaky legs. A sudden flare of pain made it very hard to think, and tears welled up. If she had hit much harder, she would have broken bones. But she could hear soft footsteps heading toward the exit. Marcus was trying to leave.

Drawing her pistol, Miri cocked the hammer and spun around. She fired before she even had a shot lined up.

When her vision cleared, she saw a bullet hovering about an inch away from her brother's forehead. Marcus was snarling now. She recognized that hatred in his eyes. That last move was a betrayal that he could not forgive. "You would try to kill me?" he hissed. "Me?"

"If I had to."

Miri pointed her gun at the ceiling and fired several times. Pieces of rock fell down on Marcus who used the spear to keep them from striking his head.

Seizing the opportunity, Miri charged forward, dropped

to her knees and slid across the floor. She raised her weapon and fired again, releasing another bullet that failed to reach its target.

But like everything else, it was just a distraction.

Closing the distance, Miri stood up and tossed her gun away. She grabbed the spear with both hands, trying to wrest it from her brother's grip. A swift kick to the belly made Marcus wheeze.

Miri pulled the spear away from him.

With a quick twist of her body, she swung the butt-end into his cheek, stunning him. She poked him in the stomach, eliciting a yelp and forcing him to double over. Then she hit him in the face again. If she could keep the momentum...

Marcus stumbled, raising a hand to shield himself. Growling like an angry bear, he flung that hand out toward her.

Something hurled Miri backward with incredible force, slamming her against the wall. She whimpered and fell to land on her feet, barely holding onto the spear. There was no way she could win this. Not against a Field Binder.

The spear...

Now that she was holding it, she could sense its power. There were little bundles of awareness in her mind. She knew that she could trigger them with only a thought, but she wasn't sure what they would do.

Marcus drew his gun.

Spinning around, Miri ducked behind a pillar and pressed her back up against it. Her heart was pounding, her lungs burning.

The roar of gunfire made her flinch.

A bullet drove itself into the wall across from her, and then that wall exploded, throwing bits of rock at her. The kinetic force flattened her against the pillar just before those rocks pummeled her.

One smacked the side of her head, leaving her dizzy and disoriented. She fought to hold onto consciousness. "You can't win this, Sister!" Marcus shouted. "Relinquish the spear, and I will let you live!"

"Never!"

"So be it."

Marcus's next shot went into the wall on her right. Without warning, she was tugged sideways, out into the open. It took every scrap of willpower she had to stay on her feet. Drunkenly, she turned around.

Marcus was striding toward her, lifting his gun in one hand and pointing it right at her. "Last chance," he said. "Surrender."

Miri staggered and lost her balance. Falling on her ass, she threw the spear at him.

Her brother leaned to one side, and the spear went right over his shoulder, striking the pillar with a loud, clear ring and bouncing off. It landed on the floor, out of reach. Now, she was at his mercy.

Marcus stood up straight, towering over her. His face was twisted into a snarl of contempt. "You're a traitor," he said. "And treason is punished with death."

He took aim with his pistol.

Miri knew that he would do it; ever since he was a boy, her older brother had been the sort of fool who embraced a black-and-white morality. The Prelate had given him an order – retrieve the Spear of Vengeance – and he would see it done. No matter the cost. But he was hesitating. The struggle was eating him up inside; she could see it. Marcus did not want to pull that trigger.

But what could she do?

One of the rocks that had come loose from the wall... The gravity from Marcus's bullet had pulled it over here as surely as it had Miri, and now it was within arm's reach. She grabbed it and threw it at him.

Marcus flinched, raising a hand to protect himself.

Curling up into a ball, Miri sprang off the floor to land with her fists up. When her brother dropped his guard, she kicked high and struck his chin with the tip of her boot. Marcus stumbled, raising the gun in a shaky hand.

Turning her shoulder toward him, Miri gasped as she felt a bullet rush past her to bury itself in the wall. She kicked out to the side, driving her foot into his stomach. The impact sent Marcus sprawling backward until he collapsed against the pillar.

Once again, he tried to raise his weapon.

Lightning quick, Miri drew a throwing knife and tossed it. The glittering blade tumbled end over end, sliced a gash across Marcus's hand and forced him to drop the gun. He screamed in pain.

Miri ran for him.

She jumped, spreading her legs wide and then bringing them together like scissor blades to trap Marcus's head between her knees. Falling over sideways, she took him down with her.

Miri rolled him over until he was flat on his back while she perched on top of him. The gun he had dropped. Miri snatched it up and shoved its barrel in his face. His eyes widened. "It's over, Brother," she said. "You've lost."

"So it would seem."

Miri closed her eyes, fat beads of sweat rolling over her brow. Every breath was laboured. "I don't want to fight you anymore," she admitted. "But you're not taking that spear out of here. Come back with us."

"You know I can't do that."

"I can't let you up until you agree."

Marcus had tears on his cheeks, but he never looked away, and he never blinked. Not even for an instant. "And I can't betray my oath to Aladar," he said. "Stand aside. I'll let you live. You can go into exile with the others."

"While you and Daresina conquer the world?"

"That is the destiny of our people."

Hissing air through her teeth, Miri seethed with rage. "Horse shit!" she snarled. "We can choose our own path."

Marcus reached to grab the barrel of her pistol, pressing it hard against his forehead. "I'm going to walk out of here, Miri," he said. "I'm going to deliver the spear to Daresina as promised. And the only way you can stop me is to pull that trigger."

"I won't do it."

"Then I suppose we know which of us has true conviction."

Gravity changed, and Miri was pulled off of her brother. She flew through the air and crashed into the wall with a grunt. Flopping onto her back, she tried to break free, but the bullet held her pinned to the stone.

Marcus, who was unaffected by the change, stood up and dusted himself off. He turned to her slowly. "I didn't want to do this," he said, extending his hand to point his ring at her. No hesitation this time.

He was going to kill her.

Miri fired first.

Three deafening gunshots made her ears ring, and Marcus spasmed each time a slug pierced his body. His arms flailed as he danced backward, and then he fell to the floor, lying in a pool of his own blood.

Miri tried to get up, tried to run to him, but the Gravity-

Source held her firm against the wall. "No," she sobbed. "Oh, Sweet Mercy, no!"

Marcus let out one last gurgling breath, and then he went still.

"No! No! No!"

Desa appeared in the doorway, gasping when she saw Marcus. She ran to Miri, and her proximity lessened the gravity that held Miri trapped. Climbing down off the wall took a little effort.

"What happened?" Desa asked.

Miri trembled as tears spilled over her face. "I didn't want to," she whimpered. "He was going to…"

"He was going to take the spear?"

Miri wiped the tears away with the back of her hand. "And give it to Daresina," she clarified. "He said that Aladar would use its power to conquer the world."

Desa looked horrified; her face was deathly pale. "Terrible weapons," she whispered. "That was what she said."

"Who?"

"It doesn't matter," Desa said. "Let's get you outside. When the Gravity-Source is depleted, we can…We can see to it that he is properly buried."

The old stablehand, a fat man in overalls and muddy boots whose gray hair fell past his shoulders, hovered about six feet above the hay-strewn floor His legs kicked, and his hands clawed at his neck to loosen the invisible vise there.

Standing before him in a sleeveless, black dress, the Weaver stretched a hand out toward him. "Once again," she said. "A month ago, you sold horses to a group of people who were passing through here."

The old fool's face was turning purple.

"Where did they go?"

"Na...Na...Na..."

The Weaver arched a golden eyebrow. "Yes?" she prompted. "Out with it, man! I haven't got all day!"

She had traveled north to New Beloran and then west along the Vinrella, following it all the way to High Falls. After weeks of searching, she had discovered no sign of Desa and her friends. So, there was nothing left to do but double back and return to the last place she knew they had visited.

Hedrovan.

Interrogating the locals produced little in the way of useful information. That bloody innkeeper said that she had overheard one of Desa's party talking about buying horses, which brought her here, to a lowly stablehand who squirmed in her grip.

He looked about ready to faint.

With an exasperated sigh, the Weaver released her hold on the man and let him fall to land on his knees in the middle of the barn. He bent forward, massaging his throat. "Needed good horses," he croaked. "Good horses for a long journey."

"A long journey where?"

The old man forced himself to sit up and blinked at her. "Didn't say," he wheezed. "But he mentioned the Halitha. I think they were headed south."

Covering her mouth with one hand, the Weaver considered that. "South," she murmured. "To Ithanar...What could they possibly want there?"

The answer became painfully clear to her after only a moment's thought. "No," the Weaver hissed. "They couldn't. She wouldn't." Of course, she would. There was no line that Desa would not cross in the pursuit of her goals. Well, the game had just become much more dangerous.

"I shall have to bid you good day, sir," she said. "As much as I would like to, I'm afraid I can't remain. It seems a trip to Aladar is in order."

27

Tommy laid the last rock down on Marcus's cairn and then stepped away. They had buried him at the edge of the forest, on the north side of the temple. A fitting place, Desa thought. He would get lots of sunlight. Strange that she should feel so...hollow inside. Marcus had betrayed her. She should be angry! She should feel *something*, but there was only a hole where her emotions should be.

Desa stood at the foot of the mound with her hands clasped in front of herself, her head bowed respectfully. "He was a good man." She had no idea why she felt the need to eulogize him – if anything, that task should fall to Miri – but the words were coming out, and she didn't try to stop them. "A man who did his duty as he saw it. Perhaps misguided at times. But...He cared."

She stepped aside.

Tommy was the next to approach, removing his hat and holding it against his chest. "There were days when I wanted to pull my hair out," he said. "'What does this man have against me?' I'd ask myself. And yet, in a way, I owe Marcus.

And not just because he saved my life a time or two. He made me into a better person. A stronger person."

He left, and Kalia took his place, awkwardly shifting her weight from one foot to the other. "I didn't know Marcus as well as some of you," she began. "But in our short time together, I could see that he was brave. Always willing to be the first one of us to walk into danger. We would not have survived this journey without him."

She opened her mouth as if to say more, then snapped it shut again and moved aside, making room for Dalen. The librarian crouched next to the cairn, reached out to touch a rock and said, "I am sorry, my friend."

Miri took his place and shuddered. Sobs wracked her body, and she covered her face with both hands. "I can't!" she moaned. "I can't!"

The late afternoon sun was starting its descent toward the treetops as they parted company. Desa needed time to think, and she suspected that the others did as well. In the corner of her eye, she saw Tommy and Dalen guiding Miri to a place where she could compose herself. That was for the best. Desa wanted to say something to comfort the other woman, but she feared that she would only make things worse.

With the spear in hand, she marched back to the pyramid and climbed the steps. Halfway up, she turned around and sat down with the weapon balanced across her knees. She ran her hand along the smooth metal.

Was it worth it?

She feared that she would never have an answer.

Kalia shuffled up the steps with her head down. Desa could see it in the sheriff's face; she was concerned. Not for herself, no doubt. For Desa. Still, she began the conversation with her usual pragmatism. "So, what do we do next?"

"Return to the *Al a Nari*, I suppose," Desa answered. "At some point, we will have to go back to Eradia and track down Adele. I don't expect that she'll make that easy."

Kalia sat on the next step down, turned so that Desa saw her in profile. She nodded slowly, taking that in. "You don't intend to return to Aladar?"

Desa looked down at the spear in her lap, noting her reflection in its shimmering surface. Sunlight glinted off the metal. "I can't risk it," she said. "Vengeance isn't a god; she's just a form of life that we don't understand yet. Which means this isn't magic. It's technology."

"Which means it can be duplicated."

"Precisely," Desa said. "I had hoped that my people would be able to study it, to discern how the spear is able to renew its connection to the Ether on its own. But now that Marcus has exposed Daresina's intentions…"

Shutting her eyes tight, Desa drew in a rasping breath. "Maybe we can give it to the *Al a Nari,*" she mused. "After we've used it to stop Adele, I mean."

"You trust them?"

"More than I trust my own people."

Kalia nodded.

Desa passed the spear to her, and the sheriff's eyes widened the instant her hand touched it. "I can feel them," she mumbled. "All of the Sinks and Sources Infused into this thing…So many!"

Desa stood up, dusting her hands, and paced down the stairs. "So many," she agreed, pausing after a few steps. "Some of them manipulate forms of energy that we haven't even discovered yet."

"How is it that I can sense Infusions I didn't create?"

Tilting her head back, Desa blinked as she considered

the question. "I don't know," she muttered. "It should be impossible."

When she turned around, Kalia was staring off into the distance. "Maybe we should take it to Aladar," she said. "If someone can learn to duplicate this thing...Think of what it could mean for humanity!"

"That's *all* I can think about!" Desa said. "When I confronted Vengeance, she told me that we would one day learn how to harness Adele's power. And we would use it to make weapons. The wasteland we saw, the dead forest: Vengeance claimed it was the result of a war that destroyed humanity."

Kalia lifted the spear up in front of her face, frowning as she studied her reflection. "And you think that this is the first step on that journey?"

"Look at what it did to Marcus."

The sheriff stood up with a sigh and then shook her head slowly. "Don't be a fool," she snapped. "You heard what Miri said: Marcus was planning his betrayal from the moment we left Aladar."

"Does it matter?" Desa countered. "Even if we can be trusted with this power, we won't be here forever. Sooner or later, that spear will fall into the hands of someone who will misuse it. And I have no idea what to do.

"I'd suggest destroying it, but I suspect that is beyond our ability. Hiding it is also unwise; hidden things tend to be found sooner or later. Without Vengeance to guard the temple, leaving it here will all but guarantee that some opportunistic treasure hunter will discover it someday."

"A conundrum."

"Yes," Desa breathed. "One we'll have to deal with much sooner than we would like."

. . .

The forest was warm and muggy, but Miri still remembered the chill from this morning. She welcomed the heat as if it could warm the ice inside her heart.

Miri sat on a rock with hands on her knees, hunched over and crying. Hot tears rolled down her cheeks. "I didn't want to do it," she said. "Why did he have to be so stubborn?"

Dalen wrapped an arm around her shoulders, pulling her close so that she could rest her head on his chest. "I know," he whispered. "It wasn't your fault."

"Damn right, it wasn't!" Tommy snarled as he paced along a dirt path. "I hate to speak ill of the dead, but what was that idiot thinking?"

Miri sat up, sniffling and wiping her tears away. "He was thinking that his Prelate gave him an order," she croaked. "And my brother was never the sort to defy an order."

Tommy marched along the path with arms folded, shaking his head in disgust. "The Almighty burn that Daresina!" he spat. "We should have expected something like this from her!"

"Shut your damn mouth!" Miri shouted.

Tommy blinked and then rounded on her. His mouth hung open as he shook his head. "You're *defending* her?"

Miri bent over with her elbows on her thighs, pressing the heels of her hands to her eye-sockets. "Of course, I'm not defending her!" She looked up to squint at him. "But I just killed my brother! So, I really don't care to discuss Aladri politics right now!"

"I'm sorry," Tommy muttered.

"Don't be," Miri whispered. "I'm not mad at you."

Miri got up and started to walk. She had no destination in mind; she just had to *move*. Her intention was to slip past

Tommy, but somehow, she went to him and fell into his arms.

Tommy held her close with one hand on the back of her head, whispering soothing things that didn't exactly register in her thoughts. The individual words weren't important. What mattered was that she wasn't alone.

"It's my fault," Miri said.

"No, it isn't."

"I should have found another way."

With a heavy sigh, Tommy put his hands on her shoulders and stared directly into her eyes. "No," he insisted. "Let's be honest about this, Miri. Your brother was a zealot. He would have killed you."

"Thomas is right," Dalen said behind her. "We both know it."

She spun around, intending to hurl angry words at him, but those words died when she saw the sympathy in Dalen's eyes. He took her hands in his and leaned in close to kiss her forehead. "I can't imagine what you're going through," he murmured. "You've had to do something that no one should ever have to do. But don't lose sight of one very important truth."

"And what's that?" Miri asked.

"What you did today probably saved millions of lives."

At that, she started crying again and fell against Dalen. He held her tight for a little while as she sobbed into his shirt. Tommy came up to join them, and then they were both holding her, both whispering soft reminders of their love. It didn't take the sting away, but at least she wasn't alone.

Miri could not have said how long she stayed like that. The minutes seemed to pass like hours, but eventually, her tears subsided. They didn't stop comforting her, however.

They were a wonderful pair, her two boys. Sometimes, she thought that a woman like her didn't deserve to be so lucky.

"I'm sorry," a delicate, feminine voice said from somewhere nearby. "I hate to interrupt this tender moment."

Miri stiffened.

She knew that voice.

Stepping free of Dalen's embrace, she found Adele Delarac standing between two trees, dressed in an elegant, black gown that left her shoulders bare. The young woman was smiling the coldest smile that Miri had ever seen.

Miri reached for a throwing knife.

"Ah, ah, ah," Adele said, waggling a finger at her. "Let's not be rash. Y'all couldn't last five seconds against me anyway."

Tommy was backing away from her, moving slowly toward a towering tree with drooping branches. He had left his bow propped up against its trunk. "We'll see about that," he muttered under his breath.

Planting fists on her hips, Adele frowned at him and shook her head. "Haven't you learned your place yet, boy?" she asked. "How many times am I gonna have to teach y'all the same sorry lesson?"

In the blink of an eye, Miri had her pistol out of its holster, cocking the hammer as she pointed at her enemy. She fired once.

Adele's hand came up in an almost dismissive gesture, and the bullet became a puff of smoke about an inch away from her body. Several more rounds suffered the same fate. Miri knew that a gun was useless against this woman; she didn't care.

"I'm sorry," Adele said. "This fight is beneath me. But since y'all are so eager for violence, I brought someone who would be most happy to oblige."

A flash of yellow in the trees caught Miri's eye. Thick bushes parted to reveal a tall woman in flowing robes, a woman with tanned skin and auburn hair that she wore in a braid. Miri recognized her. Andriel: one of the Elite Guard.

"It's true," Andriel said. "I saw the cairn. They killed him."

"Yes, they did," Adele purred. "I reckon you'll want a word with them then." She vanished, leaving them alone with one very angry Field Binder.

28

The sound of a gunshot had Desa and Kalia running for the forest. Side by side, they bounded down the pyramid steps and through the soft grass. Miri and the others were out there somewhere, but so far as Desa knew, she and her friends were the only people within thirty miles of this place.

Something was very wrong.

As soon as they entered the forest, the ground changed. Desa found herself sliding through muck, ducking under branches and leaping over ditches. The trees stood so close together they almost seemed to crowd in on her.

"You don't think..." Kalia began. "You don't think that Miri might have done something rash?"

"Like what?"

The sheriff hopped over a root with the grace of a loping deer and landed on the other side, never breaking stride. "She was feeling very guilty," Kalia said. "You don't think that she might..."

Desa shook her head. "Not for an instant," she growled.

"Miri isn't the sort who would take her own life. And that means that we have-"

Her words cut off when she slipped under a branch and stepped onto a narrow path that ran from left to right from her perspective. It wasn't the trail that got her attention. No, it was the fact that they were no longer alone.

Tall and radiant in her black gown, Adele stood on the path. Her smile was cold enough to turn summer into winter. "So good to see you again, my dear."

Desa turned to face her, clutching the Spear of Vengeance so hard her knuckles whitened. "You made a mistake coming here," she hissed. "Where are my friends?"

Adele shrugged and then tittered. "Not far," she purred. "But I'm afraid they have problems of their own."

Kalia fell in beside Desa, slowly drawing her pistol from its holster. "You caused quite a bit of havoc in my town," she muttered. "We have a score to settle."

"I'm sorry," Adele said. "And you are…"

Desa raised her weapon, allowing its glittering tip to catch the sunlight. "You know what this is?" she asked. "You must or you wouldn't have come here to stop me."

"Yes, I know what it is." Adele's blue eyes were fixed on the spear. For all her bravado, she made it a point to stay out of stabbing range. "It won't help you."

"No?" Desa asked. "Then why bother coming here?"

Spreading her skirts, Adele performed an elegant curtsy. When she straightened, her rictus grin returned. "I thought it was time we settled things."

"I couldn't agree more," Desa replied. "But let's be clear on the rules. I stab you with this, and you die. No miraculous healing, no transferring your essence to another body. This spear pierces your flesh, and you're gone."

"That's the gist of it, yes."

"Excellent," Desa said. "Then let's begin."

Kalia's hand snapped up, aiming the pistol and firing several rounds. Every one of those became a small puff of smoke before it struck Adele's body, but the third one was a Heat-Source. Transforming it to smoke didn't change that. The sheriff triggered it.

Adele screeched, throwing one hand up to shield her face. Blisters scorched forearm, marring the delicate skin. "How dare you?" she shrieked. "You impudent, little desert rat!"

With a dismissive flick of her wrist, Adele summoned kinetic energy.

Kalia was flung sideways, hurled through the forest at blinding speed. She collided with a tree and then dropped to the ground, lying in a heap. "No!" Desa yelled. The other woman's mocking laughter set her blood on fire.

Desa thrust the spear at her, unleashing a jagged bolt of lightning that made the air sizzle. Adele raised a hand and caught the electricity in her palm, gathering it together into a pulsing ball of blue energy.

She threw it with a growl.

Triggering her Gravity-Sink, Desa jumped and turned belly-up in the air. She felt the heat as the ball sped past beneath her, then flipped over to land on her feet.

The roar of an explosion behind her and a spray of wood chips told her that the lightning had hit a tree. Some of those chips scratched her back, and she hissed. Worse, yet, she heard the crackle of flames.

Raising the spear, she pulsed the Gravity-Source within it.

Adele was yanked forward, forced to stumble drunkenly over uneven ground. The woman cursed as she came running in a headlong dash toward Desa. Only an instant. That was all it took.

Desa swung the spear for her head.

Half a second before metal sliced through flesh, Adele vanished with a slight whoosh of air. She was just gone.

Desa turned around, searching.

Flames consumed one of the larger trees from its roots to its crown of leaves. Panic welled up inside her; she had not intended to start a forest fire. The spear was too powerful. Without warning, something sliced cleanly through the burning tree, causing its top half to fall over with a loud creak.

Desa jumped out of the way, landing in a thick patch of soft mud. She raised her weapon to defend herself, but no further attack came.

The tree hit the ground with a deafening crash that seemed to make the world shake. Fire spread from its limbs to nearby vegetation. In a few minutes, that blaze would be out of control.

Desa touched the spearpoint to the burning wood, triggering a Heat-Sink. Those flames vanished in a wave that expanded from her until there was nothing left but smoke and charred bark. This was no ordinary Sink. It responded to her needs. She was able to drain thermal energy from the ignited air and not from the plant life. "Kalia!"

Hopping over the fallen tree, Desa scrambled through the muck. The sheriff was still lying face-down, but she was groaning. That was a good sign. It meant that she was not only alive but conscious. Desa ran as fast as she could.

Adele was suddenly standing in front of her, blocking her path. Blisters still covered her arm. Her dress was rumpled and there was murder in those sapphire eyes.

Invisible hands lifted Desa off the ground, unseen

fingers digging into her neck, choking her. Her vision dimmed, and silver flecks danced before her eyes. Heartbeats only, but she was already clinging to life by a thread.

CRACK! CRACK! CRACK!

Desa fell to the ground, landing in a crouch. Instinctively, she rubbed her smarting throat with one hand.

When her vision cleared, she saw that Adele had turned her back and now stood with one hand extended toward Kalia. The sheriff was on her feet again, pistol in hand.

Three bullets now floated in the air, half an inch away from Adele's outstretched fingers. At her command, they began a frantic dance, encircling her body in lopsided loops, picking up speed with every pass.

Two shot off toward Desa, one toward Kalia.

The spear's Force-Sink made short work of the first pair, draining them of kinetic energy until they were perfectly inert. They fell to the ground a second later. Thirty paces away, Kalia stood with her forearm up, iron bracelet exposed. The bullet she had stopped also fell to land at her feet.

Adele screamed in frustration and disappeared.

Popping open the cylinder of her gun, Kalia took a moment to load it with fresh ammunition. "She'll be back," the sheriff panted. "You know it."

"I think a change of venue is in order," Desa replied. "Let's get out of the forest."

Together, they ran in the direction of the temple. Open ground was best. It offered less cover but Adele would have fewer opportunities to drop a tree on them. The woman had had time to learn her powers; she used them more effectively than Bendarian had.

They were almost to the clearing – the black pyramid visible in the gaps between trees – when roots wriggled out of the ground and coiled themselves around Desa's ankles. Another set held Kalia immobilized. She staggered, arms flailing, as she tried to stay upright.

Adele materialized before them. Her laughter was like a soft, delicate chime. Extending her hands, she launched two streams of fire. One toward Desa and one toward Kalia.

Raising the spear up in a guarded stance, Desa used its Heat-Sink to douse the flames. They flickered out of existence about a foot away from her. But she still felt the searing air.

Kalia, however, had no Heat-Sinks on her person. Shielding her face with one hand, she squealed as fire scorched her arm, then fell to her knees and moaned.

Adele wore a wicked grin.

Rage boiling within her, Desa lashed out, releasing kinetic energy that hit the demon bitch like an oncoming train. Adele was thrown backward, tossed out into the open.

Desa plunged the spearpoint into one of the roots that held her and used a focused burst of kinetic energy to shatter the wood. Once free, she immediately ran to her lover. Terror made it hard to think. If Kalia was dead...

The sheriff rolled onto her back, staring up at Desa. One side of her face was covered in burns, and she couldn't open one eye. "Go," she rasped. "Stop her."

"I won't leave you!" Desa bellowed.

"If you don't put her down, she *will* come back here to finish the job. Go!"

Desa couldn't argue, not when she knew the other woman was right. Their only hope was to end this once and for all, and then maybe...Maybe time in the Ether's loving embrace would heal Kalia's wounds. She couldn't think about that now. She had to focus on the immediate threat.

. . .

Heart pounding, Tommy watched as Andriel stepped out of the bushes. The woman carried a metal staff like the one Radavan had used and wore several rings on each hand. Sinks and Sources, no doubt. "You killed Marcus?" she asked in a dangerous voice.

Gripping her pistol tight, Miri kept the weapon pointed at the other woman. She backed away slowly. "I did what I had to do," she answered. "He left me no choice."

"How's that?"

"He betrayed us."

A sad smile stretched across Andriel's face, and she shook her head slowly. "So, he did his duty then," she said. "Because we know Desa Nin Leean feels no sense of loyalty to her people."

Tommy stepped forward with his bow in one hand, staring the woman down. "It's not that simple," he said. "Daresina wanted to use the spear to make weapons."

"To protect Aladar."

"She would have used them as weapons of war."

Andriel's gaze fell upon him, and his fear was like a fist around his heart, choking the life out of him. "What do *you* know about it, boy?" she spat. "You will forgive me if I don't take the word of country oaf on matters of Aladri policy."

Dalen had his hands up in a placating gesture. "Just come with us," he urged. "And we will explain everything."

If Andriel heard a word of that, she obviously didn't care. "Miri Nin Valia," she said, extending a closed fist to point a ring at her. "I charge you with high treason, the punishment of which is death."

Tommy put himself in front of Miri.

Lightning erupted from Andriel's ring, streaked through the air and winked out right in front of his shirt. The woman pressed her attack for several seconds, then let her arm drop with a sigh. "Interesting," she said. "You've learned a thing or two, boy. But you are a buzzing fly. No more than a nuisance."

"Don't be so sure about that," Tommy said. On some level, he knew that what he was about to do was incredibly stupid, but if the only way to take the target off of Miri's back was to put one on his own, he would do so gladly. "I killed Radavan."

Andriel's eyebrows shot up. "You?" she whispered. "You killed Radavan?"

"Shot him through both legs."

"Then I shall bring two criminals to justice."

Andriel pointed her staff at him.

Planting his feet firm in the mud, Tommy triggered his Force-Sink pendant and felt the kinetic energy that she unleashed draining away into the Ether. "Go!" he shouted at Miri and Dalen. "Both of you! I'll deal with her."

His two lovers turned and ran deeper into the forest, leaving him alone with Andriel.

"A foolish choice, boy," she said. "I-"

With almost inhuman speed, Tommy grabbed an arrow, nocked it and drew back the string. He loosed, and the arrow was a blur for half a second before it settled to a stop right in front of Andriel.

He turned and ran for the nearest tree, using the distraction to find cover. Pushing his shoulder up against the bark, Tommy panted. Oh, he was in it now. Miri would not be there to help him this time. "Not bad, boy!" Andriel called out to him. "I must commend Desa's training."

Training.

He fell back on everything he had learned. Desa had taught him to listen, to rely on his ears as much as his eyes. The chirping of birds, the sighing of the wind: it was so hard to find anything specific in all that noise. But what was that? The slight slurp of a boot in the mud? He couldn't place it exactly, but then, with the right tactic, he wouldn't have to.

Choosing the right arrow, Tommy nocked it and aimed around the tree. He pulled back the string and let it fly.

The shaft sank into the muck some fifty feet away.

And Tommy triggered its Gravity-Source.

With a yelp, Andriel went stumbling backward, away from her tree. Her arms flailed as she tried to stay on her feet. Two seconds only. Then the woman triggered what must have been a Gravity-Sink.

Tommy drew his pistol and fired several rounds. Every one of them stopped dead in front of Andriel, but she was frightened now. No doubt he had used up most of her Force-Sink. She stretched a hand out toward him.

Tommy ducked behind the tree.

Tendrils of lightning struck the trunk, scorching it black. The bark caught fire, and the flames spread upward.

Holstering his gun, Tommy chose another arrow. Peeking around the tree gave him only the briefest glimpse of Andriel before a throwing knife came whistling his way. He slipped back into cover, and the knife sped past him.

The next thing Tommy knew, he was being dragged backward, away from the tree. He triggered his Gravity-Sink, but it was already too late. He was out in the open now.

He heard a whoosh of air above him and looked up to see a momentary flash of yellow. Andriel descended on him. She whacked him on the head with her staff. Everything went dark, and the world seemed to spin. He was dimly aware of dropping his arrow.

Losing his balance, Tommy fell over. He groaned as he tumbled down a shallow slope where roots dug into his body. *Do something,* he screamed inside his head. *She'll rip you to pieces if you give her the advantage.* In his desperation, he reached into his pocket and found a coin.

The tree he had used for cover was now a flaming torch; he could see it when his vision cleared. Andriel didn't seem to care. This whole forest could burn as far as she was concerned.

She stood at the top of the hill with a smirk on her face. "Now," she said, drawing another knife. "What do you think this one will do?"

Tommy whipped the coin at her.

Andriel crossed her forearms in front of her face, bracing herself for a sudden blast of kinetic energy, but nothing in her experience could have prepared her for what Tommy had planned. He triggered the Sonic-Source that he had created weeks ago in Hedrovan.

Andriel sank to her knees, clapping hands over her ears to shut the sound out. Even from this distance, the buzzing of insects was painfully loud. For Andriel, it must have been deafening. And her scream only made matters worse.

Tommy stood up, pulling a Heat-Sink arrow from his quiver. He aimed not for Andriel but for the burning tree. A well-placed shot sent the bolt right into the centre of the blaze, and when he triggered the Sink, those flames dimmed. But not completely. He had to use a second arrow to finish the job.

The fire had spread to the tree's closest neighbour, but his two Sinks had been powerful enough to snuff it out. They even left a coat of frost on the blackened bark.

He killed the Sonic-Source.

Andriel looked up at him, pulling her hands away from her ears to reveal blood on her palms. There were tears on her cheeks. For the first time since her arrival, she looked afraid.

Tommy retrieved another, set fletchings to string and drew. He pointed it directly at his enemy. "Don't you even move," he said. "I don't want to hurt you, but you so much as flinch, and so help me..."

He wasn't sure if she heard him – or if she could hear anything – but she understood the message nonetheless.

Spear in hand, Desa emerged from the forest with teeth clenched. "You and me," she growled. "We end this!"

Adele was lying in the grass near the base of the pyramid, grimacing as she massaged a sore shoulder. The bitch could feel pain – Desa already knew that much – but this was the first real indication that pain might slow her down. She began thinking of ways to use that to her advantage.

Adele shifted. There was no other word for it. One moment, she was sprawled out in the grass, the next, she was standing at the top of the stairs, blocking the tunnel that led into the pyramid. She spread her arms wide, threw back her head and laughed. "Yes!" she bellowed. "Let's end this!"

Desa didn't use the spear.

With her free hand, she drew her pistol, cocked the hammer and aimed for the other woman's feet. She fired four slugs, driving each one into the black stone. Adele gasped, dancing back to avoid being hit. That wasn't Desa's plan.

The last bullet was Infused.

Desa triggered it.

Streaks of electricity shot up toward the golden-haired woman, striking her like angry snakes. Adele caught each one, of course, absorbing the energy, redirecting it into the sky. But while she was doing that, she wasn't going on the offensive.

Desa sprinted through the grass as fast as she could, huffing and puffing with every step. She scrambled up the stairs with reckless abandon.

Trembling with the effort of containing all that energy, Adele held both hands out over the sparking bullet. Each bolt that struck her made her squeal. When the Source sputtered its final burst, Adele deflated. Then she looked up at Desa with raw hatred in her eyes.

Gripping the spear in both hands, Desa tried to stab her.

Adele twisted out of the way, backing up along the ledge. Her hair was smoking, and there were rips in her dress. "You," she spat, "are a dangerous, little vixen, aren't you?"

Climbing onto the top stair, Desa turned to face her enemy. On her left, she felt cool air flowing out of the tunnel. "I've had enemies who bested me," she said. "But you are the first who made me feel like a fool. Congratulations."

"It was a fun romp, wasn't it?" the other woman murmured.

Desa swung at her head.

Adele brought one arm up to intercept the blow, Soft flesh became shimmering metal that stretched from fingertips to shoulder. The spearpoint bounced off that living steel with a reverberation that made Desa's joints ache.

Adele flung her other hand out.

Kinetic energy hurled Desa backward. Her feet slid along the top stair, and she lost her balance, landing on her backside.

Adele stretched a hand up toward the pyramid, fingers curled as if she were grasping something. Cracks formed in the black stone, and then an avalanche was raining down on Desa.

She raised the spear and triggered its Force-Sink, making every one of those rocks hover above her head. With only a thought, she switched to the Gravity-Sink so that the rocks would stay aloft while she applied a surge of kinetic energy to each one...

...And sent them hurtling toward her enemy.

Adele vanished half a second before a storm of stones pummeled her, allowing each one to slip past and fly off the edge of the pyramid. The sound they made as they hit the ground made Desa flinch.

When they were gone, the other woman reappeared. Her left arm was flesh once again, but green veins ran along it. Something about that tickled Desa's memory, but she had no time to ponder it. Adele stretched out her hands and let loose a tempest.

Desa triggered her Electric-Sinks – the one in her bracelet and the one in the spear -absorbing the blast. Electricity winked out before it struck her body. Adele screeched, channeling every drop she could summon. And then she collapsed, putting one hand on the wall to steady herself.

Desa got to her feet, clutching the spear in a tight grip. This wasn't working. They could hurl death at each other for hours to no avail. She needed a plan. But what? *Field Binding is just a tool,* she remembered telling Tommy. *You must learn to outthink your enemies.*

With one hand, Desa reached into her pocket, closing her fingers around a small bit of metal. With the other, she threw the spear.

It landed point-first in the stone, five feet away from Adele.

The other woman smiled greedily, her eyes lighting up with the thrill of triumph. "Giving up your only advantage?" she asked. "A pity. I was having so much fun."

Desa tossed the coin she had retrieved.

Gleaming metal reflected the sunlight as it tumbled through the air. Adele caught it without thinking. And Desa triggered the Force-Source that she had Infused into the coin. Never touch another Field Binder's weapon.

Adele's hand exploded with a spray of blood.

The other woman sank to her knees, throwing her head back and howling with grief and rage. She clutched her bloody stump with the other hand, rocking back and forth as if in shock.

Desa took one step forward.

She froze when Adele looked up at her. The woman's eyes were orange with thin, vertical slits for pupils. When she opened her mouth, Desa saw two pointed fangs. "You *whore!*" Adele screamed.

She stood up, despite the loss of blood, and black smoke fountained from the stump at the end of her arm. It coalesced into the shape of a hand, transforming into flesh. Not creamy, pale flesh like the rest of Adele's body. Instead, dark, green scales went halfway up her forearm, and every nail was a sharp claw.

"You ruined my vessel!" Adele shrieked.

Something lifted Desa off the ground again and slammed her against the front wall of the pyramid. Not once, not twice, but *four* times, each harder than the last. Her bones were broken, and she could already tell that she was suffering internal bleeding. But Adele wasn't done. No, not at all.

Desa was flung like a rag doll.

She landed on her side and tumbled down the stairs,

grunting with every bump. Finally, she reached the bottom and then flopped onto her back. The pain was almost enough to make her black out. She couldn't move; her muscles refused to obey her commands. Sweet Mercy…

She was going to die.

Desa had to fight to hold onto consciousness. So long as she was awake, there was still a scrap of hope…A scrap. After thirty seconds of valiant effort, she came to wish that she hadn't bothered.

Adele stood over her, holding the Spear of Vengeance in her scaly hand. "This?" she snarled in a voice dripping with disdain. *"This* is what you thought would save you?"

Glowing cracks spread out along the length of the spear, white-hot light spilling through them. Desa was dimly aware of a soft, hissing sound. And then the spear exploded, shards of metal flying in all directions.

Something fell onto Desa.

Crystals.

Tiny shards of some crystalline structure that looked so very similar to the glittering mass on top of the pyramid. She almost thought that she could feel the Ether pulsing through them. She had no time to consider it, however.

Head thrown back in exultation, Adele laughed with manic glee. "You thought to best me with my sister's weapon?" she exclaimed. "You pitiful wretch. You are nothing but the dust under my feet!"

Her orange gaze snapped down to Desa. Snake eyes without a hint of mercy. "But now it's time to end this. Goodbye, Desa."

In that last moment of desperation, Desa reached for the one thing she knew she could count on, for the one ally that had never let her down.

She reached for the Ether.

The world changed in an instant; a universe of spinning particles stretched on before her eyes. Adele was there too, and like a Bendarian, she was a human-shaped mass of darkness. A void that the Ether could not fill.

Not without a little help, anyway.

Desa reached out to her old friend and forced the Ether into the gap. Adele screamed in terror.

When Desa released the Ether, the other woman was stumbling, trying to stay on her feet. She had her hands up in front of her face, and when she lowered them, Desa saw something remarkable.

Blue eyes.

"Desa?" Adele panted. "Desa, it's me! Adele! Your Adele! Oh, Desa, you don't know what it's been like! I was in there, trapped inside my own body, unable to stop it while it wreaked havoc on the world! It's gathering its strength. I can feel it! In a few moments, it will possess me again. Please, Desa! You must help me!"

With a shaking hand, Desa drew her pistol from its holster.

Adele seemed to be oblivious to the motion. She was sobbing, tears flowing over her flushed cheeks. "It used me," she whimpered. "I didn't know what it would do! I thought I could use the power to heal this world. I thought...No! No! Not again!"

With her last ounce of strength, Desa aimed the pistol and fired. Once, twice, three times. Adele flinched as each shot went through her, flailing about. She fell to her knees in the grass, blood staining her once beautiful dress. "But..." Adele whispered. "I was your soul mate."

Then she disappeared.

Alone and fading, Desa closed her hand around one of the crystalline shards. She wasn't sure what made her do it.

Curiosity, she supposed. This substance had been inside the spear? Was that what allowed it to take multiple Infusions? It seemed to throb in her hand. Or was it in her mind? She couldn't tell. Awareness was fading. But she was certain that what she held was a smaller version of the crystal on top of the temple. The crystal that amplified the Ether.

The Ether...

Could it be?

With a monumental effort of will, Desa squeezed the shard until it shattered. Light suffused her hand. A rainbow of colours – red, orange, yellow, green, blue and purple – oscillating in an endless cycle. It spread up her arm and over her body.

Desa arched her back, gasping as the air filled her lungs. The pain was fading. She felt her strength returning as her wounds healed themselves. The fog receded from her mind.

Desa opened her eyes, and they too glowed with a rainbow of colours before returning to their natural shade of brown. She felt refreshed. As if she had just woken up from a deep, peaceful sleep.

"Kalia!" she exclaimed.

Gathering a few of the shards, she ran into the forest. The sheriff was still lying in the dirt, as still as a corpse. Only the soft rasp of labored breathing told Desa that she was still alive.

Kneeling next to her, Desa took her lover's hand in both of hers. "Come on, darling," she pleaded. "Stay with me."

She squeezed the other woman's hand until the crystal shattered. The rainbow flowed up Kalia's arm and over the rest of her. The blisters on her face began to fade, leaving smooth skin in their place.

Desa sniffled, tears spilling over her cheeks.

Eyes fluttering, Kalia smiled up at her. "Hello, gorgeous," she whispered. "What happened."

"You saved me," Desa answered. "And then I saved you."

Kalia touched her face as if to prove that the blisters were truly gone. She rolled up her scorched sleeve to expose unblemished skin along the length of her arm. "How?" she asked. "How did you heal me?"

"It's the Ether," Desa said. "These crystals are the Ether itself, solidified and given physical form! When you break one to release its energy, the concentration is so potent, it's as if you spent several days in the Ether's embrace."

Kalia sat up, running fingers through her hair. She blinked at Desa. "The others," she said. "We need to find them."

"Yes, we do."

29

"Just keep walking," Miri said.

She had the barrel of her pistol pressed hard against Andriel's back, forcing the yellow-clad woman to stumble along the narrow path that ran between tall trees. They had been walking for nearly two hours; the sun was about halfway to its zenith, and yet Desa was already tired.

By the time she and Kalia found Tommy and the others last night, it was already too late to start the long journey out of the forest. They had slept outside the pyramid, with at least two people on watch the whole time. So far as Desa could tell, they had taken anything that Andriel might use as a Sink or Source – a quick scan of her through the ether had confirmed as much – but the Elite Guardian was still crafty.

Desa had used one of the crystals to restore Andriel's hearing, a fact that vexed her. They had gathered as many shards as they could, but each one was precious. She didn't like wasting one on someone who had tried to kill her people.

Andriel looked back over her shoulder, her mouth twisted in a contempt. "Traitors," she growled.

"Yeah, yeah," Miri replied.

Desa shuffled along with her arms hanging, her eyes fixed on the ground under her feet. "We'll have to decide what to do with her," she grumbled. "Even if we could return to Aladar, there are hundreds of miles between here and there. Far too many opportunities for her to make trouble."

Twisting around, Andriel walked backward along the path. The woman's hands were bound behind her back, but her smile was still vicious and cruel. "If you were to try," she said. "You would be executed on sight."

"Maybe we could leave her with the *Al a Nari*," Tommy suggested. "They might teach her some compassion."

Desa felt her mouth tighten, then shook her head in dismay. "I don't like the thought of foisting problems on someone else," she countered. "There must be some other option."

Andriel shrugged and then looked up at the heavens. "There is one option," she said. "One that would prevent me from causing you any more trouble."

"I'm not going to kill you!" Desa snapped. "Not unless you give me no other choice."

"Marcus always said you lacked conviction."

With a hiss, Miri thrust her arm out and pressed the gun against Andriel's forehead. "He said much the same to me," she replied in a dangerous voice. "Look what it got him."

That was how they spent most of their day: trudging through the woods, making plans and verbally sparring with Andriel. Desa saw no dead trees, which gave her no end of relief. Perhaps Vengeance was well and truly gone from this world.

Adele, however, was still out there. Somewhere. Desa didn't believe for an instant that she was dead.

All of their plans had been for naught. The spear was gone; they had no weapon that they could use against Adele when she inevitably decided to show her face again. She was at a loss for what to do next, and that scared her more than any physical threat ever could.

There was one path forward if she dared to take it. She could seek out Mercy and hear what the goddess had to offer. A trip to the desert wasn't a prospect that she was looking forward to, but then Kalia had been gone from her home for almost four months now; she probably had friends and family that she would like to see again. That might be nice.

Morning blossomed into afternoon, and the air became uncomfortably warm. Once again, they had to wade through ankle-deep puddles. Desa was fairly certain that the pond they skirted was the same one they had seen on their way in. Some of those colourful frogs were quite breathtaking.

She caught her first glimpse of one of the snakes that Rojan had warned her about, a black-and-red serpent coiled up at the base of the tree. It was Dalen who first noticed it, but once he did, everyone felt the need to creep past without making too much noise.

Come nightfall, they made camp near the path. Once again, they needed two people to keep watch on Andriel. Desa and Miri took the first shift, Tommy and Dalen the second.

Their journey the following morning was much the same as it had been the day before: narrow paths and deep puddles, trees with drooping branches. It was slow going, but Desa was energized by the prospect of finally getting out of this forest.

It was well past noon by the time they finally reached the open grasslands. True to his word, Rojan was waiting for them.

His people had set up a small encampment of tents. Desa could feel Infused tools drawing on the Ether nearby, providing heat for cooking or light for reading or even just keeping the air cool.

Andriel's mouth dropped open when she felt what must have seemed impossible to her. "They can Field Bind," she whispered.

Dalen stepped up beside her with an arrogant smile. "You're going to find that a lot of your assumptions about the world are wrong."

"Come on," Desa said.

"She can stay with us," Rojan declared.

He stood over Andriel with his arms folded, frowning down at her. The yellow-clad woman was sitting on a stool in the middle of his tent. "The Council will have much to teach this one, I think."

Andriel looked up at him, and her eyes burned with the fury of a thousand suns. Her mouth twitched, but she said nothing. Emotional control. Marcus had been much the same. Sometimes, Desa wondered if it was a failing that she shared.

In dungarees and a blue shirt with the top button left undone, she sat on a stool of her own, sharpening a knife. Clean clothes! After four days of sweat and grime, a fresh shirt was nothing short of miraculous. "You're sure?" she asked. "I don't want to burden your people with our problems."

"There is no burden," Rojan said. "From what you have told me, her talents are considerable. The world would be well served if she put them to better use."

Desa nodded.

She thought the conversation was over, but Rojan glanced in her direction and arched an eyebrow. "Perhaps," he began, "you should remain among us as well. There is much we could learn from each other."

Grinning, Desa felt a sudden warmth in her cheeks. Her head sank with the weight of her regret. "I wish that I could," she said. "But I failed. Again. And someone has to stop *Hanak Tuvar*."

"You didn't fail."

"Oh no?"

Rojan shook his head. "The spear was a creation of Vengeance," he replied at last. "Perhaps the world is better for its absence."

Andriel opened her mouth to speak but clamped it shut again before uttering a word. Clearly, she did not agree with that assessment. Desa wasn't sure that she did either. The spear was their last hope.

She said as much, but Rojan only laughed. "There is always another way," he insisted. "And you brought back something much more valuable."

He drew aside his blue cloak and then reached into his pocket to retrieve the shard of crystal that Desa had given him. "This," he said, "is far, far more valuable than any weapon."

Setting her knife and stone down on the floor, Desa stood up and nodded. "That must be what allowed the spear to take multiple Infusions," she said. "I still don't know how it was able to renew its connections to the Ether without a living mind to guide the process."

"There is a living mind here," Rojan told her.

"I'm sorry?"

Rojan held up the shard, allowing it to catch the light from a glowing, metal plate that was tied to the tent wall with thick ropes. The crystal glittered with all the colours of the rainbow. "You don't know what this is, do you?"

"It's the Ether," Desa mumbled. "Somehow, the Ether was given physical form. I didn't think it was possible."

"This is so much more than just the Ether!" Rojan exclaimed. "It is a piece of Vengeance herself. My people have legends about these crystals. The bones of the gods, we call them."

Scrunching her eyes tight, Desa gave her head a shake. "I'm sorry," she stammered. "You're telling me that these shards are...pieces of Vengeance? As in a fragment of her body?"

"That is a good way of putting it, yes."

"So, that little sliver..."

Rojan smiled with pride. "Yes," he said. "This shard contains a small portion of Vengeance's intelligence. A living mind, as you put it. That is how it can renew the spear's connection to the Ether."

"I was not expecting that," Desa breathed.

"As I said, we have much to teach each other."

A FEW HOURS LATER, with the sun a red ball on the horizon, Desa strolled through a narrow lane between two lines of tents. The *Al a Nari* she passed all smiled or nodded in respect. She greeted each one with a wave or a smile of her own, but Sweet Mercy, she felt awkward. Desa Kincaid was not good with people.

She found Kalia at the edge of the camp.

The other woman was a silhouette against the red sky, wrapped up in a light blanket. "Hello there," she said as Desa drew near.

"Contemplating the future?"

Glancing in her direction, Kalia grinned. The wind teased her hair, sending soft strands flying. "Celebrating," she said. "We survived."

"Not all of us," Desa muttered.

Kalia held her hand, and that simple, soothing gesture took away some of her pain. But not all of it. Marcus. The man had been such a cantankerous, bullheaded oaf. As stubborn as a mule on his best day. But he was a good friend.

Desa closed her eyes, tears spilling over her cheeks. "I'm sorry," she whispered. "It's just..."

Kalia pulled her close and kissed her on the forehead. "You have nothing to be sorry for," she murmured. "I know what he meant to you."

Desa sighed.

On some level, she was furious. By the Eyes of Vengeance, what was Marcus thinking? If he had just talked to her, told her what he was planning, she could have talked him out of it. Or could she? *The man was willing to kill his own sister to follow orders,* she noted. *Can you reason with someone like that?*

And then there was the reality that she didn't want to acknowledge: that she should have seen it coming, that she should have noticed that something was amiss before it got that far. Twice now, she had failed to notice the threat right under her nose. No, Desa Kincaid was not good with people.

Kalia just held her for a little while, and that was enough.

Their tender moment was interrupted by the sound of footsteps, and when Desa turned, she saw Miri coming toward her, flanked by Tommy and Dalen. "So," Miri said. "Have you decided where you'll be going next?"

You, Desa noted. *Not we.*

She took a moment to compose herself, then cleared her throat and nodded. "Rojan has convinced me to stay with the *Al a Nari* for a little while," she answered. "They have information that may prove invaluable to us. About Adele's power and the crystals that we found. Dalen, you'd be a great help in deciphering their ancient texts."

The young man shut his eyes and shook his head. "I wish I could stay," he replied. "The chance to learn about their culture would be a once in a lifetime opportunity. But I promised my love that I would go with him."

"As did I," Miri added.

Cocking her head, Desa studied Tommy for a long moment. "You're leaving?" she asked. "Where will you go?"

"Hedrovan," Tommy said. "I have a promise to keep… And a grave injustice that needs correcting."

Desa strode forward and threw her arms around him, squeezing him tight. "Good luck," she said softly. "I know you can do it."

Tommy returned the hug, gently patting her on the back, and then finally, he pulled away. "Thank you," he said. "Not just for the vote of confidence. For everything."

"Oh, don't start," Desa grumbled. "You'll have me tearing up."

"We can't have that."

They wouldn't be leaving until tomorrow morning, but Desa still felt like this was goodbye. She started to cry as she watched the three of them walking away. A moment passed before she realized that Kalia was still there.

"Sorry," Desa said. "I guess…I guess you'll be leaving too. Back to Dry Gulch."

"No."

"No?"

When she turned, Kalia was smiling in the fading twilight. The other woman leaned forward to brush Desa's lips with hers. "No," she said. "No, I go where you go, Desa Nin Leean. You're stuck with me."

"Well. That makes things a little easier."

30

The Weaver examined herself in a mirror. The same face she had always known stared back at her: creamy, pale skin, high cheekbones, golden hair spilling over her shoulders. Adele's face. But not completely.

Her eyes were orange now, with thin, vertical slits for pupils. She pawed at her chin with her left hand, a hand now covered in scales. No, this would not do at all.

Stepping back, she opened her robe ever so slightly to expose her midriff. The bullet holes were gone – healed by her power – but a spiderweb of green veins tarnished her skin.

This vessel was useless to her now.

No one would believe that a woman with snake eyes was a benevolent god. Fury bubbled up until she had to resist the urge to punch the mirror. This was precisely the outcome that she had been trying to avoid!

Each use of healing changed her body just as it had for Benny, transforming her into a creature of the Nether. In truth, any use of her power, no matter how small, had the same effect, but the process was accelerated whenever she applied that power to her own flesh. As a vessel, Adele might have served for years if she had not been forced to repair the damage inflicted by three shots to the chest.

Engaging Desa directly had been a bad idea.

But then, she had tried killing the woman by proxy, and every attempt had failed. Azra, Bendarian, the attack on Aladar: all disappointments that frustrated her to no end. There was just no getting rid of this stubborn splinter in her foot.

Desa Kincaid: the bitch who refused to die.

She-

The world changed around her, the walls of her bedroom fuzzing, fading until they were gone. Now, she was in what appeared to be a cell of some kind. Stone walls with a heavy, wooden door. The only furnishing was a simple, wooden stool.

She recoiled at the sensation of a grimy floor under her bare feet. What was this place? Why had she come here? It was her own power that transported her – she knew that – but she had not willed it.

The door swung open.

A tall man with black hair and a thick mustache stepped into the room, frowning at the sight of her. "Sit," he said, gesturing to the stool.

The Weaver knew this man well. The sight of him stirred up feelings that belonged to Adele, and yet those emotions were a part of her now. "Uncle Timothy!" she said. "So, nice to see you!"

"Your father has been beside himself ever since you disappeared last spring," he said. "If only he had known…Sit."

The Weaver drew herself up, lifting her chin to stare

down her nose at him. "I choose to stand, thank you very much."

With a sigh, Timothy Delarac reached into his pocket to retrieve a black crystal about the size of his palm. "Sit!" he growled.

The Weaver sat, folding her hands in her lap and staring expectantly up at him. She had not intended to do it. Her body had moved of its own accord, and though a part of her mind screamed in rebellion, she was helpless to resist.

Turning on his heel, Timothy paced a line across the width of the very narrow cell. "Adele, Adele, Adele," he muttered. "What a mess you've gotten yourself into. If I had known that you were spying on my meetings with Bendarian...But then, you did use that twisted second sight of yours, didn't you?"

For the first time since claiming this vessel as her own, the Weaver felt fear. What did he know? How was he able to control her? This reunion no longer amused her. She tried to summon lightning, tried to strike down her uncle, but nothing happened. The power was no longer hers to command.

"What have you done to me?" she asked.

He looked over his shoulder, his mouth twisted in a sneer. "What have we done to you?" he mocked. "No more than what we planned for Bendarian. Did you think that he just happened to discover the ancient texts of *Hanak Tuvar* in my library? No, child. We spent years grooming him, preparing him to become the vessel."

"Who's we?"

"We," Timothy began, "are a society of informed gentlemen. Those wise enough and worldly enough to set the course for this great nation. We have been seeking a way to harness the power of the Nether ever since the founding of the Eradian Empire, one hundred and fifty years ago."

He spun to face her with hands clasped behind his back, smiling maliciously. "It cannot be wielded without great cost," he said. "As you have learned to your sorrow."

The Weaver flinched.

"But," Timothy went on. "It can be harnessed indirectly." He held up the black crystal, forcing the Weaver to raise her hand as well. As he waved the crystal back, the Weaver moved her hand in perfect imitation.

This couldn't be happening.

"What do you want with me?"

"What do I want for you, Adele?" he asked. "A comfortable life with a suitable husband. But you've made that impossible."

He stepped forward and went down on one knee. There was such sympathy in his clear, blue eyes. "It was never supposed to be you, Adele," he said. "Bendarian was a jumped-up son of a struggling fur trader who spent most nights in his cups. He came to us with the secrets of the Aladri, and we saw an opportunity."

Gently, her uncle laid a hand on her cheek. She tried to pull away, but she couldn't. "His first attempt to free the Nether was an abysmal failure," Timothy went on. "A patch of land stripped of colour where every living thing is feral."

The Weaver shuddered.

"Parliament has ordered the area sealed off," he muttered. "We have soldiers guarding the border. Quite the nuisance, really as it has hindered trade with the northern towns. But it worked. Bendarian gained partial access to the power. Enough to make a second attempt. It was I who put the idea of using the Temple of Mercy in his head. You were never supposed to know about that."

Timothy stood up, and every last drop of sympathy seemed to drain out of him. "It was never supposed to be you, child," he said. "But you have you made your bed, and now, you will serve your purpose.

He turned his back on her, striding out of the cell, but the Weaver caught him just as he walked through the door.

"What purpose is that?"

Her uncle looked back with a greedy smile. "War, child," he said. "First, we conquer Aladar, and then we expand until the Empire stretches to every last corner of the world. We will bring civility to the savages, and the spirit of Eradian ingenuity will propel humanity into a brighter tomorrow. The future is manifest destiny."

EPILOGUE

The crescent moon hung low in the night sky, a chilly wind sweeping over the city of Hedrovan. Autumn was nearly over, and the end of the season brought with it a slow-down in trade. No one wanted to sail the Sapphire Sea during the stormy season.

An arrow landed in the mud without a sound, and once it settled into place, the Sonic-Sink within it created a region of utter silence.

In unrelieved black from head to toe, Tommy stood upon the roof of *The Golden Sunset*. He had placed the arrow directly in the middle of the inn's backyard, halfway between the barracks that housed the women slaves and the barracks that housed the men.

The only light came from lanterns that were hung above the doors on each of those small outbuildings, one to his left and one to his right. He could see the uniformed men standing guard at those doors. Two for each barracks.

With muted footsteps, he loped across the inn's slanted rooftop, his movements silenced by a second Sonic-Sink that he wore on his person. He chose the building on his left. He would free the women first.

Triggering the Gravity-Sink in his pendant, Tommy leaped and descended gracefully onto the outbuilding's roof. He landed in a crouch, bow in hand. A quick scan of his surroundings told him that the guards had not noticed, or if they had, they had chosen not to react.

He dropped off the side of the building, allowing gravity to regain its full strength the instant his feet touched the ground, and crept around to the front. Before he stepped into view, he switched from the Sonic-Sink to a Light-Sink that squelched the glow from the lantern.

"What the-" one of the guards yelped.

"You have two options," Tommy said, stepping out into the open. "Leave now. Go back to your families and find a better line of work. Or die."

Their only answer was the sound of footsteps running away. Drawing an arrow from his quiver, Tommy nocked it and pulled back the string.

When he killed the Sink, he caught a brief glimpse of both men fleeing, running across the yard as fast as their legs could carry them. The denizens of this horrible city were a superstitious lot. At times, it annoyed him, but if it saved him from having to do violence, he was grateful.

Tommy returned the arrow to his quiver and fished a safety pin out of his pocket. "Quick and quiet," he muttered to himself.

Turning his back on the retreating men, he stepped up to the door and slid the pin into the lock. He backed away to a safe distance and then triggered his Force-Source.

The lock exploded, shards of metal flying off in all directions. One almost smacked him right in the face, but it stopped about an inch away from his nose, stilled by one of his pendants.

He let it fall to the ground.

Stepping over the shard, Tommy marched forward and yanked open the door. The lantern light was enough for him to see a long, narrow room with two lines of bunk beds on either side. Every one of those bunks was occupied, and he heard the soft rustle of blankets as several women sat up to find out what was going on.

"Ladies, I suggest you hurry," Tommy said. "We don't have much time."

Nobody moved.

Clenching his teeth, Tommy shook his head. "I'm here to free you," he explained. "Do you want to go or not?"

They needed no further coaxing. The first woman hopped down from a bunk on his left, slipped sandals onto her feet and ran out the door. After that, it was a flood of half-dressed girls charging out into the night, all chattering with one another. He urged them to silence. With any luck, the arrow that he had planted in the middle of the yard would prevent the guards at the men's barracks from hearing. But he didn't want to take any chances.

He turned around…

And found four uniformed men in the middle of the yard, standing under the bare branches of an elm tree. Each one of them had a pistol in hand. Of course. The pair that he had scared off didn't flee. They went for reinforcements. Several girls screamed at the sight of them.

One man stepped forward, raising his gun and pointing it directly at Tommy. He cocked the hammer and fired. The barrel flashed, but what should have been a deafening roar was only a soft *pop*.

A bullet appeared in front of Tommy, floating in the air. Heat wafted off the sizzling metal.

All four men exchanged glances.

Tommy triggered his Light-Sink, bathing himself in darkness, and he ran. Never be where your opponents had last seen you. As he scrambled through the soft mud, he took another arrow from his quiver.

He twisted to face the guards, killed the Sink and drew back his bowstring.

One man rounded on him.

Tommy put a bolt in that fellow's chest before he could get his gun up. Stumbling, the poor fool fell on his backside with hardly any noise. The very instant his body hit the ground, Tommy cloaked himself in shadow again.

He ran through the yard on nimble feet, sweat coating his brow. With a quick hand, he retrieved another arrow.

Light returned, and all three remaining men glanced around the yard, searching for any sign of him. The first one to spot him pointed a finger in Tommy's direction and shouted, but neither one of his companions heard a thing. His words were muffled by the Sonic-Sink.

An arrow struck the poor bastard right between the eyes, causing him to flail and topple over backward. The other two turned around.

Shrouding himself in darkness once again, Tommy ran right past them, headed toward the men's barracks. He would have to be careful. The lantern would dim as he drew near, and one of the guards might notice.

It was time to end this.

The next arrow he chose was special, Infused with a connection to the Ether. Stopping in his tracks, Tommy lined up his shot, aiming for a spot in the centre of the yard. He killed the Light-Sink.

Both men spun around to face him.

Tommy loosed.

His arrow landed at their feet, and he triggered the Electric-Sink that he had placed within it. Lacking an abundant source of energy nearby, the Infusion feasted on whatever it could find, including the electrical signals that ordered a heart to keep pumping. Both men stiffened, falling face-down in the muck. Quick and quiet. No lightning. No flashy tricks that might be visible from a nearby window.

He didn't like it -- not one bit -- but he had given those men a chance to save themselves, and leaving them alive would only allow them to raise an alarm. Any man who was willing to risk his life for he cause of *slavery* deserved whatever he got.

One of the girls ran up to him, panting. She was just a tiny slip of a lass, barely more than fifteen. Her eyes were so wide Tommy thought she might die of shock. "What do we do now?" she asked.

"First, we free your brothers," Tommy answered. "And then we start a revolution."

Dear reader,

We hope you enjoyed reading *Bullets and Bones*. Please take a moment to leave a review, even if it's a short one. Your opinion is important to us.

Discover more books by R.S. Penney at https://www.nextchapter.pub/authors/ontario-author-rs-penney

Want to know when one of our books is free or discounted for Kindle? Join the newsletter at http://eepurl.com/bqqB3H

Best regards,

R.S. Penney and the Next Chapter Team

∼

You might also like:
Displaced by Stephen Drake

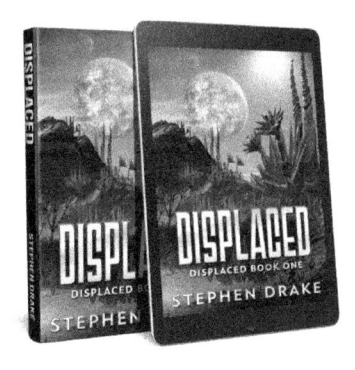

To read the first chapter for free, please head to:
https://www.nextchapter.pub/books/displaced

CPSIA information can be obtained
at www.ICGtesting.com
Printed in the USA
LVHW050502041120
670657LV00004B/507

9 781715 647407